P9-CEZ-569

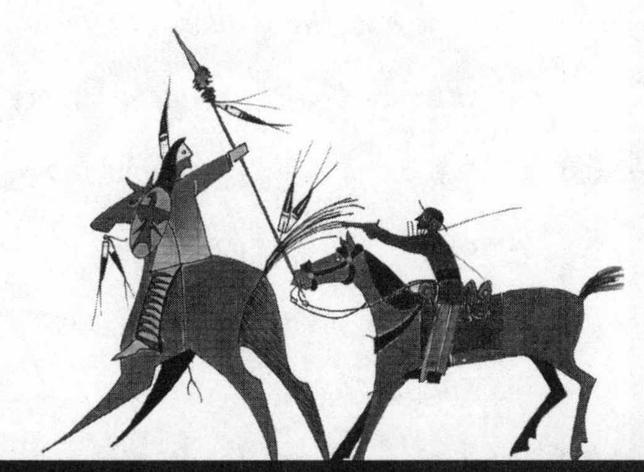

THE LONG KNIVES ARE CRYING

OTHER BOOKS BY JOSEPH M. MARSHALL III

Hundred in the Hand: A Novel

The Day the World Ended at Little Bighorn: A Lakota History

Keep Going: The Art of Perseverance

Walking with Grandfather: The Wisdom of Lakota Elders

The Journey of Crazy Horse: A Lakota History

The Lakota Way: Stories and Lessons for Living

The Dance House: Stories from Rosebud

On Behalf of the Wolf and the First Peoples

Winter of the Holy Iron: A Novel

Soldiers Falling into Camp: The Battles at the Rosebud and the Little Bighorn

How Not to Catch Fish: And Other Adventures of Iktomi

Joseph M. Marshall III

THE LONG KNIVES ARE CRYING

A Novel

FULCRUM
GOLDEN, COLORADO

This is a work of fiction. Names, characters, places, and incidents either are the product of the author's imagination or are used fictitiously.

Library of Congress Cataloging-in-Publication Data
Marshall, Joseph, 1945-
The long knives are crying : a novel / Joseph M. Marshall III.
p. cm. -- (Lakota westerns)
ISBN 978-1-55591-672-5
1. Indians of North America--Fiction. 2. Teton Indians--Fiction. 3. Little Bighorn, Battle of the, Mont., 1876--Fiction. 4. Rosebud, Battle of the, Mont., 1876--Fiction. I. Title.
PS3563.A72215L66 2008
813'.54--dc22
2008028530

Printed on recycled paper in the United States of America by Thomson-Shore, Inc.
0 9 8 7 6 5 4 3 2 1

Interior design by Jack Lenzo
Cover image: "Long Knives." Prismacolor pencil and India ink on antique ledger paper dated April 3, 1936. © 2008 Donald F. Montileaux

Fulcrum Publishing
4690 Table Mountain Drive, Suite 100
Golden, Colorado 80403
800-992-2908 • 303-277-1623
www.fulcrumbooks.com

In Loving Memory of My Grandmothers,
Annie Good Voice Eagle Two Hawk
and
M. Blanche Roubideaux Brave Marshall,
Mothers of Lakota Warriors

Mila Hanska Ceyapelo

Nantan iyayapi, mila hanska ceyapelo
Nantan iyayapi, nantan iyayapi!
Nantan iyayapi, nantan iyayapi!
Nantan iyayapi, nantan iyayapi!
Mila Hanska ceyapelo!

The Long Knives Are Crying

They went on a charge, the Long Knives are crying
They went on a charge, they went on a charge!
They went on a charge, they went on a charge!
They went on a charge, they went on a charge!
The Long Knives are crying!

One of the Lakota victory songs, perhaps the most well known, from the Battle of the Little Bighorn. It has been sung for many generations and will be for generations to come. This version is performed by the Good Feather Singers, a Lakota drum group from Boulder, Colorado.

GLOSSARY

Translated Lakota names for current or historical Euro-American names for landmarks and places in south-central and north-central Wyoming and elsewhere.

Lakota	**English**
He Wiyakpa or He Ska (Shining Mountains or White Mountains)	Bighorn Mountains
Makablu Wakpa (Powder River)	Powder River
Canku Wakan Ske Kin (The Road Said to Be Holy, or Holy Road)	Oregon Trail
Hehaka Wakpa (Elk River)	Yellowstone River
Mnisose or Mnisose Tanka (Muddy River or Great Muddy River)	Missouri River
Paha Sapa or He Sapa (Black Hills or Black Mountains)	Black Hills
Makizita Wakpa (Smoking Earth River)	Little White River
Maka Ska Wakpa (White Earth River)	Big White River
Unjinjintka Wakpa (Red Berries Creek)	Rosebud Creek
Maga Wakpa (Goose Creek)	Goose Creek
Cahota Wakpa (Ash Creek)	Reno Creek
Mato Tipi (Bear's Lodge)	Devils Tower
Wakpa Sla or Wakpa Sluslute (Greasy Grass River)	Little Bighorn River

MAPS

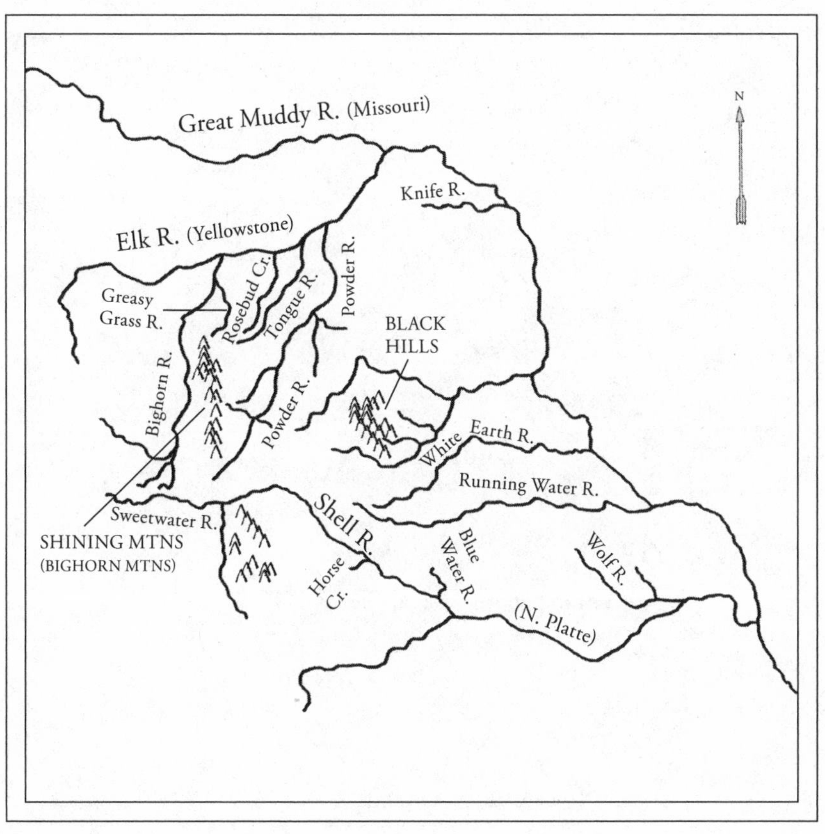
N
Great Muddy R. (Missouri)
Knife R.
Elk R. (Yellowstone)
Greasy
Grass R.
Rosebud Cr.
Tongue R.
Powder R.
BLACK
HILLS
Bighorn R.
Powder R.
White
Earth R.
Running Water R.
Shell R.
Sweetwater R.
SHINING MTNS
(BIGHORN MTNS)
Horse
Cr.
Blue
Water R.
Wolf R.
(N. Platte)

Great Muddy R. (Missouri)
Knife R.
Elk R. (Yellowstone)
Rosebud Cr.
Tongue R.
Powder R.
Greasy Grass R.
(Little Bighorn)
BLACK
HILLS
Battle of
the Rosebud
White Earth R.
Smoking Earth R.
Bighorn R.
Fort Robinson
Battle of the
Little Bighorn
Red Cloud
Agency
Spotted Tail
Agency
SHINING MTNS
(BIGHORN MTNS)
N
.....Modern-day State Lines

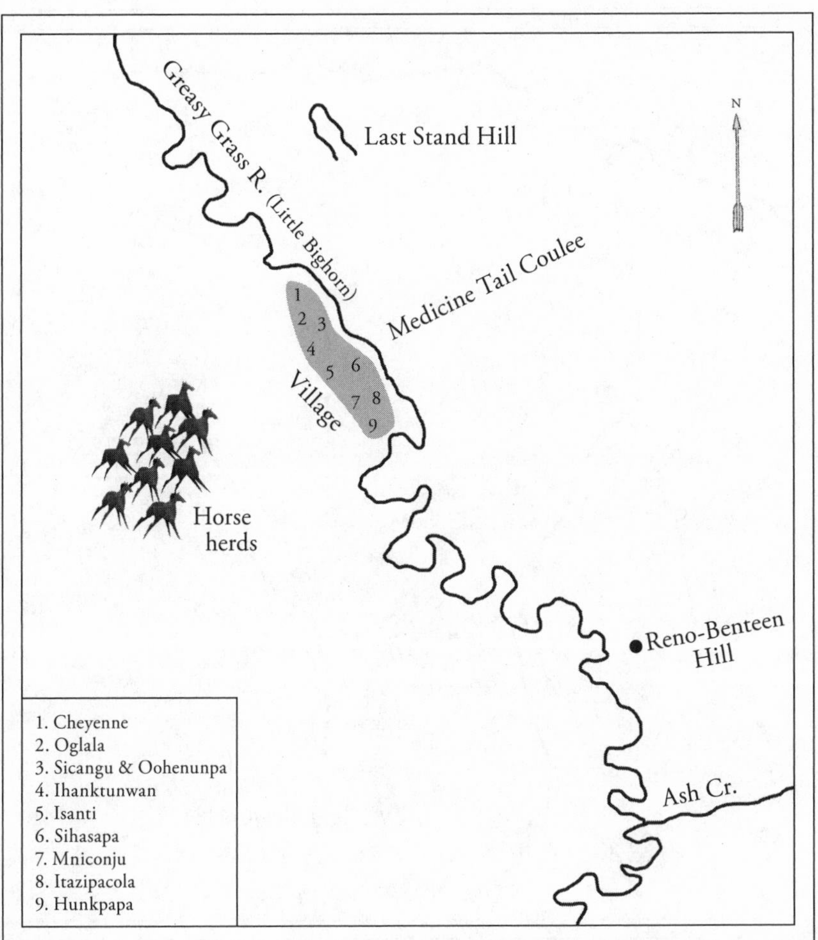
Greasy Grass R. (Little Bighorn)
Last Stand Hill
N
Medicine Tail Coulee
1
2 3
4
5 6
7 8
9
Village
Horse herds
Reno-Benteen Hill
Ash Cr.
1. Cheyenne
2. Oglala
3. Sicangu & Oohenunpa
4. Ihanktunwan
5. Isanti
6. Sihasapa
7. Mniconju
8. Itazipacola
9. Hunkpapa

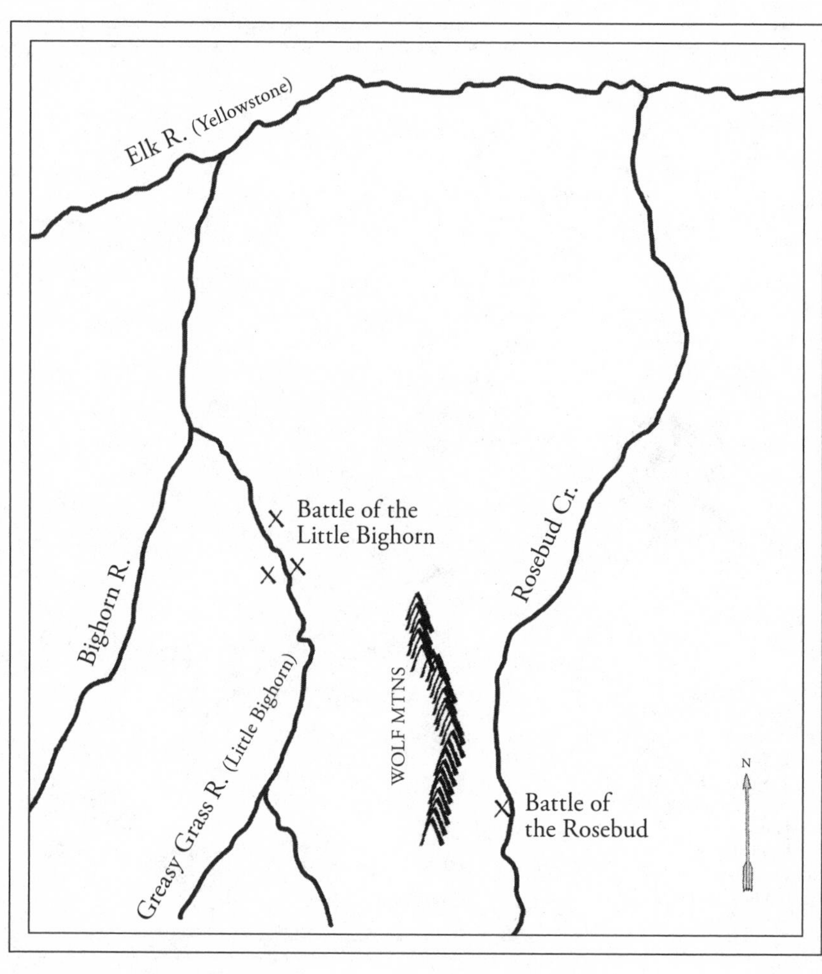
Elk R. (Yellowstone)
Battle of the Little Bighorn
Bighorn R.
Rosebud Cr.
Greasy Grass R. (Little Bighorn)
WOLF MTNS
Battle of the Rosebud
N

LAKOTA CALENDAR

The annual calendar used by pre-reservation Lakota was based on the thirteen lunar months. The names for the months were based on characteristics or occurrences in nature consistent with the weather and time of the year. Names were not universal, however, in that different Lakota groups would often use a different name for the same month. Furthermore, the lunar months did not begin or end on the same days as in the Gregorian calendar.

Wiotehike (Moon of Hard Times)	late December to mid-January
Tioheyunka Wi (Moon of Frost in the Lodge)	mid-January to mid-February
Cannapopa Wi (Moon of Popping Trees)	mid-February to mid-March
Istawicayazan Wi (Moon When Eyes Hurt)	mid-March to mid-April
Magagluhunnipi Wi (Moon When Geese Return)	mid-April to mid-May
Ptehincala Sape Wi (Moon When [Buffalo] Calves Are Red)	mid-May to mid-June
Wipazuke Waste Wi (Moon When Berries Are Good)	mid-June to mid-July
Wicokannijin (Moon When the Sun Stands in the Middle)	mid-July to early August
Wasutun Wi (Moon When Things Ripen)	early August to early September
Canapegi Wi (Moon When Leaves Turn Brown)	early September to early October
Canapekasna Wi (Moon When Leaves Fall)	early October to early November
Waniyetu Wi (Winter Moon)	early November to early December
Waniyetucokan Wi (Middle of Winter Moon)	early December to early January

OYATE KIN (THE PEOPLE)

Dakota

Mdewakantunwan—people of Spirit Lake
Wahpekute—leaf shooters or to shoot among the leaves
Wahpetunwan—people living among the leaves
Sissetunwan—people of the marsh

Nakota

Ihanktunwan—people of the end
Ihanktunwanna—little people of the end (meaning a smaller group)

Lakota

Oglala—to scatter
Sicangu—burnt leg or burnt thigh
Hunkpapa—those who camp at the end
Mniconju—to plant by the water
Oohenunpa—two boilings or two kettles
Itazipacola—without bows
Sihasapa (sometimes Siksika)—black soles or black feet

CHARACTERS

Warriors

Ashes—Oglala; older son of Little Bird and Stands on the Hill
Bear—Sicangu; cousin of Horn Tail
Bearface—Oglala; father of Sweetwater Woman
Bear Robe—Oglala scout
Bear Tail—Sicangu; decoy rider at Spotted Tail agency
Bird—Sicangu widower from Spotted Tail agency
Black Coyote—Cheyenne; husband of Buffalo Calf Road
Black Lance—Oglala buffalo scout
Black Moon—Oglala war leader
Black Wolf—Oglala; son of Tools, keeper of the eagle feather banner during battle
Blunt Arrow—Sicangu scout and warrior
Bobtail Horse—Cheyenne war leader
Bull Bear—Oglala war leader
Cloud—Oglala warrior; later known as John Richard Cloud
Comes in Sight—Cheyenne war leader; brother of Buffalo Calf Road
Crazy Horse—Oglala warrior and leader
Eagle Dog—Sicangu at Spotted Tail agency
Fast Horse—Sicangu; brother-in-law of Yellow Wolf
Fire Crow—Cheyenne; messenger for Two Moons
Flood—Oglala warrior
Flying By—Oglala warrior and horse trainer; Good Hand's father
Gall—Hunkpapa war leader
Goings—Oglala warrior and scout; cousin of Cloud
Good Hand—Oglala warrior
Good Road—Oglala war leader
Good Shield—Oglala warrior
Has No Horse—Oglala warrior and scout
Hawk Eagle—Hunkpapa warrior; Sitting Bull's messenger
He Dog—Sicangu warrior and leader; close friend of Crazy Horse
High Wolf—Oglala warrior
Horn Cloud—Oglala warrior
Horn Tail—young warrior from the agency; cousin of Bear
Horned Eagle—young Sicangu warrior
Little Big Man—Oglala warrior; friend of Crazy Horse
Little Bird—Sicangu warrior; married into Oglala family; friend of Cloud
Little Dog—young Sicangu warrior
Little Feather—young Sicangu, also known as "Bug"; grew up on Spotted Tail agency; an informant for White Hat Clark
Little Hawk—Oglala; younger brother of Crazy Horse; deceased
Lone Bear—Oglala warrior; close friend of Crazy Horse; deceased
Lone Hill—Oglala warrior
No Coyote—Oglala; son of Goings
Old Coyote—Crow warrior who seeks revenge against Cloud
Pointed Red Hill—Dakota leader
Rabbit—Oglala warrior; cousin of Cloud; deceased
Rain in the Face—Hunkpapa warrior
Red Bow—Mniconju warrior; warning rider

Red Cloud—Oglala leader who took his people to an agency near Ft. Robinson
Red Hand—Oglala warrior
Red Horse—Sihasapa warrior and messenger
Red Lodge—Oglala; son of Yellow Leggings
Runs Close—Oglala; cousin of Little Bird
Spotted Tail—Sicangu warrior and leader who took his people to an agency near Ft. Robinson; uncle to Crazy Horse
Stabs—Hunkpapa warrior
Taken Alive—Oglala warrior; friend of Cloud
Tall Bull—Cheyenne warrior and scout
Touch the Clouds—Mniconju; cousin of Crazy Horse; reputed to be seven feet tall
Two Bulls—Oglala warrior
Two Hawk—Sicangu; brought his family from Spotted Tail agency
Two Horns—Oglala; younger son of Little Bird and Stands on the Hill
Two Moons—Cheyenne warrior and leader
Walking Eagle—Sicangu warrior; brother of Yellow Earring
White Bear—Sicangu; brought his family from Spotted Tail agency
White Eyes—Sicangu; decoy rider at Spotted Tail agency
White Wing—Sicangu warrior and scout; messenger between Cloud and Crazy Horse
Wolf Eyes—Hunkpapa warrior and scout
Yellow Earrings—Sicangu warrior; brother of Walking Eagle
Yellow Eyes—Oglala warrior
Yellow Wolf—Oglala warrior and scout; friend of Cloud

Elders

Big Voice—Oglala; father of Rabbit
Black Shield—Oglala leader
Brave—Sicangu at Spotted Tail agency
Eagle Man—Hunkpapa
Eagle Road—Cheyenne medicine man
Elk of the Four Winds—Oglala; carries the embers from the council lodge
Fontonelle, Logan—part-white Omaha warrior and leader
Grey Bull—Oglala elder
High Eagle—Oglala elder; medicine man
Kills Two—Sicangu
Last Horse—Sihasapa
Red Butte—Dakota
Red Shirt—Oglala
Runs Above—Sicangu at Spotted Tail agency
Shadow Wolf—Cheyenne; old Dog Soldier
Shakes the Hill—Oglala; old medicine man
Shivering Crane—Blue Cloud or Arapaho
Sitting Bull—Hunkpapa medicine man and leader
Star Boy—Sicangu at Spotted Tail agency
Swift Bear—Sicangu; leader at Spotted Tail agency
Tools—Oglala; father of Black Wolf
Worm—Oglala; medicine man and father of Crazy Horse

Women and Children

Badger—Sicangu; horse guard
Black Shawl—Oglala; wife of Crazy Horse
Blue Stone—Sicangu; old woman at Spotted Tail agency
Buffalo Calf Road—Cheyenne; wife of Black Coyote and sister of Comes in Sight
Corn—Oglala; old woman who sometimes stays with Crazy Horse and Black Shawl
Gathers Medicine—Oglala; older wife of Goings
Good Plume—Sicangu widow
High Voice—Oglala widow
Little Creek—Oglala widow
Looking North Woman—Oglala; wife of Black Shield
Looks Back Woman—Oglala; friend of Black Shawl
Plum—Oglala; wife of Yellow Wolf
Red Leaf—Oglala; wife of Grey Bull
Red Quill—Oglala
Red Shawl Woman—Hunkpapa; mother of Hawk Eagle
Song—Oglala; older daughter of Sweetwater Woman and Cloud; later known as Katherine Fontonneau
Stands on the Hill—Oglala; wife of Little Bird
Star Woman—Oglala; mother of Sweetwater Woman
Sweetwater Woman—white woman raised by Star Woman and Bearface; wife of Cloud; later takes the name of Agatha
Swimmer—Oglala; horse guard
They Are Afraid of Her—Oglala; deceased daughter of Crazy Horse and Black Shawl
They Are Afraid of Her—Oglala; younger daughter of Sweetwater Woman and Cloud; later known as Anne Hail
Walks Alone—Oglala; sister of Plum; wife of Fast Horse
Walks in the Night—Cheyenne; younger wife of Goings
White Crane—Oglala widow
White Dress—Sicangu; wife of Two Hawk
White Hill Woman—mother of Rabbit
Willow—Oglala; deceased grandmother of Cloud
Yellow Leggings—Oglala; mother of Red Lodge; sings Strong Heart songs during the Greasy Grass battle

Long Knife Scouts

Bloody Knife—Arikara; Custer's favorite
Bouyer, Mitch—"half-breed" Sioux attached to the Seventh Cav.
Broken Hand—Crow; given food by Cloud and Crazy Horse; later hired by the Seventh Cav.
Curly—youngest Crow attached to the Seventh Cav.
Left Hand—Crow; attached to the Seventh Cav.
White Man Runs Him—Crow; attached to the Seventh Cav.

Whites and Long Knives

Benteen, Capt. Frederick—company [troop] commander, Seventh Cav.
Blake, Pvt. Ezra—Seventh Cav.; gets separated from the column
Brisbin, Maj. James—officer under Maj. Gen. Alfred Terry
Cooke, Lt. W.W.—aide-de-camp to Lt. Col. George Custer
Crook, Brig. Gen. George—commanding Ft. Fetterman column
Custer, Elizabeth—George Custer's wife; also known as Libbie

Custer, Lt. Col. George Armstrong—commander of Seventh Cav.; held brevet or temporary rank of major general in the Civil War
Custer, Capt. Thomas—company [troop] commander, Seventh Cav.; George Custer's brother
Gibbon, Col. John—commanding Fort Ellis column
Grant, Pres. Ulysses S.—eighteenth president of the United States
Harris, Jake—white trader traveling with Ben Wilkins
Higgins—pvt., Seventh Cav.; gets separated from column
Holliman, 2nd Lt. Edward Monseet—aide to Gen. Crook
Kellogg, Mark—civilian reporter from *Bismarck Tribune* accompanying Seventh Cav.
Keogh, Capt. Myles—company [troop] commander, Seventh Cav.
MacAllister, Sgt. Maj. Benjamin—noncommissioned officer under Gen. Crook
Manfred, Capt. Charles—from Fort Ellis; captured by Lakota warriors
Mathias—Seamus Murphy's assistant
Murphy, Seamus—government stenographer
Reno, Maj. Marcus—second in command, Seventh Cav.
Reynolds, Charley—Custer's guide and scout in Seventh Cav.
Sheridan, Gen. Philip—commander of Dept. of the Missouri
Sherman, Gen. William Tecumseh—commander in chief, US Army
Terry, Maj. Gen. Alfred E.—commander of the Dept. of the Dakota from Fort Abraham Lincoln
Varnum, Lt. Charles—commander of Indian scouts, Seventh Cav.
Wainscote, Sgt. Ira—noncommissioned officer from Fort Ellis; captured by Lakota
Weir, Capt. Thomas—company [troop] commander, Seventh Cav.; ally of George and Tom Custer
White Hat Clark—Lt. W. P. Clark at Ft. Robinson
Wilkins, Ben—white trader traveling with Jake Harris

PROLOGUE

June 23, 1920

John Richard Cloud stood, hat in hand, at the fence in the east ditch alongside the road and gazed into a long, wide, shadowy gully that stretched away from the narrow highway. They were on the Crow Reservation, enemy country. He had not seen a Crow Indian for more than forty years, though he knew they were still around. Something stirred inside him, an ancient, inherent sense of wariness. It was an instinctive response left over from the old days, when he and other Lakota warriors had ridden into Crow territory.

But things had changed, and there was no way to avoid the fact that their destination, the site of the Battle of the Greasy Grass, was on land that now belonged to the Crow tribe. He knew a Crow war party would not charge out of the gully, but part of him almost wished it would.

He sighed and looked up to the ridge above the gulch where a thick stand of tall pine trees covered the jagged crest. Behind him and below the road was the town of Lodge Grass, Montana. On the narrow shoulder of the road, his grandson Justin Fontonneau was putting a spare tire on the car. They had been chugging along steadily, albeit slowly, when a tire blew. Justin finished and lowered the jack, then stood and walked around the car to inspect the other tires.

"This tire is torn and the tube has a hole in it," Justin said. "I think we ran over something sharp. I want to mount the other spare before we go."

Justin was twenty-two, a strong young man who stood just over six feet tall and bore a striking resemblance to his grandfather. In April he had been honorably discharged from the US Army after a three-year enlistment that included service on the battlefields of France in 1918.

A few yards from the car, Katherine Fontonneau and Anne Hail, Cloud's daughters, sat on a blanket beneath the shade of Anne's umbrella.

"Dad," Katherine called out, "come sit with us while Justin finishes fixing the tires."

"You might as well sit and rest while I work," the young man said, taking a new tube and tire casing from the car.

Acquiescing to the heat, Cloud walked over and joined his daughters.

Both wore calico dresses and had their long black hair pulled back in a French bun. Their complexions were fair, thanks to their mother, Agatha, who was not Lakota.

They had spent the night in a hotel in Sheridan, Wyoming, after getting past a nervous desk clerk who had reluctantly let Cloud through the front door. Breakfast in the dining room had drawn more than a few annoyed glances from other patrons. After ignoring that often-comical angst, the family drove north out of town and onto a gravel highway. After two hours, the right rear tire blew and temporarily brought a halt to their odyssey back in time. Starting from the northern part of the Rosebud Sioux Indian Reservation in South Dakota, they had driven more than four hundred miles in just over a week.

In March, Cloud had started talking about wanting to see the Powder River country east of the Bighorn Mountains and the battlefield on the Greasy Grass River where the Lakota defeated Custer. Anne and Katherine had talked him into waiting until Justin was home from the army. Cloud's neighbor and good friend had loaned them his car, a 1919 Packard. Fortunately, it had two spare tires.

"This was our territory back then," Cloud pointed out, waving his arm in a sweeping gesture, "all the way to the Elk River. I guess it is called the Yellowstone River now. But the whites gave the land to the Crow, maybe because the Crow scouted for them against us."

"It's on the government map I got from the agency," Katherine told him, "the Crow Indian Reservation."

Cloud grinned. "Enemy territory. We better watch out."

Anne pointed south. "I think I remember this part of the country," she said. "I remember Mom and Great-Grandma Willow taking down the lodge whenever it was time to move. My job was to put the picket pins in a bag." She paused and gazed at the grass near her feet. "I remember when Grandma Willow died."

"Yes, that was in 1871, I think," Cloud recalled. "We took her to a small hidden plateau above the Tongue River and put her beside my grandfather."

"How old was she?" Katherine asked.

"Around eighty, she thought," Cloud replied. "She remembered hearing about Lewis and Clark when they came up the river. She was thirteen or so then."

"She outlived her children," Anne said softly. "That must have been hard."

"I never heard her say that," Cloud said, "but I know she thought about my mother and uncle a lot. She would tell stories about them from when they were children."

"Speaking of stories," Katherine said, "what happened after the Battle of the Hundred in the Hand? You said it was the coldest winter you could remember."

"It was," Cloud affirmed. "Deep snow, and so cold your spit froze before it hit the ground." He paused, letting the memories fall into place. "After the battle, I couldn't do much except walk. It was a month before I could ride a horse without hurting. My cousin Goings and the others kept my family supplied with meat. All of Crazy Horse's people had a lean winter. Men had to travel far and for days just to find deer and elk. The soldiers in the fort stayed inside until spring."

"When did they finally leave?" Katherine asked.

"Not until the following year," Cloud replied. "The summer before, they surprised us after they got new rifles, breechloaders. They could fire as fast as they could pull out one shell and load the next. We cornered several wagons on the road. There were thirty or so soldiers. Red Cloud decided to attack, but the soldiers held their own. They took down their wagon boxes, put them in a circle, and hid behind them. We charged several times, but we could not overrun them. After several good men were killed, Crazy Horse finally called it off."

"Is that where Taken Alive was wounded?" Anne asked.

"Yes. A bullet went through his leg, above the knee. That leg was weak for the rest of his life. After that day, though, he never took part in any action led by Red Cloud. He never said anything against him, he just stayed away from him."

"And Red Cloud went to Fort Robinson the next year?" This was from Katherine.

"Yes. After he signed the paper at Fort Laramie in 1868, the whites set aside some land for him to live on near Fort Robinson. His people followed him. Before that, the soldiers had left the forts, and some of Red Cloud's followers said he had defeated them. I do not know if that is true, but he never fought against the whites again."

"So after he went to Nebraska, the only people still out here were those who were with Crazy Horse and Sitting Bull?" Katherine asked.

Cloud nodded. "Spotted Tail took many of the Sicangu, my father's people, to Nebraska. I think over half of the Lakota nation was living near Fort Robinson. So when Long Hair came to the Black Hills in 1874 and said there was gold, there were not enough fighting men with Sitting Bull and Crazy Horse to chase out the whites who came like flies to a dead carcass.

"By then, the hide hunters had killed off most of the buffalo. First, they took only the tongues, then the hides, because they sold them back East somewhere. Later, other whites came and took all the bones. My cousin went along on a trip to Wash'ton one summer, and he said he saw a pile of buffalo bones near the railroad in some town. Omaha, I think. A pile higher than a square house."

"My word!" Anne exclaimed.

Justin had finished mounting the tube and tire casing on the second spare rim and brought it and the hand pump down to the ditch. After he attached the pump to the stem of the air valve on the rim, he sat back to rest.

"In the army I met a man whose grandfather was a hide hunter," he said. "He told everyone how his grandfather would sit on a hill above a herd a hundred yards away or more with a long-barrel Sharps, a .60 caliber, and kill them, sometimes forty or fifty in a day. Then the skinners came and took the hides and left everything else." Justin paused, a little anger emerging with the memory. "That man was proud of what his grandfather did."

Cloud nodded solemnly. "I remember a few times when someone found carcasses after the hide hunters left. Everyone hurried to take what was still good. Sometimes they had to cut away some of the meat and leave it. All the old women cried when they saw the buffalo, naked and dead, scattered across the prairie.

"Then they were harder to find. Buffalo scouts kept track of the herds; they knew all the trails. But after a while, the buffalo did not come, and we knew it was because there were not as many as before.

"The fall before Custer came to the Black Hills, Taken Alive, Yellow Wolf, Goings, and I looked for a long time, days and days. We came up here," he said, waving his arm, "even past the Yellowstone River, before we found anything. But that was too far to take a hunting camp. After that year, it turned worse. We had to travel farther to find just a handful, sometimes only five or six."

"So what did you hunt?" Justin wanted to know.

"Deer, elk, and antelope. Mountain sheep, sometimes. But there was no way to replace the buffalo. The women could patch lodge covers with elk hide, but there were not enough buffalo hides to make new lodges.

"Still, we meant to stay away from the agencies no matter what. Living free and being hungry now and then was better than having the whites tell us what to do."

Justin started pumping air into the tire as a truck rattled by, its driver paying no attention to the people by the road.

"Grandpa, what about the people at the agency in Nebraska? How did they live?"

"They had to stay there, I know that," Cloud said. "No hunting. The whites gave them food—beans, rice, and flour, I think. Blankets, too. All brought in by wagons. For meat, they had longhorn cattle. There was nothing for the young men to do. The way of the hunter and warrior was over. A few of them would sneak away, though, and bring news up to us. We would send word back with them for our relatives. They thought we had it rough, and we felt sorry for them."

"Dad," said Katherine, "you never gave in, did you?"

Cloud nodded slowly. "There was no other way. Your mother being white, we were both afraid they would take her away if we went to Fort Robinson. So we went part of the way with Crazy Horse in the spring of 1877. Then we went east toward the White Earth River. Yellow Wolf and his wife went with us. You, too, were there. You were born in March. I can still see you in your cradleboard lying across the withers of the horse your mother rode."

Justin stopped pumping and tested the firmness of the tire, then glanced at his grandfather, who was staring off into the distance.

After a moment, Cloud sighed and leaned forward, elbows resting on his knees. "My grandfather would say that life was not worth living unless we had to defend it now and then," he said. "That is what we had to do. It was hard for us to find food and stay hidden. We had be alert all the time and watch for white people. But it was good, too. You girls grew up free. You played along the rivers. You grew up happy and strong."

"I cannot remember ever being hungry," Anne said. "Winters were rough, but we always had food, and you and Mom told us stories."

"We can go now," Justin interjected gently.

In a few minutes, they were reloaded and on their way again. Cloud stared out at the passing landscape. The last time he had laid eyes on the hills and trees here, it had been from the back of a good horse.

Cloud lost himself in his memories as the miles slowly slid by. When they finally stopped, it was at a strange gate—made of iron, he thought—that crossed over the road. After a short pause, Justin drove through it and followed the road up a hill. Cloud recognized the area, but not the building to the right of the road, or the stone monument at the end of the ridge. They parked beyond the monument and got out of the car.

The old man sighed deeply, his thin shoulders straight as he stared at the strange square obelisk rising from the end of the ridge east of the Greasy Grass River. The last time he had stood here, dead soldiers and dead horses were scattered on the dry, dusty slope. Now, two large, light-colored blocks of stone sat atop a square base of raised earth. The monument did not fit in with the bristly soap weeds, sparse grass, and thistle stalks all around it. All the plants and the land were just as he remembered, but now there were fences and a narrow gravel road leading up to the ridge.

Immediately below the monument on the west face of the slope was a fenced area with headstones. Cloud wondered if the soldiers who had been killed here were buried where they had fallen. It was on this ridge where one of the two final skirmishes of the first day of battle occurred. In the recesses of his memory, Cloud could hear the last rifle blasts reverberating down the valley.

"Grandpa," Justin said, "I saw a painting of the battle. It shows Custer with a pistol in each hand and completely surrounded by warriors. Is that how it was?"

Cloud turned his tired eighty-one-year-old eyes toward his grandson. Justin had achieved the rank of sergeant in the army during his enlistment. He had fought in France in the worst of the trench warfare. Cloud felt a bond with the young man. They were both warriors in the truest sense of the word, having earned that distinction in the unfettered violence of combat. One of Cloud's last battles had ended here, on this ridge now known as Custer Hill.

"No," Cloud replied. "Maybe thirty or forty soldiers made it this far," he pointed to the headstones, "where those markers are. None of them were standing, and they did not fire very much. Maybe they were low on bullets. We were all around, taking good aim. There were several shots, like the last beats of a drum, and then it was quiet. All the soldiers were dead."

"So that was 'Custer's Last Stand '?"

"Not much of a last fight for them. Most of them were on foot. Some were helping the others, carrying them, I mean."

Cloud fell silent, staring out over the land. That summer of 1876 was always in the back of his mind, like a friend standing outside the door, waiting to be invited in, and sometimes like an enemy lurking in the shadows. Now, with each passing moment, the memories became clearer and clearer.

Days before, fifty miles to the south, they had fought the Battle of the Rosebud. There had been other battles—the Hundred in the Hand, the Battle of Red Buttes, near the Shell River, and the revenge raids south of the Shell after the murders of the Blue Clouds, also called the Arapaho, at Sand Creek. That was more than fifty years ago now.

Cloud's old eyes noticed that there was writing on the square monument, and he shook his head. The whites were fond of their monuments, like the one south of Prairie Dog Creek they had seen only two days ago. That one had been raised in memory of the Long Knives from Fort Phil Kearney who had been killed in the Battle of the Hundred in the Hand. But the words on that marker did not tell the truth. He wondered if this square monument told the true story of this battle.

He turned and saw his daughters. They were looking out over the land.

Anne pointed west toward the river. "Dad," she said, "where was the village?"

"You should remember," he reminded her. "You were nine that summer. It was south, on the west side of the river." A thought rushed through his mind. "What day is today?" he asked.

"The twenty-third," replied Katherine. "Today is June twenty-third."

A distant look drifted into Cloud's eyes. "On their calendar, the first day of fighting was June twenty-fifth," he said quietly.

Cloud nodded as he slowly brought himself back to the moment at hand. He glanced toward the monument. "What does it say, those words?" he wanted to know.

Katherine shaded her eyes against the bright summer sky. "Names, Dad. They are the names of the soldiers who died here."

Cloud shook his head, turned away, and began retracing the path toward their car. Katherine, Anne, and Justin followed.

"Drive that way," Cloud said, pointing south.

The road was narrow and fairly straight until it bent slightly west before it went down into Medicine Tail Coulee. From there, it rose gradually behind the eastern slopes of the ridges above the river and then opened onto a narrow plateau. They drove another half mile or so, to yet another stone monument, but a smaller one this time.

"This is where the first soldiers dug in," recalled Cloud. "They were still here when we left the next evening. All they could do was watch us go."

Justin parked the car and pointed to a high point farther south. "That hill can probably give us a good view of the valley below, if we feel like walking."

Cloud stepped out of the car and began walking across the grassy meadow before everyone else could react.

Anne managed to grab a jar of water before she and the others got out too. She watched her father, his stride long and certain. "It's been a long time since he's been excited about anything," she observed.

Katherine found the umbrella she liked to use as a sunshade. "I know," she agreed. "I think it's good. But lately there has also been a different look in his eyes, almost like he's looking at everything for the last time."

Anne nodded pensively and glanced toward her nephew, who took off his coat and hurried after his grandfather. "Yes. Last week, before we came," she recalled, "he was on the hill above our house every morning by sunrise. He was just standing there, looking around."

They stared for a moment longer at their father walking away from them. He seemed to blend into the landscape. After another moment, they hurried to catch him.

After a five-minute meandering walk through the soap weeds, the family stood on the crest of the hill. To the south, west, and northwest was the broad green floodplain. They could see where Ash Creek flowed into the Greasy Grass, or Little Bighorn, River.

Cloud pointed east toward low hills and broken ridges. "The village was there, four, five miles away, maybe, for about one month. Sitting Bull did a Sun Dance there. That's where he had his vision of soldiers falling from the sky into a Lakota village. Our horses ate the grass down, so we moved to this spot." He waved an arm to indicate the floodplain west across the river. "The lodges were pitched among the cottonwood trees all the way north to the Medicine Tail crossing."

"Yes, I remember now," Anne told her father. "So many lodges. I tried to count them, but the trees got in the way. I was playing with someone, I think, and we followed her dog into the Cheyenne camp. That would have been north of ours."

Katherine gazed down at the giant cottonwood trees standing on the floor of the valley. "Sis," she said, "where were you when the soldiers came?"

"Mom and I were making jerky in front of our lodge," she recalled. "I don't remember where Dad was."

"I was near the horse herd," he told them. "I was trading horses with Good Hand. We heard shots to the south."

Justin pointed to a grassy mound of earth. "That looks like a good place to sit, Grandpa," he suggested.

Cloud nodded and sat down. His grandson followed.

"Yes. We will sit here, and I will tell you what happened."

After removing his coat, he untied the black bandana from his neck and wiped his face. He gazed across the land below them and across the river. But Justin knew it was not the land he was seeing. He had seen that kind of look many times on the faces of men who reluctantly look deep within themselves, carefully approaching the dark memories of battle.

As Katherine and Anne joined them, a warm, gentle breeze crawled up from the river along the bottom of the valley. It was nearly noon.

Cloud turned his gaze east toward the outline of the Wolf Mountains. Suddenly, he saw a long line of mounted Lakota and Cheyenne fighting men riding up the broken slopes. He could feel the horse beneath him as it picked its way up the narrow trail.

"People forget," he began, "that we fought a column of Long Knives before Long Hair attacked us. We fought them on Rosebud Creek, fifty miles from here, eight days before we killed Long Hair. We rode through the night and fought them all day. Then we rode through the night again to get back."

Cloud plucked a blade of grass and stared at it. "But when Sitting Bull sent out the call, a lot of Red Cloud's and Spotted Tail's people broke away from the agencies and joined us." He paused to sort through the memories that swirled behind his eyes like windblown leaves of autumn. "It was good," he murmured. "When we got together, we were powerful again. When the enemy came, we defeated them. But after the battle, we had to fight a different kind of power in order to survive, so that there would always be Lakota in the world."

Anne leaned forward, offering a drink of water. "What do you mean, Dad?"

Cloud smiled as he took the jar of water. "I will tell you," he said resolutely. "I will tell you. This is a good day for remembering."

CHAPTER ONE

Message in the Winter Moon—November 1875

High above the frozen river, the Lakota sentry hidden inside a tangle of deadfall gazed intently at the horse and rider below him on a wide plateau. His expression changed little as he noted that the buckskin horse was following the game trail along the north bank of the meandering ribbon of snow-covered ice, moving in a westerly direction. Using his field glasses, the man in the brush pile quickly confirmed his hunch: the rider was a Lakota wrapped in a buffalo robe.

Yellow Wolf put away the field glasses and, as he blew on his hands, considered what to do. He had taken his station just before sunrise, and despite wearing winter moccasins, a thick elk-hide shirt and leggings, and warm buffalo-hide mittens and a robe, he still had to flex his legs and move his arms to stay warm. Although the sun had brought some warmth, the midafternoon air of the Winter Moon definitely had a sharp bite. An annoying breeze sneaked into the deadfall, forcing him to adjust his robe. Wiggling his toes and stretching his back, he was glad for the opportunity to leave his cramped quarters.

He did not recognize the rider, but he did know a good horse when he saw one. The packs hanging on either side of the tall, sturdy buckskin were an indication the man was on a long journey. Yellow Wolf guessed he was either Sicangu or Hunkpapa Lakota. There was only one way to learn which.

Easing his slender frame out of his hiding place, Yellow Wolf made sure the buffalo robe did not catch on a branch. In the crook of his left arm, he cradled a breech-loading rifle inside its thick elk-hide case. Nearly forty paces behind the brush pile stood his horse, a muscular gray neatly blending into the tall, leafless shrubs and the mottled hillside behind him. Within a few moments, Yellow Wolf was mounted and heading for the trail leading down to the river.

The rider on the plateau instantly spotted the horse and rider as they appeared against the skyline. Under the buffalo robe, he grasped the handle of the six-shooter tucked into his belt. He knew he was in the area where the Crazy Horse people were said to be, and he also knew that the Crow occasionally raided from the north. But the outline of the horse and rider did not strike him as that of a Crow. He kept his hand on the pistol, just in case, as he reined in his horse and stopped to face them.

Yellow Wolf pushed the wolf-hide covering off his head and raised a hand in greeting.

"Friend," he called out, "where are you coming from?"

Hawk Eagle relaxed and said, "I came from the northeast with a message from our headman."

"You have come far," Yellow Wolf said. He openly admired the tall buckskin gelding the Hunkpapa was riding. "That is a good horse you have."

"Yes," Hawk Eagle agreed. "He is a gift from our headman. He gave all the messengers a horse."

"Then you must be carrying an important message," Yellow Wolf assumed. "I will take you to Crazy Horse. I am Yellow Wolf."

"I am Hawk Eagle," the messenger replied. "I am glad you found me. I was sure I was in the right area. I have never been this far west. It is beautiful country."

Yellow Wolf smiled. "Nearly a thousand of us think so, and some of us think it is worth dying for."

"That is what our headman told us. He said if anyone did not think our homes and our land were worth dying for, they should go to the agency and get fat on the white man's food and pray to his god."

The Oglala nodded. "Our headman says the same."

"I have never met him," Hawk Eagle admitted. "I was there when we chased some Long Knives around up on the Elk River two years ago. They were guarding some other whites who were measuring the land the strange way they do. I saw your headman in the distance, but I never met him."

"You will today," Yellow Wolf promised.

A biting breeze forced them to pull their robes up tighter around their necks.

"We are not far from Crazy Horse's camp," Yellow Wolf said. "How long have you been traveling?"

"Twenty days," Hawk Eagle replied wearily. He had tied the twentieth knot into the braided cord attached to his arrow quiver this morning. "The weather has been cold, but there has not been much snow."

"See any buffalo along the way?"

Hawk Eagle shook his head. "No, I did not see any at all."

"What about whites and Long Knives?"

"I saw none of them, either. I came north of Bear's Lodge in order to stay away from the white trading post on the Elk River. I was told to avoid that place, so I did."

"That was a wise thing to do."

Hawk Eagle chuckled. "It is easy to hide from the Long Knives, because they do not know the country. They do not know where to look."

"True enough," Yellow Wolf agreed. "They just move over it like a cloud of locusts, eating everything in their way."

Both men laughed, though they knew the hard truth behind the metaphor was anything but funny.

Yellow Wolf urged his gray into a lope. Hawk Eagle let his horse match the pace, and together they swiftly glided over the frozen ground, the sound of their horses' hooves more of a clatter than a thud.

The Crazy Horse camp was one of nine winter camps, with nearly a thousand people altogether. All were situated on the north side of the Tongue River, nestled against a hill or the slope of a gully, out of the north wind. The snow was not deep, though more was sure to fall in the months ahead.

Soon, Hawk Eagle could see some hoofprints on the ground, and more and more as they rode on, and wood smoke came on the breeze. As they gained a bench at the top of a gentle slope, lodges came into view, and he counted twenty. A dog or two barked at the sight of an unfamiliar horse and rider. Warhorses and buffalo runners picketed near lodge doors looked with interest at the buckskin, some issuing inquisitive whinnies.

Despite the cold, people were outside, engaged in various activities. A few young women wrapped in elk robes were hauling in wood for the night. At the north edge of the circle of lodges, two men were butchering an elk hung from a sturdy, leafless aspen before an audience of hungry dogs. A group of men stood talking around a fire in front of the council lodge, but they ceased their conversation at the approach of Yellow Wolf and Hawk Eagle. A group of small boys with cold, ruddy cheeks playing an arrow-through-the-hoop game stopped to stare.

The two riders reined in their horses at the council lodge. Yellow Wolf called out to Little Big Man, who had been sizing up the newcomer through narrowed eyes.

"Cousin, where is our headman? Our visitor here has a message from the holy man of the Hunkpapa."

Little Big Man's expression softened a bit. He was a short, compact man with quick movements. He wore a colorful capote, a coat obtained in trade, instead of an elk or buffalo robe. He pushed the long hood back from his head, revealing coal black hair and a weathered face. Without turning, he pointed with a thumb toward the end of the wide gully and the horse herd.

"He should be back soon," he told Yellow Wolf. "He was checking on one of his horses."

As Yellow Wolf and Hawk Eagle dismounted, Little Big Man turned to the younger man at his side. "Perhaps you can take word to the old men."

As the young man left, Hawk Eagle stepped forward. "My name is Hawk Eagle. My mother is Red Shawl Woman. My father died of the bowel sickness a year ago. He was Oglala."

"Yes," acknowledged Little Big Man. "I know your family. I am Little Big Man. You have come a long way. There is a fire in the council lodge. You can rest there. Our headman and the old men will come." He motioned for a teenage boy in the group around the fire to come closer. "Take his horse to graze in that grove of aspen. There is still grass there."

"Thank you," Hawk Eagle said to the boy as he untied a long bundle from the horse's neck rope and tucked it under his arm.

Yellow Wolf led him into the spacious council lodge. "Sit," he said. "Someone will bring you food."

Hawk Eagle did not have to be persuaded to go into the warm lodge. Inside, he untied the strings of the heavy buffalo robe, folded it, sat, and leaned back against a willow chair. He closed his eyes for a moment, happy to be out of the cold. The warmth and the simple comfort of the willow chair felt good. Yellow Wolf added wood to the fire and left.

Hawk Eagle had spent the previous night in a gully beneath a makeshift shelter. Although he had kept a small fire going, it did not actually warm him. It had only kept the cold at bay. Hawk Eagle was looking forward to a good night's rest in a warm lodge.

A soft rustling caught his ear as the door was pushed aside. Carefully balancing a kettle, a woman entered and gave him a motherly smile. In her other hand, she carried a coffeepot. As she bent to place the pot to one side on the bed of coals, he noticed that there were flecks of gray in her hair. From a bag under her arm, she deftly took out a bowl, spoon, and a metal cup.

"Elk stew," she explained, ladling it into the bowl. After handing him the bowl and spoon, she turned and poured coffee into the cup.

"Thank you, Aunt," he said, savoring the aroma of the stew and coffee. It had been days since he had had a hot meal.

She nodded. "The fire will warm you on the outside, and the food will warm you from inside. There is plenty," she said, pointing to the kettle. "Eat all you want."

After she left, Hawk Eagle slurped down the stew, disregarding the spoon, and sat back to sip the hot coffee. It had been a long, long journey. He put the cup aside and closed his eyes.

Sometime later, Hawk Eagle opened his eyes, realizing he had dozed. Two men stood before him. The one on the left had brown hair in two long braids, and a thin scar ran from the left side of his mouth back to his ear. His expression was polite, though his eyes were dark and inquisitive. He was dressed plainly beneath his elk winter robe. Hawk Eagle knew who he was: Crazy Horse, though he did not have the demeanor of a warrior, much less that of the greatest fighting man among the Lakota. The man beside him, also wrapped in an elk robe, was taller and darker. Hawk Eagle sensed a definite air of tough competence from him. He scrambled to his feet to greet them.

"I am Hawk Eagle," he told them. "I came from the northeast with a message from our headman."

"How is he, your headman?" Crazy Horse asked.

"He is well," Hawk Eagle replied. "The winter has been hard, but our people are doing well."

"Good, that is good to hear," Crazy Horse said. He turned to the man at his side. "This is my friend Cloud."

Hawk Eagle acknowledged the taller man. "Yes, I have heard of you as well."

"Sit," Crazy Horse invited. "I know you must be tired, but the old men will want to hear what you have to say."

"I am ready."

They filed in one and two at a time, all the old men from the village and two or three from the closest villages as well. By sundown, over thirty men were in the council lodge, including Crazy Horse and several warriors such as Cloud and Little Big Man. By the time everyone had arrived, Hawk Eagle felt refreshed, though somewhat intimidated by the gathering of old warriors, many of whom Sitting Bull had mentioned by name. Sitting in the group were two medicine men: Worm, the father of Crazy Horse, and High Eagle.

Grey Bull, nearly sixty years old but looking strong and distinguished with his nearly all-white braids, opened the meeting. "A young man has come to us after traveling many days," he said in a resonant voice. "He brings word from the Hunkpapa people, from their headman, whom we all know and respect." He turned to Hawk Eagle. "We are glad you have arrived safely and are anxious to hear what you have to say."

Hawk Eagle nodded, somewhat shyly. "Please thank the woman who brought me food," he said. "I have not eaten that well since I left my mother's lodge. I hope my horse is feeling as good as I am." A few chuckles flowed through the room. "Yes," he went on, "I do carry a message. My headman sent four of us. Two rode east toward the lands of the Dakota and Nakota. One went to the people of Spotted Tail and Red Cloud, at the agencies near the Smoking Earth River.

"We are all to say the same to all our relatives: that our headman wants all the people to gather together after the winter breaks. He says it is far past time for the Lakota people to drive the whites away from our lands."

Murmurs of affirmation filled the room. Hawk Eagle unwrapped the bundle made from the hide of a mountain lion and revealed a war arrow and a pipe in its bag. He took the arrow and held it out to Crazy Horse.

"My friend, my headman told me to put this in your hand," Hawk Eagle said. "It is one of his, a gift to you and to honor the courage of those who follow you."

Crazy Horse took the arrow. Beneath its two feathers was the mark of Sitting Bull: four narrow green bands around the shaft. "Thank you," he said. "It shall be placed high on the west wall of this lodge, to honor he who has sent it to us."

West, of course, was the direction where the Thunder Beings lived. West was the direction of power. It was the home of the Buffalo People as well.

Hawk Eagle cleared his throat and took the stem of the pipe and the black shale bowl from the bag decorated with dyed quills. "This pipe," he said, "he gave me to carry as a sign that the words of his message are sent with a good heart. He told me to smoke it with all of you. He asked me to ask the father of Crazy Horse to fill it and light it."

He passed the stem and bowl to Worm.

Worm took the pipe and fitted the stem to the bowl. Then, holding a bundle of sage over the fire, he waited for the gray smoke to rise as the sweet, pungent scent filled the room. Then he smudged each pinch of tobacco before he placed it in the bowl. With the burning ember on the end of a twig, he lit the pipe and offered it to the powers of Earth, Sky, each of the Four Directions, and finally to the Creator. After a short prayer, he took the first puff and passed the pipe to the man seated to his left.

When everyone in the room had smoked, Worm dismantled the pipe, emptied the ashes into the fire, cleaned the bowl, and passed the stem and bowl back to Hawk Eagle.

Grey Bull turned to the messenger. "Tell us, Nephew, the words you bring from your headman."

Hawk Eagle nodded and nervously cleared his throat. Now it seemed so long ago, but for many evenings he and the other young men sat with Sitting Bull as he gave them the message he wanted the important men among the Lakota to hear. "These are the things you must say, and in this way," he had told them. Hawk Eagle and the others had memorized and rehearsed the words until they could practically say them while asleep. But now, sitting at the back of the council lodge in the village of Crazy Horse, in the spot reserved for honored guests, he felt overwhelmed by the task he was given to do.

He cleared his throat again. "My friends and relatives," he began, feeling every eye in the room on his face, "my headman told me to say this to you: In life there is change, some good and some bad. From the childhood of our elders, change that we did not ask for has come, like a fire that slowly weakens the strongest oak tree. That change has already divided our nation, fooling many of our people into accepting it. Now they are living under the control of those who bring the change near the mouth of the Smoking Earth River, at those places called agencies. If we do not resist more strongly, we will all be under the control of those who bring the change.

"The Black Hills, the center of our world, is like the dog that cannot rid itself of fleas. That sacred place is infested with those who seek the yellow metal that drives white men crazy. We know that our relatives who live in the shadows of the great Shining Mountains understand our thinking, because they—like us—still live as free people. And it is those of us who are still free that are the best hope to keep our lands and our old ways. We must rescue our relatives from the agencies and help them to see their mistake. We must cleanse them of their softness toward the white men.

"I invite all who have like minds and hearts to gather so that we may talk. In the old days, our old ones talked about everything that lay in their path. That is what we must do now, because if we allow the white men to take our lands from us, the thing that lies in our path now is the end of our ways. The white men have already done too much damage.

"I will bring my people to the Chalk Buttes when the winter breaks and spring comes, at the end of the Moon When Geese Return. I will pray that all good Lakota people will join us."

Hawk Eagle dropped his gaze to the bed of glowing coals in the fire pit after he finished. He had never been much of an orator, but Sitting Bull had selected him because he was dependable, as were the three other messengers. But the other three were better at speaking in public. He suddenly realized he was sweating a little and reached up to wipe his brow. He did not have to look up to know that each man in the room was contemplating the words he had just spoken on behalf of his headman.

Grey Bull cleared his throat. "I have heard your headman speak several times. His words have always been good and wise, as they are now. We here have talked of the same concerns he has. They are ours as well."

Hawk Eagle noticed that Crazy Horse nodded in agreement as the older man spoke.

"I can say," Grey Bull went on, "that we will join you when spring comes."

A chorus of low affirmations rolled through the lodge like distant thunder.

Later that evening, a boy brought in an armload of wood, smiled shyly at the small group of men still in the lodge, and exited. His movements were quick and quiet as he slipped out the door. On the north side of the room sat Grey Bull and High Eagle. Cloud, Crazy Horse, Little Big Man, and Hawk Eagle sat on the opposite side. Everyone else had gone home long before.

"It is good to visit, to hear what is going on in your country," Grey Bull said to Hawk Eagle. He stood and pulled his well-worn elk-hide robe over his wide shoulders. "But I need to go home before that old woman thinks I have wandered off somewhere again," he joked, his eyes twinkling.

Amid good-natured laughter, everyone else took the hint and stood.

Crazy Horse looked briefly at the visitor. "This morning, before you arrived, one of our buffalo scouts came back. He found a small herd in a hidden valley west of here, about a half-day's ride. If you are not too weary, we would be glad to have you along. We will leave in the morning, when the light is good. I have a horse I can lend you, so yours can rest."

Hawk Eagle nodded. "Good!" he said. "I will go with you."

Sweetwater Woman was still awake and working on a pair of winter moccasins when Cloud returned. He paused to tie the outside door securely and then did the same to the inside door, taking a moment to stuff the space between them with grass for added insulation. The air outside was cold.

"Everyone is talking," she said to him, "about the messenger. Are the Hunkpapa ready to go to war?"

Cloud shook his head as he removed the buffalo-hide coat and folded it. "It may come to that," he replied. "Many of us have been thinking that we need to do something. Going to war against the whites may be the thing."

Sweetwater Woman paused and leaned back against her willow chair, putting aside her bone awl. She looked at the small form curled under a buffalo robe between the fire pit and the south side of the room. A stream of reddish brown hair was partially visible beneath one edge of the hide.

"She has never seen a Long Knife or any white man up close," she said.

Cloud removed his moccasins and looked over at their sleeping daughter. She would be nine soon, in a month. She had been born in the Middle of Winter Moon in the winter of the Hundred in the Hand. Sweetwater Woman was right—although they had been close to Fort Laramie a few times in the past nine years, she and Song had stayed far away from the whites. For good reason.

Sweetwater Woman was terrified that she would be taken by the Long Knives if they saw her, thinking they must rescue her. She knew the Long Knives would assume she was a captive of the Lakota. Song, because she was half white, was not as light skinned as her mother, but Sweetwater Woman did not want to take the chance of some nosey white man seeing either of them. So she stayed away from the Long Knives. Although Song had asked why her mother's skin was so pale, it had been only childish curiosity, nothing more. Someday, however, there would need to be an explanation. And Sweetwater Woman would give it, when the time came. In the meantime, like any other Lakota woman in the Crazy Horse band, she wished all the white people would go away.

"Do not worry," Cloud told her. "If we go to war against the whites, it is to drive them away, out of our lands."

Sweetwater Woman smiled and began to put away her sewing things, then turned to gaze fondly at the form curled beneath the buffalo robe.

"Tomorrow, we are going after buffalo," Cloud said, glancing up at his hunting bow and quiver of arrows.

"It would be good to have fresh buffalo meat," she replied, finishing her task.

"We will," he assured her. "We will, so sharpen your knives."

CHAPTER TWO

The Hunters

Two old men stood at the edge of the encampment as the hunters rode out. Below them in the wide valley a mist hung over the river, a meandering, silvery white cloud. In the distance to the west, the black ridges of the Shining Mountains were a broad jagged line between the gray of land and sky. Black Shield and Grey Bull watched enviously as the line of riders followed a game trail until they disappeared into the mist. It was difficult for the two men to admit they were elders and not quite as physically capable as they once had been, but they found solace in the memories of their own hunts.

Without speaking, they turned and walked toward the inner circle of lodges. Only a few horse guards and dogs were awake at this hour of the morning. Several warhorses picketed at the doors of their owners hardly noticed their passing. At a lodge with the faded sketch of a coyote howling over the door, Black Shield untied the door and invited his friend to enter.

"I hope young Black Lance is right about that herd he saw," Grey Bull commented as he took a horn cup of tea from Black Shield's wife, Looking North Woman.

"I hope there are enough to feed us all," said Black Shield. "We need at least twenty to feed everybody in all the camps," he pointed out.

"If the buffalo are there, our hunters will find them. But that is not what worries me most," Grey Bull fretted.

"Yes, I know what you mean. There could be other hunters, like the Crow."

Grey Bull nodded grimly and sipped his tea. "There was a time when there was enough, more than enough, to feed all the nations. When I was a boy, I went east toward the Great Muddy with my father," he recalled. "Where the White Earth River meets the Smoking Earth, we saw something I will never forget: two herds. There were so many, they covered the land like a robe, from one skyline to the other. But that was only the beginning." He used his hands to illustrate, his fingers extended to represent the front of two herds flowing together. "They came together, like this." His fingers entwined. "One herd going south, and the other going west.

They passed through each other and kept going."

Black Shield and Looking North Woman sat quietly, in silent reverence, envisioning the image Grey Bull so aptly described.

After a few moments, the older man spoke again. "Who would have thought they would be gone in my lifetime?" he asked sadly. "When they ran, they shook the Earth, and we felt powerful. They were our power. After all, we are the Buffalo People. Now we pin our hopes on twenty."

Black Shield reached inside a bag decorated with faded quills, pulled out a bundle of sage, and held one end of it over the coals in the fire pit. As white smoke twirled upward, a wispy ribbon rising and wavering, the old man muttered a prayer.

Grey Bull cradled his horn cup between his palms, staring into the hot liquid. "It is hard not to hate them for causing all of this," he said, "but sometimes I wonder if we, too, caused it, in a way, by not fighting harder or sooner. I have heard old Turning Bear say more than once that we should have stopped the wagon people. After they attacked us over that sickly old cow,* we should have burned the fort to the ground and fought every column of Long Knives they sent. We should have tracked down and killed every hide hunter with a long gun." With a deep sigh, Grey Bull leaned back against his chair.

Black Shield had been nodding slowly, introspectively. Every man in the Sitting Bull and Crazy Horse bands carried the same thoughts and the same anger within him, and perhaps some of those languishing at the agencies near Fort Robinson did as well.

"I think Sitting Bull is doing a necessary thing," he said, "and I think many of our people will listen to what he has to say. But I also think something should have been done years ago."

"Is it too late?"

"Spotted Tail thinks so, and Red Cloud does too."

Grey Bull shook his head. "Of the two, I would be more interested in Spotted Tail's reasons for taking his people to the agency. What has it been, seven years since then? There is no one who is more of a warrior than him, except for our headman. My brother was with him at the Blue Water when Woman Killer Harney attacked. It was Spotted Tail who told me how fiercely

* Grattan Incident near Fort Laramie in 1854.

my brother fought before he was killed. But he never said anything about what he himself did. I heard it from others. After he was stabbed, he pulled the sword out of his shoulder and killed the soldier who stabbed him, and eight or nine others, before he was wounded again. That is a man! And when a man like that lays down his weapons, I would like to know exactly why."

Black Shield cleared his throat. "I think he saw something when he was in the white man's prison at the place called Leavenworth. He fought with us after that, when we went south to avenge the Cheyenne and the Blue Clouds after Sand Creek. After that, he helped us rescue the Loafers, those who were living near the white fort, when the Long Knives were taking them to prison. A man like that does not put away his weapons unless it is for a good reason."

"Yes," Grey Bull agreed, "but his reasons do not have to be ours. We are here because we want nothing to do with the Long Knives or any whites. Our reasons for living as we do are just as strong as his for living among them."

"True," said Black Shield, "but how long can we live without the buffalo?"

Near midday, the fog finally lifted. The warmth of the sun was a welcome change from the dampness of the cold, but their cover was gone. Keeping to the low areas, the hunters had cleverly used the fog to hide themselves.

Squinting in the bright light, Black Lance pointed to a stand of cedar atop a low ridge and looked at Crazy Horse. "There is a wide creek bed beyond that ridge," he said. "Good grass under the snow, and out of the wind too. They were there yesterday."

Crazy Horse glanced at Cloud. "We can take a look," he suggested. "If they are there, we will make some plans. If not, we will keep looking for them."

Gaining the low ridge, the hunters dismounted and worked their way through the thick stand of cedars. In the shallow valley to the west, they saw several cows.

"The rest are probably beyond that bend," Black Lance pointed out. "This creek comes out of the foothills; it goes a long way back, and it is narrower farther to the west."

Cloud pointed to the nearest animals. “The snow is deep there,” he said, “up to their bellies.”

That fact had not gone unnoticed. The cows, dark shapes against the bluish white hues of the snowfield, were close enough for the men to see well without using their field glasses. Fortunately, there was no wind to speak of, and all the animals had their heads down, browsing, shoving aside snow with their noses or scraping it away with their front feet.

Cloud turned around and looked at their horses standing quietly in the brush below them. Among them were two big grays, big wagon horses captured two summers ago in a raid against the Long Knives up on the Elk River. These horses had been brought along to haul meat.

“If we use arrows, we will be chasing buffalo the rest of the day,” Cloud said. “Whatever we do, we should not wait. A breeze could spring up any time.”

Crazy Horse looked toward the other men, Yellow Wolf, Taken Alive, Hawk Eagle, and Good Hand, and nodded. “How many bullets do we have?” he asked.

Taken Alive had the least: nine.

Crazy Horse turned to Cloud. “What do you think?”

“One man should stay here with the horses and keep watch,” Cloud replied. “The rest of us should move in close, crawl, I mean. Get in place so that each of us has a clear shot. Start shooting and stay hidden. If they do not see us, they probably will not run.”

“I will stay here,” offered Taken Alive.

At the Wagon Box Fight, eight years before, a bullet had gone through his right leg just above the knee. Since then, the leg had been weaker. No one, not even Crazy Horse, was a better fighter from the back of a horse than Taken Alive. But on foot, it was another matter.

“Good,” Cloud said. “Once we start shooting, if anyone else is around, they will come to see what is going on.”

Taken Alive nodded. “If you hear me shooting, it will not be at buffalo,” he said, looking around at all the men. “Remember that.”

Everyone understood his meaning.

The hunters shed their outer coats and robes so they could move easily through the brush. Then they checked their rifles. Everyone had at least a breechloader. Crazy Horse had a repeating rifle as well, but he preferred the single-shot breechloader for its knockdown power, especially for hunting buffalo. He would carry that and sling the encased repeater across his back just in case something other than coyotes or wolves was also hunting.

Each man took out a wolf cape—a full hide, from head to tail—and tied it on. When they crawled, it would look like wolves moving through the brush—if the buffalo saw them at all. If so, the buffalo would not run, but would form a circle to face the wolves. This ancient method would allow them to get close enough to take a shot using a bow and arrow.

The plan was simple. The buffalo were browsing in a meadow west of the narrow, meandering creek, now frozen solid. Staying in the brush and the trees east of the creek, the hunters would find open shooting lanes. Cloud and Crazy Horse would start shooting first.

Cloud and Crazy Horse moved out, working their way through the short, leafless brush. As soon as they were out of sight, Good Hand and Black Lance followed their path. Yellow Wolf and Hawk Eagle would be last. Yellow Wolf and Taken Alive had been watching the ridgelines and hilltops to the north.

"What do you think?" the younger man asked. "You think there are Crow over that ridge there?"

Taken Alive was glassing the ridges. He spoke without lowering the field glasses. "They get hungry too," he replied.

Yellow Wolf adjusted the six-shooter in his belt. "I think if they were around, they would have killed all those buffalo by now."

Hawk Eagle nodded in silent agreement.

"I hope you are right," returned Taken Alive.

Then, with hardly a whisper of sound, Yellow Wolf and Hawk Eagle were gone. By the time Taken Alive lowered the field glasses and looked toward the brush, he was alone. He glanced toward the horses, well hidden in the bushes. They were standing calmly, though Yellow Wolf's buckskin was testing the wind. Taken Alive watched until he was certain it was nothing more than curiosity.

Taken Alive listened intently as he kept the field glasses on the skyline. Now and then, he stole a glance toward the horses. For the time being, he was impervious to the cold.

Cloud and Crazy Horse were two shadows in the brush; only the soft swish of their feet shuffling through the snow hinted at their presence. Crazy Horse paused and pointed to an opening in the trees. Beyond the bend of the creek were more buffalo. The men crouched down for a moment. Then they moved on again.

Keeping to the trail left by Cloud and Crazy Horse, the other hunters followed quietly behind. Good Hand and Black Lance found a plum thicket and burrowed in between the stalks. From there, they had a good view of five of the cows.

Black Lance loaded his rifle and whispered, "Yesterday, I noticed there were no calves. Now that we're so close, I can see that this is a herd of cows, old cows. It means there are no bulls around."

Good Hand studied the cows in the meadow. Black Lance was right—no young ones, only mature cows. *What does that mean?* he wondered. *What if those are the last buffalo left?* He sighed. He propped his rifle on a branch and stared sadly at the cows.

Yellow Wolf and Hawk Eagle were the last in line and would not need to go as far. An arrow's cast from the cedar grove, they turned left off the trail and found a dead log in a small clearing. From there, they had an unobstructed view of the browsing buffalo. Yellow Wolf motioned for Hawk Eagle to get into position, then crawled to a small rise and brushed away the snow. Within a few moments, both men were ready to shoot.

Cloud rested his rifle on the lowest branch protruding from the trunk of a mature, leafless chokecherry shrub. A stone's throw away, Crazy Horse had fashioned his own shooting rest by tying two dry branches into a fork. He turned to Cloud and nodded.

Boom! The first shot was muffled by the distance.

Taken Alive flinched and resisted the urge to look down the valley. A sharp grunt came from somewhere in the meadow.

Moments later, more rifles blasted, one after another. *Boom-b-b-boom! Boom-boom-boom! B-b-b-boom!*

Then there was a brief silence, followed by a faint thrashing sound from the meadow.

Taken Alive kept his eyes on the ridges. He had a feeling that something—or someone—else was there, a feeling reinforced when he heard a soft snort from one of the horses. A quick glance back revealed all of them with their ears forward, staring toward the ridges to the north. Yet he also knew they could just be reacting to the gunshots.

Taken Alive turned back to probe the brush and trees along the ridge behind the hunters. A man would hide where there was cover, not out in the open. He was about to sweep left when a speck of a shadow moved in a stand of leafless aspen. He concentrated on the area for several long moments. Nothing. But he knew he had seen something. A rabbit, perhaps—or so he hoped. He looked back at the horses again. They were still looking north.

He took a quick look toward the meadow. All of the cows he could see were down. Two hunters, Yellow Wolf and Hawk Eagle, rifles ready, were moving cautiously toward the downed animals. Farther up the meadow, Black Lance and Good Hand emerged from the trees.

Two more shots blasted through the stillness. Someone was finishing off an animal.

Now for the hard work. The dead buffalo had to be gutted, skinned, and butchered. The men would be working late into the night, and they knew coyotes and wolves would come around, but those beings would only hang back in the night and wait for the human hunters to leave. Whatever or whoever else might be hiding out there would also wait for the darkness. Taken Alive was sure of it.

Cloud and Crazy Horse quickly implemented the next part of their plan. Yellow Wolf and Good Hand were sent back to the village to bring more men to help cut up and load the buffalo and more horses to haul the meat. If all went well, they would return to the buffalo camp by midday tomorrow.

Harnessing the two wagon horses, the remaining hunters set themselves to the hard, mundane task of gutting and hauling the carcasses to one area. They had killed seventeen buffalo, all mature cows. Each was bigger, and probably much heavier, than one of the wagon horses. Luckily, the snow cover made it easier to drag the carcasses, and after the third or fourth one had been moved, there was a packed and bloody trail to follow. By the time the sun was slipping down the western horizon, all the carcasses were below the cedar ridge. The wagon horses were exhausted, standing quietly with the others horses, heads hanging low.

There was nothing to do now but wait—and eat. Fresh liver and kidneys were roasted and voraciously consumed. As the hunters settled in around the fire inside the cedar grove, they heard the inquisitive yelps of coyotes and the distant howling of wolves from the gullies and ridges all around.

"As soon as our fire goes out, they will move in," Taken Alive commented. "But I have yet to see coyotes drag a buffalo carcass, though they might eat a lot."

Cloud chuckled. "We can share. I remember the big hunts. We all do. They were not that long ago," he said pensively. "The coyotes and wolves waited behind the hills. The women would leave choice cuts of meat, kidneys or liver, for the ancestors, they said, and they knew the coyotes and wolves would come and eat—for the ancestors. We have not hunted buffalo that way, with all the people doing their part in the hunt, for several years now." He pointed to the meadow where the carcasses were dark blots on the pale background of snow in the rapidly fading light. "Today, we killed seventeen," he went on. "Before, we would take hundreds so we could have meat for the winter. I feel bad for killing those today—they have just as much right to live as we do."

"My father told me that no one has asked him to train any horses as buffalo runners this year," Good Hand said. "What does that mean?"

Crazy Horse sighed. "It means things are changing. We are the Buffalo People without buffalo."

Taken Alive stirred the coals in the fire with a long stick. "I wonder what the ancestors think," he said. "I mean, about the buffalo. They have to be sad, and maybe angry. Maybe they are angry with us for not stopping the hide hunters."

Crazy Horse stared off into the fading light. "I am angry with us," he said, his voice low and hoarse. "We should have done more. We should have chased those stinking hide hunters and killed them all."

There was no argument or need for further comment. Every man agreed. But what was to be done now? A silence fell on the camp.

Around them, even the nearest trees and ridges were fading into the deepening shadows of dusk. Soon it would be dark, and there would be no moon that night.

Crazy Horse shot a glance at Taken Alive. "Coyotes and wolves will not bother us, we know that. But whatever you saw up there might. We will let the fire go out later on and wrap up in our buffalo robes. If we bring the horses into the grove, they will let us know if anything comes close."

The others nodded.

Taken Alive looked up at the hillside. He knew there had been something or someone else up there.

"One other thing," said Cloud. "The coyotes will come in, and probably wolves too. If anything else comes close, like two-leggeds, those four-leggeds will leave. So as long as we can hear the coyotes and wolves, no one else is around. On the other hand, if any two-leggeds want all the meat for themselves, they know they have to kill us all."

"Crow," Crazy Horse surmised. "They are probably Crow. We are not that far south of the Elk River. But it is probably a single scout, or only two or three, and they know there are five of us. If they outnumbered us, they would have tried something by now. Or it could also mean they are low on bullets."

"It means we do not sleep," Taken Alive said wryly.

"True," Cloud agreed. "But it also means we have a lot of meat we did not have this morning."

Taken Alive nodded. "And meat brings scavengers."

CHAPTER THREE

One Bullet, One Chance

Cloud had been hearing the sound long before he realized what it was. Someone was crawling in the snow and trying to use the snarling of the wolves tearing at the buffalo carcasses in the meadow to cover his noise. For the most part, the horses were standing quietly. Now and then, however, they stomped nervously or snorted in reaction to the wolves. The intruder was timing his movements to blend in with the sounds the horses and wolves made.

Sneaky, thought Cloud. *I wonder if anyone else is hearing it.*

As if in answer, a pebble bounced off his buffalo robe. It had come from the direction in which Crazy Horse was sitting.

Reaching down, Cloud took two tiny pebbles from the pile near his foot, quietly lowered his robe, and tossed first one and then the other toward the shadow against an old tree stump. Two stones meant he got the message.

The night air was cold, not bitterly so, but cold enough for Cloud and the others to have wrapped up in buffalo robes. There was no wind, fortunately, only an errant breeze now and then. That favored the Lakota. A cold, still night amplified the slightest noise. The other favorable factor was the snow cover. It reflected even the lowest light and revealed anything dark against the pale background.

Cloud could discern shapes, certainly well enough to tell a shrub or a tree trunk from the outline of an animal or a human. He knew someone was less than a stone's throw to the east, probably in the open areas, since moving through brush would be noisy. He knew Crazy Horse knew as well.

Cloud could visualize what the wolves in the meadow were doing from their snarls and yelps. The dominant animals, likely a male and female, had staked their claim and kept the others away. At first, judging from the intensity of the growls and snarls, it sounded like a hundred wolves fighting to the death. But Cloud knew it was a family of perhaps a dozen or so. As the younger and less assertive members moved to other carcasses, the confrontations diminished to only occasional warning growls. Now and then, he heard the cracking of rib bones in their powerful jaws.

Even as Cloud listened to the wolves gorge themselves, he kept his gaze on the shadows in front of him, knowing Crazy Horse was doing the same. More than likely, Taken Alive, Black Lance, and Hawk Eagle were alert as well.

Slowly, Cloud lifted the heavy robe off his shoulders and grabbed his tautly strung bow. He had leaned it downward across his chest, the tip of its lower limb against the instep of his right foot. Turning it, he laid it across his legs, placed two arrows into the palm of his left hand, and placed the third feathered shaft on the string.

Hawk Eagle saw nothing but dark, undefined shapes in the dim light, but more than anything, he sensed the presence of intruders. There was more than one, he was certain. But Crazy Horse was right: if there were four or five or more, they would have attacked long before now. Still, knowing that did not make him feel less anxious. Whoever was out there was probably willing to take a chance, and anything could happen. He wrapped his hand around the handle of his six-shooter. The hardest thing was waiting for something to happen.

A shadow to the left of a tree seemed to change shape, elongating, and then it slowly stretched upward. Cloud's fingers tightened around the nock of the arrow and the bowstring. He lifted the bow into shooting position, and he saw one of the horses turn its head, responding to something in the bare shrubs and trees below the camp.

The shadow blended in with the trunk of a tree. Cloud drew back the arrow on the string and prepared to snap off a quick shot. He heard a soft, whispery scrape, and then rhythmic footfalls, as something slid across the snow—someone was running, lightly, away from the camp. He released, sending the arrow in the direction of the footfalls. To his right, he heard the soft twang of a bowstring. Crazy Horse had taken a shot too.

They waited. The wolves fell silent. Several of the horses turned, looking off toward the soft noises. After several moments, the horses seemed to relax.

Cloud took a deep breath. A low query came from the darkness behind him.

"Did you hear that?" It was Hawk Eagle.

"We heard," Crazy Horse whispered. "They have gone, I think."

"The wolves are gone too, it seems," Cloud pointed out in a low whisper.

"They also heard," said Crazy Horse.

"The horses are quiet," Cloud told them.

On more than one occasion, Cloud had slept at the very feet of his horse, sometimes more than one horse. It was a common practice with hunters and warriors because horses were better sentries than any human could be. At the moment, the horses were telling them that there was nothing, or no one, close by.

"We should wait," suggested Crazy Horse.

The hunters bundled themselves back up in their buffalo robes. Each of them was lying or sitting on a thick mat of dry grass. Inside the heavy robe of winter hair, a man could be safe from the cold, even in a wind. Each was also wearing thick winter moccasins made from smoked elk hide. Smoking made the hide water-resistant, and dry grass stuffed into the toes of the shoes provided additional insulation.

They settled in to wait out the rest of the night, though they were not completely certain that the mysterious intruder or intruders would return. Most of the men dozed but did not fall into a deep sleep. Years and years on the trail as hunters and warriors helped them perfect that ability, and it often meant the difference between hearing the stealthy approach of an enemy in time or not waking up at all.

In time, the wolves were back in the clearing below, feeding again, though not as noisily. Cloud kept his eyes open as long as he could, watching the shadows and shapes in front of him. He listened for any sudden movement or noise the horses might make. He had put aside the bow and grabbed the handle of his six-shooter. Even as he felt himself dozing off, he kept his attention on the horses.

The night passed in between fits of dozing and periods of wakefulness. In a while, and ever so slowly, the landscape became more defined as the light grew from the east. The wolves had gone, but now there were higher-pitched, more strident yelps. Coyotes had been patiently waiting for their share of the meat and moved in on the heels of the departing wolves.

Cloud stood slowly and stretched his legs and back, looking around at the cold camp. Most of the horses were dozing. Behind him, Hawk Eagle and Black Lance followed his lead and roused themselves. Black Lance immediately set about starting the fire. Behind Crazy Horse, Taken Alive was rubbing his leg, trying to work the stiffness out of the old injury.

With six-shooter in hand, Crazy Horse walked down the slight incline behind the horses while Cloud went around to the other side. Behind leafless sumac shrubs a stone's throw from the camp, they found an impression in the snow where a man had lain on his stomach. Starting somewhere farther up a slope to the north, he had crossed the frozen creek and crawled to that point.

"He is good, whoever it is," Crazy Horse decided, "but it looks as though he was alone."

Why would someone take such a risk? Cloud wondered. Then, just ahead of the depression in the snow, he spotted something that answered his question: a broken arrow. He bent down and picked it up. It was a Crow arrow, but a broken arrow meant no fight.

"He went to all that trouble and risked getting shot to put this here," he said, holding up the two pieces of the shaft. "I think he wants to talk with us."

Crazy Horse nodded and looked at the slopes and groves of trees around them. "If you are right, sooner or later he will show himself again."

The smell of wood smoke wafted through the grove as Cloud and Crazy Horse returned to the camp.

Cloud tossed down the pieces of the Crow arrow. "Keep an eye out," he advised. "Someone out there wants to talk to us."

Taken Alive took the feathered half of the broken shaft and studied it for a moment. "If he shows up, I might shoot him just for keeping me awake all night," he groused.

Meanwhile, Black Lance had been making snowballs. After he had a handful, he took out his sling, placed one in the leather holder, whirled it around his head, then loosed a snowball toward the coyotes that were now visible in the meadow below them. The snowball splattered near them, and although they were momentarily startled, they quickly returned to tearing meat off the carcasses. Their hunger was more powerful than their fear of the humans in the cedar grove.

Gathering the remaining snowballs, the young man walked down the incline, took up a new position, and sent more icy missiles toward the ravenous creatures among the line of carcasses.

Although they dashed away each time a snowball splattered near them, the coyotes dashed back just as quickly to continue feeding, seeming to understand that their opportunity for fresh meat was short-lived.

Taken Alive shook his head in mock exasperation as he put a pot of snow over the fire. After the snow melted and the water boiled, he made tea.

The last stubborn shades of night were fading in the west, and the morning grew brighter with the promise of sunrise glowing over the eastern horizon.

Hawk Eagle brought more wood for the fire and settled down next to it. The sky was clear, and a cold day lay ahead, a cold day of hard work to finish the butchering they had started the day before.

Cloud unstrung his bow, encased it, put the arrows back into the quiver, and hung the weapons in a tree. He kept his rifle and six-shooter at hand.

Crazy Horse was standing next to a young cedar, gazing at the slope to the east. The barrel of his rifle protruded from beneath his buffalo robe. He turned and glanced at Cloud.

"Feel like going for a ride?"

They flanked the hill to the east, first angling south of it and then circling north, staying inside the cover of the aspen and oak until they were several hills east of their camp. When their horses suddenly showed an interest in something their weak human senses could not perceive, they stopped. Both horses rolled their ears forward and gazed intently into a thick grove of leafless aspen on a south-facing slope.

Crazy Horse lifted his field glasses from a hide bag and glassed the aspen grove on the hillside three hundred paces away. After several moments, he paused, then handed the field glasses to Cloud.

"The west end of the grove," he told Cloud. "Looks like an eagle's nest on the ground, and smoke is rising from it."

Cloud found the dark spot among the aspen. It was a well-hidden brush shelter, but the telltale smoke could not be hidden, thin though it was. Someone had taken the trouble to find dry wood to make as little smoke as possible. Cloud had a sense that they had found the night visitor to their camp—or at least they had found his camp.

A moment later, a figure rose out of the brush shelter and walked east to a tall thicket. In another moment, he led a horse forward out of the thicket.

Crazy Horse smiled. "This man knows what he is doing," he said. "Not bad for a Crow."

"Perhaps," Cloud replied. "But how good can he be? He does not know we are here, does he?"

Crazy Horse chuckled as they watched the man lead his horse through the trees to a small clearing and mount. "What are you willing to wager that he is heading for our camp?"

"Nothing I want to lose."

They rode forward to keep the distant rider in view, though they stayed inside cover as much as possible, weaving through trees and thickets. The rider wore a dark coat, probably made of wool. Cloud knew that the Crow frequently traded with whites, which probably explained this man's coat. But the Lakota also knew that the Crow were friends to the whites. What that had to do with the man they were following, he was not certain, but the combination of Crow and whites was not to his liking.

Weapons were not visible anywhere about the man, but at this distance it was difficult to see in detail. Just because they could not see a rifle did not mean he was not carrying a gun of some kind under his coat. In any case, they had the advantage for the moment, because the man did not know he was being followed.

The men stopped for a moment. Cloud turned and looked around, making sure there was no one else in the area. Crazy Horse quickly glassed the rest of slope of the aspen grove, spotted another horse in the thicket, and mentioned it to Cloud.

"Think there are two of them?"

Crazy Horse shook his head. "No. I think this man is hunting alone and has a packhorse with him." To make sure, he glassed the area thoroughly but found no other sign. "But keep your rifle ready, just in case."

Both men pulled their rifles out of their elk-hide cases before they resumed following the lone hunter.

Taken Alive was the first to see the horse and rider moving down the slope toward their camp. He motioned to the others. Rifles ready, they spread out in the grove.

Taken Alive stepped close to Black Lance. "I will keep an eye on our visitor. You two," he said, pointing to Hawk Eagle and Black Lance, "watch our flanks. I do not want anyone sneaking up while we all are watching one man."

Hawk Eagle and Black Lance immediately took positions to cover the open meadow behind them and the tree line to the north and south.

The lone rider raised both hands and rode slowly toward the camp. Taken Alive saw the rifle case hanging from the girth rope around the gray horse. There was a rifle in it. Given the age-old animosity between the Lakota and the Crow, this man was taking a chance. But Taken Alive was curious. Anyone, Lakota or Crow, who could sneak in close to any camp was a good man. He wanted to see him up close.

In another moment, two more riders topped the crest of the hill. Taken Alive recognized them immediately. He relaxed a bit, though not much. Cloud and Crazy Horse were behind the approaching rider, and probably had been for some time.

The man was Crow, no doubt about it. His horse accoutrements and especially the design of the beadwork on his rifle case were very familiar. As he came closer, his physical features became more discernible. He was a young man, a brave young man. A hand slowly reached up and pushed the hood off his head to reveal a narrow, pleasant face with a long nose and a wide mouth. A thick scar from the corner of his right eye to the edge of his mouth added to his air of self-assurance.

Taken Alive motioned him up into the grove, and then for him to dismount. Cloud and Crazy Horse arrived as the young man dismounted and led his horse to an open area and waited. If he was afraid, it was not evident in his expression or demeanor. He stood patiently.

As Cloud and Crazy Horse entered the clearing, a flicker of recognition flashed in the young man's eyes. Cloud looked at the man's gray horse with an appraising eye and gestured for him to join them at the fire.

The stranger took the cup of tea offered by Taken Alive and sat. With a twig he scratched an image, an upright hand, onto the frozen ground. Next, he drew a line across the hand, then tapped his chest.

"Broken Hand," said Cloud. "I think his name is Broken Hand."

No one, not even the longest-living elders, could say when the Lakota and the Crow became enemies. There were stories that many, many generations in the past, the Crow had been part of the Lakota, and there were many similar sounds and words in the two languages. Still, in the present day, they were enemies, and probably always would be.

Especially now, since many Crow worked as scouts for the Long Knives. But at this moment, five Lakota men were curious about the surprisingly calm young Crow man sitting at their fire, sipping their tea.

Putting down the cup, Broken Hand pointed toward the buffalo carcasses, made the sign for hunting, and imitated pointing a rifle. He had been hunting for buffalo; likely he had found the same herd. After a short pause, he made the sign of trade, moving his open palms back and forth.

"He wants to trade for meat," concluded Crazy Horse. Crazy Horse repeated the sign and held one hand, palm up and fingers spread, the sign for a question, meaning "What will you trade?"

The young man looked toward his horse, pointed, and imitated aiming a rifle. He was offering his rifle in trade for meat.

Cloud motioned for him to bring the rifle.

Broken Hand stood and walked to his horse, untied the case, and returned to the fire. Sitting back down, he opened it and pulled out a repeating rifle similar to the one Crazy Horse carried, and handed it to Cloud.

Everyone around the fire had seen such rifles. It was a lever action and could fire at least seven shots before it had to be reloaded. Every Lakota warrior wanted such a weapon, including those staring at it now in covetous silence.

Crazy Horse glanced at Cloud. "We know he is alone, and he does have a packhorse with him, so he was probably hunting and came across this herd."

"We did not kill them all," pointed out Taken Alive. "He could have followed the others that got away."

Cloud worked the lever action, but no bullet slid into the chamber. He did it several times, but there were no bullets.

The young Crow seemed to sense the situation and reached for the small pouch hanging at his belt and handed it to Cloud.

Cloud felt the small hard object inside and immediately knew what it was. Opening the pouch, he dropped a single bullet onto his palm.

"One bullet," Crazy Horse said, incredulous. "One bullet is all he has."

Taken Alive shook his head. "This bothers me," he said somberly. "This young man's people hunt north of the Elk River, either elk in the Beartooth Mountains or buffalo on the open lands. They used to come south into our territory, but it was only to raid or take horses, not to hunt buffalo."

"This is what the old ones have been saying," Crazy Horse reminded them. "Our old enemies, like the Crow, made us strong, but the new one makes us all weak." He nodded toward the young Crow. "His people may be friends with the whites, but that does not keep them from going hungry because the white hide hunters have killed so many buffalo."

A moment of silence passed. The young Crow glanced inquisitively at the men sitting around him.

"What shall we do?" asked Taken Alive. "We have no way of knowing this man's story, except for what we think we see. He could be lying. Maybe he has a bag full of bullets hidden back at his camp."

"One thing is certain," Cloud pointed out, "he is alone and seems willing to part with a good rifle for meat. If food was not important to him and his family, he would not be risking his life. I think we interfered with his hunt, but he was not going to fight us—"

"Because he has only one bullet," Crazy Horse said. "One bullet, one chance to bring down meat. I think all he was doing was trying to take meat home to his family. That is what we are doing, and in that way, we are no different."

"At that, he cannot take a lot of meat by himself," Taken Alive said. "Even if he does have a packhorse, he cannot haul an entire buffalo. No horse can."

"If he uses both horses and drag poles, he can haul most of one carcass," suggested Hawk Eagle. Then he added, "I cannot believe I am trying to solve a problem for someone who would not hesitate to kill any one of us if we met him in battle."

Cloud sighed. "We are not on a battlefield now," he said. "We have families, and so does he. We all get hungry. I think we should make a trade with him. Whatever happens tomorrow, happens."

Cloud looked at the young Crow, lifted the rifle, and pointed toward the meadow where the buffalo carcasses lay in two rows, then he made the hand sign for trade.

Broken Hand smiled and nodded.

By the time Yellow Wolf and Good Hand arrived, just past midday with five more men and ten packhorses, Broken Hand had managed to load one side of ribs and a hindquarter on the drag frames behind each of his horses. Cloud had to explain the presence of the Crow hunter to the new arrivals. The main reaction was curiosity, and the Lakota regarded Broken Hand with amused or indifferent stares. But Little Bird, in particular, said very little and watched the young Crow with a cold stare. His uncle had been killed in a fight with the Crow many years before.

Cloud and Crazy Horse escorted Broken Hand to the top of the nearest hill, just in case someone other than Little Bird had secret thoughts of revenge. But no one followed, mainly because there was too much work to be done. From the top of the hill, they could see many more hills and plateaus. The young hunter had a very long walk ahead of him, but he was taking meat home.

At a nod from Crazy Horse, Cloud dismounted and handed the encased repeating rifle back to the hunter. Broken Hand was clearly puzzled.

"For today," Cloud said, knowing the young man could not comprehend his words, "we are friends. The meat is a gift from us. There is no need for a trade."

After a moment, the young man took the rifle and raised his hand in a gesture of friendship. Cloud and Crazy Horse did the same.

Broken Hand took a deep breath and nodded slowly. With a smile and another wave, he turned and led his horses down the hill.

CHAPTER FOUR

An Unseen Uneasiness

After the carcasses had been quartered, the hunters had to use twelve sturdy horses to transport the meat home, taking two days to return. They stopped twice overnight, and the loaded drag frames had to be arranged in the middle of the camp with several fires burning around the perimeter to keep the wolves and coyotes away. The hunters knew that neither they nor their meat were in any imminent danger from those four-leggeds. The fires and posted sentries kept them from getting too close and frightening the horses.

The sixteen buffalo hides were given to those who needed to patch their lodges or replenish robes, but the cold weather made it impossible to work on them. So, although some preliminary scraping had been done by the hunters, the hides were rolled up tightly and allowed to freeze until the warm days of spring.

The meat was distributed among the nine winter villages of the Crazy Horse band. Grey Bull guessed that, if used sparingly, the supply would be enough for twenty to thirty days. It was little in comparison to the large autumn hunts, when meat could be made to last everyone through the winter, but, whether a little or a lot, the people were happy to have fresh buffalo to eat. It had been a few years since hunters returned to any village with buffalo meat loaded on drag frames behind horses. If nothing else, that sight lifted everyone's spirits and invoked memories of good times past.

Hawk Eagle stayed until the weather cleared. On a cold, bright morning, he finished preparations to begin his long journey home. He wore his new elk-hide coat, a gift from Crazy Horse and his wife, Black Shawl. His buckskin gelding seemed to sense that a journey lay ahead; his eyes were wide and eager and his ears were alert. A tightly bundled buffalo robe was tied down across the horse's withers, and hanging down his left shoulder was the hide-encased rifle. On the opposite side lay the encased bow and a quiver of arrows, and two folded rawhide cases, one filled with food and the other with Hawk Eagle's personal effects. A contingent of dogs and small boys watched him closely until Cloud, Taken Alive, Crazy Horse, and Yellow Wolf appeared, all bundled against the crisp morning air.

Cloud handed him a bag of buffalo jerky. "Try not to eat it all in one day," he teased.

"Your wife is a good cook," Hawk Eagle replied. "I just might."

Crazy Horse handed him a long, slender bundle. Hawk Eagle knew it was one of his war arrows.

"A message for your headman," Crazy Horse told him. "You can tell him that some of us will go east and meet you during the Moon When Geese Return. None of us will be there later."

Hawk Eagle nodded. "He will be glad to hear that, and I will be glad to see all of you again."

Taken Alive tossed over a small bag that Hawk Eagle deftly grabbed in midair. "Bullets," explained the older man. "We decided that each of us could spare one or two, just in case you run across some Long Knives. If you have to shoot any, tell them those are from us."

Soft chuckles ran through the group of men.

"I am grateful," the young man said, holding up the bag. "If I have to put my rifle sights on a Bluecoat, I will think of all of you."

"Take care of yourself," Yellow Wolf called out as the Hunkpapa mounted.

With a nod, smile, and wave, Hawk Eagle turned his eager mount east and urged it into a fast walk. After several moments, he was gone from view.

Since he had arrived, the message from Sitting Bull was the topic of conversation throughout the Crazy Horse camps. There was little disagreement with the Hunkpapa medicine man's intentions. Sitting Bull's attitude toward white people was well known among all of the Lakota bands. He had always urged Lakota leaders not to sign any paper that the white peace talkers put in front of them. Of course, most had not listened, and now thousands of Lakota were living at the agencies—if you could call eating stringy meat from longhorn cattle and getting permission to hunt from a white agent of the Indian Bureau living. The fact that his people, like the Crazy Horse people, were not sitting on their hands at the white-controlled agencies attested to his hard-line position. The only question in some minds was why he had waited so long to send out a call.

Cloud and the other men lingered in the cold after the departing figure faded from view. Although none of them would admit it, they were sad to see the young Hunkpapa leave. He was the kind of young man who was easy to like. He smiled easily and worked hard.

But there was something else. An uneasiness hung in the air this morning, accentuated somewhat by Hawk Eagle's departure. The successful buffalo hunt had been a bittersweet windfall. All of the hunters, to a man, were happy to have found fresh meat, but there was the nagging thought that they had further depleted the numbers of dwindling buffalo. Elk in large numbers were available, but hunting them was different. Buffalo moved in large herds, so autumn hunts usually yielded enough meat to last through a winter. Elk did not always move in large herds, and hunters had to travel deep into the mountains in the summer and fall to find them, and the yield was not as great, because elk could not be taken in large numbers. For the past four or five years, elk meat had been the staple for the Crazy Horse people, which meant that many of the able-bodied men were away hunting most of the time now. Starvation was not an imminent threat, but no man, woman, or child was even a little overweight. There were days, and there would be again, when a daily portion of meat was no more than a mouthful. Yet there was also the constant reassurance that, sooner or later, the hunters would bring home meat of some kind.

But the uneasiness that hung in the air this morning had more to do with the future and the white people. Stories among the Lakota affirmed that whites had first come into their territory more than a hundred years before. That was along the Great Muddy River, and the first Lakota to lay eyes on the strange newcomers were the Sicangu. After that, there had been a few more, mostly traders who, for the most part, had been friendly and harmless. Seventy years ago, a group of them traveled by boat up the Great Muddy, and there had nearly been a fight when the boatmen took a young Lakota hostage. After an anxious day or two, they freed the hostage, then continued north and wintered with the earth-lodge people, the Mandan. In the spring, a scout spotted the large wooden boat with the white wings going south, slipping past the Sicangu camps during the night.

So whites had been part of Lakota life for several generations, but in the past twenty years the troubles with them, because of them, had become worse and more frequent as Lakota people died and Lakota lands were lost. Whatever else had been lost, Crazy Horse and Sitting Bull were determined not to lose their freedom.

But one fact could not be ignored: most of the Lakota nation had given up their freedom. They were now agency people, living under the control of the Long Knives and other whites. To some among the Sitting Bull and Crazy Horse people, that unsettling reality seemed to be a glimpse of the future.

High Eagle, the medicine man, joined the group, his shrewd eyes sweeping over them. There was something on his mind. "I wonder," he said, "what the people at the agencies think of Sitting Bull's message. It might be good if we can learn what the Spotted Tail and Red Cloud people are saying, especially those who do not want to be there."

"Why do you say that?" Crazy Horse asked.

"Because we will need more than the few hundred warriors we have between us and Sitting Bull," the medicine man replied somberly. "The Long Knives may not ride well or shoot straight, but they do not need to because they can keep sending more and more, and because they have more guns and bullets."

Crazy Horse nodded. "You are right, Uncle. Maybe we can send a man south to slip into the agencies and listen."

Yellow Wolf stepped forward. "I will go," he offered. "My wife's sister is there. Her mother worries. Besides, she will know what has been happening."

Taken Alive jabbed the young man's side playfully. "Maybe you should ask your wife first," he joked.

The younger man grinned. "Plum will go with me," he said, "so she will not have to hide from you while I am gone."

Taken Alive grinned good-naturedly.

"When can you leave?" Crazy Horse wanted to know.

"Maybe yet today," replied Yellow Wolf.

"Good," said Crazy Horse, nodding thoughtfully. "At this time of the year, it might take you ten days—if the weather holds and there is no new snow."

"When you get there," offered Cloud, "it might be wise to wait until dark, and then go into one of the Spotted Tail camps first. Above all, the white agents or the Long Knives cannot know that any of our people are there."

"We have clothes that will help us blend in," Yellow Wolf assured him. "And we will sneak in at night. It should not take us more than two or three days to hear what is happening."

"Sitting Bull's messenger probably sneaked in," High Eagle assumed, "but I am sure by now that word has spread like a prairie fire. You will not have to listen too hard, I think."

That evening, as the sun was going down, Hawk Eagle was making camp just below the head of a narrow gully. From the Crazy Horse village, he had traveled northeast, and by the time the afternoon light was fading, he was halfway to the Elk River, or the Yellowstone, as the whites called the river that eventually poured into the Great Muddy. He had covered a lot of ground, thanks to the fast-walking buckskin.

When Hawk Eagle had stopped late in the afternoon and found the secluded gully, he picked it because it was far off any trail used by man or beast. He put the finishing touches on a heat reflector shaped like half a tiny lodge and fashioned out of dry brush. Not only did it direct the heat in one direction, it would also partially hide the glow of the fire once the sun went down. After he gathered kindling and then enough fuel to last through most of the night, he started a fire using a flint and striker. Choosing not to cook any of the meat he had, he began boiling water for tea. The smell of cooking meat might attract beings—four-legged or otherwise—that he did not want to encounter. While waiting for the water to boil in the metal cup, he worked on a sleeping shelter. He did not want anything elaborate, just shelter from the wind. Voices came on the breeze as he worked; coyotes and wolves were already starting their nightly hunts.

An easy stone's throw away, the buckskin was busy browsing the grass, chewing noisily and pausing to glance curiously toward the distant sounds of barking and baying. Unconcerned, he returned to browsing.

By the time the sun was below the western horizon, Hawk Eagle had settled in for the night. He reclined on a bed of grass and twigs and chewed on a piece of jerky, taking an occasional sip of peppermint tea. He had left the Oglala camp reluctantly. Cloud had invited him to stay the winter, but he had already been away from home for thirty-three days and did not want his grandmother to worry any more than she already had.

He chewed on the buffalo jerky Sweetwater Woman had made for him. He had not expected to see a white woman among the Oglala people, especially the Crazy Horse band. But when Cloud had told him the story of how his wife had come to live among them, it was easy to understand the circumstances. The red-haired woman was a Lakota in every way, that much was easy to see.

Sitting Bull and his nephew Gall had told stories of Crazy Horse, who was outwardly quiet but inwardly the fiercest warrior among the Lakota, according to Sitting Bull. That was why Hawk Eagle was still puzzled over the incident with the Crow, Broken Hand. Crazy Horse had not only given him almost an entire buffalo, he had also returned the rifle—a very good repeating rifle—the Crow had traded for the meat. But times were hard for all human beings because of the white people. Hawk Eagle also wondered if the Oglala headman's calling to be a Thunder Dreamer had something to do with the kindness he showed an enemy. Thunder Dreamers were supposed to act in ways that other people would not, or could not. Kindness toward a Crow was certainly the last thing any man would expect from a Lakota warrior who showed no quarter to those ancient enemies on the field of battle.

Hawk Eagle shrugged to himself and looked around. Day was fading fast. In a while, he would tie one end of the long picket rope to the buckskin's ankle and the other end to his own ankle. Then, if the horse wandered too far, he would know it. But all good Lakota horses were trained to the picket rope. They knew it meant they were to stay close to their riders.

His thoughts returned to Crazy Horse and the others, especially the men he had hunted with. He liked them and had come to respect them. If only there were ten thousand more like them. Then they could drive the whites out easily. But he wondered if that would bring the buffalo back. Still, if no more whites also meant no more buffalo, he was willing to live with that.

With a sigh, Hawk Eagle leaned forward and dropped more wood onto his fire. There was a long, cold night ahead, not to mention all the cold days of travel before he reached home. But he had agreed to Sitting Bull's request knowing that he was also agreeing to a long, hard journey. And there was another reason: he had wanted to meet Crazy Horse. He had not been disappointed. Gall and Black Moon, both accomplished warriors themselves, had likened Crazy Horse to a small whirlwind that could grow into a tornado. Hawk Eagle was at first taken aback with the man's quiet demeanor, but there was an air of strength and self-assurance that was just below the surface. It reminded him of his grandfather's admonition never to antagonize a mountain lion.

Hawk Eagle smiled and added several small pieces of wood to the fire. With such men to lead them, the Lakota could drive out the whites. And the sooner, the better, he thought.

Two days' ride to the south of Hawk Eagle's camp, another pair of Lakota hands put wood on a low fire. Yellow Wolf stirred the glowing coals. The shelter he had built was somewhat more elaborate than the one Hawk Eagle had put up. They had found a natural opening in a chokecherry thicket, and he wove long, sturdy twigs into it to fashion a windbreak. The branches of the thicket also diffused the firelight a bit.

From their village, he and Plum had ridden west and then turned south before they came to the Powder River Road, the road the whites once used and called the Bozeman Trail. No whites had used it since the autumn after the Wagon Box Fight, which occurred the summer after the Battle of the Hundred in the Hand. Yellow Wolf had been nineteen that winter, and Plum eleven. Her memories of that time were not as detailed as his, so she asked a few questions as they rode along. His answers were brief, and she sensed that he did not want to talk much about either of those battles. He did briefly mention Taken Alive being wounded in the Wagon Box Fight and his friend with the one arm being killed at the Hundred in the Hand. She remembered where the Long Knife town with log walls had been. Her father had taken her there a few years back. She recalled that there was nothing left but charred wood.

In the late afternoon, they found a secluded bend near a frozen creek and made camp. The Shining Mountains were a wall of jagged shadows to the west, one long line of darkness.

Plum handed her husband a cup of tea and a small bowl of pounded buffalo meat mixed with berries and tallow. It was a staple for hunters and warriors traveling in the winter.

"Good," he said in appreciation. "I was hoping for this."

"I brought plenty," she told him, "depending on how much you eat each day, that is."

Yellow Wolf chuckled. "We will make it last," he assured her, "but it will not be easy."

She smiled and then glanced out into the growing darkness. "I am glad you brought me along," she said.

"I would not have come without you. This is one time we can travel together."

She busied herself putting away the food, her face growing serious. After a moment, she sighed. "What do you think life will be like for our children?" she asked. "When we have children, that is. My grandmother is afraid there are hard times ahead for us." This was a worry that was often on Plum's mind because she wanted children.

Yellow Wolf stared into the deepening dusk. "Who knows what will happen in the years ahead? Maybe your grandmother is right. I hope not. But then, I think that is why Sitting Bull is sending out his messengers, because he sees hard times ahead if we do nothing."

"Will we all have to live at the agency?" she fretted.

"Not me, not you, not our family," he replied with cold determination. "I was born free, and I will die free. So will our children."

Plum looked at her husband. She believed in him because of the fire of determination that burned in him. She believed he would do everything to stay free and away from the agency. Whether or not he could stop the future from turning bad, she did not know.

"It is strange, then, that we are going to the agency," she pointed out.

"Yes, it is, in a way," he agreed. "We will not be there long. Our headman is curious about what our relatives down there think of Sitting Bull's message. But Cloud warned me not to reveal ourselves to too many people."

"What will happen in the spring? Do you think many of them will go to the gathering?" she wondered. "I mean, they will have to leave the agencies, and if that happens, what will the Long Knives do?"

Yellow Wolf slowly shook his head. "I do not know," he replied, almost to himself. "That is the strange thing, because there are far more Lakota at the agencies than there are Long Knives, or all the whites put together. They could overrun the whites at any time. I wonder about that all the time—why our people just stay there as if they are in a corral like those longhorn cattle. Some...some kind of unseen power keeps them there."

"My brother-in-law, my sister's husband's younger brother, came up here last spring, remember? He said it was easy to slip away," Plum said.

"Yes," he allowed. "It is for one or two people, but for ten or twenty or more, it may be more difficult."

A cold breeze crawled along the watercourse and shook the leafless branches of their thicket and made the flames sway over the coals. Plum turned to glance toward the horses picketed behind them between the thicket and a low sandstone ledge.

"My mother said to bring my sister and her family back with us," she told her husband. "I hope they will listen to us."

"Who knows?" he replied. "But I, too, hope we can talk them into coming back with us. I think we can."

The resonant song of a wolf rose on the breeze somewhere in the foothills to the west, reassurance that not everything had changed.

CHAPTER FIVE

Civilized Men

Half a continent away, his task finished for the evening, a lamplighter in a cold city climbed down the ladder from the last pole and extinguished the taper on the end of the slender rod. A perfunctory glance over his shoulder reassured him that all the lamps along the street were still burning. Picking up his ladder and the small box of coal he had purchased earlier, the old man shuffled off to his meager apartment not far away. If he was lucky, he would stay warm through the night, until he had to awaken in the predawn darkness to extinguish the twenty-four lamps he had just finished lighting.

There were endless rows of houses and boxes of dim light. The frigid air kept most people indoors. As the night deepened, the yellow glow from the lamps and the lights from windows defined the sprawling city. An occasional covered carriage rolled along the streets, the clop of shod hooves mingling with the metallic grind of the carriage's wheels against stone. It was impossible to take in the whole of the city with one glance, day or night. Washington, DC, was that kind of place—part of it was always hidden from view or perception.

On this night, in a small, dim office hidden deep within the bowels of a large building several blocks west of the White House, a clerk finished the document he had rewritten and wiped off the end of his quill pen. It was a simple document, no more than two pages. He pushed his metal-frame eyeglasses back up his nose and squinted middle-aged eyes at his work. His handiwork was straight line after straight line of words in cursive letters with even, uniform loops and straight backs. At the bottom left were a date and the simple title "Commander in Chief, United States Army."

The clerk knew the man: General William Tecumseh Sherman. As far as Seamus Murphy was concerned, if President Grant was considered a butcher during his military career, then Sherman was the Butcher of Atlanta. Unknown to the few clerks who worked in the same department with Murphy, Seamus had been born in South Carolina and his younger brother had fought for the Confederacy. There had been no word of Paddy Murphy since

1864, except that his name may have been on the lists at Andersonville, the infamous prison camp for rebel soldiers. Although Murphy worked hard for the meager salary he was paid as a government stenographer, his heart was secretly still loyal to his beloved South. He hoped there was a day coming when the Butcher of Atlanta would roast in hell.

Murphy reread the document to double-check his work, though he knew he had made no mistakes. But, of course, that would not preclude the document from being returned with deletions and notes in the margins, just as the previous two copies had been.

A chill went up his back, partially in sympathy, knowing what Sherman had done in his march to the sea. The document was a letter urging President Ulysses S. Grant to issue an order to the western Indian tribes to submit to the authority of the United States by January 31, 1876. Furthermore, Sherman wanted the army to have the authority to gather up all of the various Indian tribes in the West, and he was strongly recommending that the army be placed in charge of the agencies.

Murphy glanced at the calendar on the wall. January thirty-first was less than two months away. According to Sherman's recommendations, any Indian not under the control of the government by that date would be deemed a hostile and an enemy of the United States. Perhaps, Murphy thought, General Sherman was planning to wage total war against the poor Indians.

He rang the bell sitting on the lefthand corner of his small wooden desk, and in a few seconds a teenaged Negro boy appeared in the door.

"Mathias," Murphy said, acknowledging the boy with a smile as he placed the letter between two sheets of unmarked parchment, "take this up to General Sherman's secretary, and do not leave until he has read it. He may have a word for me."

"Again?" whined the boy, his face pinched. "This is the third time this evening, suh."

"Yes. Yes, I know, Mathias. It may not be the last. So be on your way now."

The boy took the document and was gone, his footfalls on the wooden floor fading as he went down the hall.

Murphy rose and went to the coal pail next to the small iron stove, took two fist-sized pieces out, opened the door, and tossed them in. The basement was always cold, which explained the wool scarf draped over his thin shoulders. He waited by the stove, soaking up its heat.

Footsteps came from the hall as he stood waiting.

Mathias poked his head through the door with a wide smile on his face. "The gentleman thanks you, suh. He says we can leave."

"In that case," replied Murphy, "we should do precisely that before anyone changes his mind."

As Mathias and Murphy left the building through a side door, Sherman pushed the letter across the desk toward his friend General Philip Sheridan in a well-appointed office that reeked of cigar smoke. "I believe, Philip, this will meet the president's approval."

Sheridan held the letter close and read it over quickly. "You realize, of course, that it will be my responsibility, as commander of the Department of the Missouri, to carry this out once the president issues the order."

"Please, Philip, I wrote the letter based on your recommendation."

Sheridan took a match from the round brass container at the edge of the desk and relit his cigar, then blew the smoke toward the ceiling. "Yes, of course. You and I both know that we must take this action. The longer Sitting Bull and Crazy Horse defy us, the more encouraged the malcontents at Camp Robinson will become. Thousands of young bucks are there, William, and some of them are not happy with their lot in life."

Sherman rose from his chair and lifted the gray wool coat draped over the back. He was not in uniform. "Can you blame them?" he asked. "What do you expect them to do?"

"I expect them to accept that they are defeated. I expect them to learn that survival among us is the best they can hope for."

Sherman took a moment to put on his coat. "I had a firsthand look at those people we've labeled malcontents, or savages, or any term that describes our low opinion of them. I sat across from them, I walked among them, first at Medicine Lodge and then at Fort Laramie. They are human beings, Philip. Backward, perhaps, but human beings. Some of them looked at us as though we had crawled out from beneath a rock. I have often asked myself what separates us from them."

"Plenty!" Sheridan protested. "We are civilized, sir. We are a nation of laws!"

"By that, do you mean without a doubt that they have neither civilization nor laws, Philip?"

"You know that as well as I do!"

Sherman paused, a bemused expression growing in his eyes. "In that case, Philip, show me the law, if you please, that states it is legal for us to kill Indians!"

Sheridan drew himself up to his full height, which still left him half a head shorter than his superior. "The president will issue the order you requested. If the Indians do not comply, we need no such law, William. You know that! That order will be all we need!"

Sherman chuckled. "And you know as well as I do, Philip, that they will not understand the order. They will not know what it says, what it means. And those who do will not obey it."

"That matters little, General," Sheridan said, stiffening into formality. "We brought civilization to this land, and we must indoctrinate, or remove, those who stand in the way of our mission to finish the job."

"Civilization? Indeed! Perhaps that explains why brother fought against brother for five years. We fought a war that nearly tore this nation apart because we are civilized?"

"We are reindoctrinating our own people who thought they could tear this nation apart, sir. What chance does an Indian have at understanding what civilization is?"

Sherman regarded his friend and subordinate with a gaze void of expression. This discussion had occurred many times before. Although Sherman was encouraged by Sheridan's commitment to duty, he was always somewhat taken aback by the vehemence with which his opinions were delivered. But in the end, it would not matter. The Indians were destined to lose. They were outnumbered and outgunned. The only question was, who should be in charge of them?

General Sherman had lately fallen somewhat from the president's favor, so he was not as effective at pressing his case that the army should be in control of the Indians. Lately he was worried, because it seemed that the Bureau of Indian Affairs was gaining favor. Bureaucrats in the Interior Department and the politicians who supported them could not understand that there was still a significant possibility that the Indians might mount a military insurgency. At the moment, he was most worried about those on the northern plains, because of Sitting Bull and Crazy Horse. He had a feeling something was stirring.

Sherman motioned toward Sheridan. "Philip, there is something I have been thinking about, something I think we should talk about in the carriage."

Sheridan was visibly relieved and stepped to the door. "Sergeant," he called out, "my carriage.

"I believe this is the coldest night so far this season," commented Sheridan as the carriage rolled up and the men climbed in. He was making conversation, trying to gauge whether or not he had crossed a line. Sherman was his friend and always would be, but Sheridan was worried he had somehow offended his superior.

"Yes," replied Sherman, somewhat wearily. "I seem to feel the cold in my joints more and more. I shall not think about what that means."

Sheridan chuckled. "You are not alone," he said. "I believe it is a consequence of all our years in the saddle."

Sherman nodded. "We have several minutes, and I have a thought I would like to share with you," he said suddenly.

Sheridan waited, almost breathlessly.

"I am certain, as are you, that Sitting Bull and Crazy Horse will not report peacefully to the agency," Sherman went on. "Therefore, I believe we must be prepared. I am of the opinion that we should make a plan to put forces into the field and capture the last remaining bands of free-roaming Sioux. If they fight, we should have sufficient strength in the field to crush them."

"I have already been working on such a plan," Sheridan informed the commander in chief. "I believe we should involve Major General Alfred Terry commanding the Department of Dakota. We will need to dispatch him to Fort Abraham Lincoln. Of course, we should also include the Department of the Platte under Brigadier General George Crook and the troops at Fort Fetterman in Wyoming."

"Yes," replied Sherman, "we cannot overlook Crook, our most experienced Indian fighter. He from one direction, Terry from another, and perhaps another column or two. This is assuming that Sitting Bull and Crazy Horse will not wander far from their usual territories."

"I think it may be necessary to go after one and then the other rather than attacking both at the same time. My feeling is, if we defeat one, the other will capitulate," Sheridan added.

"This must be carried out as quickly and as orderly as possible, Philip," Sherman sighed. "We have been killing Indians for a long time. It has been a messy business, and I am tired of it."

"Then they should have the common sense not to run from us and force us to attack," insisted Sheridan. "If they run, soldiers are duty bound to do what they must to carry out their mission."

"As I said, Philip, it has been a messy business."

The carriage turned off the street onto the lane in front of the White House and stopped. After saluting smartly, a soldier opened a door for the generals and then let them into the building through the main door on the south side.

Sherman handed his card to a secretary who approached officiously. "General Sheridan and I are here on matters concerning the Department of the Missouri," he informed the man.

"Of course," the young man said, bowing slightly. "Follow me, please."

He led them to a luxuriously appointed anteroom. "Gentlemen, please make yourselves comfortable," he said, indicating the chairs and divans. "I shall speak to the president."

The generals had barely removed their heavy wool overcoats when the secretary reappeared. "Gentlemen, the president will see you. Please, you may go in."

In the middle of a somewhat spartan room, President Grant walked around a wide mahogany desk, genuinely pleased to see his former comrades in arms. "William! Philip!" he called out effusively, hand extended.

A dark wool shawl was draped around his stooped and thinning shoulders. His face looked worn and haggard in the yellow light of the kerosene lamps. There was energy in his handshake, however, as he greeted the two men in turn.

"Mr. President," Sherman said, "thank you for seeing us at this late hour."

"Not at all. I have been looking forward to this since your note came this afternoon. I am having Halsey brew up some tea. Would you care for a cup?"

"Of course," replied Sherman, speaking for Sheridan as well.

Grant waved to a sitting area near the stove next to the wall. Firewood was piled in the bin next to it. "Come join me here," he said. "I cannot stand the smell of coal burning," he said, pointing to the wood. "I much prefer wood. It has a more natural smell."

As they seated themselves, Grant pointed to the leather folder in General Sherman's hand. "I take it, William, you have something for me."

"Yes, I do. Philip and I have refined our recommendation and are pleased to have you consider it," Sherman explained, handing over the letter.

Putting on his reading glasses, the president carefully read and reread the letter.

After he finished, he stared off across the room for a moment, then spoke. "Yes," he said softly. "Yes, this will do. However," he said, "there must be one change. This order must come from the commissioner of Indian Affairs. If it comes from me or the army directly, it will seem too heavy-handed for liberals who decry that we do not treat the Indians well."

He turned his gaze toward Sheridan. "Philip, is the army on the plains prepared to carry out this mission?"

"I firmly believe so, sir."

Sherman cleared his throat. "Mr. President, we have also been talking of a plan for a forceful military campaign against the Sioux."

"You must not expect them to comply with the order you are asking me to issue," Grant replied, waving Sherman's letter.

"No, sir, I do not," Sherman affirmed, glancing briefly at Sheridan. "I would not, were I in their place, if I understood it at all. I am afraid that chiefs such as Sitting Bull and Crazy Horse do not give credence to our authority. They refuse to accept the inevitable. That is precisely the reason for an aggressive campaign. We need to subjugate the Sioux, and we will, but we also need to demonstrate our power to the other tribes in the West."

Grant leaned back, one elbow on an arm of the chair as he stroked his bewhiskered chin thoughtfully. "William, you are correct, of course. We need to put an end to this business in the West. The newspapers have been criticizing me for our treatment of the Indians. I believe they can learn to become productive citizens, once they shed themselves of their tribal ways and thinking."

"First, however," interjected Sheridan, "we must get their attention. Crazy Horse and Sitting Bull are simply defying us. As long as that attitude persists, we are compelled to take a forceful approach."

The secretary entered with a pot of steaming tea and cups atop a wooden tray and served the three men. He stepped back. "Will there be anything else, sir?"

"Ah, yes, Halsey, as a matter of fact, there is." Grant handed Sherman's letter to the young man. "Draft an order for my signature to the commissioner of Indian Affairs according to the general's recommendations here. You need not finish it tonight, but I would like to see it by tomorrow afternoon."

"Of course, sir. I will have it ready for you." With a bow, the young man exited.

The president lifted his cup. "To victory in the West," he said softly.

"Hear! Hear!" the generals spoke in unison.

Sherman sipped his tea and stared thoughtfully into his cup, and next to him, Sheridan's face glowed with boyish anticipation.

CHAPTER SIX

Two Rifles

Night passed, cold, moonless, star filled, and clear at first, until bands of clouds slipped in from the southwest. Yellow Wolf slept lightly, as he always did when on the trail. As pale light grew in the east and the shadows around the camp turned into discernible shapes, he heard his horse's soft, inquisitive nicker. Both horses were mere steps away, standing patiently. Next to him, Plum stirred slightly. They were beneath a large, smoked buffalo hide stretched over a frame and set in the middle of the thicket.

Yellow Wolf shifted slightly and felt the encased rifle next to his leg. Close to his head was the six-shooter. After watching the horses intently for several moments, he called softly, "It is good. It is good. We will be up soon." He saw their ears perk up.

From the retreating darkness came the howl of a wolf, a victorious howl, it seemed. It had probably had a successful hunt.

Yellow Wolf lay for a while longer, already planning the route they would travel this day. The rising sun painted the overhead clouds with pink and orange and then pale red. Another cold day lay ahead. He reached behind him and squeezed his wife's leg.

"I am awake," she mumbled. "Build a fire, and I will make tea."

Far to the north, west of a small frozen tributary that eventually flowed into the Tongue River, Hawk Eagle watched the same painted sky and, like Yellow Wolf, reveled in its beauty. The new day's cold breath washed over his face as he pulled the buffalo robe away.

"Thank you, Grandfather," he prayed. "Thank you for this day, and for making me a Lakota."

By midday, bundled against the sharp cold, Hawk Eagle was kneeling below the crest of a hill and looking north, blending in among the bristly soap weed just in case someone might be looking in his direction. Just beyond the distant horizon was the broad valley through which the Elk River flowed. He would turn east before that valley. No sense taking a chance of running into any whites who might be traveling in the area.

Hawk Eagle crawled through the soap weed to the edge of the bluff. Staying prone, he glassed the landscape farther to the west, taking his time. He was allowing his buckskin to rest, having pushed him harder than usual. If he saw no signs of people, he intended to make a fire and boil water for tea. Not to mention that it would also be good to be warm, even if only for a little while.

As Hawk Eagle surveyed the cold, gray landscape south of the Elk River, Yellow Wolf and Plum reached the western edge of a vast grassland where herds of white-bellied antelope dotted the plains. On their present course, they would be south of the Black Hills in less than three days. From there, it was another two or three days to the agencies, though the Spotted Tail people were farther to the east.

On any other day, Yellow Wolf would have hidden near a water hole and lured an antelope or two within range. His favorite method was to use a white flag on the end of a pole; since the prairie goats were extremely curious, they couldn't resist seeing what was waving in the breeze. But on this day, because there were bigger issues than food, the antelope were safe from the young Lakota's deadly marksmanship. As the herds spotted the horses and riders moving across the grassy flats, they dashed away in flowing waves.

Cold gripped the northern lands under a bright sky. As the curious antelope kept a wary eye on the interlopers in their midst, two hunters with rifles in hand followed the bloody trail of a fatally wounded elk into a deep gully on the eastern slopes of the Shining Mountains. The animal was instinctively heading for deep cover farther up into a draw. Farther down the slope, Little Bird's unerring bow shot had sent a heavy hunting arrow deep into the cow's vitals, a quartering shot from the right side.

Goings and Little Bird were in no hurry. Besides, the thin snow cover on the slope prevented rapid movement. There was plenty of daylight, and the cow was losing blood.

Goings paused and looked back down the slope. Far below, he could see five horses picketed inside a grove of leafless aspen. With them were two teenage boys, their sons No Coyote and Ashes.

From up the slope, inside the gully, came a sudden tearing crash in the underbrush. Goings turned to see his friend nodding somberly. The elk had gone down. The long climb up the slope had hurried its demise.

"We will need to quarter it so we can carry it out of that gully," Little Bird pointed out. "Unless we can bring a horse up here to drag it out."

"In the meantime, I think it would be a shame to let the liver and kidneys go to waste," Goings grinned. "I will get a fire started."

Little Bird moved down the slope a bit and cupped his hands. "Bring the horses up!" he called out.

The two boys waved and started out of the grove. Little Bird moved back up the slope, past Goings, who was busy gathering wood for a fire. At the opening to the gully where the elk had gone down, he paused to make sure his rifle was loaded.

Partway into the gully, he knew they would need a horse and a long rope. The brush was much too thick for them to manhandle even the pieces of a quartered carcass through. Fortunately, the cow had fallen near a narrow crevice in the gully floor and not in it.

Little Bird wove his way through the brush as quietly as he could. Once he reached the elk, he stood for a moment to catch his breath. Then, from the small bag hanging from his belt, he took out a pouch of tobacco. Sprinkling a pinch over the ground, he said a silent prayer of thanksgiving. Taking out his knife, he severed the artery on the side of the neck and the femoral artery near the flank. Steam rose from the warm blood as it stained the snow.

Little Bird did not know what compelled him to look up at a bare patch of rock high on the west side of the gully. Perhaps it was the sunlight striking it. But look he did. Behind leafless aspen branches was a stretch of vertical rock that, from where he stood, seemed about the size of a yearling colt.

Stepping around the carcass, he slowly walked through the brush and stopped for another look at the rock. From about a stone's throw away, he could make out dark scratches on the surface. A few more steps forward and the dark scratches seemed to be two similar outlines. Intrigued, Little

Bird moved even closer. Then he realized that the outlines resembled the heads and shoulders of men. He heard Goings approaching from the mouth of the gully, but he could not avert his gaze from the rock face.

When they were younger, Little Bird and a cousin had once stumbled across paintings inside a cave a day or two south in the rimrock country. The boys were trying to find shelter from a sudden summer cloudburst. Moving along a rock wall, they had found a vertical opening, then suddenly found themselves inside a cavern wide and high enough for them and their horses. After the storm had passed and the sky had cleared, light illuminated the cave. On the walls and the ceilings were paintings of human figures and animals—deer, elk, buffalo, and eagles. Several drawings depicted groups of hunters armed with long lances charging a strange beast Little Bird had never seen. The beast had ears like ragged wings and what looked like long, curved fangs on either side of a protuberance. Over the years, other people visited the cave and stared at the drawings, especially those of the strange beast. But no one, including the elders, could ever identify it. No such animal existed, not even in the stories.

The scratches on this rock face did not resemble any kind of an animal, and Little Bird wanted a closer look. But that would have to wait. They had an elk to gut and butcher. With a puzzled glance at the rock face, Little Bird turned and walked toward the carcass.

"What were you looking at up there?" Goings asked, a little concerned. This area had holes and small caves here and there used by bears hibernating for the winter. Now and then, a hunter roused a sleeping bear.

"Something up there on that rock," Little Bird told him. "Watermarks, maybe. We can take a closer look later, after we butcher that elk."

Goings squinted up through the trees but could see nothing. Behind them, they heard a horse snort apprehensively at the smell of blood. The boy Ashes had led the packhorse, a sturdy gray gelding, to the edge of the brush. He looked inquisitively toward his father.

"Hold him there," Little Bird told his son. "If the rope is long enough, you will not have to bring him any closer. Get the neck rope ready."

Laying their rifles aside but within easy reach, the two hunters went to work. With swift, sure, and expert strokes, they butchered the elk. Steam rose up from the intestines as they slid onto the snow. True to his word,

Goings found the kidneys and liver and set them aside. When the neck was separated from the trunk of the carcass, they tied the back legs together and used the packhorse to drag the elk to the end of the gully.

By the time they finished, the sun was dipping down toward the ridges behind them. The two men decided to camp where they were for the night. It was an ideal location, far from any trails and with an even steeper slope standing guard behind them, one only a mountain goat could climb. Furthermore, the warm air, at least air that was not bitterly cold, would rise from the valley floor.

After Ashes and No Coyote finished gathering wood for the night, Little Bird motioned to his son. "Come with me," he said. "There is something I want to look at before the sun goes down."

He led Ashes across the floor of the gully and stopped when the rock face on the west side came into view. The angle of the sun made the lines on the rock more visible.

"There," he indicated. "What does that look like to you?"

The boy gazed for a moment. "People," he said. "It looks like two men, side by side, from the chest up."

His initial assessment validated, Little Bird looked for a way to climb up the cliff.

"When leaves are on the trees, it would be hard to see it," Ashes pointed out. "Do you want me to climb up there and get a closer look?"

"Yes, but be careful. There is snow on the ledges."

Tossing aside his heavy buffalo coat, Ashes wove his way through the brush, past the leafless aspen trees, and scampered up the face of the cliff, seemingly without effort, his tight, long braids swinging as he climbed.

Little Bird smiled. *To be young again would be a good thing*, he thought.

The boy worked his way sideways along a narrow ledge unseen from the ground. In a scant moment, he came to the front of the rock face and the strange lines.

"Someone scratched on the rock," Ashes called down. "This is a drawing of faces. Faces with beards like white men have."

"What did you say?"

"These faces have beards, it looks like," the boy confirmed.

"Did you say white men?"

"These are faces of men wearing pointed hats."

"Son, do you think you could draw them for me after you get down?"

"Yes, I think so."

Little Bird heard Goings and No Coyote approaching.

"What is it?" Goings called out.

"Faces scratched on the rock," Little Bird explained. "That is what Ashes thinks it is." He turned and called to the boy. "Come down! Come down and draw it for us on the ground."

With a final look at the faces on the rock, Ashes worked his way back along the ledge and down the rocks. After a few moments, he pushed through the brush and retrieved his buffalo coat.

Little Bird scraped away the snow and exposed the frozen ground, then handed his knife to the boy.

Kneeling, the boy scratched the outlines, then the hats and faces, of the figures on the rock. The hats were not unlike those that some Long Knives wore, with a crown and brim. But these hats had a pointed crown, and the brims were bent or curved upward. There was no mistaking the heavy beards.

"Is that it?" asked Goings.

Ashes sat back for a moment, then added square shoulders and the middle of the torso.

Little Bird turned to Goings. "The only beards I have ever seen were on white men. I could not grow one if my life depended on it."

"What does this mean?" wondered Goings.

Little Bird shrugged. "That white men were here, no more."

Goings had a thought. "I have a small piece of tanned hide. If Ashes can draw it again, we can show it to the old ones back home. Perhaps one of them can tell us what it might mean."

Ashes nodded. "I can use some charcoal. To draw it, I mean."

By the time the shadows were getting long and starting to slide across the rolling foothills and toward the open prairies, the boy had replicated the drawing on Goings's hide.

"I have never seen a hat like that on any white man," No Coyote pointed out.

"How many white men have you seen?" Ashes asked.

No Coyote chuckled. "Not many, I guess."

Wolves and coyotes were beginning to howl and bark, a sure sign that night was falling. Two snug, dome-shaped shelters had been built; the men took advantage of the heavy brush available. They would not be overly warm during the cold night, but everyone would be comfortable.

They had all taken bites of the raw liver and kidneys. The pieces were dipped in the bile from the gallbladder, making for a delicacy that was not often had these days. After that, they were cooked along with a large piece of flank meat.

"Father," said No Coyote, "when we go home tomorrow, will we pass by the place of the battle? The Hundred in the Hand?"

Goings shot a quick glance at Little Bird and then looked into the fire for a moment. "We might."

"Will you tell us about it? About the fighting?" No Coyote's eyes were bright with anticipation.

Goings glanced at the boys. "Yes, we can, but first you need to check the picket lines on the horses and bring more firewood. And remember, while we are telling you about the battle, it is your task to keep the fire going."

The boys nodded eagerly and hurried away to see to their chores.

Little Bird looked at his lifelong friend. "I wonder what battles they will have to fight?" he wondered.

"I am afraid it will be different for them," Goings replied pensively. "When we were their age, our fathers and grandfathers told us stories about good fights with the Crow, the Pawnee, and the Shoshone. Now, if those people are not gone, they work for the Long Knives. Our headman was born in the Year a Hundred Horses Were Taken. Some of the old men still talk about that raid against the Shoshone. Now our sons want to know how we fought the whites. Things are different. It is a different world they are inheriting."

"We have always had enemies," Little Bird observed. "That is why we were taught to be fighting men. Up until now, we knew our enemies well. They were honorable, until they put on the blue coats to scout for the Long Knives and fight with them against us. They are now telling the Long Knives what they know about us; they have sold their honor. And now we face an enemy we do not know well. In a few short years, Ashes and No Coyote will take their places with the next generation of Lakota fighting men. We have taught them as well as we know how. But we need to teach them one more thing, something our fathers did not have to worry about: we must tell them never to trust the whites, and to tell their sons, and all the sons to come. Never trust the whites."

The fire crackled in the ensuing silence. Overhead, the sky was turning a dark blue and stars began to appear. True to their training and heritage, Ashes and No Coyote worked efficiently and quietly. Of course, they wanted to hear about the Battle of the Hundred in the Hand from their fathers, who had fought in it. At the ages of fourteen and fifteen, Ashes and No Coyote had been five and six when the battle had occurred, nine years ago, on a bitterly cold morning in the Middle of Winter Moon. They remembered that time because many people had pitched their villages up and down the Tongue River valley. They remembered the excitement and the anxiety. They were a little older when the Long Knives finally left the log town, two years after the battle. The outpost had been burned to the ground. They knew their fathers had fought in it because their mothers had told them so. And, more than once, their mothers had also said, "When your father thinks the time is right, he will tell you about it."

The boys came back to the fire, each with a high armload of wood. After carefully putting down the loads, they sat down, side by side, and glanced politely at their fathers.

Goings turned to his friend. "I hope you can talk a long time," he said, a twinkle in his eye. "That is a lot of wood."

"If talking is hard, then I will sing," replied Little Bird, smiling broadly. "But you can start," he said to Goings.

Taking up a sharpened wood skewer, Little Bird stabbed the flank roasting over the coals and sliced off a piece. Putting the end in his mouth, he deftly bit off a chunk and chewed, savoring the tender meat.

Everyone took pieces of the flank and ate. Ashes took the initiative and poured cups of steaming peppermint tea from the small pot.

"I know you have heard of the son of Big Voice," Goings began, after taking a sip.

Both boys nodded. "He lost his arm in a fight against whites," said No Coyote.

Goings nodded. "He did lose his arm. But it was not really a fight. It was in the days before he became a warrior," he told them, nodding toward Little Bird. "We were there, along with our friends Cloud and Taken Alive."

No Coyote and Ashes were intrigued.

"Now remember, we do not speak the names of the dead. But we do talk about their deeds. The deeds of this young man are worthy of keeping him in stories. If you know his story, then you will know about the Battle of the Hundred in the Hand." Goings paused, gathering the memories as he took another sip of tea.

"It was along the Powder River Road, the summer before the battle. Bozeman Trail, the whites called it. We were watching seven white men with five pack mules. My friend Cloud had decided we would let them pass because all of them had rifles and we did not. For some reason, the son of Big Voice thought he could talk to the white men because he knew how to speak their language. He got on his horse and rode toward them. When he got close, they fired, although he had no weapon. A bullet hit his elbow, at the joint." Goings touched his own elbow to show the two wide-eyed boys.

"We opened fire with the two rifles we had," he continued. "My friend Cloud did a brave thing that day, a very brave thing. He jumped onto his horse and galloped toward that wounded boy—even though the whites were firing! He got down, picked him up, put him on his horse, jumped up behind him, and galloped away!"

Goings took a deep breath and paused. Little Bird took up the story.

"I have never seen such a thing in my life," he said. "That boy's arm was in two pieces. Only the skin kept it together. Cloud was going to cut it off, but we said no. We wrapped it as best we could, then we took turns carrying him, riding double with him. We rode day and night until we got home. Wore out our horses. Anyway, our medicine man, High Eagle, had to cut the arm off at the elbow, but he saved the boy's life."

No Coyote and Ashes had stopped eating. Occasionally, they glanced at each other, but mostly they stared into the fire.

"Do not get into the habit of staring into the fire," cautioned Little Bird. "It makes you blind to the night. If an enemy were to come at you out of the darkness, you would not be able to see him."

The boys nodded and averted their gazes from the flames.

"Now," Little Bird continued, "most boys would have quit. What else can you do when you lose an arm? Your right arm, at that. At first, I think that boy probably wanted to quit, to lie down and die. But Cloud talked to him and gave him a six-shooter, because a rifle was of no use to a one-armed person. Or so we thought. Cloud took him along and taught him things. Taught him that even a one-armed boy could stand on his own two feet. By the time autumn came around, that boy became a man. He had turned into a warrior. He was deadly shooting a rifle with his left hand. He wanted no pity, and he gave none. In the end, he saved Cloud's life in the battle. In the end, he died a warrior, even though he did not start out that way. You could do much worse than follow the footsteps of the son of Big Voice."

The two men continued the story of their friend Rabbit, and the two boys listened, enthralled. On this night, although they could barely remember him from when they were small boys, Rabbit found another place to live—in the hearts of two would-be warriors.

Far to the south, a low fire burned at the back of an overhang cut into the bank of an old watercourse. Over the ages, a lazy creek had carved through the sandstone bank, then finally dried up, leaving a space as deep as a man was tall. A grown man had to walk in a crouch to fit inside. But with a fire burning, it was a cozy shelter for the night, and Yellow Wolf had improved it by covering the opening with brush and grass. That kept the heat in as well as blocked the glow from the fire.

Plum had happened to glance left as they rode down the dry creek and saw a shadow against the bank, a shadow that turned out to be a shallow cave. But others had used it sometime in the past. Smoke from earlier fires had blackened the ceiling, though there were no ashes or debris on the sandy floor.

"We came far today," Yellow Wolf said in between mouthfuls of meat. It was their first hot meal in two days, a pot of soup from the buffalo meat Plum had brought along. Seasoned with wild turnips, the soup was invigorating, as good for the spirit as it was for the body. "I think we can reach the agencies in two days. But we will go north of the outpost at Robinson."

Plum nodded as she ate.

"As Cloud said, the Spotted Tail people are east of the outpost,"

Yellow Wolf went on. "That is where your sister is. But we will find a place to hide until dark. We do not want too many people to know we are there."

"We can probably stay with my sister," she said.

"We will need to," he agreed.

Farther north, Hawk Eagle had gone as far as a good horse could travel in four days. But now he had no thought about where he would spend the night. Two white men had more or less decided that for him.

He was not shivering yet, but he knew he would be soon. Since just after sunset, he had been watching them in the gully below him, and he was annoyed that he could not have any of the coffee he had smelled earlier. Ordinarily, he would have cut a wide berth around any whites he saw, but these two had repeating rifles.

Hawk Eagle wanted those rifles, and if he waited too long to do anything, his fingers would be too cold and stiff. But he had a plan, again dictated by the two white men. They were drinking down a large bottle of liquor, and had been since sundown. They were at that stage where their motions were exaggerated. More importantly, their reactions were slowed. How much that increased the odds in his favor, he was not certain. They would have difficulty handling their rifles, but each still had a six-shooter tucked into his belt beneath a heavy overcoat. There was one factor firmly in Hawk Eagle's favor: they did not have dogs. A dog would have raised an alarm long ago.

Hawk Eagle noticed that their fire was going down. It was time to move.

"Harris," said the older of the two, trying to focus his close-set eyes, "I think we need more wood on the fire. Your turn."

Harris looked toward the fire and then at Ben Wilkins. The old man had an annoying habit of telling him what to do, but it was cold. And, if anything, Jake Harris liked his comforts. He unfolded his lanky frame, stood, and lurched toward the pile of wood next to the fire. Wilkins was right, there were barely any flames. Carefully arranging several split pieces over the coals, he returned to the box he had been sitting on.

"Ben," he said, "how far are we from the trading post?"

"Oh, 'bout another day, I s'pose. 'Bout sundown tomorrow, we be pullin' in."

"Good. I be tired of sleeping on this damn cold ground!"

"Speakin' of that, I expect we should turn in," suggested Wilkins. "But we should keep the fire goin' through the night."

They lingered a moment, dulled by the whiskey flowing through their veins. The fire grew brighter as the wood caught, illuminating the camp. Wilkins was the first to notice something odd, a shadow at the edge of his vision. But before his hand touched the handle of his six-shooter, the shaft of an arrow transfixed his throat.

Harris heard a strange gurgling noise, but it took a second or two to look up and see the old man pitching forward, an arrow through his neck. In the next moment, he suddenly couldn't catch his breath. Then the pain was unbearable, then there was nothing.

Hawk Eagle emerged into the firelight. After a moment, he retrieved his arrows. He had to pull hard to extract them. He wiped them off on the old man's coat, then put them away. Next, he set their wagon horses loose. The horses would survive, he was certain. They would find forage and water. He also found four boxes of bullets and a bag of coffee beans. Then he grabbed the two repeating rifles and disappeared into the darkness.

After a long walk in the cold, moonless night, he found his own camp and built a fire, a high, roaring fire to keep the cold away. He made tea and thought about what had happened. For the first time in his life, he had killed white men, and he did not regret it. Nor did he feel satisfaction or enjoyment. It was simply a thing that had to be done. Now he had two repeating rifles.

Hawk Eagle took off his thick mittens and grabbed one of the rifles. Pulling the handle down and back up, he loaded a round into the breech.

Whatever Sitting Bull had in mind, Hawk Eagle was ready. He was ready before, but now he was even more so. And now he was even more anxious to be home.

CHAPTER SEVEN

Bearded Faces

Black Shield leaned back against the willow chair and glanced around at the circle of men sitting with him in the council lodge, among them High Eagle and Worm. The sons of Goings and Little Bird sat beside their fathers. Also listening with great interest were Cloud, Little Big Man, Taken Alive, and Grey Bull. Crazy Horse had gone off somewhere, perhaps to think, after his friend He Dog had taken his family east to join Two Moons and his Northern Cheyenne. They were planning to go south to the agencies. Two Moons was known for his friendliness to the Long Knives, and He Dog's people were mostly women and children and he wanted to keep them safe, he had said. The news from He Dog had been a surprise, especially to Crazy Horse.

Black Shield carefully handed the charcoal drawings on the piece of hide to a very old man sitting next to him, Shivering Crane, of the Blue Clouds. The old man took the hide and draped it over a gnarled hand. He lifted it up to his old eyes and studied it closely. "In the past, our people lived far south of the Shell River," he began in a tired, raspy voice. "There was trade with many people. There were stories from the Pawnee, who heard stories from other people farther to the south. Those stories were of white men who came up from the south long ago. Those white men wore pointed hats, pointed hats made of shiny iron."

Heads nodded in the council lodge. "Yes," Grey Bull said, "I have heard the same, Grandfather." He was using the title of respect even though he was not related to the old Blue Cloud. "My grandfather saw such an iron hat when he was a boy. Someone took it from a Pawnee lodge after a raid. Where the Pawnee got it, no one knew."

Shivering Crane cleared his throat. "Those kind of white men are said to be the first of their kind to come. It is said that other human beings who live in the hot forest country, very far to the south, had to fight them. Not only did those white men wear iron hats, they wore iron shirts and had guns." The old man paused, and frowned slightly. "It is said that those white men killed many human beings. But they also brought horses. At least they were good for something."

A few wry chuckles filled the air.

"How far north did they come?" asked Taken Alive.

Shivering Crane handed the sketch back to Black Shield. Many lines crisscrossed the old man's face, like roads that showed he had traveled far and lived a long life. His hair, thin though it was, hung in two snow white braids.

"It is not known if they came up into our lands, where we lived once," he said. "I do not think so. But I heard other people tell of them going into the sand country, the hot country to the south, where there is no winter. The people who lived there fought them and took their horses or ran them off."

Grey Bull leaned forward. "How long ago did they come, these white men with pointed iron hats?"

"I have lived nearly eighty years," replied Shivering Crane. "My father, almost the same. The Iron Hats came before the time of my grandfather's grandfather."

Black Shield pointed to the tanned hide with the sketch draped over his leg. "So who scratched these pictures on a rock in the Shining Mountains?" he asked.

"Someone who saw such men," suggested Worm. "Or one of them, an Iron Hat, I mean."

Little Big Man huffed. "I do not think it is possible for them to have come this far north!"

Grey Bull held up a hand. "Is it possible that the drawings on the rock were made before our people came here?"

Little Big Man shook his head in exasperation. "I myself do not think this is important enough to waste our breath on," he said impatiently. "There are bigger things for us to worry about."

Black Shield ignored the younger man's outburst. "I think it is good to hear about what happened before our time, to know as much as we can about the people who went before us. The roads they traveled yesterday can help us see ahead to tomorrow."

Little Big Man lowered his gaze.

"Some, or perhaps many, of the big things we worry about today probably began yesterday," Black Shield went on. "Perhaps our ancestors had to worry about the same things." He shot a glance toward Little Bird and Goings. "Who knows how long those bearded faces have been on that rock. But there they are. I take that as a reminder—white men have been around for many generations. Too long, as far as I am concerned. Those bearded faces tell me that the Hunkpapa holy man is right: it is time to do something about all the bearded faces, such as those infesting the Black Hills like so many hungry locusts."

Murmurs of affirmation arose briefly, but Little Big Man was silent.

A cool breeze prowled the valley as Cloud walked toward the horse herd with Song skipping at his side. She was bundled against the cold in a long elk coat, her large eyes looked dark beneath the light-gray coyote-hide cap.

"Are we going to see the horses, Father?" she asked brightly.

"Yes, I want to see if they remember what we taught them."

"Can we ride?"

"Yes, we can ride down to the water holes."

"I want to ride to the mountains, Father. Can we do that?"

"Not today. Maybe on a warm day we can go on a long ride."

"Will it be warm tomorrow?"

"Hard to say. Maybe—"

The sharp clatter of galloping hooves on frozen ground carried through the valley. Cloud stopped and looked back toward the village. No one galloped that way on frozen ground unless there was trouble. He saw a flash of movement in between the lodges on the far side. He grabbed Song. "We have to go back."

With Song in his arms, he trotted back toward the outer row of lodges as the hoofbeats grew louder. In the village, he saw several men gather and look toward the northeast.

A man slid his horse to a stop in front of the council lodge, a body draped over the withers of the sorrel. Good Shield, the rider, looked half frozen. His face stiff from the cold, he called out, "This is Red Hand! He is shot!"

Taken Alive, Goings, and Little Bird moved forward out of the small crowd to pull the inert form down from the horse.

"Take him into the council lodge," said Worm, who, with High Eagle, suddenly appeared at his side.

As Good Shield jumped down, Goings grabbed the horse's rein and motioned toward a young man. "Walk him until he is cooled down, then water him."

Inside the council lodge, the medicine men quickly cut away the injured man's shirt, revealing an entry wound on the right side below the ribs. A bigger hole just above the hip bone was left by the bullet's exit.

Cloud pushed his way into the lodge. "What happened?" he asked.

Good Shield looked up from beside Red Hand. "We cornered two Long Knives north of here, a little ways from the two thin buttes." He pointed to the wounded man. "He got shot, and Horn Cloud told me to bring him back. He and Lone Hill are still there. The Long Knives are on foot; their horses ran off."

Cloud looked around at the men gathered in the lodge just as Little Big Man entered. "Get your weapons," he said to them.

Good Shield jumped up. "I need a fresh horse."

"Get one, then meet us outside," said Cloud.

As the men left the lodge, two women entered. Worm looked up and recognized the wounded man's wife and her mother. Fear and worry pinched the young woman's face.

"He is alive," Worm assured her. "High Eagle is preparing a poultice to stop the bleeding. Your husband will recover."

Relief blossomed over the young woman's face. She sat down next to her husband, who was beginning to stir, and caressed his face as High Eagle placed a wet poultice over the wound sites.

Several lodges away, Cloud put his weapons near the door and took the bag of dried meat from Sweetwater Woman. In answer to the anxiety on her face, he took a moment to sit next to Song, who had been watching him closely. "If it is even the least bit warm tomorrow," he told his daughter, "you and I will go for a ride."

"Can Mother come along?"

Cloud looked up at this wife. "I hope so, but only if she wants to."

"Are you going somewhere, Father?"

"Yes, I am, but I will be back."

She nodded and smiled.

Cloud stood and took Sweetwater Woman in his arms. "I know you will worry," he whispered in her ear. "But remember, I will always come home."

Later, Sweetwater Woman heard the muffled thud of hoofbeats as the men's horses loped their way out of the village. There was an air of urgency. She took a deep breath and stepped to the food containers stacked against the wall. From one, she took out a braid of wild turnips. "Want to help me?" she asked Song. "I want to make stew."

In the council lodge, Worm glanced at High Eagle as the drum of hoofbeats faded. He leaned forward with a braid of sweetgrass and held it over the hot coals in the fire pit. Soon, a sweet scent, somehow reassuring, filled the room. A thin wisp of smoke from the braid whirled lazily upward toward the vent at the top of the lodge. With it went Worm's silent prayer.

Maintaining a northeasterly direction, Cloud and the others kept their horses at a low lope, not wanting to sweat them on a cold day. Now and then they slowed to a brisk walk. As the tops of two low buttes with thin crests came into view, Good Shield turned to Cloud.

"They are south of there. Horn Cloud and Lone Hill are on a bare ridge above a wide gully. There is a low ridge on the other side of a creek, a frozen creek. The Long Knives are behind a bank. They took cover there and left their horses in the open. We ran the horses off with a couple shots."

After crossing two low, wide drainages and entering a gully, Cloud called a halt and dismounted, then motioned to Good Shield. "Draw the area for me, on the ground here," he said.

As the warriors dismounted and gathered around, Good Shield drew a rough map using the tip of his knife. An east-west ridge was where Horn Cloud and Lone Hill were. Below them, in the gully cut by the creek, were the Long Knives. To the east and west was rough, broken terrain.

Mounting again, the men rode north and then heard the distant, thin crack of a rifle. All urged their horses into a gallop.

Good Shield led them along a meandering creek until he recognized a low hill to the northwest. After circling to the east of it, he pointed to a ridge in the north. "There," he said. "They are among the rocks and soap weeds."

"Where are Horn Cloud and Lone Hill's horses?" Cloud asked.

"Below them, to the south. We hobbled them."

Cloud touched Good Shield's arm briefly. "Go to the men on the ridge. Tell them we are here." He indicated Little Big Man. "He and I will circle to the west and flank the Long Knives. The others will go east and get in position."

"Is our plan to kill them?" asked Little Big Man.

"They have guns and bullets," replied Cloud with a wry smile. "That is what I want."

Little Big Man nodded grimly, a slight frown forming on his face at Cloud's enigmatic reply. Then his expression changed, and it was not so easy to read his mood. His attitude toward white people was well known. It was also known to some that Little Big Man was no friend to Cloud. But the reason for this was not clear, though some suspected that it may have something to do with Cloud's wife, who was white.

Taken Alive cleared his throat. "My friend," he said to Cloud, "if it is all the same, I will go with you." He nodded toward Goings and Little Bird. "The last time, they tried to leave me behind."

The two men grinned but said nothing. Taken Alive's ploy was obvious to them, and they had also understood immediately why Cloud wanted Little Big Man with him.

Cloud nodded. "Good." He turned to Good Shield. "We will wait for you to reach Lone Hill and Horn Cloud before we move."

Nodding, the young man urged his horse forward.

Sergeant Ira Wainscote finished counting the bullets left in his ammunition belt. He had long ago disdained the standard-issue bullet case, saying it was too awkward to wear. "Twelve," he said to Captain Charles Manfred, who looked younger than his thirty years despite his thick, light-brown beard. "My six-shooter is also fully loaded, so I have eighteen rounds in all."

Manfred glanced at Wainscote and then looked north to the long slope rising slowly to the top of the ridge. He stared at the spot where they had last seen their horses, galloping over the ridge. Their spare ammunition and food was in the packs, not to mention the dispatches for Fort Fetterman.

Wainscote pulled off his gloves and blew on his hands to warm them. Both men wore heavy wool overcoats and thick bear-fur caps, but the biting cold attacked every body part not protected. In comparison to Manfred's, the sergeant's beard was dark, almost black.

"I have seven left for the Spencer," replied the captain, "and six in the revolver. So, between us, we have thirty-one rounds, though I suspect the revolvers are no better than throwing rocks."

"Well," grumbled the sergeant, "do not sell them short just yet. When you use up the rounds for the Spencer, you will be damn happy to have that army Colt. But, hell, we'll likely freeze to death before them damn heathens get us."

"I like your cheerful outlook, Ira. Warms me to the bone."

"It is what got me to Fort Ellis. You, I heard, *asked* to be posted there," Wainscote teased, knowing that the captain had petitioned for duty in the West.

"After two years at Fort Belvoir, I wanted some adventure," Manfred said, grinning.

"Rat spit! Saturday night cotillions and breathless young ladies in hoopskirts were not adventure enough for you, Charles? So, given our current fix, what is your take on that adventure thing?"

Manfred chuckled wryly as he turned and cautiously edged up over the rim of the bank with his field glasses. "Hard to see where they are," he commented, ignoring the sergeant's jibes.

"Charles, tell me again. What sacred mission are we performing here, at the risk of our asses and our future well-being?"

"You know damn well, Ira. The colonel could not wait for the telegraph to be repaired, so we are taking—we *were* taking—dispatches to Fort Fetterman."

"Yeah, smack through the middle of Sioux territory!" The sergeant exhaled sharply, his breath misting in the cold air. "Speakin' for myself, sir, I think I will turn my footsteps back toward Fort Ellis. Especially considerin' that, in fact, we are on foot, Charles!"

"Not to worry, I shall be behind you."

The rim of the creek bank, no more than six inches from the captain's head, suddenly exploded, projecting pieces of frozen earth. Manfred ducked down instinctively, his face stinging from the dirt. The distant crack of a rifle followed in an instant.

Manfred wiped the dirt out of his eyes under the probing gaze of Sergeant Wainscote.

"Are you hurt, Charles?"

"No! Damn, that was a good shot at that range!"

"Yeah, them damn heathens is full of surprises." Wainscote stared at the long incline to the west of them. He estimated it was more than a hundred yards to the crest, a long way to run. "You good at runnin', Charles?" he asked.

"What? What do you mean?"

"How fast can you run without trippin' over your feet?"

From the top of the ridge, Lone Hill, a lanky, intense young man, looked hard at the creek bank below. The man's head had been barely above the edge.

"Close, very close," observed Horn Cloud. "Even if you did not get him, they will stay down. They have nowhere to go." He turned to Good Shield, who had just arrived. "What is Cloud's plan?" he asked.

"To get the guns," the man replied.

"So Red Hand is still alive?" Lone Hill wanted to know.

"Yes. When we left, High Eagle and Worm were with him."

"My feet are cold," said Lone Hill, wiggling his toes inside his moccasins. "I hope something happens soon."

"I think Cloud and all of them are in place. They have to do something, I think, before dark," Good Shield reasoned.

Captain Manfred stared incredulously at the sergeant. "You want us to make a run for it, up that?" He pointed to the virtually bare slope. "That's more than a hundred yards! They will have a clear view of us. There's no cover. None!"

"Yeah, but we will be moving targets," Wainscote pointed out. "If we spread out wide, it will be hard for them to pick one of us to aim at. One of those heathens is a good shot, but I'm guessing the other is not."

"Ira, I damn well agree we have to do something, and soon," the captain replied, "but that's a lot of open ground. If we have to move, we need to move from cover to cover."

"In that case," the sergeant responded immediately, "there seems to be some kind of gully to the east of us, 'bout sixty yards. Less open ground. Hell, it has to be better cover than what we got now."

Manfred looked to the east. The sergeant had a point, it seemed, since the creek bed they were in eventually curved around a hill. "We don't know what's beyond that, Ira."

"Who said life is a sure bet, Charles? You knew we were taking a helluva risk when you agreed to the colonel's request. I'm surprised we made it this far!" The sergeant blew on his hands again. "Here's the other thing: in the next few minutes, or sometime during the night, or tomorrow, those damn heathens will come for us. They can afford to wait, and the odds shift big in their favor once the sun goes down because they know the land, the ground."

"You're right, Ira. I say we run like hell for that gully to the east."

Wainscote grinned. "Now you're talkin'! I think we should sling these damn rifles over our shoulders and lead with six-shooters. If we have to go out, we go out standin' up!"

Manfred took a deep breath. "Right!"

Working quickly, they loosened the rifle slings and then hung the heavy weapons' barrels down across their backs.

The captain pulled his fur cap down tight. "Ready when you are, Ira."

Wainscote nodded. "Since I'm sitting on the east side, I'll lead the way. Stay back a bit. Keep a space between us—that way, it's harder for them to pick a target."

Drawing his six-shooter, the sergeant turned, staying low, and crawled to the end of the bank. Manfred pulled out his six-shooter, finding it awkward to hold with his thick winter gloves on. Pulling them off, he quickly stuffed them in the overcoat pocket. There was no turning back now, he realized.

He heard a scrape against the cold ground. True to his word, the sergeant was running straight up. Manfred held his breath, waiting for the blast of a rifle from the top of the ridge. None came. He cringed inwardly because that could mean they were waiting for him. Throwing caution aside, realizing that the longer he hesitated, the harder it would be to take that first step, he leapt up and sprinted for all he was worth.

He felt, and heard, the sharp hum of a bullet fly behind his head. In the next instant, he heard the crack of the rifle. He was vaguely aware of the ground erupting somewhere to his left. Somehow, he coaxed his legs to run faster.

The bend of the hill didn't seem to be getting closer no matter how hard he ran, but before he knew it, he was sliding down an incline to the bottom of a narrow gully. Relief coursed through his body as he saw Wainscote lying against the incline, still panting from his sprint.

"We…we made it!" blurted Manfred.

Wainscote nodded woodenly, staring at something in the gully. Manfred turned and nearly choked on his spit. Kneeling and almost casually pointing rifles at them were two men, two Indians with mildly amused expressions. Manfred only then noticed that the sergeant did not have his six-shooter. He assumed that the sharp downward motion from the man standing in front of him meant for him to lay down his weapon, which he did, slowly.

"What…what do we do, Ira?" he whispered.

"Make no sudden moves," came the whispered response.

CHAPTER EIGHT

Attack on the Powder River

Goings and Little Bird had been following a winding gully. They had reached a narrow bend when they heard running footsteps, and they knew who it was, who it had to be. The first Long Knife, in a blue overcoat, slid down the bank, nearly colliding with Little Bird. Before the man could get his wits about him, Little Bird snatched the six-shooter from his hand and pushed him to the ground.

More running steps followed, slapping the cold ground. A shot cracked from the top of the ridge. The second man slid down the incline, oblivious to the two Lakota warriors kneeling on the other side of the gully. It was almost comical, the way he turned to stare at them, his eyes widening as his excitement turned into shock. Little Bird motioned with his rifle barrel for the man to put down the six-shooter. Cautiously, the man complied.

"Get the six-shooter," said Goings.

Keeping his rifle pointed at the man directly in front of him, Little Bird slowly stepped forward and slid the Long Knife's six-shooter away with his foot. "I think we should signal the others," he said. Then, picking up the revolver, he raised it to the sky, cocked, and fired three times.

Bang! Bang! Bang!

Goings kept his eyes on the two Long Knives. Both were sitting at the bottom of the gully, legs drawn up and hands on their knees, staring at them warily, fearfully. Rifles hung across their backs.

"Notice something about them?" he said to Little Bird.

Little Bird shook his head.

"Their beards. In those fur hats, they look like the drawings on the rock face."

Little Bird nodded. "They all look the same, in fur hats or iron hats," he growled. "Fur hats, iron hats, no hats, they all annoy me."

Hoofbeats could be heard faintly in the distance, then grew louder as they got closer. Horses were coming up the gully they had followed. At the same moment, Cloud, Taken Alive, and Little Big Man appeared at the top of the bank. Their sharp eyes took in the scene. Little Big Man started smiling, but it was not a friendly smile he wore as the three men came down the bank.

Sergeant Wainscote's heart sank. Now there were five, and the hoofbeats he was hearing probably meant there were even more of them. He was right. Without turning his head, he glanced to the right and saw the others, three more, mounted or leading horses. Suddenly, the gully was downright crowded. The possibility of freezing to death was growing slim.

"First, we take the rifles," said Cloud.

He handed his rifle to Little Bird. Stepping to the light-haired man, he pulled the rifle off his shoulder and tossed it to Goings. Moving over, he took the rifle from the dark-haired Long Knife and stepped back, examining the weapon.

"These are new," he commented. "They must have the bullets on them."

"I will search them," Little Big Man volunteered. He pulled the light-haired one to his feet and swiftly unbuttoned the long overcoat. Undoing the belt, he tossed it aside. Attached to it was a holster and a small square case. Swiftly, and none too gently, he searched, then took out a round and shiny metal object on a chain, and a small leather case. Tossing them aside, he shoved the man back down and jerked the dark-haired man to his feet.

From him, he took another belt with a holster and the attached case, a pouch of tobacco and a small pipe, a small box with something inside that rattled, and a sheaf of folded papers.

Little Big Man stared into the dark-haired man's eyes. For a moment, the man held his gaze, but then quickly averted his eyes. Without warning, the angry warrior shoved the Long Knife to the ground. The man landed with a thud.

"Not only do they smell," Little Big Man sniffed, still glaring at the dark-haired man, "they are not intelligent. What are they doing out here, just two of them?"

Pain jolted up from his right elbow, which had absorbed the blow when he fell. Wainscote hoped the man who had searched them was not the one in charge. If so, they could measure the rest of their lives in mere minutes. He had never seen, or felt, such a murderous glare from anyone. The loss of his pipe, tobacco, and matches, and the captain's watch, did not enter his mind. He hoped that the tall one with the cool, measuring eyes was in charge. He was no one to be trifled with either, but he was in control of himself.

It took no more than a few seconds for Manfred to realize that nothing in his twelve years in the US Army could have remotely prepared him for this moment. He had long since been of the opinion that soldiers grossly underestimated Indians. Popular opinion was mistakenly based on the individuals seen up close—half-breeds or those who hung around the forts, or the scouts hired to work for the army, all of them proof that no man respects anyone or anything he has tamed or conquered or controlled. But by no stretch of the imagination were the eight Indians he saw before him any one of those. These men were self-confident, obviously at ease in an environment he feared, and all of them had a no-nonsense air about them. There was a wildness in them, but he sensed they were not reckless. He was afraid, but the one who had searched them scared him the most. That one looked at them as if they were bugs he wanted to squash under his feet.

Little Big Man backed away a few steps and looked over his shoulder at Cloud. "What do you think?" he asked. "What should we do with them?"

Cloud had been checking the bullet cases. "Not many bullets," he said. He looked closely at one of the captured rifles. It looked familiar, a breechloader similar to the one he carried, but newer. "Which direction were they traveling?" he asked Lone Hill.

"South," the young man replied.

"Probably following the Elk River," said Little Big Man.

"I think so," Cloud agreed.

"We will never know why they are here," Goings pointed out. "But it is as Black Shield said: they are everywhere."

"But what should we do about them?" Little Big Man persisted.

"We have their rifles and six-shooters," Cloud said evenly. "Let them go."

"No!" Little Big Man spun on his heel but did not approach Cloud. Anger distorted his face. "No!"

Cloud met Little Big Man's fierce stare. "What do you think we should do with them?"

"Kill them! They are nothing but white men!" Little Big Man spat vehemently. "They would kill us! They shot Red Hand!"

Cloud stayed calm. "Then kill them," he said. "Me, I do not think they are worth two bullets."

Little Big Man took a step forward. "Then tell me, friend, what would you do to these two worthless imitations of human beings?"

Goings and Little Bird exchanged glances and then stepped forward on either side of Cloud. Taken Alive shook his head slowly at Good Shield, Lone Hill, and Horn Cloud, silently signaling them to stand fast.

Cloud closed the breech of the rifle he had been inspecting. "Think about it," he said, his tone level. "They have no horses. If we take their weapons, they are as good as dead." He turned toward Lone Hill. "Which way did their horses go?"

Lone Hill pointed north.

"Maybe someone should take a look over that ridge," Taken Alive suggested. "If they are close, catch them, and take whatever they are carrying."

"I will go," Lone Hill said.

"Me too," said Good Shield.

As the two younger men rode away, Cloud stepped past Little Big Man, ignoring his seething anger, and gazed curiously at the two white men. He noticed that Little Bird had a bemused smile on his face. "You know something?" he said, glancing at him.

Little Bird nodded. "Goings was right. They do look like the drawing on the rock."

Manfred took a slow, deep breath. He and the sergeant had come close to dying, that much he knew. He also knew it wasn't over, by any means. The tall one in the elk-hide coat was a steady one, and thankfully he seemed to be in command. The captain allowed himself a small grain of hope, but

"I think we should go a little farther and find something out of the wind," Wainscote decided. "Make a shelter if we have to. We'll gather kindling and firewood. We got some plannin' to do."

"I was thinking, Ira, we have to get to the Yellowstone."

"You read my mind, Charles."

Manfred nodded, a flicker of uncertainty in his blue eyes. A cold breeze moaned through the gully and shook the thin stalks of grass poking from the snow. He could feel the cold slicing through his clothes.

The same breeze that had made the Long Knives shiver was at the warriors' backs as they rode south. Robes and coats pulled high and tight, they put their horses into a fast walk. Almost at once, a metallic, rhythmic clinking began to annoy them. Lone Hill pointed to the canvas bag on the horse he was leading. Halting, he opened the bag and pulled out a small skillet, a metal plate and cup, and a small, soot-blackened pot with a lid. Horn Cloud found similar items on the other horse. Repacking the items, they rolled the bags as tightly as they could and then tied them snugly onto the fork of the saddles. The noise was reduced considerably once they started again.

Switching from a quick walk to a low lope now and then, they managed to cover ground quickly. Occasionally, one of them would glance back toward the north, though not because they were expecting to see Long Knives. Looking back at a trail was an ingrained habit of the warrior. Being alert and aware was key to staying alive. It was how Lone Hill and Horn Cloud had spotted the two Long Knives.

Good Shield moved out ahead, and Little Big Man brought up the rear. Taken Alive moved off to one side, enough to keep Little Big Man in his peripheral vision with only a slight turn of his head. He did not expect trouble, but it was wise never to assume trouble would not come, especially after Little Big Man's outburst over the Long Knives. Taken Alive respected Little Big Man as a man and a warrior. But Little Big Man was also known for losing his temper. That was the basis for his caution.

Cloud had tied one of the captured rifles to the neck rope of his gray gelding. Draped across the withers was the black belt with the bullet case attached. Taken Alive had the other rifle and belt. But the rifles were not

Cloud's immediate concern. It was unusual for Long Knives to travel alone or in small groups, especially in the winter. If anything, they traveled in columns of fifty or more. There had to be a reason these two today were in Lakota territory. He had a feeling they might have come from the trail that the whites used along the Elk River. It was at least two or three days to the north.

He glanced back toward the two captured horses led by Lone Hill and Horn Cloud. Perhaps something in those packs might provide a hint at what the two Long Knives were doing so far into Lakota territory.

He would not have stopped Little Big Man from shooting them. They were as good as dead, in any case, and he did not care whether they lived or died. The odds were against them. Nights were bitterly cold this time of the year, and without a fire they probably would not survive more than a night or two. They would not even have a chance to starve. In the end, it would be the Long Knives' own ignorance that would do them in. He was certain of it.

Two less Long Knives was a good thing. The trouble was, there always seemed to be more. And the news that awaited them when they arrived home confirmed that grim reality.

Worm approached as Cloud and the others were dismounting. He seemed to have been waiting for them. "My son and High Eagle just left," he told them. "They took eighteen men with them to help Two Moons and He Dog along the Powder River. Two Moons sent a messenger—Long Knives attacked them, and they are in a bad way. My son wants you to follow with as many men as you can, and to take food and robes too."

Two Moons, of the Northern Cheyenne, and his people, along with He Dog and several Lakota families, had been on their way to the agencies and had been camped along the Powder River. At dawn a few days ago, according to Two Moons's messenger, Long Knives—probably more than a hundred strong—had swept down on the village out of the gray morning light.

Cloud picketed his tired horse at the lodge and hurried to the herd to catch his big bay warhorse. When he returned, Sweetwater Woman had a bag of food ready for him to take, and a larger one to help feed the Cheyenne and Lakota who had lost their food supplies. Checking his weapons quickly, he kissed his daughter and embraced his wife for a long moment.

Soon, Sweetwater Woman heard the clatter of hooves on frozen ground for the second time that day as her husband rode away into the fading light with Taken Alive, Goings, Little Bird, Little Big Man, and several others. Like Cloud, most of them were taking extra food or robes, as Crazy Horse and his men did earlier.

"Mother," Song asked apprehensively, in a tiny voice, "where is my father going now?"

"Toward the Powder River, to the east. Some of our friends, the Cheyenne, and our Lakota relatives were attacked by Long Knives, so your father and the others are going there to help them."

"Will they come here and attack us, those Long Knives?"

"No, do not worry. Crazy Horse has told the sentinels to stay out and guard the camps until he returns. So we are safe." She grabbed a deer-hide robe and wrapped it around the girl. "Come, we need to bring in wood for the night."

On the way out, Sweetwater Woman glanced down at a bundle to the left of the door. Inside was a six-shooter. A few days ago, Cloud had cleaned and reloaded it, and showed her how to pull back the hammer and aim. She wished she would have paid closer attention.

Fortunately, Cloud and the others knew the country to the east well enough to find known trails. They pushed hard, even after the sun went down. By the time all of the daylight had faded from the western rim of the sky, they spotted the glow of a signal fire far ahead. When they came to it, a voice called out to them from the darkness.

"My friends!"

"Yes!" Cloud responded. "We must be catching up with our headman!"

"He is not far ahead, resting his horses." A figure wrapped in a buffalo robe and leading a horse emerged from the darkness, walking into the dim glow of the dying fire. It was Has No Horse, a young man who smiled easily. Pulling out a bone whistle, he blew on it four times. "If they hear that, they will stop and wait," he said.

Mounting effortlessly despite his heavy buffalo robe and the rifle in his hands, Has No Horse led them off into the darkness. No one spoke as he kept to a trot, slowing down only after they came to a long downward incline. At the bottom was a narrow creek bed, and soon dark shapes materialized in the darkness.

Crazy Horse and his men were dismounted, each man pressed against his horse, a good way to keep warm without a fire.

"The fire was just about to go out when they came," Has No Horse reported.

"Good," Crazy Horse spoke from the front of the line of men and horses. "How many are you?"

"Ten," Cloud told him.

"Did you find any excitement to the north?"

"No," Cloud replied. "Horn Cloud and Lone Hill had trapped two Long Knives. We took their guns and horses. If they are smart, they will find a hole in the ground to keep out of the wind. If they happen to find a bear, at least they will be warm before they die."

Soft laughter arose in the darkness.

"How are your horses?" Crazy Horse asked.

"Strong and willing."

"Good. We will go on then."

They rode through the night, with several of the men who knew the area best taking turns in the lead. As pale light in the east separated earth from sky, Crazy Horse called a halt. The shadowy grove where they stopped turned out to be a stand of lodgepole pine, the fresh scent accentuating the cold air. Men went to work quickly to gather fuel, and soon several fires were burning. Those who had brought along tin cups scooped clean snow and boiled water for tea. Everyone ate their trail rations, the mixture of dried buffalo meat and dried, pounded chokecherries. Several bundled themselves in buffalo robes and curled up to get a little sleep before they pushed on again.

Sitting by a fire with Crazy Horse was Two Moons's messenger, a young man named Fire Crow. He was on the edge of exhaustion. After two days on a cold, hard trail to deliver his message, he had insisted on leading the Crazy Horse warriors back to the lower Powder River area. He was a strong and competent young man with broad shoulders. When Cloud arrived, he nodded a greeting and took a bag of dried meat from him with a tired smile.

"This young man says we should be able to find the camp by sundown," Crazy Horse told his friend. "They were moving as fast as they could in this direction. After the horses are rested and watered, and we get whatever sleep we can, we can start again."

By midmorning, they were back on the trail, alternating between a steady, fast walk and a trot. The land was bright as the sun reflected off the snow, forcing everyone to pull a wolf- or coyote-hide cap low over his eyes to protect them from the glare. Has No Horse and two other men were sent ahead to scout in the event that Long Knives might still be lurking somewhere. But nothing, not even old signs, could be seen. Snow had fallen since Two Moons had been attacked, and any tracks now had been left recently by birds and other animals large and small. Nothing resembling the print of a shod Long Knife horse was seen. Nonetheless, they remained watchful as ever, especially given the reason they were on this rescue mission.

In the middle of the afternoon, Fire Crow recognized a ridgeline, and shortly thereafter a faint whiff of wood smoke drifted to them on the breeze. Has No Horse came back and reported that a camp was just over the next ridge.

A meager camp it was. People were gathered around fires outside and in the lodges. All the nearby gullies and meadows had been scoured for fuel. Even the tops of lodge poles had been broken off and added to the fires to help with the fuel shortage. A ring of boys and young men guarded the horse herd of about three hundred, which had been driven into a steep-sided draw. Warriors were positioned in high places in order to have a good view of anyone approaching.

The Crazy Horse warriors quickly distributed the food and robes they had brought along, and High Eagle offered his help to the wounded, but, as he had feared, frostbite had taken a toll.

Crazy Horse sought out Two Moons and He Dog and listened somberly to the grim story of the attack. More than a hundred horses had been driven away. Several lodges had been destroyed, and much of the food supplies as well. They were down to eating whatever rabbits and squirrels could be caught or snared. Worst of all, several people were wounded, some of them children, and two young men had been killed.

"I have always been a friend to the Long Knives, to all the whites,"

Two Moons said acidly, huddled under a thin gray blanket. He had given away all of his warm robes. "Perhaps I should have listened to those of you who warned me never to trust them."

No one had imagined that Long Knives would be so far north. Because of that and the bitter cold, no sentries had been posted. The attack came from the bluffs above the village, forcing the people to scatter into the gullies and breaks, or whatever shelter they could find, and hide as best they could.

Nevertheless, Cheyenne and Lakota warriors had regrouped and driven off the Long Knives with a determined counterattack, forcing the attackers to leave behind some of their wounded and dead. After the Long Knives were gone, Two Moons sent one of his scouts to find Crazy Horse.

"My people no longer want to go to the agency," He Dog said, his bare hands gripping the stock of his rifle. "We will go back with you to stay. This reminds me of the fight over the cow almost thirty years ago, when a good man was killed simply because he wanted to keep the peace. Peace is something no white man understands."

Crazy Horse looked at his friend. He and He Dog had been boys when soldiers had come to Conquering Bear's village near Fort Laramie. They had come to take a Lakota prisoner, a man who had killed a white man's cow. But as his old friend Hump had told him later, Long Knives needed very little reason—real or imagined—to kill human beings. They had paid for their foolishness that day. All but one of the thirty soldiers had been killed after they had opened fire first. But the Sicangu people had paid a higher price, for their man Conquering Bear was fatally wounded and died days later.

Two Moons knew about that incident. He stared coldly into the fire. "When spring comes, we will go with you to the White Buttes, and I will listen to what the Hunkpapa medicine man has to say, and I will add our story to all those that are told of the white man's treachery," he promised. "It is the only way I can look our children in the eye again."

"We will be glad to have you back with us," Crazy Horse assured the angry Two Moons. "We have to show our relatives on the agency that life is a challenge best lived freely, not under the boot heels of white men."

Two Moons nodded grimly. "Tomorrow would be better for us to travel," he said. "A night's rest would do us all good, especially the wounded."

The decision was made to wait until morning to travel. Two of the Cheyenne families were in mourning and had decided to take their loved ones to the Shining Mountains for burial. Many of the warriors from the Crazy Horse camps took over the sentry duties, and some went hunting. Boys were sent to search the gullies and draws for more fuel. The afternoon air was bitter cold, and the night was certain to be dangerously so.

Close to sundown, two scouts who had been following the Long Knives returned from the south. The column was marching south, they said, more than a hundred men, and showed no indication of turning back. Good news for the worn and weary Cheyenne, but no one would be foolish enough to let down his guard again. Crazy Horse decided to leave nothing to chance and sent Has No Horse and two scouts to keep an eye out in the event the Long Knives did turn back.

After he checked on the injured and wounded, High Eagle went from lodge to lodge. He took time to visit with everyone, especially the children. Many times, there were wounds to the spirit that were not always easy to see. Too often, they were the kind that could last a lifetime if nothing was done about them.

The medicine man was invited into the lodge of Fire Crow and found it nearly bursting at the seams. Four families, most of them made up of children, were huddled together around a fire. There was no grass to stuff between the dew cloth and outer lining, so the lodge was not as warm as it could have been. Nevertheless, small brown faces framed by black hair smiled shyly as he greeted them.

"I heard this was the warmest lodge," he told them, a twinkle in his eyes, "so I might just stay here."

He stayed for a while, visiting with everyone, asking questions, and talking about anything but the cold or Long Knives. Pulling a small twist of sweetgrass from a bag, he laid it at the edge of the small fire. Thin gray smoke rose upward in a slow and perfect spiral, capturing everyone's attention, the sweet odor filling the room. It was the scent of reassurance and peace.

"There is food," High Eagle said gently. "And we will find enough wood to keep everyone warm tonight. All you need to do is eat and sleep."

Rejuvenated by a little food and their spirits buoyed by the presence of thirty Lakota fighting men, the Cheyenne and He Dog's people rested as best they could, better than they had in several nights. But a certain amount of wariness would not go away easily, and perhaps ever, in some cases. Many would awaken at the slightest noise and hold their breath until they remembered that warriors were awake and on watch in the cold night and that the enemy would be stopped if they attacked a second time.

Cloud, Goings, and Taken Alive found an overhang at the top of the gully and fashioned a shelter by piling rocks to build a wall. Inside, the fire at least kept the cold at bay. They coaxed one of the camp dogs inside with them, knowing it would hear anything that approached.

"It is hard to believe that Long Knives were this far north in cold weather," commented Taken Alive. "Something different for them."

"Something about that bothers me," Goings contemplated. "There has to be a reason for them to be up here."

"You mean other than attacking women and children?" Taken Alive spat.

"I think he might be right," Cloud said, nodding at Goings. "Maybe they were scouting."

"A hundred of them?" Taken Alive scoffed.

"Yes, that is how they do things. They are afraid of this land, so they go out in herds—mobs," Cloud retorted. "They cross the land in lines of wagons."

"If there were a hundred of them, or more, they outnumbered Two Moons's and He Dog's men, and they had more guns," Goings said. "And they were still driven away. Someday, they will attack at the wrong place, at the wrong time."

"I hope there will come a day," Cloud said quietly, "a day when we meet them face-to-face, warrior against Long Knife. When that day comes, they will learn that it takes more than a horse, a gun, and bullets to be a true warrior. They are not true warriors. They are only killers."

"Be careful what you ask for," Taken Alive cautioned. "On the other hand, maybe you are right—maybe. But I hope it is a really warm day when it happens."

After a few chuckles, they rolled up in their buffalo robes. Through the night, they took turns grabbing snatches of sleep until dawn.

As the sun came up, the people broke camp and turned their faces back to the west, toward the Shining Mountains. They set a pace the wounded and injured could comfortably withstand, and one that also helped the horse herders keep the animals together.

Hunters caught up on the second day with three deer, providing an excuse for a prolonged rest and a feast of fresh meat. Three days after that, the Two Moons and He Dog people finally rejoined the Crazy Horse people, reaching the easternmost village on a bright and cold afternoon. They were welcomed with open arms.

Two days later, Has No Horse and his scouts returned and reported that no Long Knives had followed them.

CHAPTER NINE

Fast Horse and Walks Alone

As Two Moons and He Dog and their people were settling back in along the Tongue River camps with the Crazy Horse people, Yellow Wolf and Plum reached the hills north of the Long Knife outpost called Fort Robinson.

Hiding out and staying in one place during the day was difficult, but it had to be done in order to avoid being spotted. They had to take turns sleeping, and they could only build small fires so that any smoke would be hard to see from a distance, but at least they could be warm now and then. And it was not always easy to keep the horses calm and quiet. Finding a good, secluded place to hide was as much of a challenge. After walking all night long, they had to find a gully that could hide two horses, with forage for them as well. Fortunately, because Plum kept track of the moon's cycle, as all women did, they knew when it would be full. Taking advantage of its light, they traveled east for three nights, circling north of the bluffs above the outpost. Even more fortunate for them were two cloudless nights in a row, though it was cold.

Occasionally, they heard dogs barking and the faint bawling of cattle, all sounds carried on the restless breezes that wandered aimlessly over the prairies. The farther east and away from the outpost they went, the less they heard them.

During a cold dawn, as the waning moon dipped toward the west and the sky was the deepest blue, they found an old creek bed with banks high enough to hide behind. As he gathered kindling and wood from among some low shrubbery, Yellow Wolf smelled smoke. Ducking down among a patch of snake berry bushes, he gauged the direction of the breeze. It was from the south.

As the sky brightened in the east and the first rays of the sun slid over the horizon, he caught sight of thin columns of smoke to the south. Slowly, more and more wavering columns were revealed as the light grew brighter. Yellow Wolf knew they had found the lodges of the Spotted Tail people. He told Plum as he climbed down into the gully.

"Will we go there today?" she asked hopefully.

He nodded. "Soon we should change into white-man clothes," he said, "in case we are seen by Long Knives or any whites."

Throwing caution aside, they decided that a pot of elk stew was in order. They had not eaten a hot meal for more than six days. They were also feeling the effects of getting only short snatches of sleep for the past three days.

"Are they allowed to hunt for fresh meat?" she asked as they waited for the stew to finish cooking.

"I do not know," he admitted.

"Who would stop them? Can anyone stop them if all the people here just decided to leave?" she asked. "Are there that many Long Knives and whites here? Are they that powerful that men like Spotted Tail and Red Cloud do their bidding?"

"I have thought of those things myself many times," he replied. "I have asked Cloud and old men like Black Shield and High Eagle. They do not understand it any more than I do. There are many men with Spotted Tail and Red Cloud. Several thousand. Why they do not simply pack up their families and leave..." Yellow Wolf paused and sighed deeply.

Plum pointed to the horses. Both were suddenly gazing intently toward the south. Yellow Wolf rose quickly and stood between them, stroking their noses to keep them from neighing. In a while, they relaxed.

"They hear or smell other horses," he told her. "We may be near a road. We need to change our clothes."

They stared at one another after they finished changing into the clothing they had brought along. A strange transformation seemed to have taken place. Plum wore a blue calico dress beneath a dark gray coat, and a dark scarf tied over her head as her mother had advised her to do. Her face was narrow, and it seemed to Yellow Wolf that she had shrunk.

He had to tie a rope around the top of his gray trousers to keep them from sliding down. Whoever they were made for had to have been short and wide, since the cuffs were well above his shoes, which felt strange. Looking down, he noticed that the left shoe was narrower. The faded brown shirt was already making his skin itch, and the black wool coat was almost too small.

He looked up and saw the expression on his wife's face as she stared at him. "Do not worry, it is me," he told her.

"Now I know why I do not like white people," she said. "It's their clothes. I feel like I want to escape."

He started laughing. "I have heard that white women wear an iron basket or belt, or something, beneath their dresses."

"That is hard to believe. How can they have children?"

He took the rumpled gray hat and put it on his head.

It was Plum's turn to laugh. "You are not the man I once knew!"

He shrugged and said, "We should fit in around here without too much trouble."

In a while, they sat down to eat their stew, noticing immediately that their clothes were no match for the biting breeze. Yellow Wolf watched the horses closely. They would know if anyone used the road to the south, which was likely.

"I know they told us to wait until dark, but I think it would be better not to," he decided. "We can gather wood and arrange some packs on the horses. That way, I can hide my weapons, and anyone who sees us will think we are hauling firewood."

"Where do we go? I do not know where my sister's lodge is."

"Yes, we will be taking a risk. Cloud said it is difficult to know who is on the side of the Long Knives and who is not. I think we will just walk into the village as though we belong and see what happens."

"Why can we not wait until dark? I am worried. What will the Long Knives do to us if we get caught?"

Suddenly, Yellow Wolf was reminded of Walks in the Night, Goings's Cheyenne wife. She was a gentle woman, and she always had the haunted shadow of fear in her eyes. Fear of Long Knives, of any white person.

"I have a task—we have a task to do," he said gently. "I am anxious. But this is what we can do. Gather wood, as I said, then wait until there is no one on the road, then cross it. South of here is a creek. I can see by the trees. We will follow the creek, staying in the trees. I promise no one will see us."

Plum nodded silently, though her fear persisted, like the cold breeze seeping through her clothes. "I am anxious too," she said. "I have not seen my sister for a while."

By midday they were south of the village and situated in a broad, uneven meadow. They caught only glimpses of the village through the trees, but Yellow Wolf did not see any activity. Even the dogs were strangely silent. Suddenly, he realized what had been bothering him since he had seen the first line of lodges: there were no horses picketed in front of them.

Staying in the trees, as he had promised Plum they would, and following the creek, they came to a well-worn trail that led down to a watering hole. He veered off into a thicket and decided they should wait there. Sooner or later, someone would come for water or bring a horse to drink. The question was who to trust.

He decided to slide his six-shooter out of the bundle and tuck it into his waist. "Just being sure," he explained to Plum. "We will wait and see who comes."

"There is something strange here, I mean, the way it feels," Plum said, looking about warily. "Like there is no…no life."

He had been trying to put his finger on something, a feeling. She seemed to have a better sense of it. "I thought it was these clothes," he replied, "but I think you are right. It does feel strange."

They settled in the thicket. It was better to wait, Yellow Wolf decided, but he felt uneasy nonetheless. He didn't like not having complete control over a situation.

He saw the sorrel's ears point forward and felt Plum grab his arm. Someone was walking down the trail. More than one person, as a matter of fact. A woman and a child were carrying iron buckets, and the small girl also had a hand ax.

"Grandmother," she said, "do you think there will be ice?"

"Perhaps," replied the woman. "You can break it if there is."

Yellow Wolf had noticed that the narrow creek was frozen at the edges. Cold as it was, the weather down here was not as harsh as it was in the Tongue River country. Up north, the rivers and creeks were frozen solid.

A scarf covered the woman's head and one hand held the gray blanket draped over her thin shoulders. The girl wore a long coat. He didn't recognize either of them.

At the water's edge, the old woman waited patiently as the girl swung the ax, making more noise than progress against the narrow shelf of ice. Yellow Wolf nodded to Plum, then pushed his way out of the thicket.

"Can I help you with that?" he asked, approaching slowly.

The girl paused, and the old woman turned toward the voice. Although there was no concern or surprise on the woman's face, neither was there a sign she recognized the man approaching. Maybe it was someone from the Red Cloud agency. She had never been there.

Yellow Wolf took the bucket from her and bent to the slow trickle of the cold creek between two borders of ice and dipped into it. When he had filled it, he pointed to the other bucket. "If you give me that one, I can fill it for you too," he offered.

Smiling shyly, the girl picked up the bucket and gave it to him.

He took the bucket and motioned for Plum to join them. The old woman smiled as Plum pushed the branches aside and emerged.

"Grandmother," she said, "we will carry the water back for you."

"Thank you," said the old woman behind a slight smile. She noticed the two horses with packs and bundles of wood.

Yellow Wolf decided to take a chance. "Grandmother," he said casually, "my wife and I came to visit. She is looking for her sister."

"What is her name?"

"Walks Alone," Plum told her.

The old woman's eyes brightened. "Yes, I know her." She motioned to the girl. "Granddaughter, go to Walks Alone's lodge and ask her to come here. Just say that. Tell her I need her."

Yellow Wolf smiled as the girl hurried away. "Thank you, Grandmother."

Plum brushed away a bit of snow from the edge of the low bank. "Sit here," she invited. "Your granddaughter, what is her name?"

"We call her Two Birds. She is always flying about," the old woman said as she took a seat. "I live with her and her mother, my daughter. My name is Blue Stone."

"My mother is Little Grass," Plum told her, "and my father is Stands There." She pointed to her husband. "He is Yellow Wolf."

"My mother is White Horse Woman. And my father is No Lance," he said.

"Yes," said Blue Stone. "I know your families. You have traveled far to come here."

Yellow Wolf took another chance. "So did Sitting Bull's messenger."

The old woman nodded. "They are still talking about him and the message he brought."

Soft voices drifted from the direction of the village, and soon footsteps scuffed on the path. Plum turned to look, unable to hide her anticipation. Down the path came Two Birds, leading a young woman by the hand. The woman was thin in the face and had a slight limp. She glanced toward the two horses in the thicket as she descended the path to the water, and then noticed the man and woman with Blue Stone.

Plum stood, unable to contain herself. "Sister!" she called out.

Walks Alone stopped, momentarily puzzled, but recognition came in the next heartbeat. Her hands flew to her mouth. "It cannot be!"

The sisters embraced, clinging to one another through soft sobs. After several long moments, they pulled apart, smiling through the tears.

"Where did you get these clothes?" Walks Alone asked. "What are you doing here?"

Plum laughed as she brushed away her tears and nodded at her husband. "The clothes were his idea," she said, divesting herself of responsibility for the way they looked. "And we came to see you."

Shortly, Yellow Wolf learned why there were no horses picketed in front of any of the lodges. There was a corral east of the village on the other side of the creek, similar to those made by whites. Posts set into the ground supported four rails made of oak. It was large enough to hold the eighty or so horses that he was able to quickly count. At Walks Alone's urging, after removing the packs and ropes, they turned their horses in among the village's herd. Yellow Wolf knew someone would notice them sooner or later, but he decided not to question his sister-in-law's obvious sense of caution.

Luckily, there was not much activity in the village, so they did not arouse any curiosity. Yellow Wolf hauled the water to Blue Stone's lodge. He noticed that many of the lodges were made of canvas, and they rattled strangely in a strong breeze. Looking around quickly, he saw only four or five buffalo-hide lodges, patched many times, he noted.

"My husband went hunting early this morning," Walks Alone explained as she hung a kettle on the iron tripod over the fire. "To the south, after deer. He set snares for rabbits too. Many of the men do; sometimes it is the only fresh meat we have. There are no more prairie dogs around here. We ate them all long ago."

"Does he have a rifle?" Yellow Wolf asked.

She shook her head. "No, he hunts with a bow. He said he would be back by sundown."

Plum dug into her pack and pulled out a flat container of dried buffalo meat and a short braid of wild turnips. "We brought as much as we could carry."

Walks Alone sighed. "Thank you."

"What about the cattle?" Yellow Wolf asked. "How is the meat?"

"It has a different taste," she told her brother-in-law. "You can get used to it. But that is not the problem. There is never enough. I hear they are brought up here from the south, sometimes on the iron road. They—the white men at the agency—tell us that there is a hard winter to the south, so the cattle cannot be brought north. So there is no meat. We are low on flour as well."

Yellow Wolf had arranged their bundles near the door so that his rifle was hidden. He kept the six-shooter hidden under his coat. He noticed that although his sister-in-law's lodge was one of the few made of buffalo hide, it was shorter and narrower than the others.

"Your lodge," he said, "it is smaller than the others."

"Yes," she replied as she mixed flour and water in a kettle. "We cut it down last summer. We do not need all the room, and it is easier to heat. Six poles were left over, so we used them for firewood. Other people have done the same."

Her husband, Fast Horse, came home before sundown with two large rabbits already skinned and gutted. He was understandably taken aback at the unexpected visitors, but he seemed pleased, especially when he caught the smell of buffalo soup seasoned with wild turnips. "That is a good smell," he commented gratefully. "It reminds me of a life we once had."

After finishing a bowl of soup, he leaned back against his chair and got to the heart of the matter. "It seems to me," he said, "the two of you did not travel all the way from the Shining Mountains this early winter just to bring us buffalo meat—although I am glad for that." Fast Horse smiled as he poked at the fire. He wore a black scarf around his neck, tied in a knot at his throat. A thin scar along his left jawline attested to unspoken adventures in the time before the agency. He was a tall, pleasant-looking man with wide-set eyes, a strong jaw, and a quick smile. The worn winter moccasins on his feet hinted at a rebellious nature. He had followed Spotted Tail to the agency because he trusted the man. But lately he had secretly begun to question the wisdom of anyone who said life on the agency was the way of the future.

"There is always a reason for everything," Yellow Wolf replied cautiously.

"I wonder what the reason is for men to sit on their hands," Fast Horse replied. "There was a time I could not wait to chase the buffalo. Now I cannot wait to chase a few rabbits."

"On the other hand," Yellow Wolf pointed out, "while we can chase buffalo whenever we want, there are very few left to chase."

"These are strange and difficult times," Fast Horse declared wistfully.

Yellow Wolf told them about the buffalo hunt. "The meat we brought is from one of those cows," he said. "I pray they were not the last buffalo on Earth."

"Surely the Great Spirit would not allow that to happen," Fast Horse added. "The Buffalo People without buffalo is the same as a man without a soul."

"One of the hunters with us was the man who came from the Knife River country with a pipe and a message."

Fast Horse nodded. "Yes. One came here as well, as you know."

Yellow Wolf kept his silence. He had taken a chance by mentioning Sitting Bull's messenger to Blue Stone at the creek because he sensed she was someone he could trust. He liked Fast Horse, but he didn't know where the man's loyalties lay. Mentioning Hawk Eagle without referring directly to the message he carried was, he hoped, a way to find out.

The man looked toward his wife. "Perhaps you can boil some of the black medicine for our visitors," he suggested. "I must admit, it is one of the few things the whites have that I like. We can have some with the fried bread."

Smiling, Walks Alone pulled out a bag of coffee beans. Pouring a few onto a flat pounding stone, she took a stone hammer and quickly pulverized the beans, repeating the process until she had enough to boil in a pot. Plum took it upon herself to flatten pieces of dough and cook them in the hot skillet.

As she worked, Fast Horse stared at the fire. "My friend, you have taken a risk coming here for the reason I think you came. You people are the so-called wild ones. Everyone down here, even the Long Knives and the other whites, talks about you and the Sitting Bull people. There is a young Long Knife named Clark, called White Hat. He is always asking people about those of you up north. He knew almost immediately that Sitting Bull's man was here among us."

"Crazy Horse warned that there are those who seek favor from the whites," Yellow Wolf asserted.

"True, and it is not easy to know who, exactly. Some of our men have put on the blue coat and work for the Long Knives. There are others who are the eyes and ears for White Hat, here and at Red Cloud. So, if anyone asks—and someone will—you are here to visit. Nothing more. But White Hat will be suspicious because you are one of the wild ones. I do not know how long you plan to be here. Not too long, I hope."

"We had to hide the young man who came from Sitting Bull," Walks Alone revealed. "White Hat wanted to make him a prisoner, to put him in a house with the iron bars."

Yellow Wolf inwardly breathed a sigh of relief. Now he could be somewhat certain that Fast Horse and his wife's sister could be trusted. Nevertheless, he had a thought to talk to someone like Swift Bear or Runs Above, as Cloud and Crazy Horse had suggested. Those men would definitely have opinions regarding Sitting Bull's message.

He cleared his throat. "What about Swift Bear and Runs Above? What is their thinking about Sitting Bull?"

The aroma of boiling coffee filled the room. Strangely enough, it was a reassuring aroma. Plum helped her sister pour the steaming liquid into metal cups and pass out the fried bread.

"Perhaps we can arrange something," Fast Horse said, nodding thoughtfully.

In the corral, a young man walked slowly toward his horse, speaking softly and keeping the rope halter and lead rope behind his back. But the wily, nondescript little bay was inherently suspicious of people. He pushed into the middle of the herd.

Bug, the people called the young man. Twig thin, his clothes always hung loosely on his small frame. His overly large eyes gave him a constantly startled appearance and thus earned him his second name. Most forgot that his real name was Little Feather, passed to him by an uncle. Everyone here and at the Spotted Tail camp knew him by his nickname. "Hey, Bug," some would say, "can you tell me if there is a flea on that hawk up there?" Or they'd make some other derisive comment at his expense. Sadly, it was a fact of life for Bug.

But he was learning the white man's language. The more words he could remember, the more hard sweets he got from the one called White Hat. He did not make fun of him the way his own relatives did. As a matter of fact, the stubborn little bay was a gift from White Hat.

As the horses pushed up against the corral and moved away from him, two stayed in one corner, a sorrel and a gray, both in excellent condition despite the sparse winter forage. After a moment, it dawned on Bug that he had never seen those horses before. As soon as he caught the bay, he would ride over to the little square wooden house not far from here. The wooden house where the Long Knife called Lee came to sit and look out the window toward the Spotted Tail village. Lee would pass the word to White Hat about the two new horses.

CHAPTER TEN

Ambush

Cloud led the small group up the slope to the burial grounds. There had been no new snow for several days, so the way up was clear. Behind him, he could hear the clatter of hooves on the frozen ground. Sweetwater Woman was next in line, followed by High Eagle, and then Little Bird. Song was huddled beneath her father's buffalo robe, looking out at the wintry world through a gap as she hung on to the end braid of the horse's neck rope.

The midmorning sun was bright on the eastern sides of the snow-covered peaks and slopes of the mountains to the west, providing another breath-taking, glistening affirmation of their name: the Shining Mountains.

High Eagle sang an honoring song to Mother Earth, mingling his voice with the distant whistle of a bull elk. Little Bird nodded in rhythm with the song, giving the impression that the wolf-hide cape over his head and shoulders was dancing.

The plateau above the river was hidden behind a tree-choked bend. For that reason, it had been chosen as a burial site, and it had been here since before Cloud was born. Here were the remains of his mother and his grandmother and grandfather on his mother's side. Among the nearly one hundred others were Bear Looks Behind, Two Horns, No Tail, and Kills Crow, as well as a host of grandmothers. So, too, were Lone Bear, Crazy Horse's boyhood friend who had been killed at the Battle of the Hundred in the Hand, and, of course, Rabbit. He had also been killed in that battle, after saving Cloud's life. The bones of Little Hawk, Crazy Horse's younger brother, were not here, however. His brother had buried him in the lands of their enemies, the Shoshone. And the body of Hump had been taken back to his Mniconju relatives in the great hill country west of the Great Muddy River. Every burial scaffold here was an empty place in someone's lodge, the cause of loneliness and even regret and an occasional tear, but also, now and then, a secret smile.

This was not Cloud's first visit to the burial site, and it would not be the last. Today he was here to pay respect to Grandmother Willow. She had died in the last days of the Middle of Winter Moon.

They dismounted, tied their horses, and carried their gifts and offerings of food.

"Our relatives," said High Eagle, "you have lived in our hearts and minds since the day you left this earthly journey. We know you are well and happy in the Spirit World. We are not here to speak your names and impede your journeys on the other side. We are here to remember your time on this Earth, and your words, your ways, your deeds. We say these things with the certain knowledge that we will see you again one day, when we join you on the next journey."

They laid bundles of sage and offerings of food on the scaffolds of all their relatives and friends. Song followed her mother, wide-eyed and silent, staring up at the scaffolds.

At one of the newer burials, Sweetwater Woman paused. "Here is your great-grandmother," she told the girl. "She gave you your name before you were born and then helped to bring you into this world. It was on a day much like this that you were born, and it was on a day much like this that this good woman left us for the Spirit World."

Song nodded, then her father came and took her hand and led her to two scaffolds, side by side, and pointed to one.

"Here is your great-grandfather. He taught me how to be a good man, or tried to. He and my father showed me the way of the hunter and warrior, and he was a Crazy Dog warrior."

"Is your father here too?"

"No," he replied. "I took his body to the lands where he lived as a boy, to the east, this side of the Great Muddy. My father was a Sicangu, and, like his father, he was a Crazy Dog warrior."

"What is that, Father, a Crazy Dog warrior?"

"A Crazy Dog warrior is one who never retreats in battle. My grandfather did not, and that's how he died, fighting to the last."

Cloud moved over to the next scaffold. "And here is your grandmother, my mother. She was lost in a blizzard on the way home from visiting relatives. I learned how to be a hunter and warrior from my father, but my mother, and my grandmother, showed me what courage is. Now, come, there is one more to tell you about."

They moved down the uneven line of scaffolds and stopped before one next to a bare aspen. Cloud reached up and turned the shield with its weatherworn and tattered covering. The paint had faded, but the sketch of the warrior with two outstretched arms on a galloping horse, as though flying, was still plain enough to see.

"This is my friend," he told her. "He suffered a terrible wound and lost half of his arm." He touched his own elbow. "From here. But he did not let that defeat him. He was a better man with one arm than some are with two. He was killed on the day you were born. He was a good man and a very brave warrior. I think of him every day because he saved my life."

"Then I will think of him every day too," she said.

"Good! Your mother and I will tell you these stories again and again."

"Why?"

"Because you must know who you are. All of these people, these friends and relatives, are part of who you are, of what you are."

"I am hungry, Father. Can we eat with all these friends and relatives?"

Cloud turned toward Sweetwater Woman and smiled. "Yes. They will like that."

By midafternoon they were on their way home, expecting to be home by sundown. Little Bird took the lead as they headed northwest. A steady breeze had sprung up, but, all in all, it was still not an unpleasant afternoon. Shadows were lengthening in the wide valley, almost touching the base of the bluffs to the east. Cloud was adjusting the buffalo robe to keep the breeze from bothering Song when he heard a soft grunt. Glancing forward, he saw Little Bird twist strangely to the right.

Then came the faint crack of a rifle.

In a heartbeat, Cloud was off the left side of his horse, pulling Song down with him. "Get down! Get down!" he yelled to Sweetwater Woman and High Eagle.

Clinging grimly to his horse's long rein, he jumped down into a depression and shoved Song under its low bank. Sweetwater Woman scrambled past him and lay herself across Song.

High Eagle ran toward Little Bird, whose horse was spinning right, as the wounded man was sliding off on that side. As High Eagle reached for the reins, Little Bird fell to the ground. Behind them, a bullet ripped into the earth, then bounced away with a high whine.

"Stay here!" Cloud said to Sweetwater Woman as he covered them with his buffalo robe. "Stay down, no matter what happens!"

Twenty or so paces from them, High Eagle dragged the limp figure of Little Bird toward a slight rise no higher than a man's waist. He dropped down on the west side of it. Little Bird's horse snorted nervously, on the verge of running away.

Cloud ran toward the horse and managed to untie the encased rifle hanging from the neck rope. In the next few heartbeats, he was mounted on his own horse.

"Go!" yelled High Eagle. "Go!"

Cloud tossed Little Bird's rifle and bullet pouch toward the medicine man, who managed to catch it. With a last glance at Sweetwater Woman and Song, Cloud spun his horse toward the east and kicked him into a gallop. He had no idea how badly wounded Little Bird was, except that his friend was not moving. Still, under the circumstances, he couldn't be in better hands.

Something buzzed by his head with the sound of an angry hornet, and the pop of the rifle was not far behind. That meant he was closing the distance. The broken and uneven terrain prevented the sorrel gelding from stretching out into an all-out gallop.

The shots had come from the bluffs, but there was no way to tell whether they were from one rifle or more. He had to assume there was more than one shooter. As he glanced toward the rim of the bluff, he saw the briefest flash, which was followed by a sharp whine above him. The shot was high and probably from inside a draw. Now he had some idea of where the shooter—or shooters—was.

The north end of the bluff angled down to the valley floor with a gentle slope, but by no means was the surface smooth. Deep fissures, cut by melting snow and heavy summer rains, ran from top to bottom. Getting to the top of the bluff as quickly as possible would be in his favor, and that meant doing so on the back of the sorrel. Then he realized that the shooter would expect him to ascend that north slope.

He was closing in on the base of the bluff and did not hear any more shots, meaning he was probably below the shooter's line of sight and field of fire. If they stayed down and out of sight, Sweetwater Woman and High Eagle were behind enough cover.

High Eagle worked quickly and skillfully. A bullet had torn through Little Bird's upper right chest, entering just below the collarbone and slashing its way out by the right shoulder blade. The hole in his back was large enough to poke two fingers in, and it was bleeding heavily.

"Granddaughter!" he called out as he worked on the wounded man. "Are you hurt?"

"No," Sweetwater Woman replied, lifting her head up from beneath the buffalo robe, "we are not hurt. How is he?"

"Bad wound!" he told her. "If I can stop the bleeding, he has a chance. Stay down, both of you!"

"We will!" she assured him. Sweetwater Woman resisted the urge to look over the top of the low bank. She could no longer hear the hoofbeats of Cloud's horse, but she had heard two more shots. Her heart was beating heavily.

"Mother," came the muffled voice from inside the robe, "where is Father? Where did he go?"

"He is going to see about…about the…he is trying to keep us safe," she said, trying to sound calm. "We will wait until he comes back."

"Do not worry, Mother. He will come back."

"I know. I know."

An unearthly scream shattered the eerie stillness, and a movement to the south caught her eye. A horse stumbled and went down out of sight. Sweetwater Woman recognized Little Bird's bay mare. She fell and struggled to rise. In all the confusion, Sweetwater Woman had not noticed until now, but their horses had obviously stayed nearby.

Her momentary confusion was obliterated as she saw snow and dirt explode behind the horses, and then heard the distant pop of a rifle. They were shooting at the horses! The bay mare went down again, out of sight behind a line of sagebrush. Sweetwater Woman shifted to see where the other two were but could not.

"Stay down!" shouted High Eagle.

Song squirmed inside the robe. "Mother!"

"Shh! Stay still!"

Cloud looked west and picked out two horses loping to the southwest. He was on a crumbly ledge above a thin grove of leafless oak, where he had tied the sorrel. Laden with weapons, he had started climbing up the south side of the gully. Exposed to the warm rays of the sun as it was, there was little to no snow or ice on that side.

From this distance, the valley was empty except for scattered clumps of sagebrush and occasional thickets. He saw no sign of Sweetwater Woman and High Eagle.

He heard two more shots. That was at least five so far. The shooter must have plenty of bullets.

Near the top, he had to use his knife to keep from sliding. It was the only way to make a handhold. Fortunately, like on the valley floor, across the top of the bluff there were scattered clumps of sagebrush as far as he could see. Crawling away from the lip of the gully, he stayed low, though the ground was cold. He waited in a depression until he stopped panting and his heartbeat slowed.

He kept the rifle in its case, to protect the muzzle from dirt and debris. It could be fired while it was still covered, if necessary. He returned the knife to its case and moved the six-shooter closer to his left hip so it was out of the way when he crawled. He debated for a moment whether to leave the unstrung bow and quiver of arrows in its case, but decided against it. They might be needed at some point. And, at some point, in the interest of freer movement, he might have to remove his elk-hide coat.

Somewhere ahead of him, to the south, was the shooter. The breeze was pushier on the bluff top, shaking the grass and sagebrush, and it was colder as well. If he stood, he would give away his location to anyone who might be watching, and he had to assume someone was watching for him. As slow as it was, he decided to stay down inside the sagebrush and crawl.

A thought jarred him, causing momentary indecision: the shooter might leave the bluff and go after Sweetwater Woman, Song, and High Eagle.

However, from this distance, it was not easy to determine if someone was a man or woman, and he had kept Song under the buffalo robe. Cloud took a deep breath. There was no choice but to trust that High Eagle would remain alert.

After another deep breath, he moved ahead on elbows and knees, keeping his stomach barely above the ground. Rather than raising himself up to look around, he peered between the openings in the sagebrush. He stopped to listen and crawled again.

The muzzle flash he had seen seemed to be just below the rim of the bluff, in the middle of the plateau. But that was not an absolute certainty, since he had been galloping over rough ground and his visual perception might have been distorted by the movement.

He moved quickly, repeating the process of crawling and stopping to listen. So far, all he heard was the breeze whispering through the brush and the whistle of a hunting hawk far overhead. Somewhere ahead of him, a small animal scurried across the ground.

The rim of the bluff was a series of shallow and deep cuts, like the one he had climbed, a consequence of water and wind erosion over thousands and thousands of years. They reached to the valley floor. Cloud came to the edge of one of those cuts and turned left. He estimated that he had covered a straight-line distance of at least eighty long paces from where he had gained the plateau. He kept going, staying in the openings between the sagebrush stalks to prevent his coat or bow from catching on them.

His neck and shoulders began to feel the effort of crawling. He paused to gaze through the openings in the brush. Something caught his attention, though he was not sure what. In a moment, he realized that it was a shape that did not fit with the sharp angles of sagebrush stalks, grass, and uneven ground. It was not much, but it was enough for him to question whether it belonged or not. Motionless, he concentrated.

He was looking at a smooth edge, a curved, smooth edge, a shadow low among the sagebrush. Like him, it was not moving. When a hunter was looking for a deer or an elk in brush or trees, it was best to look for part of the animal—an ear, the point of an antler, a leg visible between branches. Cloud assumed he was looking at something similar, a part of something. Perhaps part of a man.

The muscles at the base of his neck protested at the strain of staying motionless, but he kept his gaze locked on the small piece of curved shadow. He dared not avert his eyes, not until he was certain what he was seeing.

Moments dragged by. A breeze rattled the brush next to his head.

Little Bird moaned as High Eagle checked the thick poultice of tobacco he had placed in the wound on his back. Blood was beginning to clot, a good sign. He was considering their circumstances even as he worked. By now, Cloud was probably somewhere on the bluffs. When he would return was an unknown. Or if he would. That last possibility seemed remote, but it still had to be taken into account.

He wasn't about to share his concerns with Sweetwater Woman, but it would be foolish not to do what they could to improve their situation. Although they were behind sufficient cover and therefore probably safe from the shooter on the bluff, they were still in the open and unprotected from the weather. And perhaps there was someone else in the area, someone other than the shooter on the bluff. All those possibilities had to be considered.

Little Bird was alive, and he was beginning to reach toward consciousness. Moving him would have to be done carefully. High Eagle shifted his position without exposing himself to the bluffs and studied the terrain behind them. A deep wash or creek bed was what they needed. He reached to some sagebrush close at hand and pulled off a handful of leaves. He used the leaves to blot off the blood on his hands, then blew on his hands to warm them. The cold was tolerable for now. He pulled on his mittens, made of smoked bear hide, and again studied the nearby terrain.

It moved, slowly, and was gone. For several long moments, Cloud kept his eyes on the spot where the shadow had been. It did not return. There was no way to know exactly how far away it had been, but he thought no more than forty paces of the distance a man would walk with a normal stride. Cloud remained still for several more moments before he reached up and pulled the carry strap of his bow case over his head, then slowly slid the encased bow and quiver of arrows over his right shoulder and placed them on the ground in front of him. Pausing to softly blow on his cold fingers, he pulled the bow from its case, then had to shift slightly onto his side to string it. That done, he carefully thought about his next move.

He wanted to trick the shooter into giving away his exact location. As far as he was concerned, he had two possible ways to do that; throw rocks or shoot arrows to startle his unseen adversary. He would have to get into at least a kneeling position in order to have the leverage to throw a rock the required distance, but that would mean exposing himself. He decided to use the bow.

Moving slowly and carefully, he shifted around until he was on his back, with his feet toward where he thought the shooter was. He took five arrows from the quiver. One he placed on the string, and two more he fit into the crook of his bent fingers holding the bow. He would play a game his grandfather had taught him. The game was to launch three arrows into the air, one after another, and have the third in the air before the first came back to earth. This game had higher stakes, however, than the toy bone horses his grandfather gave him. Because the ground was frozen, he thought—he hoped—the arrows would make noise.

Placing the fourth and fifth arrows next to his hip, he slowly lifted his bow to an angle that would bring the arrows crashing down behind where he thought the shooter was. The last two arrows were just in case he got lucky and guessed correctly.

He drew the stout ash bow. *Twang twang twang.* He watched only the last arrow and briefly lost sight of it, then found it as it reached its apex high above the ground, tipped to a point-down configuration, then began its deadly descent. *Thud thud thud.*

Almost immediately he heard a scrape and something like loose stones falling, and the unmistakable outline of a man partially rose from the sagebrush. Cloud came to a sitting position, nocked his next arrow, pulled, and released all in one continuous motion.

The arrow caught the sunlight as it flashed through the air, almost faster than the eye could follow. A hollow pop followed and the man jumped, instinctively grabbing for the shaft protruding from beneath his lift armpit.

Jumping to a kneeling stance, Cloud nocked, pulled, and released the next arrow. It flew as straight and true as the first one had, slicing into the base of the man's throat. As the man staggered back and fell, Cloud saw a rifle fall out of his hands.

He dropped the bow and yanked the cover off of his rifle, pausing as his legs trembled a little. Sliding off the safety, he took a few steps toward the fallen adversary. Eyes fixed on the spot where the man had gone down, he moved deliberately, aiming the rifle.

The clump of sage to his left suddenly exploded in a blur of motion. Although he instinctively brought the rifle up in a protective move, the impact drove him sideways and down. A jolt of pain in his right shoulder coincided with the pinpoints of light he saw. Without thought, he made himself roll, using the momentum that had driven him to the ground, and saved himself from the point of the buffalo horn–tipped war club that impaled the ground where he had been. But the rifle had slipped out of his hands and had landed several paces away. He scrambled to his feet and came face-to-face with the biggest man he had ever seen.

It was a white man dressed in the manner of a Crow. His brown braids were neat, he was clean-shaven, and his eyes were so light brown they looked yellow. He wore no robe or coat. The long-handled buffalo horn ax was obviously made to match his size and strength. It was as long as any rifle, perhaps longer, probably much heavier, and could easily crack open a man's skull.

Cloud threw two quick glances to the right and left to assess his footing. His rifle was ten paces away, caught in the branches of a thick sagebrush stalk. There was no way he would be able to get to it and get a shot off in time. His mind raced. Behind him was the edge of the bluff and a long fall.

He stood, feet apart, arms at his side, staring at the man, who stared back with the cold look of a killer. There was only one thing he could do.

He looked toward the rifle and then back at the man. A smile of anticipation creased the white Crow man's face. Cloud crouched slightly and then went for the rifle. For a big man, the white Crow was surprisingly nimble as he moved to cut Cloud off. In an instant, he came to a stop, realizing that Cloud had not moved more than a step before he stopped.

In that instant, for he only had an instant, Cloud reached under his coat, pulled out his six-shooter, aimed, and fired.

The man grunted, still on his feet, his big face twisting in surprise, pain, and then rage. With an ungodly roar, he launched himself toward Cloud.

Cloud emptied his six-shooter, the shots shattering the silence of the plateau. Like a falling tree, the man crashed to the ground.

High Eagle saw the rider coming through the sagebrush. "Granddaughter," he called out to Sweetwater Woman, "do not move. Someone is coming."

"Who is it?" she asked.

"At this distance, it looks like your husband's horse, but do not move. If it is not him, I will shoot whoever it is when he gets close enough."

They had heard the six gunshots from the top of the plateau. That had been a while ago, and it was natural to expect the worst.

"Is my father coming?" came the hopeful little voice from beneath the buffalo robe.

"Shh!" whispered Sweetwater Woman. "Did your father not say that he would always come back to us?"

"Yes," Song replied. "Yes, he did. He should hurry. I am getting cold."

Moments passed. Long, anxious moments.

"It is your husband!" the medicine man called out. "He looks to be in one piece."

CHAPTER ELEVEN

Bluecoats and Fleas

Yellow Wolf sipped his tea and pulled up the collar of his coat, wishing he had his buffalo robe. But there was something that bothered him more than the cold. Apparently, not all Lakota people valued the free life enough to fight for it. Much of the conversation around the fire was a disturbing affirmation of something that Cloud, Crazy Horse, and others had warned him about—there was a growing attitude that living at the agencies was how life would be for the Lakota from now on.

Six men, including Yellow Wolf, sat in a small circle around the fire in a dry wash. There was no council lodge; many of the old men still gathered to talk, but never at the same location. They knew that the agency whites—especially the young Long Knife known as White Hat—had eyes and ears among them. More than a few Lakota passed information to him, and everyone knew who they were. So any issue or circumstance they did not want the agency whites to know about was discussed in secret. Using a different secret location worked much of the time, but there were only so many places they could hide. And, since it was easier to hide a few people, they always kept such gatherings to a small number of men who could be trusted implicitly.

On this particular afternoon, those seated around the fire also included Fast Horse, Brave, Star Boy, Runs Above, and Swift Bear.

"Grandfather," Yellow Wolf said cautiously to Swift Bear, who sat across the fire from him, "I do not understand why there is any disagreement with Sitting Bull's message."

A leader among the Sicangu people for many years, Swift Bear was known for his patience. On this day, he wore a dark wool overcoat and, like many Lakota men here at the agencies, a black scarf tied around his neck. His moccasins looked out of place, but he wore them because they were much more comfortable than stiff shoes—and because it was also a quiet, symbolic statement against wholesale change.

Swift Bear had a craggy, narrow face with a strong jaw and a proud set to his wide mouth. But his eyes were his strongest feature. They could flash with a piercing gaze in an instant. At this moment, he nodded thoughtfully. He appreciated the way the young Oglala respectfully asked a difficult question. Respect for elders was something that many young people did not learn anymore, and that concerned Swift Bear. Perhaps that was a result of the new ways and new times. He held his palms to the fire, eyes narrowed, almost closed.

"Sitting Bull is a wise man," he said, his tone low. "And perhaps he is right to say that something must be done to drive the whites out. That has been his thinking for many years. I would not be honest if I said I liked white people. I do not. They are very strange in their ways. I wish they were not here." He waved his hand, a way of indicating the current situation. "But as much as my heart agrees with Sitting Bull, my head does not."

Yellow Wolf nodded. He reminded himself that he did not come to argue with anyone—especially a venerable old warrior—or convince anyone to join the spring gathering. The question in his mind was why, but he was not about to say it aloud.

But Swift Bear was a perceptive man. "The reason is reality, how things are," he said. "Our headman has traveled east to the place of power for the whites. He tells us they are so many, they cannot be counted. That is their strength, aided by the things they have, like the iron road and the message wires, and weapons. They have weapons and the willingness to use them, even against women and children. That is the kind of people they are. If we get in their way, they will not stop until they kill us all. So I, myself, do not want to give them any reason to do that."

Runs Above had been simply nodding his gray head in agreement with his old friend. His deeply lined face showed that he was the older of the two, an accomplished man in his own right, but one not given to oratory.

"Grandson," he said, briefly locking eyes with Yellow Wolf, "what my friend says about the whites is true. The other side of that truth is that there are not enough of us, even if every one of our fighting men had a new rifle and a thousand bullets. They replace themselves easily, and we cannot. We cannot keep them out of our lands. Last year, we could not stop the Long Knives when they went into the Black Hills to see for themselves that gold is there. Now there are thousands of whites there digging for the gold. They want that gold bad enough that their 'peace talkers' were willing to kill old men—and they would have, if we had not signed a paper giving them the Black Hills."

Yellow Wolf was dumbfounded. The other men around the fire exchanged apprehensive glances. Judging from their reaction to Runs Above's revelation, Yellow Wolf could only assume they all knew something he did not. Perhaps none of the Oglala people in the Powder River country knew. For that matter, perhaps Sitting Bull didn't know that the Black Hills had been given away, if that is, indeed, what Runs Above had just said.

Swift Bear studied the young man's reaction for a moment. It was good to be young and full of determination. But young people did not have the blessing, or the burden, to be able to look back on a lifetime of change. At some point, usually past middle age, everyone learned the two certainties in life: change and death. Of the two, change was always the most difficult to face. Swift Bear guessed the young man to be nearly thirty years old. When he was born, white people were beginning to nibble at the edges of Lakota territory.

"When I was a boy," Swift Bear recalled, "we were powerful. White people were still a new thing. When they first came around, they were nothing more than gnats that fly around the face. When you were born, they were like mosquitoes, starting to suck our blood. Now they are ants, helping themselves to everything we have. We can step on them, but there are always more. In your lifetime, Grandson, we lost our power. Now they are crawling around the Black Hills like fleas on a dog because we did not have the power to stop them."

"How did they take the Black Hills, Grandfather?"

"I will tell you. We turned down selling that sacred place several times. But then they took old men to meet with their peace talkers. The peace talkers had a paper for them to sign to give them the Black Hills. The old men still said no. So Long Knives with guns were brought in. They were told to load their guns and point them at our old men.

"The old men were given a choice: if they did not sign the paper, all of us at the agencies would be loaded into wagons and taken to the south country, Oklahoma, they called it. We hear that many humans from many nations have been sent there, and many have died there. The peace talkers also said the Great Father would no longer give us food—the flour, coffee, beans, and meat. The old men believed them, so they put their marks on the paper. They felt that being here, living this way, was better than dying far from home."

Yellow Wolf sighed. "What does it matter if they have a paper?" he muttered. "They are already in the Black Hills, stinking up the lands."

"Know this, Grandson," Runs Above said, his voice trembling slightly, "we did not put our marks on the paper because we old men were afraid for our lives. We did it because we know the whites are crazy enough to haul our women and children away. None of us wanted our children to suffer because of our stubbornness."

Brave and Star Boy had not uttered a word, but their anguish over this issue was plain to see. There was a sadness in their old eyes that said more than mere words could.

Yellow Wolf had come on a simple mission: to learn what the agency Lakota were thinking and saying about Sitting Bull's message. He had not expected to hear what he had heard this morning. He was forced to conclude that the gathering in the spring, if it did happen, would be made up of only the Sitting Bull and Crazy Horse people.

"Thank you," he said to the four old men. "Thank you for telling me these things."

"It does my heart good to see you," Star Boy said. "I know your family. I am glad that you wild ones are out there. Our hearts are with you, as my friend said. But there is one reality that is hardest for me to accept." He paused, interlocking his fingers, sighed, and continued. "We are no longer powerful, because we lost more to the whites than land, because they killed off more than the buffalo. We have lost our ways, the ways of the true Lakota. I know that some of our people, perhaps more than we think, are praying to the white man's god. We sit and listen like scared children when their Black Robes tell us that our way of praying is evil. So, we pray in their way, and turn our backs on the ways that have sustained us for so long. In the end, if we cannot decide what we are—Lakota or imitations of white men—we weaken ourselves."

Sparks flew up as Fast Horse dropped more wood onto the fire. Yellow Wolf could only nod. Suddenly, he felt heavy.

Brave cleared his throat. "I have heard our headman, Spotted Tail, say many times that it is time to live like white men. He does not mean that we become white men. To me, that does not mean we should stop being Lakota. My friend Star Boy is right—we are losing something just as important as land. Someday, if we are not careful, we will be brown on the outside and white on the inside. The task we face is to survive on the inside—to be Lakota no matter what happens to us on the outside."

Yellow Wolf sipped his tea, which was barely warm. Flames slowly enveloped the dry wood, but either the air was growing colder or the fire was not throwing off much heat. But cold tea and staying warm were not important at the moment. He had much to think about, much to tell Crazy Horse, Cloud, and the others back home.

Clearly, the agency Lakota were embroiled in the very issues the Crazy Horse and Sitting Bull people wanted to avoid at all costs. Yellow Wolf recalled a discussion between High Eagle and Black Shield in which they agreed with Sitting Bull's assertion that no Lakota should have ever showed up at any treaty meeting. Like Sitting Bull, they were convinced that the Lakota had lost more, and suffered more, as a consequence of trying to talk with the whites than they did by fighting them.

He felt the anguish of the men sitting with him around the fire. They didn't want to be here, in effect living a do-nothing life. They were here because they saw it as the only way to survive. Yellow Wolf didn't agree with that thinking, but he understood their rationale for it. In a sense, Swift Bear and the others seemed to be in mourning. He shivered inwardly at the implication that what had passed was the Lakota way of life.

He suddenly realized that the persistent thuds he kept hearing at the edge of his awareness were coming from a horse moving at a gallop, and it was coming in their direction. Fast Horse stood and peeked over the edge of the creek bank.

"Eagle Dog," he said, identifying the rider. "I asked him to warn us if there is trouble."

In a moment, a winded horse and an anxious rider appeared. "They are coming," he said, pointing at Yellow Wolf, "for him and his wife! White Hat sent ten men. Bear Tail just brought word. He says they are more than halfway here."

Swift Bear stepped past the fire and grabbed Yellow Wolf's arm. "You need to go now. Go east. They will expect you to go north. Go east to the second creek, and then north. Tell your headman and all your people not to forget us. Tell them to pray for us."

"We will always think of you, and we will pray for us all," Yellow Wolf replied.

"I will go back to the village with him," Fast Horse said.

"We will stay here," Swift Bear replied. "Tell White Hat's men we are here, and let them think that this young man is here with us."

Yellow Wolf looked around at the old men. "I will see you again," he told them. "Take care of yourselves."

Within a few moments, he and Fast Horse were galloping toward the village. They followed an opening through the grove of leafless oak. They came to the creek, crossed it, and followed the west bank until they could see the corral. Several men were in one corner. As the two riders approached, one of the men ran to open the gate.

Yellow Wolf saw Plum's horse tied to the corral rail, ready for travel. One of the men broke from the group and met them as they dismounted.

"They are coming for you, to take you back to the outpost," he said to Yellow Wolf. "White Hat has big ears."

"This is my friend Bear Tail," Fast Horse said to Yellow Wolf, then turned to the man. "How close are they?"

"Too close to waste any time," Bear Tail replied.

"Thank you," Yellow Wolf said to him.

"White Hat is a snake," Bear Tail said. "So is anyone who helps him."

"Swift Bear says to lead them to the dry wash," Fast Horse told the stalwart young man.

"We will, and we have a plan." Bear Tail gestured toward the other men. "Two of us will lead them away and try to throw them off, get them to chase us."

"Good," Fast Horse agreed, then pointed at Yellow Wolf. "They will go east."

Bear Tail and the others mounted and rode out of the corral. "At least you brought some excitement with you," he called back to Yellow Wolf. "Have a good journey home!"

Yellow Wolf waved and turned to Fast Horse. "We have not been able to talk, you and me," he said. "Perhaps my wife has talked to her sister."

"They have done nothing but talk," Fast Horse replied, grinning.

"Yes. She wants the two of you to come with us."

Fast Horse was not entirely surprised, it seemed to Yellow Wolf.

Running footsteps approached. It was Plum and Walks Alone, with bundles in their arms. Grabbing the bundles, the men tied them onto the waiting horses.

Walks Alone grabbed her husband's arm. "They want us to go with them!" she said, her eyes pleading.

Fast Horse looked at her and then at Yellow Wolf. "We are not ready. If we take the time to prepare, we will slow them down."

"I have put some bundles together," Walks Alone quickly replied. "We do not have much anyway."

"What about food?"

"We have a little," Plum said. "And the two of you can hunt on the way."

"This is no place for us. You are like one of these horses penned up in this corral," Walks Alone told her husband. "Blue Stone and her family can have our lodge."

Yellow Wolf nodded as Fast Horse looked in his direction.

"But we must hurry," Fast Horse said.

With a joyous cry, Walks Alone embraced her husband. "Our bundles are in the lodge. They have been ready since Bear Tail told us the agency men are coming."

Plum wiped away a tear as Yellow Wolf helped her mount.

At the lodge of Walks Alone and Fast Horse, they stopped long enough to tie a few small bundles onto their horses. As Fast Horse helped her get on her horse, Walks Alone looked sadly toward a particular lodge. It was not the way she wanted to leave. "All we have is memories of the free life," Blue Stone had said once. "Up north, our relatives still live that way. It may not be easy, but when you are free, you can face life the way you choose." *I will see you again, Grandmother*, Walks Alone spoke in her mind as her horse took the first steps toward a freer life.

Fast Horse led them east, staying in the sparse groves of oak to keep hidden as much as possible.

North of the encampment, Bear Tail and White Eyes waited next to a lone oak. They did not have to wait long. Appearing over a far rise was a group of riders, bobbing up and down as they came at a high lope. At a distance, they were dark and shadowy. As they rode nearer and nearer, their blue overcoats could be seen.

Bear Tail nodded and urged his horse into a fast walk, heading north. White Eyes followed. From the perspective of the approaching blue-coated men, two people were riding north from the village. White Eyes had taken off his hat and pulled a gray blanket over his head and shoulders. Bear Tail kept an eye on the approaching riders.

A mixture of strange feelings overcame Bear Tail and White Eyes. Under the flat-brimmed hats were long black braids. The blue-coated men were Lakota who chose to work for the Long Knives. One of them was probably White Eyes's cousin, one who had found a way to acquire a bit of power and importance, little though it might be.

"Here they come!" said Bear Tail gleefully.

Five riders were coming at a gallop.

After waiting another moment, Bear Tail and White Eyes kicked their horses and raced north. The crack of hoofbeats on the cold ground could be heard in the village, and a few curious people poked their heads out of their lodges to see what was happening.

The chase was on as the Lakota Bluecoats turned north in hot pursuit.

Five more Lakota Bluecoats entered the village and immediately approached the corral, bridles jingling and saddles squeaking.

Two men looked up from the task of scraping mud from a horse's hoof, gazing in amusement at the Iron Breasts, as the Lakota policemen were called because of the shiny metal badge they wore over the left breast of their blue coat.

"The man Yellow Wolf and his wife," one of them said, "where are they?"

The two men in the corral exchanged glances and shrugged. "I do not know them," one replied.

"We know they are here!"

"Then why are you bothering us?"

One Bluecoat urged his horse forward. "Be careful, friend! I might decide to put you in jail if I do not like the tone of your voice. Where are they?"

"I do not know of a man called Yellow Wolf," the man in the corral replied. "All I know is that there is some kind of meeting going on south of the village. I think Swift Bear is there."

A victorious gleam flashed through the Bluecoat's eyes. "If this is not so, I will be back for you." In a moment, the clatter of hoofbeats faded as the five Bluecoats hurried away, performing this all-important task for White Hat.

One of the men in the corral turned to the other. "I think it is time to have a talk with Bug," he said.

Bear Tail felt the wind on his face as he and White Eyes stayed well ahead of those in pursuit. He saw a familiar landmark ahead, a low hill with a stand of cedar. Beyond that was a wide, treeless meadow. He decided they would circle the hill and then head west.

Swift Bear, meanwhile, poured tobacco onto a small square of paper and was concentrating mightily on rolling it into a cigarette as five riders burst noisily through the trees and surrounded the dry wash. Brave, Star Boy, and Runs Above were clearly annoyed at the sudden intrusion.

"What do you want?" Runs Above demanded.

"A man," one of the blue-coated riders replied. "A man named Yellow Wolf."

Runs Above looked around at the other men around the fire. As yet, Swift Bear had not acknowledged the presence of the Bluecoats. "None of us here have that name," said Runs Above, a twinkle in his eyes.

"Do you know a man by that name?" asked the Iron Breast.

"Yellow Wolf, Yellow Wolf," mumbled Star Boy. "Yes, I do. From when I was a boy. He was a Hunkpapa, I think."

Swift Bear finished rolling his cigarette. From the fire he took a long twig with an ember at one end and carefully lit the cigarette. After blowing smoke into the air, he spoke while looking at the cigarette in his hands. "Grandson," he called out in a loud voice, "one day, I will get used to this thing, this white man way of smoking tobacco. However, I will never get used to a Lakota wearing the blue coat of a Long Knife."

The five riders exchanged uncertain glances. The only thing certain was that the old men around the fire would tell them nothing. With a nod from their leader, they rode away.

Runs Above put more wood onto the fire. "It is hard to believe," he said softly, "that life has come to this."

When they came to a creek not quite frozen over, Fast Horse turned the party north. They had stayed within cover and in the low spots, keeping their horses at a comfortable fast walk. Fast Horse, with Yellow Wolf's six-shooter tucked into his belt, led the way, while Yellow Wolf brought up the rear. Now and then, Walks Alone wiped away tears but kept her silence.

They stayed on the northerly course until midafternoon, when they found a deep depression at the base of a hill. There they dismounted and rested, taking a bit of food and water while they let the horses graze.

Yellow Wolf and Fast Horse crawled to the top of the hill and studied the trail behind them. They saw no one.

"As Swift Bear said, I think we can go west from here, but I think we should go north past the horizon, then turn northwest," suggested Fast Horse.

"Do you think they will send anyone out to track us?"

"Hard to say, but I doubt it. If White Hat's men had been able to capture you, he would have made much of it. But I think sending out trackers is a risk for him. It would be saying that he has lost control."

"What about Bear Tail?"

Fast Horse chuckled. "He will have fun with them. They might put him in jail out of frustration. But I think that will be all. At least I hope so."

Bear Tail slowed his horse. She was getting tired.

White Eyes pulled up alongside. "Think this is far enough?" he asked, grinning. They had come to an open hillside with patches of snow on it.

Bear Tail stopped his horse and looked toward the approaching riders. Grim-faced to a man, the blue-coated riders quickly surrounded Bear Tail and White Eyes and reined in their winded horses.

"Why did you run away?" demanded one of them.

"Why did you chase us?" Bear Tail shot back, grinning. "We were just going for a ride."

"Do you know a man by the name of Yellow Wolf?" asked another of the Bluecoats.

"Yes, I do," Bear Tail replied, still grinning.

"Where is he?"

"That I do not know."

"I think you are lying!" blurted the first Bluecoat.

"I do not care what you think."

"Then maybe you will care to know that we can put you in jail if it suits us."

Bear Tail looked around at the men on their winded horses. He urged his horse forward until he was face-to-face with the man who had threatened him, a man he knew.

"Friend," he said, "you can do that. I would expect that from someone who has to wear a blue coat and a piece of shiny iron to feel important."

The man glared at Bear Tail but said no more. Bear Tail and White Eyes were known to be capable men, the kind of men who could only be pushed so far. After a moment, the Bluecoat turned his horse and rode away. With the jingle of bridle bits and the squeak of saddle leather, the other Bluecoats followed him.

Bear Tail shook his head and then gazed off to the north. "Good journey, my friends," he said. "Good journey."

CHAPTER TWELVE

A Healing

Winter gripped the northern lands in the Moon of Popping Trees. Every river, creek, and pond was frozen solid. The ringing voices of iron axes sang up and down the valley of the north fork of the Tongue River as young men chopped ice to reopen watering holes that had frozen shut during the night. On the banks, other boys and young men waited with their families' horses. While some worked, others played in the cold, bright day.

Cloud watched his daughter's snow snake—a long, thin willow rod, peeled and painted—slide unerringly across the river ice toward a large river rock at his feet. The snow snake hit the rock again. He waved at Song and Sweetwater Woman, standing behind another rock some thirty paces away. Song jumped up and down. Every hit was worth one point. She was ahead three points to two, after the third of four allotted shots.

He grabbed his fourth snow snake, his final shot, and took aim at the rock in front of his wife and daughter. Even if he hit the rock, the best he could hope for was a tie. If he missed this shot, she would win. Taking off his mitten, he put his pointer finger in the shallow notch at the end of the rod. Bending slightly, he tossed the snow snake with an underhand motion. He threw too hard. The snow snake slid past the rock. Song was jumping up and down, and the bright smile on her face was plain to see.

Theirs was not the only game of snow snake. Laughter rippled into the cold air, mingling with the occasional bark of a dog or a horse's nicker. Winter was hard, but so were the people who had survived many as a society. Life did not stop when the snow flew before the howling winds and the deep cold descended; it took a deep breath and prepared itself for the renewal that always came with the spring.

After gathering their snow snakes, Song, Cloud, and Sweetwater Woman ascended the bank to the village on the plateau. The smell of wood smoke filled the air. Small boys were at play, fluttering about like flocks of birds.

A man in a buffalo robe stood at the top of the trail, watching Cloud and his family come up. It was Little Bird. Although his wound had healed, he was still thin. Only in the last month had he been able to move about consistently.

"You could have picked a warmer day to go for a walk," Cloud teased.

"Any day is a good day to be out," Little Bird replied. "I was just trying to see if I could pull my bow."

Cloud waited, noting a look of frustration on Little Bird's face. No one could ever hope to be as good with a bow as Little Bird was. He had won horses with his skill.

"There is a stiffness," he explained, "some pain when I pull it. High Eagle says I should be patient and let my shoulder heal. He says it is still healing inside."

If Little Bird admitted to "some pain," it was more than that. "I think he is right. Maybe by spring," Cloud said.

"The trouble is, the shoulder is still tender, and I think the kick from firing a rifle would…it would be painful as well. I still cannot move my shoulder freely."

"Do not worry. It will heal."

Little Bird squinted in the bright daylight. "I was just hoping to go with you the next time you went after elk, or deer."

"It would be good to have you along," Cloud affirmed.

"I am cooking a big pot of elk meat," Sweetwater Woman reminded Cloud. "My mother and father are coming over." She glanced at Little Bird. "It would be good if you and your family could come over too. There is plenty."

"I will tell my wife."

After Sweetwater Woman and Song had gone, Cloud stood with Little Bird a little while longer. They watched the activity as the people in the village went about completing their tasks and playing their games. Another winter was nearly over; spring was less than thirty days away. But they had yet to see the first flocks of geese going north.

"Do you ever wonder about those two Long Knives?" Little Bird asked suddenly. "We took their horses and their guns."

Cloud shook his head. "No, they have not crossed my mind."

"I think they are dead. It strikes me that Long Knives—all whites, probably—depend on things rather than knowledge."

"What made you think of those two?"

"I am not sure, but I thought about them after you told me about the giant white man. The white Crow, I think you said."

Cloud didn't like being reminded, however unintentionally, of his encounter on the bluff. He knew Little Bird was not purposely bringing up a topic that was sensitive to him, but the effect was still the same. He tried not to think about the white Crow and his companion, but they would not go away.

"The two Long Knives probably froze," he said. "Hard to guess if they knew how to build a fire without the flint and striker, or make a good shelter, or set snares for rabbits. They probably did not live long enough to starve."

"Ah!" Little Bird blurted apologetically. "There are other things, pleasant things to talk about. I was thinking, because High Eagle told me I could use my arm as long as I did not hurt my shoulder, I would cut some ash wood while the sap is still down. I thought I might as well make a bow or two."

Little Bird was also widely known for his skill at making bows. He had not only won horses with his skill as an expert marksman, men were willing to trade horses for one of his bows.

"When we found the picture carvings on the rock face, I also saw a thick stand of young ash," he recalled.

"Then maybe we should go there, if you think you can ride that far," Cloud suggested.

Little Bird nodded contemplatively. "I thought I would go for a ride this afternoon—on my oldest and slowest horse," he said, grinning. "Just in case I have forgotten how."

"Good. I will go with you, after we have some elk soup."

A low, gray sky blocked the sunrise the following morning and stayed until sunset. In midafternoon, Cloud led four of his horses on a long lead to a rise northwest of the village. There, the wind kept the hilltop bare of snow, leaving enough grass uncovered for the horses to graze. A wolf cape covering his head hung down over the back of his elk-hide coat, and he stood with his back to the slight breeze, keeping watch. The white Crow and his companion had been deep in Lakota territory. That was a bothersome reality.

All the horses lifted their heads and looked to the west. Cloud instinctively grabbed the stock of his breechloader inside its case, but he relaxed after a quick glance. They saw a rider whose posture and outline were familiar.

Crazy Horse reached the hilltop, dismounted, and turned his horse loose to graze with the others.

From their vantage point, they had a clear view of the hills to the north. The blue-gray landscape was broken with an occasional dark hilltop where snow had blown away. In the hazy distances to the west stood the foothills and slopes of the Shining Mountains.

Crazy Horse gazed at the panorama and took a deep breath. "I cannot imagine a day without this image to make my heart beat faster," he said.

"That will never happen, because the Earth will outlive us all," Cloud replied.

"I went to your lodge," Crazy Horse said conversationally, still gazing toward the mountains. "Your wife said you left to graze horses."

"Sometimes a man needs to talk to the wind."

"No one listens better," Crazy Horse replied. "No one makes you look inward as well as the wind does."

They stood listening to the horses eat, listening to the wind whisper over the grasses and sing through the cedar trees on the slope below them.

"This is where I want to die," Cloud said. "With my face to the west, toward where the Buffalo People and the Thunders live. And when that time comes, my only hope is that I will be a good enough man to join our warrior fathers and grandfathers, to look the grandmothers in the eye and be able to tell them that I did not turn away when it was my turn to stand and face the enemy."

"That is all any of us can hope for, in the end," Crazy Horse pointed out. "That is why we follow in their footsteps. But, I hope the end for both of us is a long way off."

Grinning, Cloud nodded. "Yes, I plan on living a long time. Long enough for the buffalo to be plentiful again, and for the Buffalo Nation to become as strong as we once were."

"Good things to look forward to."

"Yes, but you did not come up here to listen to all that."

Crazy Horse chuckled. "It is like hearing my own thoughts. But I did want to talk about a few things. After your horses are fed, perhaps you would come to my lodge."

Black Shawl prepared tea and roasted a grouse. Cloud licked his fingers after finishing the succulent meat.

"Thank you," he told her. "I have not eaten grouse for several months. It is plump for this time of the year."

Crazy Horse's wife smiled demurely. "My husband came across them yesterday. He is better with the sling than he is with the bow. But he may not want anyone to know that," she told her guest.

"Actually, my horse stepped on them," Crazy Horse added.

Cloud smiled as he sipped his tea. The most famed warrior among the Lakota was not above poking fun at himself. Very few men of his stature had the strength of character not to take themselves too seriously. It was probably the thing that Cloud liked best about his friend.

Black Shawl busied herself, knowing that the two men had something to talk about. She was still thin, Cloud noticed. A bout with the coughing sickness two years before had taken its toll physically, adding to her emotional difficulties at the loss of their small daughter two years before that. The girl was nearly four when she died of the coughing sickness. She seemed to be a frail child, Cloud recalled. During her four short years in this world, her father was quick to smile. Since she had gone, he was quieter. And he had taken to spending days alone, away from the village.

"Spring will be here before we know it," said Crazy Horse, breaking into Cloud's thoughts. "Once the weather is warmer, we will all feel restless. We will want to see what is over the next hill, around the next bend. That need to wander is in our blood. It is what the Buffalo People have taught us."

"True," Cloud agreed. "Especially when we hear the first calls of the crane or the geese."

"My father always looks forward to that," Crazy Horse said, smiling. He began to fill his short-stemmed pipe, pausing the conversation to touch the floor with the stem and then lift it to the sky. "But there is another reason to be restless this spring, I think," he went on. "The people seem to be anxious about Sitting Bull's call to gather."

There was another pause as he took a burning twig from the fire and touched it to the tobacco in the bowl. After a few puffs, the sweet aroma of red willow filled the lodge.

"I do not know that country around the White Buttes," Crazy Horse admitted, "so I wonder what the hunting is like, and grass for the horses. Perhaps we should think about sending scouts when the green grass comes."

"Yes, I think so."

"But there is something that concerns me, especially after I heard of your fight with the white Crow. They have not raided and come into our lands as much as they once did, but they will know when hundreds of us go to the White Buttes."

"You may be right. But the white Crow was a strange incident," Cloud said hesitantly. "It is hard to know if he lived with the Crow or not."

"The other man was a Crow?"

Cloud leaned back against his chair, his eyes focused on a moment in the past. "The other person was...was a woman."

Crazy Horse paused. "A woman? Which one shot Little Bird?"

"Hard to say, but she had the rifle. There was only one rifle between them."

After relighting his pipe, Crazy Horse nodded slowly as the smoke curled around his head. "What happened?"

"The first shot hit Little Bird. We dismounted, took cover. I rode for the butte and climbed it, hid in the sagebrush, and waited. I saw someone, tricked him—I thought it was a man—into showing himself. I...I got him with an arrow. I made the mistake of thinking it was one person alone. The big man surprised me—he was hiding. I had to empty my six-shooter. He was as tall as your cousin Touch the Clouds, but bigger. When I went to see about the first man—first person—it turned out to be a woman dressed like a man. Maybe she was his wife."

"If you knew it was a woman, you would have hesitated, and maybe you would be dead instead of them," Crazy Horse reasoned.

"Perhaps, but I killed a woman."

Crazy Horse tapped the bowl of his pipe on one of the stones around the fire pit to empty out the ashes. "These things happen, my friend. They will not change, or go away from our thinking. You did not intend to kill her. You were fighting an enemy who was trying to kill you. You were defending your family and your friends."

"That is what I tell myself. But I can still see her face—she was young."

Crazy Horse glanced at Cloud and then averted his gaze to the fire. "I, too, still see a face," he whispered.

"What do you mean?"

"When I was fourteen, I went to visit Sicangu relatives. It was summer, and I went along with Spotted Tail and Iron Shell on a raid into Omaha country, to the south along the Great Muddy River. We took many of their horses. They chased us, and we fought. That time, their headman was killed. I remember he rode a big blue roan, the biggest horse I have ever seen."

"You mean Logan Fontonelle, the part-white?"

"Yes. He fought hard. They all did, and they got some of their horses back. Some of us hid in tall grass, and several Omaha got in close. I took a shot with my bow. Afterward, I crawled through the grass to see—it was a girl, a young girl. I can still see her dark-brown hair in two thick braids. I still see her face."

Black Shawl came to the fire, refilled their cups of tea, and took a seat beside her husband.

"At Sand Creek, the Long Knives killed Cheyenne and Blue Cloud women and children knowing they were women and children," Crazy Horse continued, his voice low. "I have listened to Goings's wife tell her story. One of the young women killed was a friend of mine, a Cheyenne. She made moccasins for me that I still have.

"We do not kill the helpless ones knowingly. I heard a story, maybe two years ago, of a Crow woman who could shoot a rifle better than any man. Perhaps that was her on that bluff, and perhaps it was her who shot Little Bird. Whether it was her or the big man, they intended to kill you all. Do not blame yourself, my friend, for what happened. No amount of self-blame will change it."

The last dipper of water on hot stones exploded into a loud hiss inside the low, dome-shaped lodge. Final waves of stifling heat filled the interior, which was covered with thick buffalo hides. Forty-five river stones filled the center pit dug into the ground. They had been heated earlier in a deep fire pit near the lodge until they glowed red hot and were then carried into the sweat lodge. The rocks maintained their heat through the long healing ceremony.

After a final prayer, Worm called for the young helper sitting to the left of the door to open it. Cool night air swept in as the hide flap was swung aside. The moon was a thin glow behind the clouds as several participants emerged one by one from the west-facing opening of the structure as the ceremony ended. Clad only in breechclouts in the deep chill of the night, they formed a circle as High Eagle lit his pipe, took a deep puff, and passed it left to Worm. In turn, the pipe was passed to Crazy Horse, Goings, Little Bird, Taken Alive, and Cloud.

They finished their smoke as the temporary immunity to cold began to wear off and they began to feel the chill of the night. To a man, they waited until High Eagle disassembled his pipe, cleaned it, and placed it back into its elaborately decorated bag. Then they grabbed their buffalo robes and slipped on their moccasins.

Crazy Horse had asked for the ceremony as a healing for the wounds suffered by Little Bird and Cloud; one had wounds to the body and the other to the spirit.

When the medicine men had gathered all of their things and left the ceremony, they turned their footsteps toward the village. Even in the faint light of the cloud-covered moon, lodges could be plainly seen, and the smell of wood smoke filled the cold air.

Sweetwater Woman sat up as Cloud finished tying the inside door of the lodge. "How was the ceremony?" she asked.

"Good. It was good," he told her.

"How is Little Bird doing?"

"He gets better every day. Making bows is helping to heal his arm. I am very glad we cut those ash trees for him."

"What about you? How are you?" she asked tentatively.

"Good."

She pointed to the fire. "I was just thinking of putting more wood on when you came in."

After adding several pieces of knotty pine to the coals, he sat down in his chair and began to undress.

Sweetwater Woman grabbed an elk robe, wrapped it around herself, and joined him by the fire. "Tell me what happened on that bluff," she said. "Everything."

After a deep breath, he told her everything that had happened, from the moment he reached the plateau until he turned over the body of the one he had killed with two arrows and discovered she was a young woman dressed in white man's clothes. He could still see her face, a look of fear frozen in her dark-brown eyes, the shaft of his arrow protruding from the front of her neck. He could not recall how long he might have stood there, staring at her face. Then he retched and retched until his stomach hurt and he found himself on his hands and knees. Then, suddenly enraged, he grabbed the rifle and smashed it against the frozen ground until it had shattered into pieces.

Sweetwater Woman wiped away the tears he did not know were sliding down his face. "Your grandmother told me about when the horse kicked you, when you were five. She said you did not cry, you would not cry. That night, she said, when you probably thought no one would hear, you finally cried."

"When did she tell you that?"

"One day when she and I were watching Song try to walk." Moving closer, she leaned her head on his shoulder. "You did nothing wrong. You were doing what you were born and bred to do. A Lakota warrior defends his family. That does not mean something will not kick you, kick you hard, now and then. When that happens, remember, you do not have to cry alone in the night."

CHAPTER THIRTEEN

Old Men and Bears

Winter delivered a final reminder of its power with a blizzard late in the Moon When Eyes Hurt, and the following moon, Moon When Geese Return, lived up to its name. Day after day, endless flocks of snow, gray, and blue geese laced the skies, flying north in arrowhead-shaped formations. Their high, shimmering calls signaled new grass to emerge and spoke promises of warmer days to come.

After a long winter of sparse, dry grass and bark from young cottonwood trees, the horses hungrily sought out fresh shoots. They would need to gain strength so the people could make the trek east to the White Buttes.

As with the return of each spring, there was excitement and anticipation. The nomadic people who wandered over the land reveled in the movement of the seasons as well. Everyone, especially the old ones, could add one more winter as a marker on the road that was their earthly journey.

As days gradually grew warmer, creeks and rivers filled with cold runoff from the melting of winter snow. Watercourses dry since late summer ran bank to bank, burbling bright songs celebrating their brief role in the annual renewal of life. By midautumn they would be completely dry once again.

Nine camps became three as the people, anxious to shed the reminders of winter, left the confines of deep arroyos to spread out into more-open meadows, though they pitched their lodges well above the floodplains of the creeks that drained into the Tongue River. No one wanted to tempt the unpredictable moods of spring and early summer, with their penchant for flash floods.

All but one of the rituals of renewal of nature and man were observed—the Lakota buffalo scouts did not go forth. Although they might have found small isolated herds here and there, they knew the massive, numberless herds were no more. Nevertheless, High Eagle and Worm performed the ancient buffalo-calling ceremonies. They were not asking the buffalo to travel their age-old byways, however. They were asking them, pleading with them, to return from the edge of oblivion. No one, not even the oldest and wisest among the Crazy Horse people, could foresee what the years ahead would be for the Buffalo Nation without the Buffalo People.

The people had once lived deep inside in the mountains, the old story said, below the surface of the earth. One day, they came out because they wanted to live on the surface. All except for one, that is, who stayed behind. As time went on, the people flourished and were happy. But hard times came eventually, and famine gripped the land. The one who stayed behind looked out from the hole and saw that it was so. Coming out of the hole, she turned herself into the buffalo, and soon there were many of her kind, so many that the people ate their flesh and grew strong and became People Who Belonged to the Buffalo, or the Buffalo Nation. From then on, their spirit was always connected to the Buffalo People, and so, too, their destiny.

For that reason, Worm and his friend High Eagle prayed from sunrise to sunset, to connect with the spirit of the Buffalo People. It was still there, they said, but it was no longer vibrant. The two medicine men wept because they had never imagined that it would ever be so.

Some people were not surprised. An alarming reality had been creeping up on them like an enemy in plain sight. Their main source of life had been diminishing a little at a time. Now the buffalo could no longer honor their part of the ancient relationship. Many lamented this sad consequence, and even as they wondered how it could have happened, they knew the answer—it was a combination of pushy and arrogant newcomers and a failure to keep them back.

Sadly, thousands of Lakota decided that this newcomer was too powerful and gave up the old way of life. But in submitting to a different life, the immediate and ongoing consequence was the reality of no longer being masters of their own destiny. The Crazy Horse and Sitting Bull peoples could not believe that their friends and relatives with Red Cloud and Spotted Tail at the agencies were actually embracing this different life. Had they forgotten, they wondered, that the one answer to change had always been to adapt? Did they not realize that becoming agency people was not adapting? Did they not realize that it was outright surrender?

Black Shield and Grey Bull spoke of these things as they sat on a little plateau above a narrow but swiftly flowing stream. They talked as they made hunting arrows. In a small pot over a low fire was warm hide glue, which they used to attach arrow points and feathers to the chokecherry shafts. Hunting with guns was much easier, since hunters did not need to get as close to the game, but it also meant using up a limited supply of bullets. Older men were adamant that hunting should be done with the bow and arrow, not only to save precious bullets, but to keep necessary hunting and stalking skills sharp.

Making tools and weapons had always been an individual responsibility; each man made his own weapons for hunting and warfare. But in order to help preserve the supply of bullets, Black Shield and Grey Bull circumvented ancient custom somewhat by making hunting arrows for others. Since arrow length was slightly different for each man, the two arrow makers had asked for and gotten the necessary measurements from several men. Arrows were as long as the distance from a man's elbow to the tip of the middle finger of the outstretched hand, plus the width of a hand.

Generally, hunting arrows were made of hardwood stalks and fletched with three feathers, instead of the customary two for war arrows. Next to the two arrow makers were a pile of peeled, dried, sized, and straight chokecherry shafts, a supply of split turkey-wing feathers, and handfuls of wickedly sharp points made of tempered barrel-hoop iron. There were also strands of buffalo sinew for tying on points and feathers.

Before the day was over, Black Shield and Grey Bull would make nearly forty arrows. And as they worked, they talked.

"Ever since Yellow Wolf came back from the agency," Black Shield said, "I have been thinking about what Swift Bear had to say. I understand his thinking, but it bothers me. All those people at the agencies gave in. They gave themselves up to something they despise, something we all despise."

Grey Bull picked up an iron arrowhead and dropped it into the palm of his hand. "I remember what you told Cloud and me about stone arrowheads," he recalled. "Very few know how to make them anymore, because it is easier to make arrowheads out of iron. Yet these arrows we make with iron points are still Lakota arrows. Maybe that is Swift Bear's thinking. No matter what happens, our relatives down there will still be Lakota."

"Maybe," the older man replied thoughtfully, "but we Lakota were not made to live in square houses or without the freedom to travel to the horizon and beyond. If our relatives have to live without round lodges and the freedom to move, at what point is the change so deep that they start being something different? You are right, we are making arrows, and that means they are Lakota arrows, but I am part of the old way, and I will always know that there were stone points. Who is going to remind our children and grandchildren that we used to be something different?"

Grey Bull had no answer to the old man's question. For several long moments, they both worked in silence.

"As you and others have told us," Grey Bull finally said, "when the horse came, he did not make us into different people. He helped us do the same things we have always done. We still hunted and moved over the land, we just traveled farther and faster than we did before. That was a good change, so I think it is in us to find a way to grow stronger because of a bad thing."

Black Shield considered that for a moment, nodding as he thought it over. "You are right, the horse did not change us. But I think the gun did. Since it is more powerful than the bow, we all want one. I think when some of our grandfathers got their hands on one, the bow and arrow started becoming a thing of the past. Did the gun make us more powerful, the way the horse did? I do not think so. I think it weakened us as men, as hunters and warriors, because it made us dependent on something outside of ourselves. We cannot make a gun, so there is no connection to it the way there was, and is, with the bow and arrow. My generation and yours still have the knowledge to make bows and arrows. We may know how a gun works, but we cannot make them. What will happen when there are so many guns that everyone has one? I think the customs and beliefs that connect us to the bow and arrow will be lost. So, I agree, even though arrows with iron points are still Lakota arrows, the iron point is the first seed of change. It means we have lost something that was a part of us."

After a deep breath, the old man turned his gaze toward the mountains. "In a hundred years," he went on pensively, "when our great-grandchildren look at those mountains, I know the mountains will be the same. What about our great-grandchildren? Will they be Lakota in the same way we are? You are right—difficulty can teach us to be strong, but that can also change us."

"Like you said, Swift Bear's thinking is understandable," Grey Bull said. "Perhaps white people are so powerful that it is of no use to stand up to them. That is a scary reality. But I was born to this life, and I will die living it. If the buffalo are lost to us forever, I think we can change and find a way to live without them. It will not be easy, but it will not be impossible either. The important thing is to be free."

As Black Shield and Grey Bull talked and made arrows, Cloud and Crazy Horse took their buffalo runners for a long ride. Cloud's horse was a muscular little bay that reminded him of a taut bowstring. Crazy Horse rode a gray roan equally fast and nimble. Both were ten years old and had been trained by Good Hand's father, Flying By, a man who loved horses. Now that the buffalo herds were diminished and almost nonexistent, the trainer and the horses seemed to have lost their purpose, though that thought went unspoken.

The horses flew over the prairies as the riders let them stretch out and run, guided only by an occasional shift of weight with a lean to the right or left. Buffalo runners were born to run, to be the crucial link between life and death. Careening through clumps of sagebrush, down one slope and up the next, both men and horses were exhilarated by the freedom of unimpeded motion, to go as fast and as far as they chose.

Eventually, Cloud and Crazy Horse resumed a straight-up posture and the horses began to slow down until they gradually settled into a high lope. There was a surge of energy and excitement that could not be ignored. From a high lope, they allowed the horses to ease into a trot, and then to a fast walk. In short order, they recovered their wind and were reined in to a shallow wash between two low hills.

After ground tying their horses to let them rest, the two men climbed a hill covered with sagebrush and soap weed. Using field glasses, they studied the hills and skyline to the north. A warm breeze prowled the land, and it felt good to be unfettered from bulky robes. Freedom of motion was as precious as any other kind. Small bunches of antelope grazed to the northeast, and hawks and eagles prowled the skies. Cloud and Crazy Horse were watchful for two-legged enemies, but they were just as alert for bears. Now was the time the great brown bears were waking from their long winter sleep, hungry and bad-tempered.

"I was thinking," Crazy Horse said after a long silence, "we need to send two scouts east to find the best route to the White Buttes. But maybe we should wait a few days. I heard one of the old weather women talking a few days ago. She was saying that a blizzard might be coming."

Cloud agreed. "A cold night in a blizzard was never one of my favorite experiences," he said. "Unless you find a cave out of the wind, it is hard to make a fire to at least make you think you are warm. Who did you have in mind to send?"

"Yellow Wolf, and he can pick who he wants to take with him."

Below them, Cloud's horse snorted nervously. In an instant, both horses were testing the wind, their bodies tensed.

"Something is out there. The wind is from the north," Crazy Horse said as he moved slowly down the incline and grabbed the lead ropes of both horses. "But it is not a man."

Cloud panned the skyline with his field glasses as the horses grew more nervous. The antelope were running, gliding effortlessly over the ground until they disappeared over the horizon. Swiftly and skillfully, Crazy Horse fashioned and tied front hobbles on both horses and took the rifles from their cases. After a moment, he rejoined Cloud on the rise.

"There!" Cloud called out. "Two hills to the left, coming over the rise. A bear!"

At a distance of three hundred or so paces, the bear was still a dark form against the green earth, but its pronounced hump was unmistakable. A brown bear, a big one, and it was moving deliberately south toward the men and their nervous horses, and toward the northernmost of the three villages.

"He will smell us and the horses sooner or later," Cloud commented. "He does smell something and is being led by his nose."

"Yes, and in the direction he is going," Crazy Horse pointed out, "he will eventually reach the upper village. He is hungry and will stop at nothing to get food. There are no berries or grubs yet, so he is looking for meat. I bet he smells some of the elk meat on the drying racks."

One of the horses whinnied fearfully. They could smell the bear. Crazy Horse knew about bears. In most instances, it was smarter to avoid them. Some adult bears could sprint as fast as a horse for short distances.

"We have two choices," Cloud said. "We can divert it, lead it away, but it might come back, because it will remember where the food is. Or we can kill it."

"We have to kill it," Crazy Horse replied without hesitation. "It is already too close to the villages."

The bear paused on a rise and rose up on its haunches, testing the wind.

"He has found us," Crazy Horse said.

The horses knew the bear was close. Only their hobbles prevented them from galloping away in panic.

"Here he comes," Cloud said, pointing. He slid a cartridge into his breechloader. As it came up and over an intervening rise, the bear broke into a trot.

Crazy Horse loaded his own rifle. "When he is within a hundred paces, you take the first shot," he said. "I will go to the next rise, over there, and take the second shot. After that, we keep shooting, if necessary."

Neither man would go out of his way just to kill a bear. No one hunted bears just for the sake of hunting them. But there were many instances when bears had come face-to-face with humans, and, more often than not, the bear walked away from such encounters. But, by and large, no one carried any grudges against bears. They only did what they needed to in order to survive, as any other being had to do.

Crazy Horse ducked behind the rise and ran to the next one and took up his position. At the north end of a wide meadow, the bear trotted steadily, but he was on a line toward Cloud. A frontal shot, even with a .55 caliber, was a risky shot.

"You have a better shot from the side," Cloud yelled over.

Crazy Horse waved a hand and moved around to rest the barrel of the rifle on a stout sagebrush branch. Cloud aimed from a prone position and hoped the bear would react to Crazy Horse's bullet by turning to one side or the other. There was nothing for him to do but react to whatever happened.

Onward came the bear, now halfway across the meadow, his reddish brown coat vivid in the bright sun. He was unaware that he was living the final moments of his life.

Behind Cloud, the horses were fighting their hobbles, their frantic cries piercing the quiet afternoon. The bear broke into a lope. Cloud realized that he would break into a sprint to go after the horses, and there would be no good opportunity for a clean shot. There was only one thing to do.

"Get ready!" he shouted to Crazy Horse. Before the puzzled expression could fade from Crazy Horse's face, Cloud jumped to his feet, waving his arms.

"Hey! Hey, bear!"

Skidding to a stop on all fours, the bear paused for a surprised instant, then rose to his full height.

Boom!

Cloud heard the pop of Crazy Horse's bullet as it hit the bear in the chest. A bear carrying the weight of feeding all summer and autumn might have withstood the impact of the shot, but this one was thin from a long winter's sleep. The shot made him stagger, but his weakened physical condition did nothing to diminish his reaction. With an enraged roar, he regained his balance and ran toward Cloud who was down on one knee, taking careful aim.

Boom! Boom!

Crazy Horse's second shot immediately followed Cloud's first and only shot. Collapsing in midstride, the bear plowed his chin into the dirt no more than thirty paces from Cloud and moved no more.

Reloading instantly, both men waited for a moment before they approached the animal. Behind them, the horses were still snorting apprehensively. At ten paces, they could see the brownish red fur being ruffled slightly by the breeze. Somewhere overhead, a hawk shrilled.

There was no joy in the kill, no celebration, but there was a sense of immense relief. Though thin, the animal was old, a battle-scarred warrior that had likely sired many offspring.

Crazy Horse nodded grimly at his friend. "If he had not stopped, neither of us would have had a good shot." A gleam of admiration appeared in his eyes. "How did you know he would stop?"

Cloud shook his head, staring at the long black claws on one of the dead bear's extended paws. "There was no way to know," he admitted, "but I had to try something."

"Life is only worth living if you must defend it now and then," Crazy Horse spoke the ancient saying, acknowledging his friend's reckless act of bravery.

Cloud chuckled. "Especially if you live to tell about it because you have a friend who is a good shot."

After they retrieved the horses, they gutted the bear and cut out the heart to give to High Eagle. Cloud volunteered to stay and guard the carcass while Crazy Horse went back to the village to bring a wagon horse with drag poles.

Cloud walked down the incline to the bay horse to grab the water skin from the girth rope. He wanted to wash the blood off his hands. The horse was still nervous; its nostrils flared, testing the wind. Cloud assumed it was only smelling the heavy odor of the intestines on the ground next to the gutted carcass. He patted the horse's stout neck reassuringly.

Something between a grunt and a squeal erupted from the bay, and in an instant he spun and galloped away. To the drumming of hooves, Cloud could only watch as the bay disappeared over a rise, and then the hair on the back of his neck stood up. A shadow, a very large shadow, appeared in the corner of his vision.

It was a bear, rising up on its hind legs.

Cloud heard the sharp intake of his own breath as the water skin fell out of his hand.

Its fur was light brown, and it seemed to be nearly two times taller than Cloud, even at a distance of fifty paces. As it reached its full height, it let out a roar that obliterated the silence.

Cloud was immobilized by momentary indecision. His only means of escape was gone, and the rifle was fifteen, perhaps twenty, paces behind him.

Once the bear came back down on all fours, Cloud knew it could cover the open ground between them in three or four bounds. Slowly, he turned his head to see where he was in relation to his rifle. It was leaning against a thick clump of sagebrush. The only advantage he had was that the rifle was loaded. But he did not know how fast he could cover the fifteen or twenty paces, grab the rifle, aim, and fire.

If he managed to reach the weapon, then fired and missed, there would probably be no chance to reload. The bear would be on him. If he could hit the bear, he would have only an instant more to reload.

There was only one thing Cloud was certain of—he would go for the rifle. He had to. And there was no time like the present, while the bear was still up on his haunches, roaring to the four winds. Cloud reached into the bullet bag at his belt and took out two rounds, jamming them on either side of his right index finger.

Spinning on his heel, he sprinted for the rifle. Behind him, he heard a grunt and mightily resisted the urge to glance back, concentrating instead on grabbing the rifle with one swipe of his left hand. He heard claws scraping over sand and stone and tearing through brush, and then the raspy breath of the beast.

Bending low, he grabbed the stock, then slipped and lost his footing. With a jolt, he crashed to the ground and rolled, tearing through a low stalk of sagebrush and ending up on his back. He brought the barrel of the rifle around and slid the safety off.

The bear was perhaps fifteen paces away now. Cloud saw the animal's small, dark eyes in its massive head. He aimed below the jaw and squeezed the trigger.

Boom!

The rifle bucked in his hands.

A squeal of pain and rage erupted from the cavernous mouth of the beast. Blood spurted. He stumbled, swiping at his jaw.

Cloud pulled open the breech, but the empty cartridge jammed and slid only partway out. Mouth dry, heart pounding, he dug at the cartridge with the tip of his finger, but it did not budge.

Cloud realized that the bear was down, its head behind a clump of sage. Grabbing his knife from its sheath, he forced the empty cartridge out with the tip of the blade and reloaded.

Rising on trembling legs, Cloud stepped to his left in order to have an unobstructed shot at the chest behind the bear's elbow. He stopped when he noticed the chest was moving. The bear was still alive.

At the same instant Cloud raised the rifle to his shoulder, the bear was on its feet. Blood covered its chest, and its jaw hung down; Cloud's bullet had torn away part of it. His massive head turned, the little eyes looking directly at the only other living thing near it. Something inside him told Cloud to shoot while he still had a shot at the bear's exposed left side.

Boom!

With a jerk, the bear hunched up, and then launched himself. But it was the last spurt of enraged energy he would expend. His head and sightless little eyes came to rest within a pace of Cloud's feet. A realization coursed through Cloud like an icy breeze: this bear was bigger than the first one.

Cloud's heart was thudding in his chest as he fumbled to reload the rifle. With shaky steps, he climbed the low rise to take a quick look around. Nothing was moving on the land. He knew his horse was probably back in the herd northeast of the village by now, or would be shortly. Turning, he looked at the bear lying on its stomach, the front legs folded underneath. He had never hunted bears, because he had always admired their strength and ferocity. Now he was standing between two dead bears. Life was unpredictable.

He saw the water skin on the ground and went to retrieve it. Sitting down next to a clump of sagebrush, he took a drink and then poured water over his hands. He tried to finish wiping off the last stubborn patches of dried blood with a handful of grass, but could not get it all. All the while he kept the rifle leaning against his left shoulder.

It was difficult to ignore the dead bear. Not only was it very large, but it had managed to approach without a sound, even surprising the horse, to an extent. If not for Cloud's incredible luck, the bear would likely be feeding on his flesh right now. If the rifle had not been loaded…if the bear had not paused to rise up on his hind legs…if he had missed the first shot…A slight shiver traveled up Cloud's back, prompting him to take several deep breaths to calm his nerves. Images of Sweetwater Woman and Song floated in his mind's eye.

Cloud knew he would die someday, but in the past few months, it seemed that death stalked him openly. First it was the giant white Crow on the bluffs, and now two bears. Two bears in one afternoon, as a matter of fact. He reached into his bullet pouch and counted the rounds he had left. Seven, plus the one loaded in the rifle. After another deep breath, he wrapped both hands around the barrel of the rifle. Leaning forward, he rested his head on his hands.

Several young men came along to lend a hand, but more to hear the story of how Crazy Horse and Cloud had brought down the bear. They were astounded to see Cloud sitting on a rise staring down at the dead body of another bear. Crazy Horse dismounted and slowly approached.

"My friend," he said, "are you hurt?"

Cloud shook his head. "No, but my horse is gone. He ran off when the second bear came."

The horses snorted nervously as the young men gathered around, glancing at the bears and Cloud, puzzled amazement and awe keeping them silent.

Crazy Horse finally tore his eyes away from the two bears to look back at Cloud and say, "My friend, if I would have known you were going to kill another bear, I would have brought back another horse."

Cloud gave him a shaky smile and, after a moment, rose to his feet to help begin the work at hand.

CHAPTER FOURTEEN

The Heart of a Bear

The village was still buzzing with the excitement over the bears as the sun went down. Boys and young men gathered to watch as two tall, sturdy tripods of lodge poles were pitched and the bear carcasses were hoisted to be skinned. Crazy Horse had given the hearts to High Eagle, who went down to the river with them.

Crazy Horse's story of the way Cloud distracted the first bear had made the rounds several times. Of the second bear, Cloud had said only that he had to shoot it twice.

It had been years since anyone had killed a bear, and most of the children in the village had never seen one up close. Now they gathered to stare at the two large carcasses.

High Eagle found a secluded spot by the river. After gathering kindling and dry wood, he built a small fire. At the water's edge, he washed the bear hearts. Next, he dropped a bundle of sage into the flames, causing a sweet, pungent smoke to billow. A heart in each hand, he held them in the smoke, smudging them. Then, after laying them on a large flat stone, he picked up his knife and began to slice into the organs.

Goings approached Cloud, who was standing at the back of the crowd. Both carcasses seemed larger, hanging head down from the tripods, and both were mature males. The first bear was noticeably smaller, however, and, as the hide was finally peeled away, it suddenly looked pale and unimposing. Death had certainly stripped it of its dignity. Cloud felt a tinge of pity for both of the dead animals and silently asked forgiveness for having killed them.

"One of my uncles shot a bear years ago," Goings recalled. "It was in the spring. They surprised one another, and my uncle got one arrow in him, and the thing chased him. He had to climb a tree, and somehow he shot two more arrows into him. Then he had to hang on and wait for the bear to bleed to death. The thing is, you can never tell about bears. That is part of their power."

Cloud felt High Eagle's presence before he heard soft footsteps approaching. In his open palm, on a bed of gray sage, the medicine man held small pieces of meat. "Eat four pieces," he instructed Cloud. "You will take upon yourself the ferocity of this being."

Cloud took four pieces of the bear's heart and swallowed them one at a time. "Thank you, Uncle. The hide of the second bear is yours."

Cloud stayed at the back of the crowd after the medicine man left and patiently answered endless questions. He was relieved when Yellow Wolf came with his buffalo runner.

"I found him in the herd," he told Cloud. "He seems unhurt."

Cloud nodded. "Yes, he had the good sense to leave. Thank you."

Taking the long rein, he quickly inspected the horse. The neck rope was still tied on. He took the horse to the water for a drink, but he was just as much seeking refuge from all the attention. Then, rather than picketing the horse by his lodge door, he turned him loose with the herd to let him graze.

He had tried to point out that Crazy Horse's deadly marksmanship had brought down the first bear. Crazy Horse, on the other hand, had successfully fashioned his story on how Cloud had stopped the first bear's charge by confronting him face-to-face. That only added to the mystery of how Cloud had killed the second bear. "Two bears in one day," people marveled to one another.

Back in his own lodge, he settled back to enjoy a cup of tea and told his story to Sweetwater Woman and Song. After he finished, Sweetwater Woman held a braid of sweetgrass over the small cooking fire, saying a silent prayer to the spirits for keeping her husband safe.

A soft, almost timid scratch came at the door.

Sweetwater Woman peeked out and smiled. "Come in," she said to the boy standing outside. It was Two Horns, Little Bird's youngest son.

"Uncle," he said shyly to Cloud, "my father would like you and your family to come to our lodge to eat. He has something for you."

The enticing aroma of roasted elk ribs greeted the visitors to the lodge of Stands on the Hill and Little Bird. Their two sons sat off to one side, smiling shyly at Song. Cloud was pleasantly surprised to see Black Shield and his wife there as well. Stands on the Hill invited them to sit near Black Shield and his wife, Looking North Woman. After they were seated on the willow chairs, she began to serve the meal.

After the main course of roasted ribs and peppermint tea came chokecherry fruit soup. The adults conversed as they ate, while the children were respectfully silent, unless one of the adults spoke to them.

After the meal, Little Bird unrolled a long elk-hide-covered bundle to reveal a bow case and quiver made from the tanned hide of a mountain lion. A handful of arrows were in the quiver, and the bow case contained a sinew-backed hunting bow made of chokecherry wood.

Little Bird handed the encased weapon to Cloud. "It is fitting that I planned to give this to you today," he said, smiling in admiration, "this day of two bears. Four years ago, a cat stalked me while I was hunting. I climbed a tree, but that did not stop him." He paused and glanced toward the children in the room and decided to omit the details of killing the mountain lion. "I asked Two Crow to prepare the hide for me, since there is no one better. Since then, I've kept it with the intent to make a bow case and quiver out of it, and I finally have a good reason to do that. I can never repay you for saving my life, but I can give you this bow I made with my own hands."

Cloud slid the bow from its case. He had never seen one so exquisitely made. The sinew was applied evenly, covering the entire back of the bow without a single bump or blemish, and giving the weapon a slight backward curve because the sinew had shrunk as it dried. The sinew backing also added to the strength of the bow. It was longer than his other hunting bows, and the center, the handle, was wrapped with tanned otter hide with the hair side out, meaning the arrow would fly from the bow without the slightest whisper of noise to alert the game. Overall, it had a heft and a feel that Cloud's other bows did not.

"The sinew on the back is from an antelope," Little Bird pointed out. "The bowstring is buffalo sinew. So your bow has the spirit of the fastest and the strongest animals known to us. I have never made one that shot a heavy hunting arrow as fast as this one does."

As far as Cloud knew, there was no one better at making bows than Little Bird. "There is one other strength it has," he said. "It is just as important to me, and that is the skill that went into making it."

"In that case," Little Bird replied, "look at the arrows."

Cloud pulled the arrows out of the case. There were only six, but each was tipped with a point made of black stone and fletched with three goose feathers. He glanced toward Black Shield. No one could ever hope to make stone points so expertly and beautifully as he did.

"Grandfather," he said, "thank you. I am almost afraid to use these, they are so finely made."

"But you must," the old man said. "You must use the bow and the arrows to help them fulfill the purpose they were created for. Otherwise they will be things without a spirit, without a purpose."

"Yes, you are right, Grandfather. I will use them, and each time I do, I will think of you both."

Black Shield nodded, then turned toward Little Bird's sons and Song. "This is a good time to tell these grandchildren how our people came to have the bow and the arrow," he said.

"Long, long ago," he began, "we were hunters, as we are today. In those days, the hunters used several kinds of weapons to bring down animals. One of them was a spear and spear thrower. The spear was long and slender and looked much like an arrow does today, with a sharp stone point and feathers. The spear thrower was made of heavy hardwood, as long as from the elbow to the wrist." He pointed to his own arm. "The tip of the spear thrower fit into a notch at the end of the spear, and the hunter threw the spear like so, overhand, like throwing a stone. It was a very good weapon, until the bow came along.

"A hunter had a dream one night. No one remembers the hunter's name, but in his dream, he heard Moon speak to him and say, 'Look at me when I am young and I will show you how to be a more powerful hunter.' So the hunter did—he looked at the new moon. Now, when the moon, which has the female spirit, is new, it is very thin. If you look closely, it is a thin curve and is wider in the middle and narrows toward the ends. Each time any Lakota hunter strings his bow and bends it, it looks just like the new moon."

Two Horns and Ashes nodded respectfully.

"Now, the moon gave us the bow because she knew the sun had given us the arrow," the old man continued. "What is it your father tells you when he makes arrows?"

"They must be as straight as the rays of the sun," said Two Horns.

"Yes," Black Shield said, his old eyes twinkling. "Then, after the bow came, the spears became arrows and were shorter, the way they are today.

And each time you see the sun's rays—its arrows—shining down through the clouds, you will always remember that our arrows must be as straight as that."

He paused, looking at the young faces. "And do you know why we have weapons?"

The boys shook their heads.

"What makes deer so difficult to hunt?" the old man asked the boys.

"They have good eyesight," Ashes said. "And they hear very well."

"Yes. And what about the great beasts that your uncle Cloud faced on this day? What is their power?"

"Their claws," Two Horns replied. "And their great strength."

"Yes," Black Shield agreed. "Bears can smell at great distances as well. When I was a young man, I watched a bear sniffing the ground, and then it dug up moles. He smelled them even though they were so deep he had to poke his head in up to his shoulders. My cousin was wounded in a fight, and he hid in a small cave on a hillside. He said that he watched a bear on the horizon several hills away come toward him. That animal smelled the blood from the wound in his leg.

"All the four-legged people have some kind of strength, a power that sets them apart from all the others. The falcon can fly faster than all the other hunters of the sky. The wolf has great endurance, like no other. The great cat of the mountains not only has strength and speed, he can see well in the night. As does the owl, who sees better at night than anyone does, and he flies silently. And there is no one faster than the white-bellied goat of the prairie, the antelope. Porcupines have quills that can be just as deadly as knives, and, of course, there is the skunk."

At the mention of the skunk, even Song giggled.

"So," the old man went on, "we can sit here all night and talk about what makes the winged people and four-legged people more powerful than we are, and we should not forget the crawlers. But I would like to talk about what makes us equal to them, sometimes. What do you think that is?"

"Our weapons?" ventured Two Horns.

"And how do we get our weapons?" the old man asked.

"We make them," the boy replied.

"How can we do that?"

"Because...because we know how?" Two Horns asked timidly.

"Exactly. What, then, allows us to know how?"

The boy was stumped, and turned to his brother, who was equally at a loss.

Black Shield smiled knowingly, a twinkle still playing in his old eyes. "Our fang, our claw, our speed, our keen eyesight is our ability to think, to reason in our own way." He touched a finger to his head. "It may not be the best of strengths at times, but it is our strength, such as it is. But it can also be a weakness, especially when we humans think we are better than all the other beings. When it comes down to it, we are not the strongest or the fastest of creatures, so we have to rely on our minds."

He glanced slyly toward the two boys. "Can you run as fast as a rabbit? Can you catch even a mouse with your bare hands? Of course not. That is why we have learned to make traps and snares. If necessary, we can make a trap that can catch a bear. But whether we are out to trap a bear or a squirrel, we have to know where to put a snare or a trap. If we did not know these things, we would be hungry and cold and frightened. We would be poor creatures indeed."

"Speaking of knowing things, Grandfather," Cloud interjected, "I wonder if you would consider helping me learn how to make stone points. It would be a shame for that particular knowledge—your knowledge—to fade away."

"You can include me as well," Little Bird added. "And my sons too."

The old man glanced at his wife with a smile, then nodded appreciatively at Cloud and Little Bird. "That is good. I would be glad to do that," he told them. "There is not much black stone available anymore. But there is flint and another kind of stone some call arrow stone. We can go looking after the first heavy rain washes away the creek banks. When that happens, it reveals the arrow stone."

Morning came cool and gray. Cloud and Song walked down to the river and then upstream. Cloud wanted to shoot his new bow and arrows but did not want to shatter the black stone points, so they walked until they found a sandbank relatively free of large stones. In a spare quiver, he carried iron-tipped arrows.

"Father," Song said as she watched him string the new bow, "can I have a bow and arrows too?"

Cloud glanced at his daughter as he hung the new quiver at the front of his waist. He was not surprised at her question, and he was pleased. At some point, he intended to teach her how to handle and use weapons, as he had taught her mother. Like many men, he felt it was important for women to be able to hunt and defend themselves when necessary. In order to do that, they needed to learn the basics of weaponry.

"Yes," he told her, "you can have your own bow and arrows. I have a few ash staves hanging below the smoke hole in our lodge. We can pick one and make a bow for you. But if you want to learn to shoot, I think it is just as important for you to know how to make a bow. Want to learn how to do that too?"

She nodded, a broad smile on her face and eyes bright with anticipation.

At twenty paces from the bank, the first arrow was barely a flash in the air before it buried itself halfway up the shaft. The straight and unerring flight of the arrow was due primarily to the skill and experience of Black Shield, and the speed with which it flew was the direct result of the bow.

The other five stone-tipped arrows flew every bit as fast, and all embedded themselves in the sandbank in a group no larger than a man's palm. Cloud retrieved the arrows and exchanged them for the iron-tipped shafts in the other quiver. Stepping back ten more paces, he methodically shot eight arrows into the bank. He paused before retrieving them and ran his hand over the limbs of the bow. It was truly the work of a master craftsman.

In the old days, the skill to make a beautiful and powerful bow was not taken lightly, because life and death always hung in the balance for the hunter as well as for the warrior. Although every man still could make his own these days if he had to, hardly anyone had Little Bird's or Black Shield's skills. And the preference for firearms and the growing dependence on them for hunting, as well as for warfare, diminished many skills, foremost the ability to craft an adequate weapon.

Not only was Little Bird highly skilled at making bows, he was also a deadly marksman. No grown man among the Crazy Horse people was as good. That is, Cloud reminded himself, until a bullet had torn through his right shoulder in the ambush at the bluffs. But even with that, once his shoulder had completely healed, he would still be a lethal marksman. Little Bird's determination, courage, and commitment made his skills as a warrior all that much more formidable.

There were more than one hundred such men who followed Crazy Horse. Cloud knew that every one of those men, including him, would ride into battle with a rifle as his primary weapon, perhaps not by choice, as in his case, but certainly because of necessity. As lethal as the bow could be and was against an enemy who was similarly armed, it was inadequate against firearms. Perhaps the bow and arrow's time as a battlefield weapon was passing.

The reality that had been mocking him since yesterday was that he would not have killed the bear with a bow. True, he might have been able to put at least one arrow into the beast, but that would not have stopped the animal. His wife was not a widow, and Song still had her father, because of the rifle. It was a reality he was immensely grateful for, but it was a sad and foretelling reality nonetheless. If the bow and arrow were becoming things of the past, what other ancient realities of the Lakota world were being lost?

A small voice tugged at his awareness. "Father?"

Cloud glanced at Song, who was pointing off to the side. Turning, he saw Crazy Horse approaching with a horse on a lead.

"You look like someone with much on his mind," the man observed.

Cloud held up his new bow. "This, for one thing," he told his friend.

Crazy Horse admired the weapon. "How does it shoot?"

"Smooth and fast. It is the best one I have ever had."

Crazy Horse took the weapon and ran his hands over the limbs. "Yes," he said. "It has a feeling of power. Little Bird was in a good place when he made it. My father always says that the power of the bow begins with the spirit of the man who makes it."

They watched as Song pulled her father's arrows out of the sandbank.

Cloud took the bow and unstrung it, then slid it into the case. "That is very true," he said, "especially with this weapon."

"But that is not the only thing on your mind," Crazy Horse ventured perceptively.

Cloud took his arrows from Song and put them into the arrow cup and then slid it into the quiver. "I was thinking about...about yesterday, and what could have happened." He caressed his daughter's shoulder and pulled her close. "I was lucky, very lucky. All in all, if I did not have my rifle with me..."

"I know what you mean," Crazy Horse agreed, nodding. "Like you, I use the bow for hunting and carry one as a backup when we go on patrol. I think I will always have one with me. A Lakota man without bow and arrows is like...is like the bow without the arrow, or the other way around." He sighed deeply. "But in order to defeat the one enemy who now threatens our way of life, all of our fighting men must have guns—and plenty of bullets. That is the new reality. The trouble is, we can make bows and as many arrows as we need, but we cannot make guns or bullets. There, our enemy has the advantage over us."

"True," Cloud said. "But we are better fighters and better horsemen. And if we all have guns and plenty of bullets, then any one of us is worth several of them."

Crazy Horse couldn't agree more. Attitude was the best weapon of all, and men like Cloud, men who had a firm grasp of reality, were the strongest defense the Lakota had. As he and others knew, some—perhaps most—of the Lakota men languishing on the Red Cloud and Spotted Tail agencies felt the same way. He knew it was what Sitting Bull was counting on.

"I spoke with Yellow Wolf this morning," he said. "He is willing to go on a scout to the White Buttes, and Fast Horse will go with him. But I think they should wait." He pointed to the gray sky. "The weather women are right again," he said. "There is bad weather coming."

CHAPTER FIFTEEN

The Colonel

A cool morning breeze slid in from the east as Captains Frederick Benteen and Myles Keogh stood at the west edge of the parade ground at Fort Abraham Lincoln, the outpost along the western banks of the Missouri River. The brown waters of the river were roiling high with spring melt runoff. Both men were slender and less than six feet tall, thus filling the requirement for cavalry soldiers. The officers were watching a column of nearly twenty mounted troopers practice turning left into line. They were also keeping an eye on the lithe figure standing twenty yards to their left. He, too, was watching the troopers drill. That man had his arms crossed and observed the efforts of the mounted squad with a hard, narrow-eyed gaze.

"Seems to me the general is not entirely pleased with our newest recruits," Benteen commented in a low voice.

Keogh chuckled wryly. "I know for a fact that half of those men hardly ever rode a horse before they signed up at Jefferson Barracks," he said in a slight Irish brogue. "Perhaps we would be wiser to teach them to dismount quickly, without tripping over themselves. Like the Crow, the Sioux put their boys on a horse before they can walk."

"Well, I myself am a bit more concerned that they know which end of a Springfield rifle is which," sighed Benteen. "If we cannot hope to match the Sioux as mounted fighters, then we are forced to rely on firepower—given, of course, that we can provide sufficient ammunition for them to practice with."

The man up the line uncrossed his arms and approached briskly. "Gentlemen," he said in a clipped tone, stopping three yards away.

Even at that distance, he had to look up at Benteen and Keogh. He had a thin face with a long nose and a sandy mustache, the same color as his shoulder-length hair. There was even more authority in his smoky blue eyes than in his voice, which was dripping with it. And although it was a cool morning, he wore no uniform coat.

"Sir!" they replied in unison.

"Tell me, what do you think of the newest members of the Seventh?" Lieutenant Colonel George Armstrong Custer tilted his head toward the drilling soldiers. "General Terry has assigned them to us."

"I am certain that after a few days under the capable guidance of the sergeant major we should have adequate troopers on our hands, General," Benteen replied. Custer had held the brevet rank of major general during the Civil War, and it was customary to address an officer by the highest grade he had held.

Custer nodded, keeping a relentless stare fixed on the two troop commanders. "Adequate, perhaps," he replied, "but they are nonetheless still recruits. We are soon to take to the field, and our assignment will require experienced soldiers. Owing to that, I will distribute them throughout each troop. After the sergeant major is through with them, it will be up to your men to bring them further into line."

"Yes, sir," Keogh replied. "How soon are we to depart?"

"In two or three weeks, I suspect," Custer said, taking a quick glance over his shoulder as the recruits reached the south end of the parade ground and executed a sloppy turn. "That should be sufficient time for you to turn those men into basic soldiers. There should be no more than three new men in each troop."

"We will do what we can, General," Benteen assured Custer.

"You will do what you *must*, Captain, what I expect from you," Custer insisted. "We cannot afford to take an ill-prepared command into the field."

"Yes, sir. Is it true then, General? Are we to go west toward the Yellowstone region?"

"That is certain."

"I trust that Washington City was as grandiose as I hear it is," Captain Keogh ventured, alluding to the fact that Custer had only just returned from the East. Rumors swirled around that trip, that Custer had stepped on one too many toes with his accusations of fraud in the Indian Bureau.

"To be known as the Yellowstone Expedition," Custer went on, ignoring Keogh's comment about the capital. "We are to convince the recalcitrant Sioux to accept reality and report to the agencies." Custer smiled thinly.

Hurried footfalls reached them. It was a sergeant from the office of the commanding general, Alfred E. Terry. He stopped in front of them and saluted Custer smartly. "Sir! The general sent me to find you. He wishes to speak with you immediately."

Custer nodded nonchalantly. "Of course, Sergeant. I was on the way to my quarters. After that, I will speak with the general."

A warning look filled the sergeant's eyes, but no words came out to match it. "Very well, sir. I shall tell the general."

Custer turned his attention back to Benteen and Keogh. "I shall send an orderly around to remind you, of course, but I will have Officers Call this afternoon. I am certain that the general will give us our orders, and I want the Seventh to be prepared to take to the field."

Spinning on his heel, and without so much as a glance in any direction, Custer turned and walked toward a frame house with a porch.

Keogh turned his attention back to the mounted troopers, noting Benteen's cold stare in Custer's direction.

"In my estimation," Keogh said, pointing at the mounted recruits, "a long ride would do them more good than learning formation drills. Most of them simply need to learn to stay in the saddle first. We should instruct the sergeant major to do just that."

"Agreed," Benteen replied, only mildly interested.

Keogh reached into a coat pocket for the carefully trimmed portion of a cigar he had left there and put it between his lips. "I think I shall have a word with the sergeant major," he muttered. "Perhaps I will take those... those 'troopers' out for an excursion before the general has Officers Call."

Benteen nodded absently as Keogh strode across the parade ground toward the mounted soldiers. From across the yard came the sergeant major's strident, exasperated yells.

Unmindful of anything transpiring outside his own parlor, Custer took his uniform coat from his wife, Elizabeth.

As he slipped it on, she watched him with a critical gaze. "Dispatches have come from the East," she told him.

"Yes. As you know, Libbie, there is a campaign in the making. I will convince General Terry to let the Seventh take the lead, as well we should."

She sighed and crossed her arms. "I believe Alfred is a good man. He realizes the worth of the Seventh. However, do be cautious, Autie. Let him speak first."

A frown creased his forehead, drawing his heavy brows together.

"Well, whatever do you mean, dear?"

"He is the commanding officer here. I simply think you should be more mindful of that. Hold your ambitions close to your vest."

A sharp growl and then a screech from the basement interrupted the colonel before he could reply.

"Autie, I do wish you would set that poor creature free. He does so torment poor Abigail each time she has to go past him to the cool room."

An impish smile spread across his face. "Dear, he is restrained by a stout chain. He cannot hurt her."

"She is convinced otherwise, and I do not see what you value in a scrawny old bobcat."

"I assure you, dear, he will harm no one."

Adjusting his coat a final time, the colonel paused at the door to put on his hat. With a wave, he was gone.

Ten minutes later, Lieutenant Colonel Custer took a step back and lowered himself slowly into the nearest chair, his face paler by a shade.

"Sir," he said in a near whisper, his eyes uncharacteristically downcast, "I do not understand why I am to be punished for…for…for answering questions put to me by a committee."

Major General Alfred E. Terry pointed to a pile of pages on the desk before him. "According to this, Armstrong, you did much more than simply answer questions. Of all things, you accused the president's brother of being a thief!"

"I…I testified as to what I know to be fact, sir."

"These dispatches arrived here before you did, before you came back from Washington. I am being directed to take you off the duty list, to strip you of your command, Armstrong!"

The general shoved his chair back and stepped to the window, looking out toward the river for a moment before he turned and redirected a glare at the other man in the room. "I was hoping that you would come of your own accord and inform me as to what happened back there. Or did you think that the hornet's nest you stirred up would not reach this far?"

Custer's shoulders slumped. "General, I took it upon myself to try to set the record straight. I waited for several hours for the president to see me. He would not. He ignored me."

"Do you blame him?"

"No, sir. I suppose not."

"You suppose not? Do you realize, Armstrong, that, for all intents and purposes, you called into question the integrity of the president of the United States? To make it worse, the press decided it was worthwhile news! If Grant wanted to make you the commanding officer at a fort in the Florida Keys, or of an anthill in Arizona, he could! The only way you could deter that would be to resign from the army."

"I wrote a note, General, apologizing. I tried to see General Sherman, but he ignored me as well."

"You wrote a note? Did you not stop to think that nothing less than a heartfelt personal apology would do? What were you thinking, Armstrong? There is little I can do for you in this instance. Do you not realize that?"

"What am I to do, Alfred? All I know is soldiering."

Terry threw up his hands and sat back down. "Perhaps you should have considered that before you opened your mouth."

Custer sighed deeply. "Will you not speak on my behalf, sir?"

"Yes, of course. I will do what I can, but in the meantime, I have orders to follow. You are relieved, Colonel. Major Reno will assume command of the regiment."

Custer came out of his chair. "Major Reno!"

Despite the outburst, Terry gazed calmly at Custer. "Armstrong, unless you want me to follow these orders to the letter, which would mean you would never hold another command in the field, I suggest you aspire to a bit of humility. I know that is difficult for you, but I do not wish to take a stand on your behalf and then realize it was the wrong thing to do. Do I make myself clear, Colonel?"

"P-perfectly, sir. I cannot abide that my regiment will take to the field and I not be along to share in the dangers. I will do my best, sir."

"Then I suggest you send a telegram to Sherman. Humble yourself, Armstrong."

Oblivious to the usual daily activity in and around the outpost, Custer walked slowly across the parade ground. If he had hoped that the anonymity of an isolated frontier post on the edge of Indian country would soften Grant's angst, he was wrong. Who would have thought that Fort Abraham

Lincoln would be a cornerstone of a campaign against the Sioux? That was clearly Phil Sheridan's idea, and therein was a ray of hope. General William Sherman knew how valuable the Seventh would be, as valuable as the point was to the spear.

He stopped in his tracks. Perhaps he should point that out to Terry. But he forced himself not to turn around. Instead, with a resigned sigh, he headed for his house. Aspire to a bit of humility, the general had advised. So, he would take that advice.

Libbie was waiting with a pot of tea and patient silence.

Hanging up his hat, he took a seat at the writing desk in the front room. "You knew, I think," he said to her gently. "You knew what was going to happen."

"Just remember, Autie, that I, too, am in the army. Therefore, I know how it works."

"What am I to do?"

"Follow orders, like the good soldier you are. The general will put in a word on your behalf. There will be talk, but you must rise above it. Let Benteen and Reno think what they will. We must be patient, dear. We must be patient."

Amid the clink of china and silverware and the low buzz of conversation in the officers' mess that evening, Benteen grinned across the table. "Congratulations on your new command," he said to Major Marcus Reno, a man with dark eyes and a thick, dark mustache.

The major, a small, nervous man, smiled tentatively. "If I would have earned it on my merits, I would be pleased," he replied. "Winning anything by default is not always a good thing,"

Benteen leaned closer. "Nevertheless, Major, were I you, I would make the most of it."

Reno allowed himself a smile. "Of that you can be sure, Frederick."

"We are to head west, toward the Yellowstone," Benteen went on, "in a matter of weeks, perhaps days. Take a strong hand, Marcus. Make this regiment your own. Earn it, if you must, by putting your stamp on it. A firm but fair hand and success in the field would make General Terry take notice."

"What you say is true, Frederick. But our erstwhile colonel seems to live under a lucky star. He always manages to land on his feet."

The turbulent career of Custer had been the topic of conversation and speculation on many occasions by the officers of the Seventh Cavalry. The exceptions were Captains Thomas Weir and Tom Custer, and Lieutenant W. W. Cooke. One was a staunch ally of the mercurial colonel, one was his brother, and the third was the aide-de-camp. The three of them sat at a table apart from Reno and Benteen, trying to catch bits and pieces of their conversation.

Benteen nodded toward Weir and the younger Custer. "You must be especially firm with those two gentlemen, Marcus. You must watch your back around them. Replace Cooke with your own man, quickly."

Reno nodded. "I appreciate your advice, Frederick. However, I think I would sooner face the Sioux than deal with those three."

"I have a feeling, Marcus, you will have no choice on both of those matters."

CHAPTER SIXTEEN

The Broken Arrow

A lone figure stood atop the windswept plateau, oblivious to the wind and the ants crawling among the sagebrush and over his feet. What kind of good fortune or mean twist of fate had brought him here, he didn't know, and he didn't care. He had been meant to find this place. He ignored the bones of the big man, after recovering from the initial shock of finding the two skeletons. Coyotes and buzzards and the elements themselves had stripped off all the flesh, but there was no doubt about who they were—or had been.

Old Coyote had suspected for months that his younger sister and her husband had gotten themselves in trouble somewhere deep in Lakota country. His white brother-in-law had been determined to collect Lakota scalps and would not listen to anyone advising caution, perhaps because he feared no one. He was the biggest man anyone had ever seen, and he had the strength to go with his size, and perhaps a foolish sense of invincibility as well.

The fact that the big man was dead was a warning. Somehow, someone had killed him. No one stood a chance against him fighting hand to hand, and the bullet hole in his skull suggested the encounter was not that. Whoever killed him had figured the odds, probably almost immediately. The smashed rifle was a puzzle, however, as was the fact that the bullets were still in their bags. Rifles and bullets were always coveted prizes. The killer had smashed the rifle, and he did not take the bullets.

Old Coyote didn't know the name of the man who had killed his sister and her husband, but it was a Lakota. Of that, he was absolutely certain.

There were two weathered arrows with his sister's bones. He reached down and grabbed the broken shaft of one. It was a war arrow, with only two goose feathers. In the space between the feathers was a mark faded by the weather, but the faint red-and-black lines were still visible. One Lakota warrior, and only one, used those marks on his arrow. Old Coyote would search for that man. He had time. Likely, the man who had killed his sister and her husband would not know that someone would come for him, so there was time for revenge.

He didn't care about the white man, his brother-in-law. Old Coyote laid the blame on him. If the man would have come back alone, he would have killed him. Without a twinge of regret, he would leave his bones behind. The important thing was that he had found his sister's bones. He would gather them up and take her home to his mother and father so they could bury her properly.

Old Coyote rode away from the plateau, his sister's bones in the bag he had fashioned from a gray blanket. He would travel as fast as he could to his village, half a day north of the Yellowstone River.

Several days before, he had watched a line of people, Lakota people, moving camp and heading east. Perhaps they were looking for buffalo, as his people were, but they must have found nothing. There were no more buffalo. But wherever the Lakota were going, he would return and follow them.

In his hand was the piece of shaft with the faint markings beneath the feathers. He rolled the broken arrow between his fingers as he rode.

Cloud helped guide the last small group of horses into a valley between two low hills where the grass was good. He estimated that there were nearly a thousand head in all. A small creek flowed between the hills, and once the guards were in place around them, the horses would settle down. Farther down the valley to the south, the camp of more than two hundred lodges was already in place.

According to Yellow Wolf, they were at least three days from the White Buttes. He and Fast Horse had scouted and laid out a general route.

Food was an issue, however. At least eight deer or four elk were needed to feed nearly a thousand people every day. In the past, fish was only an occasional delicacy, but now fish traps were placed in every stream at every opportunity. Prairie dogs, rabbits, squirrels, and grouse were regular fare as well.

While seeing to the rigors and tasks of everyday life, the people moved steadily toward the White Buttes, toward what they hoped was an answer to the problem of the encroachment of the whites, toward the time when the buffalo might shake the earth again and the ruts left by the intrusive wagon wheels would be forgotten and grown over. But they had to eat and stay strong, so hunters were going and coming constantly. It was decided that they would camp here for two or three days so the hunters could find fresh meat.

Cloud dismounted and led his horse to the top of a rise above the herd to gaze at the animals that filled the meadow. They were a palette of colors against the greening earth: grays, sorrels, bays, buckskins, blacks, and brown-and-white, black-and-white, and yellow-and-white paints, with roans thrown in for accent. But they were more than colorful expressions. They were the symbol of a relationship with the Lakota that was just as critical and defining as the relationship the Lakota had with the buffalo. For Cloud, galloping over the land on the back of a graceful, powerful horse was the closest he felt he would come to flying. Even now, as he heard the rhythmic pounding of hooves and turned to watch a group of boys racing their mounts over a hill, he could almost feel their exhilaration and joy.

Then Cloud turned instantly and instinctively toward a movement he caught out of the corner of his eye. Taken Alive was quick to wave as he saw his friend's attitude of alertness, like a wolf ready to spring. Across the back of the packhorse he was leading was draped the carcass of a black-tailed deer. "I know ribs are your favorite, so I will drop some off at your lodge," he said to Cloud.

"We are grateful," Cloud replied, acknowledging his friend's generosity.

"Last evening, I heard the old men say to our headman that we should rest for two or three days," Taken Alive informed him. "That would be good, because there is a valley to the north of here, and it is full of blacktails. Maybe we could go after more of them before dawn."

"I am ready for a good hunt," Cloud replied, "a chance to use the bow Little Bird made for me."

"Good!" Taken Alive exclaimed, urging his horses down the slope. "My wife and I will skin and quarter this carcass and bring the ribs over to your lodge."

Dawn found them north of the camp in the valley Taken Alive had found the day before. They were waiting in a stand of blue spruce as the growing light slowly defined the landscape. They had rubbed themselves down liberally with sage to cover their human scent, and, along with water, they had brought peppermint tea to cover their breath. They stood next to their horses, their bows already strung, quivers tied to the front of their waists, and six-shooters tucked into their belts.

No conversation was necessary for the experienced hunters. If no black-tailed deer appeared in the area, they would simply move on to another likely spot. They kept an eye on the terrain they could see, knowing that their horses would see, hear, or smell any other creature before they would.

Soon, both horses looked to the left. Taken Alive had not overstated the situation. Through the trees, the hunters saw three large doe walking into the head of the narrow valley, browsing lazily on new shoots of grass. If the doe stayed on the valley floor, they would cross in front of the waiting hunters.

The hunters had not randomly picked this stand of spruce. The fresh scent of the trees would cover their human odor, and the trees themselves would hide them and the horses. Also, they were looking down a slight incline into a small meadow that was thick with new grass, the type of secluded area deer liked. Their position gave them a perfect shooting lane. A lifetime of hunting, literally beginning in their father's and grandfather's footsteps, had taught them things that now were instinctual. Like any predator, most of their actions were carried out without conscious thought.

With hand signs, Taken Alive indicated that Cloud should take the first shot. With unhurried and deliberate movements, Cloud placed an arrow on the bowstring while Taken Alive got down low and crawled under his horse's belly to the other side, so that it was between him and the approaching deer. He nocked his arrow and stayed down on one knee.

Cloud noted that none of the doe had any fawns with them, and the udders of all three were not full. A herd of old doe, he guessed.

Eventually, they were at the bottom of the gentle slope below the hunters. Taken Alive was hidden between the horses, and Cloud was kneeling behind a soap weed that hid him effectively.

Not so much as a breath of wind stirred the grass. As blacktails are in the habit of doing, the doe lifted their heads frequently to look around. One spotted the horses and stared for several long moments, put her head down to graze, and immediately looked up again. Satisfied that the horses were no threat, she seemed to settle down.

Cloud decided there was no better opportunity for a shot, since she was about thirty paces away. Smoothly, he pulled and released. As much as he had practiced with his new hunting bow, he was still surprised at how fast the arrow flew.

At the same instant he heard a hollow thud, the doe jumped sideways, then dashed frantically away.

Behind her, from the corner of his eye, Cloud saw another doe spin, then sprint up the slope. Taken Alive had taken a shot, he realized.

The remaining doe bounded over the ridge and was gone.

Cloud's doe had gone east and crossed over two ridges. He found her in a thicket and dismounted to bleed and gut the carcass after tying a bundle of sage in the branches of the snake berry bushes. He washed off his hands after he finished and sat on the crest of the gully to wait. He was ever alert, because the demeanor of the warrior was every bit as instinctual as the habits of the hunter. He watched the distant skylines all around. From a far hill, he heard the thin bark of a coyote, and from somewhere beyond a distant ridge came the drumming of the sharp-tailed grouse as it performed its courtship dance. Spring was a time of renewal, and he hoped that the journey to meet Sitting Bull at the White Buttes would bring renewal for them all.

At the sound of hooves softly scraping against the ground, Cloud's hand went to the handle of the six-shooter. Taken Alive whistled as he rode to the crest, leading the packhorse carrying his deer. They quickly loaded and tied down Cloud's doe and were headed home before midmorning.

By the middle of the day, they were within sight of the herd of brood mares. Many of them had already given birth, so dozens of long-legged colts were suckling their mothers or testing their legs with quick sprints. A pair of teenage horse guards waved as they passed. Although the air was still cool, the boys were dressed only in leggings, breechclouts, and moccasins. Taken Alive and Cloud smiled. It was good to see that the hopefulness and eagerness of boys was alive and well.

Another pair of eyes had also been watching the horse herd and trained a long glass on the two hunters as they passed in front of him. Old Coyote had spent the night crawling to the top of a soap weed–covered knob. Swathed in grass and twigs from head to toe, he blended into the crest of the knob and hoped he had not unwittingly found an anthill. His only weapons were a knife and a six-shooter.

Lakota men wore their bows and quivers across the small of their backs when they were not actively on the hunt or engaged in battle. Old Coyote concentrated on the tops of the quivers of both men, specifically on the partially exposed feathers of their arrows. The men were moving past him at no more than thirty paces away. The one leading the packhorse carrying two deer carcasses had yellow markings on his arrows. He focused on the other man, but he could see only the tops of the arrows.

Old Coyote bit his lip in disappointment. For six days, he had been shadowing this encampment on the move. There were perhaps a thousand people or more, he estimated, and as many horses. They were traveling east. Each night, he positioned himself so that he could observe the group as they passed by the next morning. Two days ago, he had been nearly trampled by horses, but, fortunately, they had walked around the clump of sharp soap weeds where he had hidden.

There were no other Lakota camps in the area. Several winter camps had been along the Tongue River north of the plateau where he had found his sister's body. Those camps had obviously gathered and were heading east. He would follow as long as he needed to. He was certain that his sister's killer was here, somewhere. Days ago, he had ridden south within half a day of the Tongue River with his cousin Singing Elk, who had gone back north with the horses.

Old Coyote had decided to go it alone because he didn't want to put up with anyone else's attitudes or shortcomings. Also, it was easier to hide and become a shadow when alone and on foot. But he suddenly realized the truth of his grandfather's words, that revenge was a lonely path. Nevertheless, he was prepared to stay with it until he found the man he was looking for—or until they found him. His parents' grief was too painful for him to let his sister's death go unpunished. If there was a way to kill her worthless husband twice, he would do it. The worst he could do to him was to leave his bones where they had fallen and deny him a proper burial.

There was no certainty of success, that all would turn out the way he wanted. Only one thing was certain: Old Coyote would stick with his task until it came to an end. Someone would die. Fortune had favored him slightly when all of the Lakota camps along the Tongue River had gathered themselves and headed east.

The two hunters rode up a slight incline and his glass passed over the carcasses hanging over the packhorse. A slight flash of color caught his eye. He moved the glass back and saw the feathered end of an arrow protruding from the side of a carcass.

There was a small spot of red between the feathers.

Cloud and Taken Alive were not the only hunters who had been successful. A steady stream of men leading loaded packhorses came home throughout the day and into the evening. Women took over as their hunters brought home the meat. They quickly and skillfully skinned and cut up the carcasses. Hundreds of meat racks sprang up all over the village as chunks of meat from hindquarters were sliced into long, thin strips to air-dry. Entire sides of ribs were roasted over fire pits with thick beds of hot coals. As the sun went down, a festive atmosphere rose with the enticing odor of roasting meat. A few drums sang here and there, blending with the ringing laughter of children. Around the horse herds, the guards looked longingly toward the village and anxiously waited for their relief to come so they could join in the feasting.

A warm, pleasant spring day turned into a cool evening, which was no deterrent for a people that spent most of their lives outside. Families gathered around the outside cooking fires, reluctant to let the day end. Grandmothers told stories until little ones nodded off to sleep in their father's or mother's arms.

In the council lodge, Crazy Horse sat with the old men. Although they were traveling through territory that the Lakota considered theirs, there had rarely been large encampments here. The harvest of deer and a few elk had been unexpected, so the old men decided that a few more days of hunting to fill the meat containers would be good for the spirits of the people, as well as for their stomachs. Not to mention that a day or two more of rest and grazing would be good for the horses as well, since grass was plentiful. The ripples of laughter and the soft pounding of drums in spontaneous celebration of a good day was reassuring to the old men. It was a sure sign that the people still had the ability to make the best of what life put before them. To a man, they all hoped, and prayed often, that the buffalo would return. In the meantime, life had to go on.

"I think the Hunkpapa people will send a scout or two ahead," Black Shield commented as he set aside his bowl of soup. "We should do that too."

Grey Bull nodded in agreement. "I was thinking the same," he said. "If no one is there yet, they can leave a sign, or wait. They will probably do the same."

"It will be good to see them," Worm mused, "to hear how life has been for them. But mostly to be in the company of people who think like we do."

Worm's sentiments were not lost on Two Moons, who still blamed himself for the losses his people had suffered at the hands of the Long Knives not two months past. Why he ever thought white people, especially Long Knives, could be trusted to act honorably was a question that would bother him the rest of his life. Vivid memories of that dawn attack near the Powder River haunted him every day, especially since some of the wounded had been children.

"I hope the Hunkpapa headman has the answer," he said. "These white people have been a scourge for too long. They showed what they were made of at the Washita River, when they killed women and children and slaughtered all of those horses. And again, at Sand Creek, going on four years ago now. Thinking of those...of those times wounds the heart all over again."

The Cheyenne headman sighed and glanced quickly at the somber faces around him. "If my young men, and He Dog and his young men, had not fought back the way they did, we probably would have had to bury more of our people than we did. Or maybe they would have killed us all. I will never think kindly of white people again. So that is why I say I hope the Hunkpapa headman has the answer. Whatever it is, I will fight, and I will die making it happen."

"We are all in this together, my friend," High Eagle reminded the Cheyenne. "Our people have been allies for a long time, long enough for us to speak one another's languages. Now there are children and grandchildren who have Lakota and Cheyenne blood flowing in their veins, as well as the blood of the Blue Clouds. I, myself, think the only way we can be defeated is to forget that we are friends. Like you, I look forward to what Sitting Bull has to say, but somehow I think it will be to remind us of things we already know. I think he will say that standing shoulder-to-shoulder and back to back is what we need to do, in one way or another."

The old men talked away the evening, of good and bad times past, of victories won and battles lost. They spoke not to lament, but to remind one another of the roads they had traveled and the strength and wisdom they had gained.

In the cool of the evening, a man led a horse slowly, deliberately, among the lodges. He wore the shirt of a Cheyenne warrior and the hairstyle as well. Like everyone else, he seemed to be caught up in the lightheartedness of the evening, smiling and nodding as he went. At one cooking fire, he took a succulent rib from a woman, nodded his thanks, and went on.

He had slipped into the horse herd just after sundown, after he had changed into a Cheyenne shirt and braided his hair in the manner of a Cheyenne warrior. A horse guard's inquisitive look had been waved away nonchalantly as he found an old mare without a colt. His only fear was that someone would recognize the horse. But what was life unless one took risks now and then? A smattering of Cheyenne was all he knew, and he could probably explain that the mare had gotten loose. Of Lakota, he knew nothing, except to recognize names. But that was of no consequence to him now; it was only a matter of time before he found what he was looking for.

The Cheyenne lodges were of no interest to him. His sister's killer had been a Lakota, and he had already passed by almost half of the Lakota lodges. He had spent the evening wandering about in no particular pattern, not wanting to look too obvious in case someone were to notice him. Turning down yet another row of lodges, he cast a quick glance at the willow tripod standing to the right of a door to a lodge in the second row from the outside, and stopped.

Old Coyote's heart pounded as he paused to stroke the mare's neck, then bent low, as if checking her leg. His gaze settled on the tops of the arrows protruding from the quiver hanging from the tripod. Straightening, he stepped closer to the tripod, reached over carefully, and pulled one of the arrows out slightly, just enough to see the painted crest beneath the feathers. From his belt, he slipped out the broken arrow he had found among his sister's bones and held it next to the other. The markings were the same, exactly the same.

He had been incredibly lucky. He had not expected to find the matching arrow for the red-and-black crest so quickly. Furthermore, no one was home at this lodge, so he was able to look at the arrows without being detected. Looking around, he made up his mind quickly.

All around him were his enemies, and any one of the men, Cheyenne or Lakota, would not hesitate to kill him if they found him out. Yet part of him reveled in the moment. Living life on the edge, to the point of taunting death, was what he had been born to do. The Lakota and Cheyenne warriors in this village would understand that.

Past the outer row of lodges, he stopped and took a seat on the ground, letting the horse stand behind him. From his pouch, Old Coyote took strands of cord and began to braid them. He would sit here for a while working on his rope. Sooner or later, someone would return to the lodge where the red-and-black crested arrows hung in the quiver on the tripod. He had seen the hunter this morning, but judging from the size of the lodge, that hunter had a family.

Sweetwater Woman helped her mother, Star Woman, take the meat down from the large rack outside and move it to the one inside the lodge for the night. Several thin strips were drying on a trellis rack high above the coals over the inside fire pit. Song helped carry some of the meat, then settled against a chair to watch her mother and grandmother hang the strips of meat from long, thin rods, then tie the rods holding the meat high on the lodge poles. They were still working when Bearface returned from the council lodge.

"Are the old men still talking?" Star Woman teased her husband.

"No," he replied, a twinkle in his eye. "There is too much good meat to eat. But the feeling is we will stay here for two more days."

"Good." his wife replied. "I won't sleep past dawn tomorrow, and we can dry this meat so it will not spoil inside the containers."

"Granddaughter," Bearface said to Song, "did you get enough to eat, or are you still hungry, like me?"

"I ate ribs," the girl replied, returning the smile.

"Listening to all those old men makes me hungry," he said, looking around for food.

"Your grandfather just wants a reason to eat," Star Woman went on.

Sweetwater Woman helped her mother braid sweetgrass. "We should go home. I want to make stew for Song's father."

"Yes," the older woman agreed. "As soon as the sun comes out tomorrow, I will hang the meat outside. You can take your share tomorrow evening. It should be well on its way to drying by then."

The drums had stopped, and people were settling down for the night. For yet another time, he unraveled the cord and starting braiding again when a movement caught his eye. Looking up, he saw a woman and a girl return to the lodge. The woman took down the shield, the lance, and the bow and arrows from the tripod and went inside.

CHAPTER SEVENTEEN

The Missing

From among the short and gnarly windblown pine trees jutting stubbornly from the rim of the butte, a man intently watched three riders who were approaching almost leisurely. They had not deviated from their course since entering the meadow southwest of a line of yellowish and bare white hills. There was something vaguely familiar about them, but Hawk Eagle could not be absolutely certain of who they were. It had been nearly four months since he had seen any of the Crazy Horse people.

Nonchalantly, he pulled his bow from its case and strung it and took an arrow from the quiver. All the while, he remained seated among the pine trees bent by years of resisting the relentless winds that frequently blew over the rims of the flat, bare hills. Gauging the distance to be about two hundred paces, he nocked an arrow on the taut string, pulled his bow, and aimed at a sharp angle upward. There was a soft twang, and the arrow streaked skyward until it disappeared from view. But he was confident that it had come to earth a hundred paces or so in front of the approaching riders. They would see it if they did not turn aside or stop. Hawk Eagle waited.

Yellow Wolf was in the middle, flanked by Fast Horse on the left and Neck on the right. They were at least a day ahead of the main camp. Yellow Wolf was nearly past the arrow when he spotted the shaft impaled in the loose dirt next to a clump of grass. It was a Lakota arrow, clean and dry, though the blades of grass near it still held drops of moisture from the early-morning dew.

"Stop," he said calmly, and reached down to pluck the arrow from the dirt. From the bottom of the sinew wrapping at the ends of the two feathers to the nock, the shaft was painted blue. Yellow Wolf glanced around. "I think I know who this belongs to," he told the others.

"Where did it come from?" Fast Horse wondered.

A flicker of reflected light from the rim of the bare hills answered his question. "Up there," said Yellow Wolf. "Somebody has a looking glass."

In a moment, a figure rose to his feet, towering above the line of bent pine trees, and waved.

Yellow Wolf returned the wave. "Come on," he said, "this is a friend of mine. I want you to meet him."

Over a small fire on the bank of a narrow, busy creek in a secluded gully below the hills, the four men made tea and waited as two of the men skinned and gutted rabbits and roasted them over the flames. Within a stone's throw, four horses were picketed on ankle ropes, eagerly tearing at green grass and eating noisily.

"The first camp is less than half a day behind me," Hawk Eagle told his friend. "The second and third camps are a full day behind them. Our headman is with the second camp."

"Our people should be here this time tomorrow," Yellow Wolf said. "The Cheyenne are with us—Two Moons and his people. So there are more than a thousand of us."

"That is about our number, perhaps a little more," shrugged Hawk Eagle. "Shakes the Hill, an old medicine man, is with the first camp and leading the way. He is to select the sites for the people to pitch their camps."

"Yes, High Eagle and Worm are doing the same for us," Fast Horse said, poking at the rabbits to see if they had finished cooking.

Hawk Eagle nodded, smiling thoughtfully. "It will be a good time, I think, but things have changed. We saw buffalo, thirty or forty or so, but we did not chase them. Our holy men said prayers for them instead, to make them invisible so no hunters will see them."

Fast Horse nodded slowly. "My grandfather said he once saw a herd of so many animals that they took an entire day to cross the White Earth River. He said he and a friend counted four thousand, just on the outside edge, and he said there had to be at least a hundred times more than that."

Hawk Eagle shook his head as he tried to visualize that many buffalo in one place. "I hope those days will come again," he said softly.

Four pairs of eyes stared into the fire and at the two lean rabbit carcasses roasting over the flames.

"Yes," Fast Horse agreed. "It would be sad to think that is the only way they will live from now on, in the memories of our grandfathers."

Sweetwater Woman saw her mother walking ahead of her, leading her dun-colored riding horse and a big bay laden with drag poles. Behind the bay came the other two horses towing drag poles. All the pack frames were loaded high but tied securely.

Sweetwater Woman glanced north. Laughter and hundreds of conversations floated to her ears as the wide swath of humanity flowed like a colorful stream. The column of people and horses was fifty paces wide and four or five hundred paces long. On either side, teenage boys and young men moved the horse herds, and on the sides of the entire column rode the warriors. There was no hurry, only the steady pace of people and horses long used to such moves. Dogs were everywhere as well. They, too, were moving steadily, a few carrying small packs. This was one of those moments when Sweetwater Woman felt strongly connected to everyone and everything.

Elders rode on some of the pack frames, their gray heads swaying to and fro with the gentle rhythm of a slow-walking horse. Some of them held small children on their laps or sat next to them. Sweetwater Woman glanced around and moved her horse to the side to see if Song was walking with her grandmother. Her daughter was nowhere to be seen. Unconcerned, because groups of children walked together everywhere in the column, she urged her horse to a faster walk until she caught up to her mother.

"Have you seen Song?" she asked.

Star Woman turned to look up with a smile. "No," she said. "Maybe she is with her grandfather, or with the group of girls ahead of us."

Sweetwater Woman looked back and around, but she could not spot her daughter in the groups of people. They had been moving since just after sunrise, and she wondered if Song might be tired and wanted to ride.

Moving to the outside edge of the column, Sweetwater Woman dropped back and glanced into the passing depths of people and horses. She saw Walks Alone, Fast Horse's wife, and called out, "Have you seen my daughter?"

The woman shook her head.

Sweetwater Woman stopped her horse and carefully peered at the faces of children passing by. This was not like Song, to be so far from her mother.

Two Horns suddenly appeared, trotting his horse, so she called out to him. "Can you find my husband?" she asked. "Tell him I want to talk to him!"

The boy nodded and waved, then loped his horse toward the end of the horse herd on the south flank of the column and then around it.

She stayed on the edge of the column, looking intently now, probing and searching, a worried knot forming in her stomach. Approaching hoofbeats did not distract her until Two Horns and Cloud slid to a stop near her.

"Something wrong?" Cloud asked, noting his wife's face pinched with worry on the verge of outright fear.

"Song," she murmured. "I cannot find her!"

"When did you see her last?"

"Just after we started this morning," she replied, still looking into the passing crowd.

The long column of mostly women, children, and elderly numbered about eight hundred, with nearly two hundred horses being ridden or pulling drag poles. It would be easy enough for a nine-year-old girl to blend in and lose herself, unaware that her parents were looking for her.

Cloud turned to the boy next to him. "Can you ride to the front on this side and look?"

Two Horns nodded.

"I will do the same on the other side."

He reached out and grabbed his wife's arm. "Stay here, keep looking," he told her. "If you see her, put her on the horse behind you. Two Horns and I will meet at the front. When we find her, we will bring her to you."

When Cloud arrived at the head of the column, Two Horns was already there, behind Grey Bull and the other old men riding at the front. The boy shook his head.

Cloud hurried over to the two medicine men. "Uncle," he said to High Eagle, "my wife has not been able to find our daughter, and we could not see her anywhere. Can you signal for the people to halt?"

With a look of concern, High Eagle nodded and lifted high his eagle-banner staff and kept it aloft. Ponderously, the long column slowed to a halt. Cloud turned, urging his horse into a fast walk just at the edge of the crowd, as did Two Horns on the opposite side.

High Eagle went to the people at the front. "Pass the word back," he said. "Cloud and Sweetwater Woman are looking for their daughter."

Like grass bending before a moaning wind, the word went back through the column. By the time Cloud and Two Horns reached the end, people were already shaking their heads, indicating that Song had not been found.

Cloud rejoined Sweetwater Woman, who was now dismounted and waiting with her mother and several other women. He shook his head, and his heart broke as his wife's tiny, pale hands flew to her mouth, her eyes pleading for an answer to the sudden, bewildering dilemma.

Goings and Taken Alive arrived, just ahead of Little Bird and High Eagle.

"What do you want to do?" Goings asked Cloud.

"Ride back toward where we camped," he said.

"We will come with you," Taken Alive announced.

"Meanwhile, we will look again here and wait for you," the medicine man promised.

Cloud dismounted and took Sweetwater Woman in his arms. "We will find her," he whispered to her. "We will find her." He wiped her tears and held her for a moment longer. As he pulled away, the circle of women—mothers and grandmothers, all—closed in tenderly. In another moment, hoofbeats pounded and then faded away into the west.

The wide swath of trail left where the drag poles scratched the ground was not difficult to follow. Four abreast, they rode at a lope, thirty or forty paces apart, scanning the area on either side. On hills and rises, they paused to glass all around. Taken Alive blew on his eagle-bone whistle, its piercing notes loud enough to startle deer. But Song was nowhere to be found.

The horse he had taken was old, and Old Coyote was correct in assuming it did not have the stamina it once did. But it was calm and responsive, which were far more important for the time being. His right arm encircled the girl. Without so much as a whimper, she sat in front of him with her tiny hands holding tightly to the mare's mane. Not once did she glance back at him as they rode steadily south. But she had put up a determined fight when he had grabbed her near the creek. Luckily, he had managed to clamp a hand over her mouth before she could utter a sound. Any remorse he might have felt was swept away by the memory of his sister's bones scattered on the windy plateau, even when he felt a tear fall on his hand.

It was next to impossible to read anything from the hundreds, if not thousands, of tracks in and around the site where they had camped for four days. It seemed that nothing but horse droppings and freshly buried fire pits had been left behind. A thorough search of all the surrounding gullies turned up nothing. Taken Alive shrilled away on his eagle-bone whistle, but only a slight breeze answered with a melancholy whisper.

Goings whistled from the edge of the meadow where the encampment had been, waving to Cloud and the others. When they joined him, he grimly pointed to a slender pole impaled in the ground. From the top hung a strip of pale blue cloth, and tied to it was the feathered end of a broken shaft and a girl's moccasin.

Cloud grabbed the broken arrow and the small moccasin. The arrow was one of his, faded by wind and rain and sun. He could feel his heart thumping in his temples. He held the moccasin tenderly.

"What could this mean?" Taken Alive asked hoarsely.

"I think it means my daughter was taken, probably by a Crow."

Goings was beginning to understand. "Could this have something to do with…?"

Cloud nodded. "Yes, it does," he hissed. "The woman and the white Crow who ambushed us."

"What kind of a person takes revenge against children?" Taken Alive spat, his voice dripping with contempt.

Cloud shook his head. "Perhaps that is not his purpose, or I hope it is not." He pondered the broken arrow in his hand. "I think this is a challenge. This is a challenge sent by a man who wants to meet face-to-face."

"Who? Where?" Taken Alive asked, incredulous.

"On that ridge, that plateau," Goings replied, looking grimly at Cloud. "That would be my guess."

"I think you may be right," Cloud agreed.

Taken Alive pointed to the broken arrow. "Yes, I see now. You left that there and someone found it, and he has been looking for you."

Cloud nodded and pointed to the southwest. "It is a full day's ride to the butte where we were ambushed."

"How can you be sure that is where he is taking her?" Little Bird asked.

"Look," Cloud replied, pointing to the row of five stones at the base of the pole. They pointed to the southwest.

"What do you want to do?" Taken Alive asked. "Just tell us."

Cloud looked at Taken Alive. "My friend, if you could take word back to my wife. I do not know what you can say to her, except that I know where our daughter is."

Taken Alive nodded, his jaw clenched. Cloud turned to Goings and Little Bird. "Follow me, but stay well back. I want this man to think I am alone."

"We will wait until you are at the horizon," Goings told him. "We know where that butte is."

Taken Alive reached over and grabbed Cloud's arm. "My friend," he said, "can you be certain that this man has taken your daughter to that butte? Perhaps he has taken her north, toward Crow lands."

"This is my best guess. This man, whoever he is, wants to avenge the woman I killed. I do not blame him for that, because he is her father or some relative. But he left all the signs for me to follow, and that butte is where that woman died. I will go there. I have no other choice. If no one is there, then I will go north into Crow lands."

"We will follow you to the butte," Little Bird assured him. "Leave sign if you can."

"There are deep cuts in the west face of the butte," Cloud recalled. "I climbed up through one at the north end. I will use that same approach. I will mark the side of it or leave my horse there. Do not use the same one. Go farther south, climb up, and circle back to the north. If anything happens to me, take my daughter home to her mother."

"You can count on it," Goings promised. "But we will all be going home together."

Old Coyote returned with another armload of dry brush and dropped it near the small, crackling fire. He had built a windbreak to shelter it, and on a makeshift spit he hung a plucked sharp-tailed grouse. Grease dropped into the fire as the bird roasted, causing the fire to hiss loudly. Nearby, the old mare grazed contentedly, though her movements were restricted by the walking hobbles on her front ankles.

The girl did not, would not, look at him directly. She sat staring at the cooking bird, her ankles and hands bound securely. She was a beautiful child with fair skin and reddish brown hair, as his sister's had been when she was still a small girl. He didn't know her name, and it didn't matter. He would give her a new name.

The girl's father would come if he found the sign Old Coyote had left for him. It was only a question of when—perhaps today yet, or tomorrow, or the day after. Or maybe he would come in the night. But he would come for his daughter, and Old Coyote would face him man-to-man, and he did not plan on losing the fight. After he killed the Lakota, he would take the girl home, north beyond the Yellowstone River to his mother and father.

"I will not hurt you," he said to her, knowing she couldn't understand him. "You cannot know my words, but you will in time. My mother and father will teach you to be a proper Crow woman—as my sister was."

As the man walked away and climbed a rock and looked around with his long glass, Song braced one bare foot against the other and pulled at the cords around her ankles. They gave a little. If she could stretch them enough, she thought she might be able to slide her feet through and then slip them through her leggings, the tops of which she had loosened with her hands when the man wasn't looking.

If she could slip her feet out, she would run, bare feet or not. She was afraid, but so far she had been able to stifle the sobs that wanted to explode from her throat. Her father would come, and other men as well. Song was somehow certain of it. This man had hung her moccasin from a pole he had stuck into the ground. Tied to it was one of her father's broken arrows. Something was happening that had to do with her father, she was sure of it.

The man had been at the little creek helping to fill water bladders. He looked like a Cheyenne, though she had never seen him around. But he had been helpful to the women and the girls, helping them fill water skins while everyone was breaking camp for the move. Her water skin had slipped out of his hands and spilled. He had quickly picked it up and began to fill it as the other girls left. Suddenly, he grabbed her and ran down a gully. Morning seemed so long ago.

The man jumped down from the rock and walked toward her. She stopped pulling at the ankle thongs. She was hungry, and the roasting bird smelled good. If she were to run away, she would need to be strong.

"I am hungry," she told him when he returned. Song pointed to the grouse.

Old Coyote was surprised to hear her speak, and he knew what she wanted. He pulled at a leg, but it did not tear away. It was not yet fully cooked.

"Wait," he said to her. "It will be done soon."

Old Coyote took the bag he had left behind the windbreak and moved away from the fire and sat down on a bare patch of ground. He opened the bag and pulled out a shirt. Pulling off the shirt he wore, he slipped his own over his head.

Song watched, though the man sat with his back to her. After he put on a different shirt, he started working on his hair, and he was doing something to his face. In a while, he closed the bag and stood and returned to the fire.

He didn't look the same. His shirt was cut differently, and the top of his hair stood up straight, but it was the paint on his face that caught her attention the most. Two wide, red lines were painted down across his eyebrows, over his eyelids, and down past the corners of his mouth. Song knew what it meant. He was preparing to fight, to face someone in battle. A shiver went up her back.

Now she knew what he was. He was not Cheyenne, he was a Crow, one of the enemy people from the north. And she had a feeling that the man was waiting to do battle with her father.

CHAPTER EIGHTEEN

Getting Down the Hill

Worm and High Eagle sent the camp criers through the column to announce that the people were to stop and pitch their lodges and wait until Song, the daughter of Sweetwater Woman and Cloud, had been found and brought home. Lines of people and horses moved north and down into a broad meadow with a creek at the eastern edge.

As Star Woman sat with her daughter, several women and girls unpacked Sweetwater Woman's lodge and pitched it skillfully and swiftly. When the sun was just past the middle of the sky, an entire encampment had blossomed.

Crazy Horse stood amid a gathering of warriors and listened to Taken Alive describe the events of the morning.

"Goings and Little Bird are following Cloud," he told them. "He will probably reach the butte before sundown. He is certain that it is one man, a Crow, who has taken his daughter."

"Why?" someone asked.

"Revenge," Taken Alive replied.

High Eagle worked his way through the circle of men. "I was there," he said, "along with Little Bird and Cloud and his family. We were returning home from visiting our relatives at the burial place. We were ambushed; someone was shooting from the rim of the butte. Little Bird was hit and, later, one of the horses. After making sure we were all safe, Cloud jumped back on his horse and rode toward the butte. They shot at him—two, three times. He climbed to the top and took out two people. One of them was a white giant, he said. He was right. He showed me the body—a white man as big, or bigger, than Touch the Clouds. Perhaps he became a Crow, because he was dressed as one. The other was a young woman."

"When my friend shot her," Crazy Horse said, taking up the story, "he did not know it was a woman. He was sick over it, but there was nothing to be done."

"Someone found the bodies and probably took a piece of Cloud's arrow that had broken off," Taken Alive continued. "That piece—along with one of the girl's moccasins—was left on a pole where we had camped. We found it this morning. Cloud is certain the man is waiting for him on top of the butte. He is probably the dead woman's father."

"We cannot let this pass," Crazy Horse declared. "I am going south to help. It would be good if all of you standing here can come with me. Likely, my friend does not need our help, but that does not mean we should not be ready to give it."

As Star Woman stepped out of her daughter's lodge to help Sweetwater Woman with her work outside, she saw a line of armed and mounted warriors approach and then stop. Crazy Horse came from another direction, leading his horse. His wife walked beside him, carrying a container of meat in her hands.

"Sister," he said to Sweetwater Woman, and then laid a hand on her shoulder, "I remember a day ten years ago when you rode with your husband up into the mountains behind the Long Knife town on Buffalo Creek. That was before your daughter was born and before we defeated the Long Knives that winter," he recalled. "I have...I have thought about that day often, each time I think of our daughter. Every Lakota is precious to me, especially one who will grow up to be the mother of warriors." He pointed to the mounted warriors. "We will help your husband bring your daughter home safe."

"I have a little meat," Black Shawl said gently. "We can prepare a stew while we wait."

Shadows were growing long on the plateau. Hawks and eagles floated on the winds high above, and meadowlarks sang their bright songs. But nothing came close. Occasionally, Song brushed an ant off her bare foot, but always she kept an eye on the man. Several times he had climbed the rock at the edge of the meadow and looked around through a long glass. Each time he returned to the fire, he said something to her that she could not understand.

"Your father will come," Old Coyote muttered to himself. "I know he will. The questions are, when and from what direction? But it does not matter. I am ready for him."

Old Coyote sighed deeply and sat back. "My sister was not like other girls," he told his small captive. "She wanted to learn how to shoot the bow, and she learned how to shoot a rifle. She was a good shot, better than some men. The only stupid thing she ever did was marry that white man." Old Coyote's eyes flashed in anger. "She would not listen to me!"

Song brushed another ant off her ankle. She was thirsty and reached for the water flask he had placed near her. After two swallows, she put it back. The grouse had tasted good. She had eaten both legs because they were small. But water was more important, her father had taught her.

Sunset was not far off. The sun hung on the edge of the jagged skyline to the west, and the air was not as warm as it had been earlier.

Old Coyote stood and draped the Cheyenne shirt over the girl's shoulders and walked to the rock for another look around. He returned and put more twigs and dry brush on the fire. On the opposite side of where she sat, he piled several stones high to make a reflector, a small wall to push the heat in her direction. Then he left to search for more wood.

Finally slipping beneath the jagged horizon, the sun painted a few stray clouds blood red before they faded into a soft orange and, last, a cool lavender. Dusk fell onto the land. Nighthawks began to prowl the skies, for the darkness was their time to hunt for insects, few though there were at this time of year. But hunt they did, because hunger never rests.

As the darkness deepened, moment by moment, the world at the top of the plateau grew smaller and smaller, seeming to exist only within the reach of the dim light from the small fire. There was no moon this night, and, although stars appeared, the land grew darker and cooler.

Song slid forward, closer to the fire. Coyotes started to sing all around, and she knew the occasional deeper songs she heard were wolves.

The man returned with more dry brush and added some to the fire. Small orange sparks flew up and floated on the soft breeze before they faded and died out. In the firelight, his face was shadowy and his eyes grew more and more wary.

Old Coyote had a thought to bring the mare closer to the fire, so he stepped quietly through the grass and sagebrush. He untied the walking hobbles, which were the reins, and fashioned a halter with them. A few paces from the fire, he tied the end of the reins to the base of a thick sagebrush stalk. In the firelight, he could see the horse's every reaction. At that moment, the horse lifted her head and stared off, listening to the shrill chorus of distant coyotes. Old Coyote watched for a moment, then returned to sit by the fire.

At first, Song thought an insect had bumped into the back of her head. It was nothing more than a light tap. But it happened again. Then a pebble landed softly by her feet. Song resisted the urge to look around. She swallowed the lump in her throat with a deep breath. It was her father. It had to be. She stared at the tiny pebble next to her bare toes and slowly reached for it. In her palm, it felt warm.

Old Coyote slid the sheath with the knife in it closer to his hip bone. The knife was attached to his belt. He had tucked the six-shooter loosely under his belt next to the knife. He wanted both weapons, his only hand weapons, within easy reach. He began to regret that he did not have his rifle, or even his short fighting lance. Large weapons were cumbersome, but he could have hidden them somewhere and gone back to retrieve them. It was of no use to lament, though. He was surprised he had come this far; he could have been found out at any time. All in all, he had been very lucky.

With every new outburst from the coyotes wailing in the darkness, the horse looked up nervously, its nostrils flaring to test the breeze. Stars now filled the dark void overhead as the last glow of dusk in the west gave way to night.

Old Coyote looked across the fire. The girl was sitting calmly with her knees drawn up. Something scurried through the brush behind him, perhaps a rabbit, by the sound of it. The horse glanced sideways but didn't seem alarmed.

Old Coyote stood and stared into the darkness, beyond the reach of the fire's glow, in the direction of the scuffling. Somewhere, probably in the wide valley west of the plateau where a meandering creek was flanked by groves of trees, an owl called softly. A shiver went up his back—it was the first time he had heard an owl this spring.

An instant after he turned back to face the fire, the first thing he saw that was not there before was the glint of a gun barrel in the firelight.

Click-click. The hammer of a six-shooter had been drawn back.

Old Coyote could hear the man's muffled voice, deep and low. The girl rolled sideways and away from the fire as the man stepped forward. A tall man, grim-faced and angry.

Old Coyote stood motionless. He knew that any sudden movement would be his last.

With his left hand, Cloud pulled a knife from the sheath at his belt and dropped it to the ground next to Song. "Cut the bindings around your ankles," he told his daughter.

Grabbing the knife, Song cut through the thongs.

"Did he hurt you?"

"No. He gave me food and water."

"I see. Now, go around to my side and go out of the light and lay down, flat, on the ground. Quickly!"

Song scrambled on her hands and knees and ducked behind a large sagebrush bush. Her father did not move, yet there was something steadfast and powerful in the way he stood, like a rock in the middle of a stream. She wanted to cry but swallowed the lump in her throat.

An eagle-bone whistle suddenly shrilled from the darkness behind Old Coyote, startling him.

"My friend," a voice called out to Cloud, "we are here!" It was Goings.

The darkness came alive with shadows. One man after another stepped into the light of the fire, until they encircled Cloud and his captive. Taken Alive stepped up next to Cloud, holding Song in his arms.

Two men, a Cheyenne named Bobtail Horse and Little Bird, stepped behind the Crow and took the man's knife and six-shooter. From behind them, another circled to the front of the man and turned to face him.

Old Coyote's knees trembled. He knew this man. A thin scar ran from the corner of the left side of his mouth back to his earlobe. He was slender and dressed plainly. He was the one called Crazy Horse. His eyes were black and intense and held no pity. A hand rested casually on the handle of a six-shooter in his belt. If the girl's father didn't kill him, this one would.

All around, more men stepped into the firelight. Cloud finally lowered his six-shooter, but the anger in his eyes did not waver.

"How many of you are there?" he asked, grabbing his daughter from Taken Alive.

For a long moment, he held her tightly, breathing in the scent of her hair. Song's small arms encircled her father's neck and she held on and finally allowed herself a few soft sobs.

Crazy Horse glanced around. "Twenty-four, I think. You did not think you would have fun with this foolish Crow by yourself, did you?"

Cloud smiled, relaxing for the first time since this morning. "Now I guess I will share the fun."

"What did you have in mind?" Crazy Horse wanted to know, tossing a cautious glance toward Song.

"Since he took my daughter's moccasins, I thought I would take his," Cloud replied.

Taken Alive stepped up. "First, I think we should send two men to let this child's mother know she is safe. Then we should feed her. Besides, I am hungry, if no one else is."

Lone Hill stepped forward, just ahead of his friend Horn Cloud. "We will go, Uncle. We know a shortcut from here."

"I am grateful," Cloud told them. "I know her mother is anxious. Tell her we will start back at daylight."

The fire burned high. Old Coyote couldn't see it, but he heard it crackling. Most of the Lakota were sitting or standing around it, as far as he could tell. He lay facedown just at the edge of the light, his arms behind him, bound tightly at the wrists. Around his neck was a noose with a cord attached to the bindings around his ankles. His ankles were drawn forward, just above his buttocks. If he relaxed his legs, he began to choke himself with the noose. He knew that, sooner or later, his leg muscles would start to cramp and he would have to straighten his legs. He had a choice: endure the excruciating pain of leg cramps to stay alive, or choke to death if he tried to straighten his legs to relieve the cramping. To make matters worse, if that was possible, he was completely naked and the night air had a chill. By morning—if he lived that long—it would be cold.

The conversation around the fire was punctuated with occasional laughter. He had to wonder how much of that had to do with him. Then he heard another sound—somewhere from the night came the soft, sobbing call of an owl.

A temporary camp materialized on the plateau. Brush shelters stood around the fire, and the smell of peppermint tea wafted on the breeze. Horses grazed nearby in the darkness. The largest shelter had been constructed for Cloud and Song, a low, dome-shaped structure covered with enough brush to block the wind. The floor space inside was covered with hides.

Wrapped snugly in a deer robe, Song sat on her father's lap eating leisurely from a plate fashioned out of bark and filled with dried meat. On her feet were new moccasins one of the men had made for her. An array of toys lay all around, crafted of whatever material was at hand by men who had daughters or younger sisters of their own. Under her arm was a doll made of twisted grass. She had just finished playing with a small hoop that could be twirled on a stick. The stick in this case had been someone's arrow, without the point, and the hoop had been made from a slender green willow cut from the small stream below the plateau.

She smiled shyly at the men as she played and ate, and the day's ordeal began to fade from her mind. Somewhere between the last bite of food and the last sip of tea and trying to decide which toy to play with next, her head fell back onto her father's chest and she slept.

Morning came, clear, bright, and chilly. Sagebrush leaves and grass sparkled with dewdrops. Several sleeping fires still burned low, but most of the men were already awake and checking on the horses. Cloud handed Song a cup of hot tea as she wiped the sleep from her eyes.

Taken Alive sat with them. "I have a comb," he told her. "I know your father will help you comb your hair and fix your braids. I do not want your mother to think we did not take good care of you. Want to borrow my comb?"

She smiled, nodded, and took the comb in her hand.

Old Coyote took a deep breath. Sometime in the night, someone had cut the cord to the noose around his neck. He was still lying facedown and naked, so very cold, yet still alive. He didn't know what to think, and then he realized that no matter what he thought, or wanted, the situation was out of his hands. The only thing he could do was wait. He knew the Lakota had talked and decided his fate.

With his ear pressed to the ground, he could hear the soft thud of the horses' hooves moving out together. There was some conversation, and then footsteps came his way.

Hands grabbed him by each arm and yanked him to a sitting position. Stiff and sore muscles in his legs protested, forcing him to grit his teeth. Four men stood around him. He kept his eyes forward and didn't look at their faces, but he knew one of them was the one called Crazy Horse. At a word from him, two of the others pulled Old Coyote to his feet.

Crazy Horse stepped directly in front of him, and Old Coyote immediately felt the intensity in the man's cold stare. He averted his eyes and looked out over the valley to the west, until he felt the tip of a buffalo-horn war club under his chin, forcing him to look directly into the merciless stare.

The Lakota war leader motioned to one of the men, who stepped closer. A Cheyenne, from the cut of his clothes.

Crazy Horse spoke, his voice low and menacing, like the long, low growl of an enraged wolf. The Cheyenne put the words into Crow, and Old Coyote understood them: "We see you, we kill you. We see you, we kill you."

Old Coyote swallowed past the dryness in his throat and nodded.

Crazy Horse glanced at one of the other men.

Old Coyote felt a tug at his braid, the end of which had hung to his waist, then saw it thrown to the ground. He felt a tug at his other braid, then saw it, too, tossed into the dirt. Then the bindings around his ankles were cut, but not those around his wrists.

The Lakota moved aside, and someone shoved Old Coyote from behind. Naked and barefoot, his short hair tousled by the breeze, he took the first shaky steps into his new life. Whether he would feel an arrow between his shoulder blades before he reached the end of the plateau, or whether he would stumble into the path of a bear or a puma, he didn't know. But he was alive, and if he made it home, his mother and father would not have to mourn for him too. He wondered if that would be worth the shame of failure.

But, first, he had to make it down the hill.

Song swayed with the motion of the horse as she sat in front of her father. Only once did she glance back out of curiosity. "Where is that man?" she asked tentatively.

"He is going home."

"Where is his home?"

"North," Cloud told her, "beyond the Elk River."

"Why did he come here, and why…why did he, ah…"

"You mean, why did he take you?"

She nodded, her head bobbing against his chest.

"I think it was because he was sad. He had a sister, I think, and…and she died."

"How do you know that? Did he tell you?"

"Yes," he replied. "Yes. In a way, he did."

"Oh."

"When we get home, you can show your mother all of your new toys."

She looked up and smiled, squinting in the bright sun.

CHAPTER NINETEEN

Men of Stature

No one knew exactly how many lodges were in the meadows near the White Buttes, but one old man took the trouble to climb up to one of the sandstone rims and look from there. He counted just over four hundred. As for the number of people, perhaps over two thousand, everyone agreed. Horses were another matter, however. Some of the horse guards thought there might be at least four thousand, a third of which were new colts.

There were three distinct camps in the flat meadows, two in a north-south line even with the buttes. The third, Sitting Bull's camp, sprawled to the east. Together, the three formed roughly the shape of an arrowhead. The Crazy Horse people were in the camp at the south end. Each camp was arranged in a precise circle, with three to four rows of lodges set up in C-shaped patterns with the openings to the east.

A festive air permeated the village. Drums pounded and people danced for three nights in a row as each village hosted the doings that went far into the night. Relatives from the far-flung reaches of the nation were happy to see one another, some after a year or more. Many children and young people were introduced to relatives they had often heard about but never met. Friendships were renewed, especially among the elderly. As the people came together, at first it seemed the days were not long enough to see and visit everyone. But after several days, the initial busyness diminished somewhat, though the excitement remained. Many of the old men were anxious to get to the issues at hand.

In the space between the three camps, several warrior society lodges had been erected. In the center of them was a new council lodge, the biggest and tallest anyone had ever seen. It was nearly thirty long paces across, and as tall, and the story of how it came to be circulated quickly. Sitting Bull had asked the older women in his extended family to cut down and sew together three old lodge coverings. Although the forty-two hides were pieced together from old lodges, the long spruce poles were new, and so was the purpose for the new-old lodge.

On the afternoon of the fourth day of the gathering, Sitting Bull invited the warrior leaders into the lodge. He had sensed something palpable in the air and wanted to take advantage of it. After all, if he was nothing else, he was shrewd. Two other shrewd, gray-haired old men had been keeping an eye on things and an ear to the ground. Sitting near the council lodge in the shade of a low frame covered with hides, Red Shirt, an Oglala, and Eagle Man, a Hunkpapa, watched—and not without a certain sense of pride—the warrior leaders arriving one by one and two by two.

"How many people are with Spotted Tail and Red Cloud at the agencies is hard to know," Eagle Man commented, "but it seems to me that we have our share of warrior leaders."

"Having enough warrior leaders is a good thing, but we must have enough fighting men to follow them," Red Shirt pointed out.

"True," Eagle Man agreed. "But it is good to see that we have such men with us here."

"And we have the greatest of them all," Red Shirt said resolutely as he pointed to Crazy Horse ducking into the council lodge.

"Yes. And we cannot forget the one man who brought us all here," Eagle Man was quick to reply. "He is gathering the warrior leaders to him, and the people are watching, as we are. Old people are the symbol of wisdom. Our warrior leaders are a symbol of our strength as a nation. When we see a man like Crazy Horse, anyone who knows him or has heard of him thinks of the victories he has won, and of the strength of his medicine. That is what Sitting Bull is doing. By bringing all these warrior leaders together, and by having all of us watch them walk through the camps, he is reminding us of our victories, our strengths."

Red Shirt chuckled. "Yes. And he is also showing his power and influence. Those warrior leaders are going to him to listen to what he has to say."

As the two old men sat in the shade, inside the lodge Sitting Bull sat quietly, waiting patiently. The Hunkpapa leader was not a tall man, and he was still fit and trim for a man approaching his sixth decade. He did walk with a noticeable limp, however, testimony to his early years as a warrior when an enemy's bullet had smashed into his right hip. Flecks of gray were beginning to streak through his hair, which he wore in two long braids wrapped in otter skins. His eyes were large and dark and missed nothing, and in combination with a long, straight nose and a wide, slightly down-turned mouth, he exuded an air of strength and no nonsense. But he was quick to smile as well, and poke fun at himself to put others at ease. All in all, no single Lakota commanded as much respect from young and old alike as he did.

As Red Shirt and Eagle Man had pointed out, among the Lakota and their Cheyenne allies were many experienced military leaders tested mightily by the fire of battle. Sadly, however, some of the Lakota leaders were at the agencies near Camp Robinson, fighting boredom instead of Long Knives or Crow or Shoshone. Fortunately, several sat in the council lodge with the Hunkpapa leader, such as He Dog, Black Moon, and Good Road. Two of the Cheyenne were the venerable Two Moons and the accomplished Bobtail Horse. Two of the best were sitting with the Hunkpapa leader: Gall, also a Hunkpapa, and Crazy Horse.

Tall and broad-shouldered, with handsome features, Gall certainly looked the part of a decisive and successful battlefield leader. At times, he was self-confident to the point of arrogance, though his confidence was well founded, partly because he enjoyed a special status as the protégé of Sitting Bull.

But no one except Sitting Bull was as well known as Crazy Horse. His battlefield exploits were legendary. Many still talked about how he and a small group of decoys baited a column of soldiers into a surround and eventual defeat at the Battle of the Hundred in the Hand. Warriors still described how he was always the first to charge the enemy and the last to leave the battlefield in raids against the Crow. Although he was famous throughout Lakota territory, many of the Sitting Bull people were seeing him for the very first time. They were surprised that he was so boyishly slender, and quiet to the point of being almost painfully shy. That characteristic endeared him to the elderly.

The presence of such renowned military leaders gave the people a feeling of strength and confidence. It was an unexpected gift, in a sense, and Sitting Bull wanted to make the most of it. After all, sitting next to him was Crazy Horse, a man whom warriors followed in a heartbeat, one respected by experienced warrior leaders older than he was. The challenge for Sitting Bull was to convince the old men that their warriors were the point of the lance that could drive away the whites, and the shaft of the lance would have to be the support of the people. But for the people to give and maintain their support, first the old leaders would have to give their unwavering support.

Not until after the pipe circled the double row of men did Sitting Bull speak. "My relatives," he began, "it is good to see all of you. I am grateful that you honored my invitation. When I sent my messengers out last winter, I could only hope that someone would take me seriously. It does my heart good to see all the people here. We Hunkpapa were here for a day before anyone else came. Three young Oglala men were already here, but when I saw my friends Worm and High Eagle come over the horizon with their people behind them, my heart danced."

Hard-bitten warriors smiled as the Hunkpapa medicine man expressed his joy at something as simple as an arrival. Yet, to him, it was not simple.

"Those of us here today may be the only hope for our nation," he said, pointing out a possibility many in the lodge had considered. "It is hard to say how many more of our people will come. With us, the Hunkpapa, are Mniconju, Oohenunpa, and Sihasapa families. There are Sicangu among the Oglala, and, of course, we are glad some of our Cheyenne friends are with us. And someone tells me that there are some Blue Clouds as well. The messengers I sent east returned with word that our Dakota and Nakota relatives will try to join us—if the Great Muddy River is not too high and if some of them were able to cross before the ice began to break up. If they cannot cross, and if no one comes from the agencies to the south, we are the only hope."

He paused to gaze around at the circle of strong faces. "But I refuse to think we are the last hope. I say that because there is another generation waiting. Although we may be few in number, our willingness to endure any hardship to stay free will make one man fight like he is three or four. That is what we must teach the next generation. For that, I look to all of you."

"We will do what we must, Uncle," Good Road said quietly. "I have two young sons. Their mother and I did not raise them up to be anything but Lakota. We have made our choices, my family and I."

"You speak a truth that will help us persevere," replied Sitting Bull. "The more of us who share that truth, the harder it will be for anyone to defeat us. That truth is just as important as guns and bullets. So, I must ask all of you, each of you, to help our fighting men to understand that truth.

If we run out of bullets and arrows, then we fight with clubs and lances. If we have no clubs and lances, we fight with our hands. The power in the man who fights to the end is the willingness to endure, whatever it takes."

"Many of us have been speaking and listening to the young men," Gall explained. "I have not found any doubt among them as to what they want to do. So we must show them the way, as you say, and we will."

"Good! Good!" the Hunkpapa medicine man exclaimed. "That will help me to convince the old men that we should stand together until we accomplish the difficult task ahead of us. Some of them do not understand the danger we face. Some of them are willing to wait and see what happens. I say we cannot wait, we should not wait, any longer."

"Uncle, what do you think we should do first?" asked He Dog.

"We have people and horses to feed," replied Sitting Bull. "Water, food, and grass are what we need. And to sleep peacefully at night. It is not likely that anyone will think of attacking us—anyone but Long Knives, that is."

"We have scouts as far as half a day out, all around us," Crazy Horse pointed out quietly. "In pairs. If they see anything we need to know, one will come back and the other will stay behind to keep an eye out. They are watching for game as well as for enemies."

"We have sentinels on the high points around the camp," Gall added. "Guards are in with the horses at night."

"Good," Sitting Bull said, absorbed in thought. "While we stay safe, the people must not want for anything. And as far as grazing, how long do you think we can stay here, near the buttes, until we have to find new grass?"

"Ten to fifteen days," Good Road estimated. "We can take the brood mares and colts to graze during the daylight to a different area each day and bring them back to the camp at night," he suggested. "And we can break them up into smaller herds. It will be a good task for the older boys. The horses we ride every day, and the buffalo runners and warhorses, we can keep close."

"In the meantime," Gall said, "we can look for the next campsite. There is a running creek southwest of here with good grass on either side of it."

"Good. If our horses are strong, then so are we," said Sitting Bull.

The Hunkpapa medicine man paused for a moment, glancing quickly around with an inner sense of satisfaction. Every man waited with rapt attention.

"That leads me to my next concern, though I think I know the answer. How many fighting men do we have?"

Crazy Horse cleared his throat. "Around three hundred. Most of us have a gun of some kind, a lot of muzzleloaders, some breechloaders. A few that can hold seven bullets at a time. Just about everyone has a six-shooter. Like always, a steady supply of bullets and powder is the difficult thing."

"Ah, yes," Sitting Bull muttered. "Bullets. I sent messengers to some of the sheep-eater people far to the western mountains. I heard they have good trade with the whites, so I thought we could do some trade with them for bullets. Very little came of it. I am afraid bullets will always be a problem."

"That is why we tell everyone to hunt with the bow," said Black Moon. "We can recover an arrow that misses, but not a bullet. And a bow is quiet. It does not scare the animals away."

"A wise approach," Sitting Bull agreed. "And how about our younger men? I know they have the skills, but what about the will?"

"Those who are fifteen, sixteen, and seventeen," Crazy Horse replied, "are the most inexperienced. They do have the skills, so we will give them as much practice as we can. Older warriors will take two or three along every time they go out on patrol."

"I am glad to hear it. That is as it should be." Leaning back against his willow chair, Sitting Bull sighed. "This is a good spring, the best I have seen in a few years. The summer grasses will be good for the elk and the deer, as well as for our horses. It is important to our future for wise men to talk. The more they talk, the more answers they will find. I must depend on you, the leaders that you are, to give us that chance."

"We will do that," Crazy Horse replied. "Our eyes and ears, our scouts, are out there. Enemies may come, but we will keep them away. All the people will be safe."

Sitting Bull nodded, his eyes bright. "We are a free people. We eat, we sleep, we dance, and we laugh. We will face our problems and our enemies straight on. For every step we take backward, we will take two forward. That has been our way since the days of our grandfathers' grandfathers. It was our strength then, and it is our strength now."

Eagle Man and Red Shirt watched the warrior leaders file out of the council lodge. A few of them paused to chat with the two old men before going on their way.

"Grandfather," they would say to each of them, "it is good to see you."

The old men smiled, pleased to be acknowledged. For a moment, each of them remembered their days as younger men, when their hair was still black and their joints were not stiff, those days when they were the first line of defense, as these men now were. "Good to see you as well, Grandson," they would reply.

Around the two old men, throughout the three camps, young and old were going about the day. Younger children played games. Older children helped with various tasks. Girls watched over babies bundled in cradleboards, or hung out sleeping robes to freshen in the sun, or helped grandmothers keep an eye on meat drying on racks. Boys took family horses to water or helped move small herds to a new grazing area. Occasional laughter and squeals of children and the muffled rumble of a horse herd being moved blended with the distant trills of meadowlarks floating across the prairie and the high, shrill cries of hawks and eagles soaring on cool breezes. It was all worth a good smoke, so Eagle Man reached for his pipe bag.

Sitting Bull waited until the last man stepped out of the council lodge before he turned to Crazy Horse. Known to but a few, the two had met during the winter when Crazy Horse had traveled northeast with his wife. They had talked for days. Crazy Horse realized that no one understood the full extent of the white problem the way Sitting Bull did.

The Black Hills were now the stronghold of gold-hungry white men. According to Sitting Bull, it would not have mattered if the Lakota had killed all those who came to dig for gold. Others would have come in their place.

In one generation, the numbers of buffalo had diminished astonishingly. No one, not even the wisest man, had foreseen that tragedy. But a tragedy just as great was the loss of sustenance for the body and the spirit for the People of the Buffalo. First came the hunger of the body, to be followed by the hunger of the spirit. They had both wept when they had talked of this reality.

Thankfully, the wagons along the Holy Road—called the Oregon Trail by the whites—had stopped coming. They had been a pestilence summer after summer, and the ruts they had cut into the earth were deep scars. On either side were graves of white travelers and the bones of their horses, cattle, and mules, but the wagon people had cast covetous eyes on the land as they passed. So the peace talkers had called the Lakota to Fort Laramie, and showed them pictures of the land, and told them where they could live and where they could hunt, so that they would be out of the way of the white people coming. That was not the worst of it. The worst was when several Lakota headmen allowed their names to be marked on the paper, giving their consent to whatever the words on the paper said. And who among the Lakota really knew what those words said? Then those headmen had pitched their lodges on the agencies near the mouth of the Smoking Earth River at the Long Knife outpost known as Camp Robinson. That was yet another bitter reality. Most of the Lakota people had followed those headmen to those agencies. But it also raised a question: did those people follow blindly or did they surrender of their own accord?

Over those wintry days, that was the question that gnawed at both of them. The answer to it would come, or not, in the days ahead.

"Nephew," said the older man, breaking into Crazy Horse's reverie, "I wanted to talk to you about the attack on Two Moons and He Dog a few months past."

"They can tell you, they were there."

"No, I want to hear what you think about where the Long Knives came from."

Crazy Horse nodded thoughtfully. "From the south. Two of our scouts followed their trail toward the Shell River for several days. There are three Long Knife outposts: Laramie, the one upriver from there, and the one north of Elk Mountain."

"I see. Any closer than those?"

"No."

"I know they could not have come from the outpost where the Heart River flows into the Great Muddy. That is a long way for Long Knives to travel in the winter, and we would have known. I hear there is a large outpost in the west, beyond the Beartooth Mountains."

"Yes, I think that is true," Crazy Horse asserted. "The same day we got word that Two Moons and He Dog were attacked, Cloud and several other men found two Long Knives north of one of our camps. They took their horses and weapons away. They came from the east or the west. They could not have come from the southern outposts."

Sitting Bull shook his head slowly, his brow furrowed in thought. "We may know where the Long Knives are, but we do not know how many."

"True, but we do know they do not do well in our country. Their big horses are not suited to the land. The Long Knives themselves are not true horse warriors. They seem to prefer fighting on foot and in large groups. They ride to the battle and then get off to fight. We fight from the backs of our horses, and our horses are trained for that. They do not know our lands. These things are in our favor, and I plan to take advantage of their weaknesses and our strengths."

The medicine man nodded slowly. "You are right, the fighting skills of our men are much better than theirs. If every one of our warriors had a good rifle and plenty of bullets, we could outfight them every time.

"That brings me to something else I want to talk about."

Crazy Horse nodded and waited.

"It is hard to know if more of our people will join us," Sitting Bull declared cautiously. "My biggest concern is the number of fighting men. We have three hundred now, and I think many of the single men will break away from the agencies, so we may have four hundred. That is still a small number, and there are still battles to be fought—if our leaders agree with me. So, if we have no more than three or four hundred, how do we make the best use of them without putting our women and children and old ones in danger?"

"Yes, I have been thinking about that," Crazy Horse replied. "Perhaps we should not wait for the Long Knives to come looking for us. Small groups of warriors can move fast, say twenty or so. We can attack their outposts, or near them, and fade into the hills before they can counterattack. We can make them chase us around. It will not be necessary to always defeat them in one battle. We can wear them down, pick them off a little at a time."

"That means enough men could stay home to protect everyone else."

"Yes. Small groups could stay in the field for half a month, then others could take their place. Men and horses could come home to rest."

Leaning back against his chair, the medicine man looked out the door.

After a moment, he sighed and spoke again. "It is time to adapt. We cannot change the difficult things that have happened. Who knows if the buffalo will be plentiful again? We can hope, but, in the meantime, we have to live with the realities that face us, like it or not. If we dwell on the losses, we will waste our energy weeping. Instead of crying, we need to change how we survive."

Crazy Horse could not have agreed more. "For our warriors, it means we do not fight for honors, or for the simple satisfaction of knowing we are better than an enemy we face on a given day." He paused to stare at the empty fire pit, and then spoke again. The hollow tone in his voice matched the cold intensity in his dark eyes. "We have to fight to kill the Long Knives and their kind. When enough of them have died, they will not want to set foot on our lands anymore."

Eagle Man and Red Shirt finished their smoke as the two men stepped out of the council lodge. The younger one was dressed very plainly, with only a single tail feather of a red-tailed hawk hanging down the back of his head. The older one walked with a limp and used a short lance as a cane. Neither was as tall as some Lakota men were, but other men did not have the kind of stature that stood higher than size or strength, as these two did.

The two old men struggled to their feet as Crazy Horse and Sitting Bull approached and stopped. Crazy Horse saw the pipe leaning against the altar stone beneath the shade.

"Pray for us, Grandfathers," he said. "We have much to do."

"We will, Grandson," Eagle Man assured him. "We will."

"Uncle," Sitting Bull said to each of the old men in turn, "it is good to see you."

"And you as well," Red Shirt replied, his old eyes shining.

CHAPTER TWENTY

Dog Soldiers and Drumbeats

Rain came with some frequency and the grasses grew. Horses were shedding the last of their winter hair and were beginning to look sleek. Lodges had to be pitched away from the low drainage areas as the rains and high spring runoff filled the smaller creeks up to their banks.

Cloud and Goings splashed across a pushy, deep creek on their way home. After spending six days as scouts, they were relieved by Yellow Wolf and Fast Horse the evening before. For those six days, they had turned themselves into shadows in the pine trees along a narrow ridge guarding a wide valley, watching the known trails to the south, trails that could be used by Long Knives. At night, to avoid giving themselves away, they built no fires, but they had more than enough dried food, and the night chill was easily tolerable. The worst part of their stint was the mosquitoes. It had been their second time on watch, but they saw no Long Knives. Nor any other two-leggeds, for that matter.

On the far bank of the creek, they stopped to let their horses water and stepped down for a quick drink themselves. Spring was in full bloom. Everything and everyone was busy, from the grasses swaying in the warm breeze to the insects buzzing about and the swallows chasing them. Cloud noticed the deep prints left by an animal with small hooves. A deer, he guessed, probably a lone old buck, since there were no other tracks about. Everything seemed to be moving, going somewhere, as they were. They would be home before sundown, he estimated, and said as much to Goings.

"I will be glad for a bed," Goings muttered, splashing water on his face. "And some hot food."

"It is possible they have moved while we were gone," Cloud said. "The grass is good and thick, but the horses are eating it down fast. High Wolf heard Worm and High Eagle talking about an area farther to the southwest, toward the headwaters of Ash Creek."

They walked for some distance, leading the horses to ease their burden somewhat, laden with robes, extra clothing, food, and weapons as they were. Each of them had a rifle tied to the neck rope on one side and two sets of bows and arrows on the other.

Since the White Buttes, the villages had moved twice, farther to the west each time. More people had come. Nearly a hundred Dakota had arrived, following their headman, Pointed Red Hill. But the nearly daily flow of one or two young men at a time from the Red Cloud and Spotted Tail agencies was cause for excitement. No one was saying that each young man was another who could stand between them and any enemy, though that was the case. They tried to focus more on the news of family and friends, and the fact that the men had turned away from life at the agency.

"If they have moved, we will be home tomorrow," Goings reasoned. "Hot food and a good bed will just have to wait one more day."

"The river valleys will have good grass all summer," Cloud predicted. "And if Sitting Bull has his way, we will be heading south toward the Shining Mountains after that."

"I hope that happens," Goings admitted. "If we can grow to a fighting force of seven or eight hundred, that is something."

When Cloud and Goings found the village site they had left eight days before, they discovered that another move west had, indeed, taken place. Most of the grass in the valley and surrounding hills had been grazed down. A wide swath of a trail left by the drag poles being pulled over the ground led away to the west. Among the grooves stretching to the horizon were moccasin prints and hoofprints too numerous to count. Looking at the trail filled them with a sense of being powerful and small at the same time.

Resisting the temptation to ride through the night, they made camp in a gully just below the crest of a hill dotted with soap weeds and sagebrush. Amid the fresh scent of new sage came the tiniest hint of wood smoke, a tantalizing indication that they were near home and their families. They arose before dawn and reached the encampment by midmorning.

Although they smelled smoke from the cooking fires the closer they came, the tops of the lodge poles were not visible until they reached a low rise. They immediately noticed several new lodges interspersed with the old. The camp was now one large circle, eight or so rows deep. Their lodges were on the west side of the circle. They would occupy this same area wherever they were encamped, until the old medicine men said otherwise.

It was the twelfth day of the new month, the Moon When Calves Are

Red. Some called it by its other name, the Moon When Horses Shed. The second seemed more appropriate now, since there were thousands of horses and the herd grew each time more people arrived. On the other hand, no one had seen any buffalo at all, much less reddish brown calves playing in the spring sun. Who knew if there were any red calves anywhere? Everyone hoped and prayed it was so.

Cloud found a picket pole ready and waiting to the right of the door to his lodge. He dismounted, quickly fashioned a halter with the long rein, and tied his horse to the pole. As he finished unloading weapons and gear, a flash of brown hair caught his eye.

Song squealed and jumped into his arms. "Are you hungry?" she asked, her nose touching his.

"Starving," he replied.

"Mother has food ready."

"Where is your mother?"

Song jabbed a finger toward the lodge next to theirs. "She is helping Grandmother sew something. I saw you coming."

There was a slight rustle nearby as Sweetwater Woman came around the back of the lodge to join them, a soft smile of welcome revealing her white teeth. She put her head against her husband's shoulder as he pulled her into a one-armed embrace.

"I have food," she told him. "Mother made soup this morning. The kettle is inside."

"Very glad to hear that," he said in her ear. "Six days of dried food and mosquitoes sucking my blood make me very hungry for hot food and warm...things."

She reached under his shirt and pinched his chest. "Food first, then I will pile all the buffalo robes on you so you can be warm."

He grinned and lowered Song to the ground. "After I eat and take a rest, my daughter and I will take this horse to water and turn him loose with the herd and find the bay."

"I know where the bay is," Song volunteered. "I saw him this morning when I went with Grandfather to check on our horses."

"Good. Did you tell him to come when I got home?"

"No. He does not listen."

"What do you mean? He listens to me. I say, 'Whoa' and he stops. I say, 'Come' and he walks to me."

She frowned, not certain if her father was serious. "But he cannot know. He…he would be confused if you used lots of words."

"What do you mean?"

"Because *come* is just one word, and *whoa* is just one word."

They ducked through the door, and Cloud wearily settled back against his chair, grateful for the familiarity of his lodge. Everything was in its place, as usual. He turned to Song and said, "So, you mean if I told the bay, 'Go to the water and have a drink,' that would be too many words for him to understand?"

"Yes."

"Why?"

"Because…because he does not speak people. He just speaks horse."

Cloud smiled at Sweetwater Woman as she handed him a bowl.

"Did he tell you that?"

Song frowned and stared at her father as if he had lost his mind. "No. I said he does not speak people words."

"Then how do you know he speaks horse? Maybe he speaks gopher. There are a lot of gophers around here, right?"

"Father, you are silly!"

"Maybe. But I am sure hungry too."

After food and a nap, Cloud took the gray gelding south of the village to the creek, Song close on his heels. As the horse drank, he turned and looked at the encampment. It was big. Not as big as the encampment near the Shell River below Elk Mountain had been eleven years ago, when Blue Clouds and Cheyenne had joined the Lakota. That had been the spring and summer after the raids south of the Shell River to avenge the murders committed by Long Knives at Sand Creek.

But he had a feeling. More people were arriving every day, which was exactly what Sitting Bull was hoping for. If that continued, Cloud was certain this gathering would come close to matching the one eleven years ago.

Just as important as the growing number of people and the number of warriors was the overall feeling among the people that was growing as well. It was not a feeling of power, necessarily, as far as Cloud was concerned.

It was more a sense of being part of something larger than one person, or one family.

He put a hand on Song's shoulder. "Daughter," he said gently, "when you are a woman and you have a family of your own, tell them about this." He pointed to the village. "Remember everything that is happening here."

Song squinted up at her father and saw a look in his eyes she had not seen before. It was difficult to describe, but she would remember it for the rest of her life. She nodded. "I will, Father. I will."

When they arrived at the herd where the riding horses were, they spotted Little Bird's sons, Two Horns and Ashes, immediately. Turning the gray loose, they walked among dozens and dozens of lazily grazing animals.

"Which one are you looking for, Uncle?" Two Horns asked.

"My bay gelding," Cloud replied.

Ashes pointed and disappeared into the herd with his long braided rope in hand. After a few moments, he returned, leading the bay.

"Thank you," Cloud said, fashioning a halter with his own rope and handing the boy's rope back.

"Uncle," Two Horns asked, "have you heard that Sitting Bull is going to have a Sun Dance?"

"No. When?"

"Next month, in the Moon When Berries Are Good. I thought the Sun Dance was done in the month of Moon When the Sun Stands in the Middle."

"Yes, usually."

"Then why is he doing one before then?" the boy wondered.

Sitting Bull was shrewd, Cloud thought. There was more to strength than weapons and warriors. The source of that strength was in the hearts and minds of every man, woman, and child. What better way to draw out that strength and turn it into a force for unity than with a Sun Dance?

Cloud smiled at the two boys. "Sitting Bull knows what he is doing," he told them. "If he wants to do a Sun Dance one month earlier than usual, then that is exactly what we will do."

An old voice caught their ears and they all turned to see a man in a feather bonnet riding slowly toward them. Cloud recognized him. It was Shadow Wolf, an old Cheyenne Dog Soldier.

"My friends!" he called out, waving the ceremonial medicine bow he held. The bow was long and made of a slender ash pole. Its handle curved inward, and the end of the bottom limb was tipped with an iron lance head. Shadow Wolf had been a stalwart and fearless warrior in his younger days, and he had the scars to prove it, along with the distant stare of a fighting man with memories that would not go away.

"How are you, Uncle?" Cloud replied.

"I am well," the old warrior chirped. "My horse is short, so he is easy to get on, and my wife still feeds me now and then. Life is good!"

Cloud chuckled. He knew the old Dog Soldier had suffered a grievous injury during a battle over thirty years ago. His horse had been shot and rolled over him, breaking a hip. Although he had healed, he walked with a slight stoop, never to stand up fully straight again. Yet he always had a cheerful disposition.

"There is much to be said for a good horse and good food," Cloud said.

Ashes and Two Horns were openly admiring the old man's elaborately decorated shirt made of tanned bighorn sheep hide. It had been made in the days when women still used dyed porcupine quills instead of glass beads traded from the whites. From the points of each shoulder, running down the length of the sleeves and across the front, were double rows of hair tassels, locks of human hair.

"The less you expect, the happier you will be," Shadow Wolf advised, reining his horse to a stop. "When the sun goes down, the Dog Soldiers will dance to honor the memories of all the grandfathers, fathers, and friends who have followed the warriors' path before us. You must come. Dance and eat with us."

"Thank you, Uncle. We will be there."

Shadow Wolf clucked to his horse, waved his bow, and went on.

Cheyenne Dog Soldiers were fierce and dedicated fighting men. Like the Lakota Crazy Dog and Red Sash warriors, they were feared by their enemies. "If your friend is a Dog Soldier," it was said, "he will fight with you to the end, or die in your place."

The moment the sun slipped behind the ragged edges of the distant horizon, the first drumbeat reverberated throughout the camp, summoning anyone not already in the center of the camp circle. Eight warrior society lodges stood guard around the council lodge, a visual reminder that fighting men were willing and able to defend the people. Along the north curve of the circle, one flew long red streamers from the very top of its poles. The streamers waved and danced in the breeze in time with the drum and the voices of the singers as they sang a victory song.

Between the Dog Soldier lodge and the council lodge, a pit had been dug and a fire burned in it. The flames were still low, since the evening was just beginning. In front of the lodge, the singers sat in a tight circle around the drum. All around the fire, a crowd had gathered and was watching the headmen of the Dog Soldier society dance in a procession around the fire. An old white-haired man, wearing a feather bonnet with a trail of eagle feathers that nearly touched the ground, led the headmen. He carried a hide bundle, a replica of the bundle that held the sacred Medicine Hat, which had been brought to the Cheyenne by their holy man Sweet Medicine in the time far past the remembering of the oldest Cheyenne in the camp.

Cloud heard the drums and the singers as he stopped at the lodge of Big Voice and White Hill Woman, the parents of his friend Rabbit. They were both standing outside, looking toward the sound of the drum, and warmly greeted Cloud.

"Aunt, Uncle," Cloud greeted in return, "it is good to see you."

"Good to see you as well," White Hill Woman replied gently. "We do not see you as often as we would like. But I know you are busy."

"I will try to stop by more often," he promised.

"Good," Big Voice said. "There is a chair at the back of our lodge. It will always wait for you."

Cloud nodded and cleared his throat to try to loosen the lump that seemed to be forming.

"How is your daughter?" White Hill Woman asked. "I hope that she is not bothered by what happened to her."

"She is well. Only once did she wake up with a bad dream," Cloud told her. "Thank you for the doll you gave her. She sleeps with it every night."

White Hill Woman smiled, her eyes glistening a little.

"I was wondering," Cloud said, "if I might borrow your son's six-shooter this evening. I would like to carry something of his in the dancing, which is to honor warriors. I will return it."

The woman nodded, unable to stop the tear that slid down her cheek. "Yes. It is kind of you to remember him."

"I think about him every day," he told them.

Big Voice brought out the six-shooter in its decorated case. "I remember the day you gave this to him," he recalled. "It brought him back from the edge of giving up."

Cloud recalled that day as well. He touched the handle of the pistol. It was a tangible connection he and they had to Rabbit.

The drum beckoned, and Cloud joined the crowd watching as the line of Dog Soldiers finished the first dance. Throngs of people were still arriving. On the other side of the ring stood Sitting Bull. Hanging farther back in the third row was Crazy Horse. He had come to honor the warriors who had gone on to the Spirit World, but, as usual, he was reluctant to be seen.

The old white-haired Cheyenne Dog Soldier who had led the procession stepped forward to speak. An expectant silence fell over the crowd as young and old waited politely.

"We invite anyone who wishes to honor the memory of a warrior to join us," he began in a strong voice. "The Cheyenne, the Blue Clouds, and the Lakota have been friends for a long, long time. Over the generations, our warriors have fought side by side. Our warriors have shed blood together and have died together. They have shown us the road we must follow. We must not turn aside from that road. To do so would be to insult the memories of our brothers, our fathers, our grandfathers—and several of our sisters, mothers, and grandmothers, as well—who have given all they could, all they had. Join us and dance to their memories. Join us!"

The entire throng moved forward into the dance circle as the drum pounded. Warriors shouted their battle cries and women trilled.

By the time dusk gave way to the first shadows of night and stars began to appear one by one in the sky, three more drums and their singers joined in. So many dancers came that the dancing arena expanded to the area that encircled the council lodge. Women and girls danced in place around the outside edge of the circle, while the men and boys circled left to right.

Sitting Bull came unadorned, except for the long red-willow rod he carried, his victory stick. Tied to it were twenty eagle-tail feathers, representing some of the battle honors he had won as a warrior. He had chosen not to wear his feather bonnet with a sash of forty feathers that reached to the ground. Other eagle feathers he had won were attached to ceremonial lances tied to the poles inside his lodge. He danced to four of the songs and then stood back to rest, cooling himself with his eagle-wing fan. With a slight smile, which did not match the sense of satisfaction he felt, he surveyed the scene. Even the flickering flames danced to the rhythm of the drum. It was as he had hoped. The feeling of strength was growing day by day.

Cloud stayed in the dance circle for one more song, moving shoulder to shoulder with Goings and Little Bird and behind Grey Bull and Black Shield. The two older men were resplendent in their feather bonnets. As he moved along the circle, the ground already matted down by a hundred pairs of feet, faces and images floated through his memory in time with the drums—Rabbit, Hump, Little Hawk, and Lone Bear, along with his own father and grandfather. He could feel their presence. Warriors, all. Good men, all. *Grandfather*, he prayed, *when my time comes, help me to be half as brave as they were.*

Accompanied by Little Bird, he worked his way back toward the spectators. They found High Eagle standing in the shadows.

"Uncle," Cloud said, taking a deep breath, "I think I will leave the rest of the dancing to the younger ones."

The medicine man smiled knowingly as the first rapid beats of a sneak-up song invited younger men to form a ring around the edge of the dancing circle. As the song was sung, they danced toward the center. It was a fitting song, with a story dance to go with it: the enemy had been seen and the warriors approached unseen, then charged to victory.

As the singers and dancers paused in between the first and second of the four rounds of the dance, Cloud stepped closer to the medicine man. "Uncle," he said, "I heard today that we might have a Sun Dance next month."

High Eagle nodded. "The Hunkpapa headman told us he and his helpers have been planning one. A group of their young men pledged last year and will fulfill their pledges this summer."

"Why next month?"

The drum pounded again, calling for the second round. The spectators surged forward, caught up in the spirit and urgency of the dance.

"There is a time for everything," High Eagle explained. "It is the sacrifice, the gift the dancers give—the gift of themselves—that is the most important. He feels the people, especially those who have been living on the agencies, need to be reminded of that."

"Makes sense to me," Little Bird declared. "Yellow Wolf was disappointed at what he heard down there. He wondered if the whites put something in their clothes that harms anyone who wears them. My grandfather said their clothes were infected with bad illnesses and killed a lot of human beings. That is how the Pawnee lost half of their people over twenty years ago. So maybe there is some kind of illness that makes people change on the inside."

"If an antelope is in with a herd of cattle long enough, he will begin to think he is one of them," High Eagle observed. "So a Sun Dance is one way to cleanse those who need to be. To remind them of who they are."

Shouts and war cries erupted from the crowd as the circle of young Cheyenne and Lakota dancers finished the second round with a flourish and the drums pounded with booming, reverberating beats.

CHAPTER TWENTY-ONE

The Mighty

With an exasperated shake of his head, the lieutenant watched one of the newest members of the Seventh Cavalry nearly slip out of the saddle as his horse jumped across the narrow creek. Lieutenant W. W. Cooke made a mental note to talk to the sergeant major about the new private. The soldier was not young in years, but a greenhorn in every other way when it came to horses. He had a nervous expression on his narrow, blue-eyed face. Cooke sighed. Who knew what this one was running or hiding from. To make matters worse, the man barely spoke English. That seemed to be the pattern the last few years. If they weren't foreigners, they were Galvanized Yankees, repatriated Confederate soldiers. But at least the former Johnny Rebs could ride. Although this man clung desperately to the pommel of the saddle, he lost his balance and went off the right side and landed with a smack on the muddy ground

Cooke waited for the soldier to pick himself up and remount. At least the private was good for breaking up the tedium of a long and uneventful trail.

His cheeks burning, the private avoided the lieutenant's mocking gaze and brushed the mud from his pants. When he risked a glance toward the officer, he noticed something flutter in the breeze among the branches in the tall cottonwood tree behind him. A piece of cloth, he thought. Then the private's jaw dropped.

Lieutenant Cooke saw the man's fear and turned to look over his shoulder, in the direction of the man's gaze, and a shiver went up his spine. In the branches above him, partially obscured by the swatch of new leaves, hung a skeleton covered with tattered remnants of clothing.

Cooke forgot about the frightened soldier as he stared at the dead man, wondering how he had died in the tree, so high off the ground. He answered his own unspoken question when he noticed the cords across the man's chest and ankles binding the remains to an upright branch. Then he noticed the tufts of light-colored hair on the yellowish skull. Probably the man had been lifted to the branch and tied there after he had been killed. It was a white man, or had been. Cooke guessed he had been killed by Indians.

The private pointed and said something unintelligible, though the fear on his face was still plain enough. Looking back up, Cooke saw what the soldier was reacting to.

The iron point of a lance was embedded in the branch, its broken shaft protruding like a pointing finger through the rib bones. *What were the odds of anyone seeing this grisly sight?* Cooke wondered. Then he realized that their Crow scouts had been leading them along a known Indian trail. And whatever Indian or Indians had hoisted the dead man up into the tree knew that white men were apt to use it now and then. Another shiver went up his spine.

Voices drifted from the thin grove of trees behind the cottonwood. Two of the scouts who had gone ahead were doubling back, coming toward them at a fast trot. The unhorsed soldier couldn't help but notice how easily the two Indians rode, totally in unison with their horses. Smiles creased their weathered brown faces when they saw the soldier covered in mud and immediately guessed what had transpired. Cooke caught their attention and pointed up into the tree.

Bloody Knife, Custer's favorite scout, reined his horse to a stop, glanced up, and saw the skeleton in tattered clothes. His eyes narrowed into a knowing gleam. "Sioux," he said, in a low, gravelly voice. "Kill, then scalp. Hair on some Sioux man's shirt."

The other scout, White Man Runs Him, leaned toward Bloody Knife and nodded almost imperceptibly toward the soldier trying to remount his horse. "Either he is muddy or that dead man scared something else out of him," he muttered in Crow.

Bloody Knife chuckled under his breath and looked at Cooke, who seemed to get the gist of the remark.

Cooke turned his bearded face away for a moment, then urged his horse over toward the hapless soldier. "Private," he said gently, "lead your horse over there and wait." Cooke pointed to a grassy knoll well off the trail and out of the path of the approaching column.

The soldier nodded gratefully and yanked on the reins of the long-suffering horse. He glanced back over his shoulder once more at the skeleton tied to the branch.

Cooke pointed in the direction from which the scouts had come. "Is it clear?'" he asked.

"No sign," Bloody Knife replied.

"Where are they? The Sioux, I mean."

The scout pointed west.

"Will we see any?" Cooke wondered.

"They show themselves when they want," Bloody Knife replied patiently.

These soldier chiefs are all the same, thought Bloody Knife, *all anxious to find Indians, especially the Sioux. As if they could do anything with them.* He doubted that even Long Hair was strong enough to deal with the Sioux. Some days ago, a feeling had come, a feeling like a cold stone that pressed against the small of his back. It refused to go away. Now he was worried, though he had said nothing to anyone.

"How far west?" Cooke persisted.

Bloody Knife grimaced and shook his head. "Maybe ten, twenty days."

Cooke urged his horse closer toward the scout. "Bloody Knife, my friend," he said, smiling benignly, "sometimes I wonder whose side you are really on. You are leading us toward them, and I think you know exactly where the damn Sioux are, but why?"

The scout locked eyes briefly with the lieutenant. For an instant, Cooke felt as if the man was looking clean through him, as if he wasn't there. He was annoyed that the man was not afraid of him.

Bloody Knife cleared his throat. "Cooke," he said, "this big land." He paused to gesture at the rolling hills and distant ridges all around them. "This good land. Sioux want to keep. They fight to keep."

Cooke nodded. What, if anything, did any of these tribes know about progress? How much were they really aware that they were in the path of a hunger that was hard to satisfy? He pitied them, and yet he despised them, as well, for their ignorance of the civilized world.

Soft thuds of hoofbeats on the damp ground interrupted his thoughts. The general's aide appeared in the grove, a captain whose name Cooke could never remember. Behind him was Major Reno, and thirty yards behind him rode Terry and Custer, side by side. Reno seemed preoccupied. Cooke guessed the major was not pleased that Custer could be so familiar with the general.

"What's the word, Lieutenant?" Reno demanded.

"The scouts saw nothing," Cooke reported, then pointed up into the cottonwood tree beneath which Reno has just passed. "Except that, sir."

Reno was not unused to such sights. Serving on the plains as long as any of the senior officers in the Seventh, he had seen his share of atrocities committed by Indians against whites. Still, Cooke noticed a brief moment of surprise and shock before the major composed himself.

"A white man, I take it?"

"I believe so, sir."

"How in the deuce did he get up there?"

"Bloody Knife is of the opinion that the Sioux put him there. After they killed and scalped him," Cooke replied patiently.

Terry and Custer arrived, immediately noticing Reno's agitation.

"What is it, Major?" Terry asked rather nonchalantly.

"I believe it's a message, General." Reno pointed up.

Terry and Custer reined in their horses and twisted in the saddle to look up into the branches of the tree.

"I think the major is correct," Custer commented dryly.

"What does it mean?" Terry asked.

Reno jumped in. "I believe it is a warning. Perhaps to demonstrate what happens to anyone who enters their territory."

A man in civilian garb arrived, taking immediate notice of the cluster of officers looking up into the trees. "Gentlemen," he called out, wiping the sweat off his brow with the back of a hand, "I hope this means we are stopping for a brief respite."

"Mr. Kellogg," Custer replied, "this is as good a time as any for a brief respite, if the general agrees," he said, glancing sideways at Terry.

Mark Kellogg was a reporter from *The Bismarck Tribune* in the territorial town of Bismarck, across the river from Fort Abraham Lincoln. His presence on the expedition was not entirely looked upon favorably by Terry.

Kellogg followed Terry's upward gaze. His face paled a little at the sight of the dead man.

Terry turned away and nodded vaguely. "I think we should take care of that unfortunate soul," he said.

"Of course," Custer agreed, turning toward Cooke. "A burial detail, Lieutenant, and quickly!"

Kellogg pulled a small notebook and the stub of a pencil from an inner pocket and quickly scribbled notes, underlining Custer's remarks.

The general's aide informed the troop commanders in the approaching column of the temporary halt. The front ranks were routed away from the tree before they stopped. Cooke took the initiative and conscripted several privates to dig a grave. Although the passing troopers saw work going on, many did not know it was a burial until news spread later in the afternoon.

Reno sat in the shade of a scrub oak with Captain Benteen, sipping water from a canteen and scowling darkly. He nodded toward a cluster of officers with Custer standing next to Terry. As usual, Custer was animated and carrying the conversation.

"It amazes me that he was reinstated," Reno hissed.

"Amazing, indeed," agreed Benteen, wiping sweat from his forehead with a handkerchief. "Nothing seems to keep him down long. Word was that he was to remain behind, not to accompany the regiment. He overcame that somehow."

"I was never one to ride anybody's coattails," Reno sighed. "I know that the rise of any officer is not based solely on individual merit, but I cannot bring myself to stand around at social affairs with an insincere smile frozen on my face."

"I quite agree, but if you had, perhaps you would be wearing silver oak leaves by now. On the other hand, any posting out here, in this godforsaken frontier, means the War Department has forgotten us."

"'General' Custer has been a lieutenant colonel for eight years." Reno chuckled without enthusiasm.

In the afternoon, under a graying sky with a promise of rain, the column encamped a few miles east of the burial site in a meadow that bent with a narrow creek. Canvas tents, already dirtied by continuous use and handling, looked dingy against the backdrop of green. Rolling hills and long ridges surrounded the campsite. After the initial frenzy of erecting tents and unhitching wagon horses, the two-thousand-man column, with its horses and wagons, settled down somewhat. Every troop assigned its own horse guards and grazed horses near its own unit. Sentries were posted on the higher points all around.

By late afternoon, the skies had turned dark and a steady drizzle began to fall, forcing canvas coverings to be erected above cooking fires. Weapons and ammunition had to be covered as well, and soldiers added the rain to the list of things to grumble about.

Crowded into Terry's tent were several senior officers, including Reno and Custer. "According to my estimate, we have progressed approximately a hundred miles," Terry stated, looking around for affirmation or disagreement. Hearing none, he went on. "We must step up our pace. I shall dispatch our Indian scouts to find a route favorable for faster travel."

He looked toward Custer. "Armstrong, I would like to send Lieutenant Varnum and your man Bloody Knife."

Custer ignored Reno's burning stare and said, "By all means, General. They are at your disposal."

"Very well. You can brief them. We need to increase our pace and cover closer to thirty miles a day. The fewer steep slopes, up or down, for our wagons, the happier I will be. I expect they will be on their way before the sun goes down."

"As soon as we are finished here, sir, I will brief them and send them out."

Under the canopy erected in front of Custer's tent, Charles Varnum and Bloody Knife listened impassively to their orders.

"We will stand down tomorrow," the colonel stated. "The general wants to give you ample time. You should return by tomorrow evening."

"May I suggest, sir," Varnum injected, "it would be good to take two more scouts. I can send a man back each day while Bloody Knife and I stay ahead of the column. If we rotate messengers, we can maintain the pace the general wants."

Custer nodded. "Very well. I will inform the general later. Proceed in that manner. You may select whatever other scouts you need."

Bloody Knife, although listening attentively, had been staring into the distance. He turned back and addressed Custer. "If we see Sioux, I will stay and send others back."

Varnum, Bloody Knife, and two other scouts rode away virtually unnoticed. The drizzle had turned into a steady rain, rattling off the canvas tents and forcing horses to stand with their heads down. Soldiers pulled down hats and caps and pulled up their collars, paying little attention to anything beyond their own wet surroundings. Tents in low areas had to be moved, as every depression in the encampment soon filled with water.

There were no campfires as night fell. The wet kindling and steady rain discouraged anyone from attempting to light a fire. Soldiers huddled inside tents, dreading their turn at sentry duty in the downpour.

The next afternoon, Curly, the young Crow sent back by Lieutenant Varnum, returned to the sight of a bogged-down camp. Attempts had been made to move wagons to higher ground, but several of them had sunk into the mud up to their axles. Curly knew that nothing short of the ground drying out would move those wagons. And it was still raining.

He found White Man Runs Him, who knew a little of the white man's language, and reported to Custer that Bloody Knife and the others were three days' journey ahead, and it was raining just as hard there.

After listening for a moment, Custer turned to White Man Runs Him and said, "I will report to General Terry. Give this man some food and a fresh horse. After he has rested, bring him to me. I want him to tell Varnum to wait a day or two."

White Man Runs Him nodded and motioned for Curly to follow him, while Custer headed toward the general's quarters.

Major General Terry sipped some tea as he contemplated the colonel's report. "There might be some wisdom in your suggestion," he said. "This rain is not letting up, and it is not likely that it will. Yes, Varnum should wait. I shall have my aide write a dispatch for the scout to take back."

"Yes, sir." Custer replied.

The general stood and walked to the opening of his tent and looked out across the soaked land as the rain rattled on the tent. Here and there, it was dripping through. "Armstrong," he said without looking at Custer, "it is easy to think of ourselves as powerful with this mighty force of men and arms. I find it disheartening that we can be immobilized by something as common as rain."

CHAPTER TWENTY-TWO

A Hawk and a Whirlwind

Stands in Timber, a young Cheyenne with a pleasant face, stood on a rise north of the village and took in a sight that made his blood stir. No one knew how many people there were in camp; only guesses could be made. He estimated there were around five thousand people, and one of his friends thought there were nearly nine thousand horses. There were so many horses that they had to be broken down into several smaller herds and spread around the encampment to graze. So many that the grass at each new campsite was eaten down to the ground in a matter of three or four days.

Sitting in front of his lodge, he had felt a throbbing, the rhythm of life that begins to rise whenever so many people come together. He had felt it so strongly that he was compelled to climb the low rise, thinking perhaps he could see it, or perceive it somehow.

He stared at the forest of poles stretching upward like long, thin, intertwined fingers from the tops of hundreds of lodges. An endless forest, it seemed. Below them walked the people of three nations—the Lakota, along with their relatives the Dakota and Nakota, and the Blue Clouds and Cheyenne. Stands in Timber drew in a deep breath. Somewhere inside of him was the feeling that he would never again see such a sight.

People and horses were everywhere. Laughter and conversations floated on the lazy breeze. Full meat racks and empty drag frames stood upright between the lodges. Children moved about in small bunches. Women worked, scraping hides or slicing meat into thin strips to hang on the racks. Babies in cradleboards were numerous, as were dogs staying as unobtrusively close to the meat racks as they could. Old men sat around in small clusters, watching it all.

Walking slowly down the rise and entering the circle of the encampment was like walking into the warm waters of a lake. He could feel a sense of belonging surround him. He followed a line of lodges until he came to the Oglala neighborhood, intending to visit with his friend Crazy Horse. They had not spoken since two campsites ago. As always, there was a crowd at his lodge. Stands in Timber took a seat on the ground at the outer edge of the small group.

Little Big Man was speaking. Next to him, Grey Bull listened patiently, but, from the expression on the older man's face, Stands in Timber knew Grey Bull was not pleased with what he was hearing.

"From what the agency people hear," Little Big Man was saying, "the outpost upriver from Fort Laramie has a large number of Long Knives. I believe those who attacked Two Moons came from there. It would be wise to consider attacking it. We have at least seven hundred fighting men here now. Is that not why we are coming together, to do something about the Long Knives? What better way than to take the fight to them? They would not expect that."

"I know the agency people hear news about Long Knives," Grey Bull spoke up, "but do we know how many Long Knives are at that outpost? My guess is that there are a thousand, if not more. And every one of those thousand has a rifle and plenty of bullets. And let us not forget their wagon guns."

Little Big Man was not dissuaded. "Many of us are ready to fight," he countered. "Our skills as fighters are better."

"But does that make their guns less powerful?" asked Grey Bull.

The younger man's eyes glowed with anger. "It can," he retorted.

Little Big Man was known for his quick anger. Almost singlehandedly he had frightened off several white peace talkers only two years ago at the Spotted Tail agency. At the meeting known as the Council to Steal the Black Hills, he rode in and challenged any Lakota who would sign the paper giving away the Black Hills to the whites. It was a brave thing to do, and fortunately no one had gotten hurt, despite the anger and tension and the Long Knives' habit of shooting first. But no one signed the paper, and the peace talkers left.

"No one doubts the fighting abilities of our men," Grey Bull replied, "or your courage. But it is a good thing to have common sense to go along with courage. We cannot afford to lose a single fighting man. To replace the loss of one experienced fighter is not easy for us. We may have seven hundred warriors here, but how many of them have the kind of experience you have, Nephew? On the other hand, we may kill a thousand Long Knives, but a thousand more will come from their country to the east. I agree with what you say—we must take the fight to them—but we must plan carefully before we do. We have to fight when we know we will win."

Stands in Timber noted that everyone nodded, silently agreeing with Grey Bull.

Good Weasel, one of the battle-scarred veterans Grey Bull had alluded to, tossed an inscrutable glance at Little Big Man. "I, too, agree with what you say. But what Uncle Grey Bull says is also true. Some of our young men have very little experience, and inexperienced men can make mistakes in the heat of battle. I think we should pick the fights we can win. Strike quickly, inflict casualties, and break off. That will give our young men experience as well as confidence."

All eyes looked toward Crazy Horse. "Our battle leaders have talked about these things, and what my friend says is the method we all agree with. The first thing we need to do is send our scouts in close to the Long Knife outposts and have them use whatever means they can to learn their numbers and the routines they have. Then we can plan how to attack."

Warfare against the Long Knives and whites was the thing most talked about by the men. Most of the younger men assumed that when the war leaders decided there were enough warriors, there would be raids against the Long Knife outposts. They didn't worry about planning the way the older warriors did. Younger men worried about doing well in battle. Many were also thinking about something Crazy Horse had been saying consistently: Fighting the Long Knives and other whites was not the same as fighting against the Crow or Shoshone. It was not for personal honor. The Lakota and their allies had to fight to kill Long Knives and destroy their will to come after them. Personal honor was no longer as important as survival.

The reasons for becoming a warrior, a fighting man, were the same: a warrior's duty was to protect family and home. But now being a warrior was even more important because the Long Knives had turned into the kind of a threat many human beings had not expected. They were like the prairie fire that consumed everything in its path. They didn't understand honor, only destruction and death.

Three men sat in the shade of a lodge not far from the group sitting with Crazy Horse. Under the watchful eye of his father, Little Dog was helping Horned Eagle clean a breech-loading rifle. The two young men were twelve when the

Battle of the Hundred in the Hand had been fought, nearly ten years ago. Now both were thoroughly trained to be fighting men, but, as yet, they had not faced Long Knives in a protracted battle.

"I remember three years ago when we went with Crazy Horse and Cloud up to the Elk River," Horned Eagle recalled. "The Long Knives numbered two hundred or so. Crazy Horse wanted to draw them into an ambush, but they would not chase us. We fired on them, they fired back. Nothing much happened."

"Remember the bunch we caught napping on a small island in the middle of the river?" Little Dog asked. "They were surprised to see us."

"That is exactly what Crazy Horse is talking about," his father said. "When I was a young man, war was different. I was with Crazy Horse's friend and teacher when we came across some Shoshone. We fought up close with lances and war clubs. Men were knocked from their horses and rescued by their friends. We fought hard that day. We did not let up, and we drove them away. On another day, maybe they would have been stronger, but that is how it goes. Only two of our men were seriously injured. Several of theirs were badly hurt. No one was killed. But when the fight was over, we felt good, we felt strong. Several of us were given eagle feathers later by the old men."

At that moment, Cloud and Goings were on the north side of Ash Creek, gazing intently at its waters flowing into the Greasy Grass.

"I have not been here in three years," Goings commented. He pointed west across the flat plain that stretched to the low hills beyond. "But the last time I was, the grass was not this tall or thick."

Cloud pointed to the rushing waters of the Greasy Grass. "It is running high. Too high to cross." He looked north. "We can go north to Dry Creek and get a good look from the slopes of those ridges. There is no need to cross that water."

Staying inside the groves of short oak and willow along the banks of the Greasy Grass, they rode north, choosing a straight course rather than following the meandering river. The ridges on the eastern side of the river rose suddenly, filled with tree-choked gullies that cut down to the water.

They proceeded slowly and cautiously, hands on their six-shooters. Staying below the ridge, they climbed to the benches above the river, then across the ridge. Below them was a forest of mostly very old and tall cottonwood trees that could hide anything and anyone.

The cottonwood floodplain west of the river was a favorite campsite for many people, especially in the summer or autumn. This year, the grass on the plain was thick and tall, up to a horse's belly, Cloud estimated.

Breezes wandered about, whispering softly as they passed through the grasses, making stalks slowly bend and sway. Eagles and hawks soared overhead, and meadowlarks and sparrows flitted among the smaller trees and brush. Cloud spotted a doe and its fawn emerge from the cottonwoods and pause at the west bank of the Greasy Grass. After a long drink, the doe moved off slowly—a reassuring sign that no one else, two-legged or four-, was in the trees. They waited a while longer before they proceeded into the open western slopes of the ridges on the east side of the river.

Far to the north, but still south of the Elk River, a young man dressed only in a rabbit-skin breechclout peered at the shadowy overhang of an old watercourse. His hair was loose and short, barely below his ears. His body was covered with cuts, scrapes, and bruises. In his hand was a long pole sharpened on both ends, worked to points by continuous scraping against stone surfaces. It was an effective weapon for defense and more than adequate for spearing fish. On his feet were slats made of pine bark tied with strips of rabbit hide. In a small bag tied around his waist, next to the cone-shaped fish trap made of willow stalks, were pieces of cooked rabbit.

The high bank had caught his eye as he was following a creek. Any kind of overhang was shelter, especially one that was out of the wind. This one had large stones scattered across the front, something he knew did not occur naturally. Someone had used this before.

Old Coyote moved forward to have a closer look. A step from the stones, he noticed an odd-shaped object behind them. He knew there was nothing or no one inside the overhang—it wasn't deep enough for anything larger than a coyote or a deer. He moved closer until he could poke the object with his spear. It fell away to the inside, and a deep, damp, musty odor wafted outward.

He looked around. If nothing else, he had learned that constant alertness was the best defense. He saw nothing, except for hawks and eagles and smaller birds.

Turning back, he crawled closer toward the overhang, and the musty, dank odor was more evident. Rising slightly, he saw something he knew was not plant or animal—a swatch of pale blue cloth.

He reached in and pushed aside the stones and moved back instinctively from the unexpected sight. Steadying himself, Old Coyote moved forward slowly to take a closer look.

Behind the stones were two skeletons. Part of the bank had collapsed on them, probably because of the rain. Tiny bits of flesh and strands of hair still clung to the exposed areas not covered by the faded blue uniforms. With the sharpened staff, he poked at the clothing, then sat back on his haunches for a moment. A thought came and he pulled more stones aside and dug around the bodies for weapons he knew soldiers always carried. He found nothing.

Using the staff, he tried to pry up the closest skeleton, but it was stuck in the earth. Having no choice, he shoved his hands under the coat and pulled up. The skeleton came apart, with the skull rolling down the slight incline. The dank odor was strong. He pried the bones up and out of the dirt, but still found no weapon.

The two skeletons were side by side. Old Coyote could only guess that they had taken shelter here sometime during the winter and had frozen to death. There were no signs of a fire. However they died, and for whatever reason they were here, he knew they were soldiers. Soldiers without weapons, it seemed. There was probably a story, one that would never be told.

Old Coyote touched the uniform coat and pulled at it. It was still intact; it had not rotted from the weather. He sat back to think. He had found clothing; if both uniforms were still intact, he could make use of them. They could be washed in the creek he had been following. The breeze was warm, so they would dry quickly. How he would explain coming home dressed in a soldier's clothing, without weapons, and without avenging his sister, he didn't know. But he was alive. That was something. It was the best he could hope for.

He had lived on mice and fish and rabbits and spent more days than he cared to remember wandering around naked. From flint he had fashioned a small finger knife using the point of a deer antler he had found. After four rabbits, he had barely enough hide to make a loincloth. But through the cold nights, shivering in a hole or against a bank, he had never felt so alive.

Old Coyote glanced at the skeletons. It would be a while before he was in that condition. He thought to bury them in the clearing nearby, then realized he had nothing to dig with. Collapsing the overhang over them would be easier. He wouldn't need the shelter now. He had clothes to wear.

Goings and Cloud kept a wary eye on the trees across the river as they followed the bank above the east side. From that vantage point, they were at the same level as the tops of the trees across the river. Deer grazed beneath the high canopy of cottonwood branches thick with leaves. Farther to the west, the open prairie was a wavering green floor that stretched to the low hills beyond.

"How long do you think it will take the horses to graze all that down?" Goings asked, pointing over the trees.

"More than a few days," Cloud replied, grinning.

To their right, the undulating ridges rose sharply above them, their slopes green with grass as well. The bank gradually narrowed and sloped down as the ridge behind ended abruptly with a steep bank, an old slide. Beyond the end of that ridge was a coulee, with a narrow watercourse that reached the river. Water flowed in it during wet springs, like now, but for most of the year it was dry. The Lakota called it Dry Creek. To the Crow, it was Medicine Tail Creek.

The two riders halted at the end of the bank above the mouth of the creek. A shrill cry of a hunting red-tailed hawk pierced the sky. Cloud glanced up in time to see it set its wings and dive.

"Look!" Cloud caught Goings's attention and pointed to the diving hawk.

They watched the hawk as it flared out, its tail feathers down in attack position as it struck something hidden in the grass. They saw a puff of fur and a small gray form roll through the grass as the hawk beat its wings to regain its balance, then pounced on the rabbit. The bird sat on its kill for some moments before it began to tear into its flesh.

Both men silently watched the hawk. The redtail had been part of the vision Crazy Horse had had as a boy. Occasionally, Crazy Horse wore an eagle feather in his hair, but more often he wore either a single tail feather from a redtail or a fan of four tail feathers. The fan pointed down, exactly like the redtail in attack position.

A breeze arose in the trees across the river, shaking the branches of the tall cottonwoods and forming a whirlwind that twisted toward the river. A column of brush and leaves rose and danced inside it. Over the river, it sucked up a white mist that dissipated quickly as it hit the eastern bank, crossing in front of the two warriors.

With a shrill, the red-tailed hawk launched itself upward and climbed swiftly, rising on the powerful winds of the whirlwind.

The whirlwind, with the hawk above it, rushed up a long, gradual slope that led away at a northward angle from Medicine Tail Creek. Higher and higher the hawk circled, until it blended into the sky. Meanwhile, the whirlwind gained the top of the slope and kept going.

Cloud glanced at Goings, who was shaking his head as he watched the whirlwind disappear over the horizon.

"Something will happen here," Goings said in a near whisper. "I can feel it. Something will happen here."

CHAPTER TWENTY-THREE

Bug

Sometime well after sunset, under the pale light of a half moon, the west-facing opening of the low dome-shaped sweat lodge was pushed open and several men crawled out of the structure. Wisps of steam flowed out with them. Last to emerge was Sitting Bull. Like the others, he walked into the narrow, deep creek behind the structure and rinsed off. Then the group gathered in a circle around the earth altar between the sweat lodge and the fire pit. Ashes still glowed in the bottom.

A helper brought a twig with a glowing ember and handed a pipe to the medicine man. Offering it to the Sky, the Earth, the Four Directions, and, finally, to the Great Spirit, Sitting Bull touched the ember to the tobacco in the bowl. The sweet aroma of red willow arose with the smoke. Passing the pipe to his left, Sitting Bull waited until every man had smoked—Worm, High Eagle, a Cheyenne medicine man named Eagle Road, Gall, Two Moons, Crazy Horse, Good Weasel, and Grey Bull.

"My relatives," he said, dismantling the pipe and handing it to the helper, "thank you for joining me. Tomorrow night, I will sweat and pray with the young men who have pledged to do the Sun Dance. It will be good if all of you can join us. The day after that, I think we should move to the area along Ash Creek. We will prepare the dance circle there."

Black Shawl was still awake when Crazy Horse arrived home. She had a cup of tea ready. Corn, the old woman who lived with them sometimes, was asleep under a robe near the south wall.

Coals glowed in the fire pit. Although the days were warm, the spring nights were still cool, at times downright chilly. With warmer weather and frequent moves during the spring and summer, no grass was stuffed between the inner dew cloth and the outer covering, but a low fire was often necessary for part of the night, especially for the older people.

Crazy Horse took the cup and sat against his chair. Black Shawl joined him, wrapping a soft deer-hide robe around her shoulders.

She was thin and had been since her long bout with the coughing sickness, and he was constantly worried about her health. But she would wave aside his concern, assuring him she would live to be a cranky old woman.

Their little daughter had died nearly five years ago, but there were still nights when he heard Black Shawl weeping softly. He had never been good at finding the right words, so all he could do was hold her when she cried. Several times, he had caught glimpses of one of They Are Afraid of Her's dolls, one Black Shawl had kept. He understood her grief. In the small bag of warrior's tools he often wore on his belt, he kept one of the toy bone horses he had made for her.

He sighed and sipped from the cup. It had been another long day. Reports from scouts were reassuring, however. No Long Knives were within four days of travel, which was as far out as the scouts were from the village.

"I have heard a lot of talk over the past few days," she said, breaking into his thoughts, "of a Sun Dance, of Little Big Man."

Little Big Man had been stirring up many of the younger warriors, convincing more than a few that now was the time to take the offensive against the Long Knives.

"Yes," he said. "Sitting Bull and High Eagle and my father have picked a spot farther to the east, along Ash Creek, for the Sun Dance. The main dancers will be several young Hunkpapa men. They pledged last summer and have been preparing since then."

"What about Little Big Man?"

"He is good in a fight," he replied, "but sometimes he acts before he thinks things through. The younger men are swayed by him."

"They are swayed because he is your friend." There was a cautionary tone in her voice. "He uses that. His words carry weight because of that."

"What is it you are not saying?" he asked.

For a moment, she stared at the glowing coals in the fire pit, then glanced toward the sleeping form nearby. "I think you should be wary of him. I do not think he will always be your friend."

An ember in the pit cracked softly. He sipped tea and leaned back against the chair and loosed a deep sigh.

"I heard something else that worries me," she went on softly. "Many are saying that you should be made the headman of all of the people, of all the Lakota bands. Some women asked me about that."

"Someone asked me too. There is a lot of talk about that. But our ways do not allow for one man to be given that kind of power. As far as I can see, if anyone is to be that headman, it should be Sitting Bull."

Black Shawl smiled to herself in the semidarkness of the lodge. "As I recall, when the old men gave you the Shirt, they asked you to be a Shirt Man and to take on the responsibility that came with it, because they knew many of the people were in favor of that. It is what the people think, what they want, that matters, does it not?"

"That is the difficult part," he replied. "They do not know what they are asking. I do not have all the answers. I have not lived long enough. I do not have the wisdom."

"Yes, but at least you know that. That is what the people see."

He finished his tea and reached to set the cup down next to the pot near the fire pit. "Sometimes I want us to take down our lodge and go find a place in some secluded valley somewhere and live by ourselves in peace."

She shook her head and grabbed his arm. "Maybe, but your sense of duty will not let you do that. Besides, the people would follow you, because we are all seeking that peace. We all want to live in peace."

Crazy Horse took another deep breath. "For that, it might mean we go to war to drive the white people away from us. That is one of life's ironies. Peace cannot be had without war."

South of the sleeping village, a young horse guard, Ashes, the son of Little Bird and Stands on the Hill, shook his head to fight off sleep. He was sitting with his back against an oak tree. From a flask, he poured water into his hand and splashed it on his face, then stood and tossed off the warm robe. The cool air was refreshing. The moon was in the western sky, and there were clouds here and there, and the first faint light was beginning to push over the horizon in the east. He felt good. It was his first night alone among the horses, and he had not fallen asleep. But he was hungry and would be glad to crawl into his bed.

At midmorning, Yellow Wolf stopped to visit with Little Bird. Ashes was still asleep as the two men sat outside the lodge drinking tea.

"He did well for his first time," Little Bird said, proud and relieved at the same time.

"You do not have to worry about him," Yellow Bird advised. "He is too much like you."

Little Bird loosed a self-deprecating chuckle. "I would feel better if he were more like his mother. When something has to be done, she is like a wolf that has caught the scent."

"Then perhaps he is the best of both of you. Like I said, you do not have to worry about Ashes. He will do well. With your permission, I would like to take him with me the next time it is my turn to scout," Yellow Wolf offered.

"That would be good," Little Bird consented. "Boys seem to listen better to anyone but their fathers. I am grateful, and he will be, too, in the end. But I know you have other things on your mind."

Yellow Wolf looked around, making certain no one was within earshot. "Yes, I do," he said in a low voice. "What is Little Big Man trying to do? Do you know?"

"Make a name for himself," Little Bird replied quickly.

"What will stop him from leading a raid on his own?" asked Yellow Wolf.

"The thought of getting on the wrong side of Crazy Horse," said Little Bird. "As long as he does not hear outright approval from our headman, he will do nothing. At least, I hope so. In the meantime, we need to talk to the young men we know and advise them to wait for whatever Crazy Horse and Gall decide to do."

"You think Little Big Man is a bit jealous of those two?"

Little Bird nodded. "I think that is part of it. If so, he can be a dangerous man. He might get in the way of what Sitting Bull is advising. On the other hand, Little Big Man knows that if he tries to do something on his own and no one follows him, he will lose face. He will embarrass himself. I hope that possibility is enough to make him cautious."

"I guess we will see what happens," Yellow Wolf sighed. "Perhaps Crazy Horse will step in."

"You can count on that," affirmed Little Bird. "Have you talked to Goings or Cloud since they returned from the Greasy Grass?"

"No, I was planning to do that today." Yellow Wolf handed the cup back to Stands on the Hill as she emerged from the lodge and thanked her. He wanted to finish straightening a bundle of chokecherry stalks he had been drying for arrows, but he also wanted to hear what Cloud and Goings had seen in the Greasy Grass valley.

At the last moment, he decided to go to the herd and catch the big gray gelding he had been training to pull the drag frames. *Might as well work with him while I can*, he thought. The gray had a calm disposition, but, although sure-footed and quite nimble, he had no speed to speak of. That made him the ideal horse to pull a drag frame and carry precious passengers. As the kind of horse that yearned for human attention, he was coming along nicely.

Just beyond the edge of the village, perhaps a lazy stone's throw away, was a line of low brush shelters erected by the single men, young or old. Yellow Wolf waved at two youngish men who looked up from the apparently difficult task of reassembling an old muzzle-loading rifle and returned his wave.

One of the horse herds was below the village to the south in a wide meadow. Halfway down a slight incline, Yellow Wolf stopped. Something nagged at him. After he stood for a moment, he turned back toward the line of shelters, some covered with canvas or hides. The two men he had seen working on the rifle were still talking to each other, bent low and trying to work out the intricacies of the uncooperative rifle. Down the line, another man was braiding strands of cord into a long rope.

As Yellow Wolf was about to turn away, he noticed a pair of shoes—shoes, not moccasins—with the toes pointed down, behind one of the shelters. One that was covered with a dark blue wool blanket. Yellow Wolf took a step up the slope to get a better look. Someone was obviously wearing the shoes. That someone was also wearing gray trousers. White-man trousers. Someone was either napping facedown or…

Yellow Wolf moved carefully up the slope, his moccasins making no sound on the soft earth. The two men working on the gun looked up at him inquisitively. He put a finger to his lips. They were puzzled but said nothing.

Angling to his right, Yellow Wolf continued to walk slowly. A pair of legs began coming into view. Whoever they were attached to was not moving.

He slowly circled back around the intervening shelter, careful not to make a sound. Coming around to the back, he saw a man bent over on hands and knees trying to peek around the shelter. Yellow Wolf moved closer a step at a time until he was behind the man in the gray trousers and brown shoes. He was also wearing a dirty blue shirt.

"That is a bad way to take a nap," Yellow Wolf said.

The man might as well have been poked with the sharp point of a lance. In an instant, he was on his feet, but tripped over something and fell back, his startled face looking up at Yellow Wolf.

Something about the frightened little man was familiar, annoyingly familiar. The clothes gave him away as one of the newer arrivals from the agency. There was a reason the man was hiding. Then he remembered—it was the eyes. Even when the man had somewhat recovered his nerve, his eyes were still unusually wide.

It was Little Feather, also called Bug. The man at the agency everyone said was White Hat's eyes and ears. Now he was here. But why?

"My friend," Yellow Wolf said with a friendly tone, "when did you arrive?"

Bug rose to his feet and brushed off his clothes. "Y-yesterday," he replied apprehensively.

"Did you come alone?"

Bug nodded.

"Have a good journey, or was it difficult?"

"N-no."

Yellow Wolf had to work at keeping a straight face. "Which one? Was it good or difficult?"

"No, no. It was good, it was good." Bug appeared to be recovering his nerve with each passing moment, though it was difficult to tell by the expression in his eyes.

"See any Long Knives along the way?"

"Ah, no. I…ah, no. No Long Knives."

Yellow Wolf smiled and started down the slope, then turned around. "How long are you staying?"

The young man shrugged. "Hard to say. I came to stay."

"I see. Do you have a gun?"

Bug nodded. “Yes, yes I do. I have a rifle.”

“Did you get it from White Hat?”

“Ye—. I mean, no. From a friend at the Spotted Tail agency.”

Yellow Wolf gazed at the nervous little man. He had a feeling about him, and it was not good. Bug was here for a reason. Yellow Wolf was certain that the man would not have chosen to come on his own. He would give odds that Bug’s rifle was like the kind the Long Knives used. Probably with plenty of ammunition to go with it. A payment from White Hat.

“I will let Crazy Horse know you are here,” Yellow Wolf said over his shoulder as he turned and walked toward the meadow. “He will be glad to hear another fighting man is here—with a good rifle.”

Bug nodded, but he looked as though he was about to throw up. Suddenly, he noticed the two men in front of the next shelter staring at him strangely. “What are you looking at?” Bug demanded. Then, losing his sudden bravado, he ducked inside his blanket-covered shelter. Sitting with his head down and knees drawn up, arms curled around his legs, he noticed that the laces on his right shoe were untied.

Yellow Wolf walked as nonchalantly as he could manage and stopped behind a grove of scrub oak. The more he thought about it, the more he was bothered by the presence of that mousy little man. True, a number of Lakota men were working for the whites at the agencies as policemen, otherwise known as “those who catch men.” Other names for them were Club- or Short-Stick Carriers because of the short hardwood clubs they carried. Others called them Iron Breasts because of the shiny iron badges they wore pinned to their chests. But those men did it openly and endured the anger or ridicule or mistrust of their friends and relatives, probably for the pay they received or the prestige of wearing a blue coat.

Bug was a different matter. He was working for the whites on the sly and had been for years, perhaps. How many people at the agencies down south had he betrayed? Yellow Wolf wondered how many other Little Feathers there were wandering around undetected through the village, listening and sitting in on conversations, fully intending to betray the people here.

He had to find Fast Horse. He knew about Bug. Together, they could talk to Grey Bull and Crazy Horse. He turned and headed for the west side of the village, resisting the urge to find the little man again and grab him by the scruff of his neck.

As Yellow Wolf headed off on his mission, Sitting Bull, together with High Eagle, Worm, and Eagle Road, sat in the council lodge with twelve young men.

"In two days, we will move again," he said. He indicated the other medicine men. "We have selected a place to do the Sun Dance, along Ash Creek, farther west of here. There are also some hills in that area, good places for the vision seeking. When we are in the new camp, we want to put four of you at a time on the hill. Starting tonight, we will sweat and pray to prepare all of you. We will do a sweat every other night until the Sun Dance starts."

The medicine man paused to look at each of the young men. Four of them had danced to the sun before, with two of those four on the verge of their third and fourth Sun Dances. Eight were pledging for the first time and were trying to hide their apprehension.

"I want to express my gratitude for what you are doing on behalf of the people," Sitting Bull continued. "As we go along, I want you to remind yourself of that. This is for the people. It is difficult to know what waits for us as a people in the years ahead. That is why we are gathering—to think, talk, and pray.

"There is one thing I know for certain: we need to be strong. But strength needs to come from more than just the warriors. There is a strength that comes when everyone thinks the same, when every man, woman, and child is committed to doing what is best for everyone. That means we must be strong of mind and spirit. That is why what you have pledged to do is important. When you dance to the sun and the people see the sacrifice you make for them, that strength will begin to grow. That is why I express my gratitude."

If any of the young men who had pledged their first Sun Dance had any doubts about their decision, they disappeared like the fog yielding to the heat of the sun.

A shadow crossed the opening of Bug's little shelter, and then another. A face ducked low and peered in.

"My friend Little Feather," called out Yellow Wolf, "come out. I want you to meet someone. Perhaps you remember him."

Bug ducked through the opening and straightened himself, reluctant to look into the face of the man standing next to Yellow Wolf. Both were much taller than him, and very broad in the shoulder. These were men who had actually seen battle, probably while he had been living by his wits on the agency. His family had gone there, along with many other Sicangu loyal to Spotted Tail, eight years ago, when he was twelve. At the agency, he had not been taught the path of the hunter and warrior. Things change, he was told. The days of the "wild" Lakota are gone. However, these people here, a few thousand, from the looks of it, didn't seem to be planning on disappearing.

He steadied himself and looked into the face of Fast Horse and knew he was in trouble.

"My friend Bug," Fast Horse said calmly, "good to see you. I take it this means you have given up the ways of the whites?"

In the interest of survival, Bug nodded.

"Good! Crazy Horse will be glad to hear that. He wants to talk to you," Yellow Wolf said, smiling.

Bug felt his legs wobbling and reached out to lean on the top of his little shelter. "Cra-Crazy Horse himself?" he stammered.

"Himself," Fast Horse nodded. "Come. We cannot keep him waiting."

Yellow Wolf bent down and looked inside the lean-to. Its floor was covered with canvas, and blankets were neatly rolled to one side. Not far from the opening was a little fire pit below a small iron grate on top of which was a new coffee pot.

Yellow Wolf pointed to a rifle lying in the back of the tiny dwelling. "That is a good-looking weapon," he said, pointing. He reached in and grabbed it. "I think we will show this to Crazy Horse as well."

Bug couldn't recall how he went from his shelter to the large lean-to shade made of slender pine poles and pieces of canvas. Beneath it sat two men, one older, one younger. The younger man, with dark-brown hair in two thick braids and a thin scar on the left side of his face, motioned for him to sit.

"I am Crazy Horse," the younger man said in a low voice. "This is my uncle, Grey Bull."

Silvery flecks of gray in the older man's hair did not match the intensity of his probing gaze. He said nothing initially, choosing instead to study the inwardly trembling Bug.

"We are glad that many people from the agencies have joined us," Grey Bull finally said in a deep, resonant voice. "I assume that your reason for coming here is the same as all the rest—they do not like how things are with the whites. Up here, we intend to stay a free people. What do you say?"

Bug took a deep, nervous breath and stared at his feet. He tried to clear his throat, but bleated like a sheep instead. "Ah…ye-yes. I think—I think they are right," he wheezed.

"We are told that you are friends with one of the Long Knives down there," Grey Bull continued. "A shrewd young man by the name of White Hat. White Hat Clark, I think."

It was a statement spoken with the conviction of truth, and one difficult to argue. He couldn't. He was friends with White Hat, at least from his side of things.

"What do you suppose this White Hat thinks of you, Grandson?" the old man asked.

"What…what do you mean, Grandfather?" Bug at least had the sense to be respectful of the old man. But it was more than respect. He had never been so afraid in his life, not even of White Hat.

"What are you to this white man named Clark? What are we Lakota to the Long Knives, or any other whites? Why is it that they say their headman is our 'Great Father' and that we are his 'children'?"

"I…I do not know."

"I believe you. What do you think this White Hat will do to you if you go back now and have nothing to tell him, except what he probably already knows—that we are gathering to do a Sun Dance. What would he do to you?"

Bug's breath became shallow and fast, and his mouth was dry.

Grey Bull leaned forward. "Do you want to find out?"

Bug slowly shook his head. "N-no." He had never felt so helpless, so powerless, ever in his young life. His shoulders slumped and his chin dropped toward his chest. "I…I would like to stay."

Grey Bull smiled. His eyes softened a bit, but his tone did not. "I am glad to hear that, Grandson. Glad to hear that, because we will need your help. Tonight, we need you to take your turn at guarding horses, from dusk until dawn. Can you do that for us?"

Bug nodded.

"Good. Some young men will come to your little lodge before it gets dark. But I want to tell you something." He pointed to Yellow Wolf and Fast Horse. "See my nephews there? They can track a mouse in the moonlight. Do you understand what that means?"

Bug nodded again. "Yes, Grandfather. I…I will wait for the young men."

On shaky legs, Bug rose and took his leave. Just before he turned, he locked eyes with Crazy Horse. In them was neither anger nor friendliness, only a piercing, measuring gaze that made his stomach turn cold.

As he walked away, he was already thinking about how he could get word to his mother and father that he was never going back to the agency.

Fast Horse turned to Grey Bull. "Uncle," he said, "that little man knows things. It is certain he has heard things or seen things that other people did not, or could not. White Hat was very good to him."

Grey Bull nodded confidently. "First, we will make friends with him. When he trusts us, he will talk."

"What about this?" Yellow Wolf asked, lifting Bug's good breech-loader.

"Give it back to him," Crazy Horse told him. "But keep the bullets, for now."

CHAPTER TWENTY-FOUR

They Have No Ears

Blunt Arrow waited until the group of people and horses that he had been watching stopped inside a grove of sandbar willows above a small creek. The creek flowed into the Powder River, which was running high. He had crossed it this morning, and the current was stronger than he had thought it would be. The group included several small children, and they would need help crossing the stream.

There was no question in Blunt Arrow's mind that they were from either the Spotted Tail or Red Cloud agency. For the past month, there had been a steady flow of people moving toward the Tongue River region. Everyone was assuming that the Sitting Bull and Crazy Horse people were there. Crazy Horse had told scouts like Blunt Arrow to be on the lookout for anyone and to point them in the right direction.

After spending several long moments checking the surrounding skyline for signs of other people, Blunt Arrow mounted his gray gelding and loped down the hill to the creek.

Two men, two women, and four small children watched him approach. Two Hawk grabbed the handle of his old six-shooter. It was the only firearm they had.

"He is Lakota," White Bear, the other man, said.

"Look at his clothes," said White Dress, Two Hawk's wife.

They stared at the rider, who was dressed in a tanned deer-hide shirt and leggings and elk-skin moccasins. Only the rifle resting across the withers of his gray horse and the six-shooter tucked in his belt were not Lakota made. It had been several years since they had seen anyone dressed in this manner. Bags decorated with quills hung on either side of the horse, and the rein and neck rope were made of braided buffalo hair.

White Bear and Two Hawk exchanged glances, suddenly embarrassed by their white-man clothes. They stepped out of the willows and raised their hands in greeting.

"Friend," Two Hawk called out, "good to see you."

Blunt Arrow stopped his horse and dismounted gracefully, a smile on his face. "Good to see you as well," he replied. "How long have you been traveling?"

"Twelve days," Two Hawk replied. He pointed toward the horses. Two were pulling drag frames. "They are old. We go every day until they are tired."

"You have come a long way in twelve days," Blunt Arrow told him. "Four or five more days and you should find the camp. It is probably somewhere along Ash Creek now. But first, we have to get you across the river."

"Are there many people?" White Bear asked.

Blunt Arrow could not help but notice that their supplies were meager, and they all looked thin and worn. Three boys and a small girl stared at him in utter, wide-eyed curiosity. All were dressed in white-man clothes.

"Several thousand, according to some," he told them. "More every day. Is anyone behind you?"

Two Hawk shook his head. "I do not think so. There were some behind us, maybe half a day, but they only had one horse. I think they turned back."

"Several thousand?" said White Bear. "I know people have been leaving the agencies. Suddenly, one day, someone or some family is no longer there."

"Yes," Blunt Arrow affirmed, "several thousand."

After following the creek, they came to the Powder at midday and set up a camp. Blunt Arrow wanted to look for a crossing. He gave the women the dried meat he had.

"I noticed you have a bow," he said to Two Hawk. "Are you any good with it?"

"Best thing to hunt with around the agencies," the man replied, smiling. "That way, the whites hear nothing."

Blunt Arrow pointed to White Bear. "He and I will look for a crossing. Maybe you can find some fresh meat."

Well downstream from the campsite, Blunt Arrow and White Bear found a straight and wide section of the river. Where it was wide, the current was often not as strong. Blunt Arrow mounted and rode slowly into the water, letting the horse pick his own way. At the deepest spot, the water was up to the horse's belly. Blunt Arrow piled stones on the opposite bank as a guide marker and crossed back over.

Arriving back at the camp, they found the women roasting several rabbits that Two Hawk had shot. The children were playing in the willows. By now, it was late afternoon. White Bear told them of the crossing farther downstream.

"After we eat," Blunt Arrow said, "we can cross and make camp on the other side. Tomorrow, you can get an early start."

"You will not come with us?" White Dress asked.

Blunt Arrow shook his head. "No. I need to stay around here for a few more days."

"What will happen?" White Bear asked. "There is a lot of talk that Sitting Bull is gathering power, that he has a plan to drive out the whites."

Blunt Arrow shrugged. "I do know this," he said, "he brought us together. With all of us together, there is a feeling of…of sharing something bigger than each of us. What he has been telling us is easy to understand: together, we are strong."

The first lodges were taken down in the early morning. Before the middle of the day, nearly seven hundred households were on the move. Most of the horses had been moved the day before. At an unhurried and leisurely pace, the move was like a lark, the people playing in the warm spring sun. Nevertheless, lines of warriors rode on either side of the wide column. Laughter and the shouts of children drowned out the songs of meadowlarks and the bright calls of the red-winged blackbirds. Thousands of drag poles sliced into the soft earth and left an obvious trail.

After a half-day's travel, the camp was set up in between low sandstone cliffs on the south side of the cold, fast-flowing waters of Ash Creek. Farther south, in a flat meadow, the Sun Dance grounds had been marked out and sweat lodges had been erected. As Sitting Bull had instructed, sweat ceremonies would be conducted every night.

Six days after the new village was in place, the Sun Dance tree was cut and hauled to the middle of the dance circle and put in place. The sacred cottonwood was not allowed to touch the ground after it had been cut until it was replanted in the dancing ground. A sense of anticipation and purpose was palpable. Even young children were caught up in it, though they didn't understand exactly why.

Under the supervision of medicine men and their helpers, the young men who had pledged to dance were put on isolated hilltops to spend several days and nights alone, taking no water while fasting and praying. A final preparation for the Sun Dance.

Every day, there were new arrivals. The fastest and easiest route from the agencies near the headwaters of the Smoking Earth River was to head south of the Black Hills and then in a northwesterly direction.

Two Hawk and White Bear followed Blunt Arrow's directions from the river crossing and found the village. The first indication of the number of people present was the number of horses. On the top of a hill south of the village, they stood in silent awe. Several herds were scattered in the low, wide valley all the way to the western and eastern horizons. There were thousands of horses. Thousands.

Three days after their arrival, the Sun Dance commenced.

For four days, the young men danced, and thousands of people gathered around the dancing grounds. For four days, the sun shone as the dancers stared relentlessly into its searing brightness while the drums pounded ceaselessly from sunup to sundown. At the center of the dancing circle was the sacred cottonwood, its branches decorated with streamers. Attached to the sacred tree by cords looped through the chokecherry skewers in their chests, the dancers gave themselves to the pain and danced, praying for their people to have the strength to persevere.

On the last day, at the conclusion of the dancing, Sitting Bull offered one hundred small pieces of his flesh, fifty from each arm. Sitting against the sacred tree as Eagle Road and High Eagle took the flesh, his blood flowed down his arms and soaked into the earth. His body stiffened as he went into a trance.

The two medicine men recognized it immediately and kept him upright until it passed. When Sitting Bull was himself again, they washed the blood from his arms and led him from the dancing circle.

Two days later, the Hunkpapa medicine man gathered the Sun Dancers, together with Worm, Eagle Road, High Eagle, Gall, and Crazy Horse, in the council lodge.

Most of the people in the ever-growing encampment had not seen a Sun Dance for many years. Children who had been born at the agencies had never seen one. Excitement over the ceremony had not waned. Throughout the camp, it was still the topic of conversation.

Sitting Bull said as much. "We have been reminded of who we are, what we are," he told the men sitting with him. "Not every Lakota will participate in the Sun Dance, but none of us should forget what it means. I am reminded each and every time. But something else happened two days ago. I was given a gift. I was able to look into the future. I saw something that gives me hope."

An expectant silence filled the lodge.

Sitting Bull pulled out a bundle of sage from a bag and leaned forward to drop some onto the hot coals glowing in the fire pit. A pungent odor rose with the white smoke. He reached into the smoke and pulled it toward him.

"Two days ago, I saw victory," he went on, "victory over Long Knives. Long Knives and their horses were falling from the sky into the circle of a great Lakota encampment," he said, pointing up. "The white men were bloody, their ears were cut off. A voice said to me, 'They do not listen, they have no ears. I give them to you, but do not take what belongs to them.'"

The silence prevailed for several long moments, then Gall, the Hunkpapa war leader, spoke. "Uncle," he said softly, "you have taught me that we should not take such things lightly. A victory over Long Knives is a good thing, but I must ask you this: Do you know if there will be a war? Or did you see one battle?"

Sitting Bull watched the last of the smoke from the sage float upward and out through the smoke flap of the lodge. "I cannot say, only that there will be a victory. Yet I think there is something else."

"The voice," High Eagle said. "We need to listen to the voice."

"You are right," Sitting Bull agreed. "I think it was saying two things. First, there will be a victory. *I give them to you* means that. I also heard, 'Do not take what belongs to them.'"

Gall glanced at Crazy Horse, who was staring ahead, an inscrutable expression fixed on his features. "Uncle," Gall asked, "what does that mean?"

"I know what it means," Crazy Horse said. "It means that victory over the Long Knives is not complete unless we do what the voice says. We must not take their guns or their bullets or their horses, or anything that is on them."

Sitting Bull nodded silently in agreement.

Gall glanced around at the others in the lodge. "That will be difficult," he pointed out. "Guns and bullets are what we need if there is to be a war!"

"True," Sitting Bull replied. "But the difficulty is not that we need such things. The difficulty is that young men will not understand why they must not take them."

"Then tell me why, Uncle," Gall insisted, "because I do not understand."

The medicine man threw up his hands. "I am not wise enough to know all the answers," he admitted. "But if there is to be a war, there will be many battles. My vision was of one battle, I think. Winning one battle is not enough. There is a reason the voice said not to take their things. The way to learn that reason is to listen to the voice."

"Our scouts have not seen any sign of Long Knives," Gall told everyone. "When will this battle happen?"

High Eagle cleared his throat and looked directly at Gall. "The important thing, Nephew, is that it will happen. The other message, though it is not as plain, is that we must be ready at any time."

Noting the stern tone in High Eagle's voice, Gall nodded but decided to say no more.

"Warriors arrive every day," Crazy Horse said. "I think we have around eight hundred, perhaps more. They all seem to be willing to fight. Many are young, however. Others have experience but have not taken to the war trail for several years. We will do everything we can to prepare them.

"Weapons are another thing. Although many have a gun of some kind, there are a number of them who have only bows and arrows."

Gall leaned forward and looked cautiously in the direction of High Eagle. "My friend has revealed a difficult truth," he said. "We need weapons, and when we have the chance, we take them from our enemies. A gun is not only a worthy prize of battle, it is necessary for a man to fight on an equal basis with any enemy, especially the Long Knives."

Sitting Bull stared straight ahead and then down at the fire pit. "Life is full of choices," he said. "The kinds of choices we make cause things to turn one way or another."

He looked for a moment at the young Sun Dancers. "I can only tell you what I saw and heard. I believe that what I saw and heard gives us choices."

He paused to look at Gall and Crazy Horse. "I must ask all of you here to give the message of my vision to our warriors. They must understand,

and if they do, then maybe they will honor it and make the right choice when the time comes."

Unable to contain his restlessness, Cloud looked across the lodge at Sweetwater Woman. "Where is Song?" he asked suddenly.

"Just outside, playing," she told him. "Why?"

"Feel like going for a ride?"

"All of us?"

"Yes. I will get the horses. The two of you can get ready."

Song rode her own horse, a steady old gelding. A bay mare was Sweetwater Woman's favorite, while Cloud decided to give his buckskin warhorse a bit of exercise.

They rode north, crossed the creek, and climbed an incline that took them to the top of the sandstone rims. Although they were at the level of the tops of the lodges, they still couldn't see the western end of the village. Turning west, they followed the crest of the rims and stopped at a point Cloud thought was in line with the center of the village. There, they took in the view below them.

People were everywhere. From this distance, faces could not be distinguished. Children were moving continuously, often in small groups. Here and there, in between lodges, women were kneeling and scraping hides staked out on the ground. Girls and young women carried bundles of firewood from piles that had been stacked around the encampment. To the south, horses grazed peacefully. Now and then, new colts dashed off in impromptu races, celebrating a sudden surge of life and playfulness, their short tails up like banners.

Sweetwater Woman reached out and touched her husband's arm. "I remember the gathering along the Shell River, eleven years ago, I think," she said. "There are just as many people here, maybe more."

"More, I think," Cloud replied.

"Where will we go from here?" she asked.

"I think to the Greasy Grass. The old men sent Goings and me to look around there several days ago. Plenty of good grass and water."

She shook her head slowly. "No, I mean, what will happen? What does Sitting Bull's vision mean?"

News of the Hunkpapa medicine man's vision had swept through the encampment faster than a hot wind.

Cloud gazed at the image in the valley below. Something about it touched him like few things had. There were moments in his life when he felt validated—when Sweetwater Woman's parents consented to his marriage proposal, and the first time he had seen his daughter. This was one of those moments. But this was more than personal validation.

"I have never felt more Lakota in my life," he said to Sweetwater Woman. He pointed to the view below them. "Because of this. I have been thinking about that vision. I want to talk to High Eagle and Grey Bull about it. I think…I think the vision means exactly what it says: a victory. It means we are strong. But I also think there is a warning. What it is, exactly, I do not know."

On a hill across the valley, two other Lakota stood next to their horses and took in the view. Little Big Man and Rain in the Face, an Oglala and a Hunkpapa, were both battle-hardened warriors ready to fight Long Knives at a moment's notice.

Many months ago, Rain in the Face had been a prisoner of the Long Knives at the outpost near the Great Muddy River. Several Long Knives held him while another beat him until he lost consciousness. Since then, he had thought of nothing but revenge. For as long as he lived, he would never forget the face of the one who beat him. One day, a speaks-white came and told him that he had been captured by mistake. He turned him loose, his nose broken and his eyes nearly swollen shut, and without his weapons or his horse. In the end, he learned that some Lakota had been blamed for a crime whites had committed. To Rain in the Face, Long Knives had no purpose that justified their existence.

It was well known that Little Big Man had nothing but disdain for Long Knives. In Rain in the Face he had found someone who agreed with his contention that the fight must be carried to the Long Knife outposts and white towns.

"Our medicine man has had a powerful vision," said Rain in the Face. "He has seen a victory. We need that victory to happen so the Lakota who have fallen under the spell of the white men at the agencies will come to their senses."

Little Big Man couldn't agree more. "Yet there is one thing that bothers me. His vision means that the Long Knives will come to us. They will attack us like they attacked Two Moons. Something must be done before that."

Rain in the Face shrugged slightly. "To attack the Long Knives—or any other whites—before that vision comes to pass would be an insult to a good man, a question against his power," he said hesitantly. "I respect him."

Little Big Man nodded, not entirely surprised that Rain in the Face didn't want to question Sitting Bull. Everyone respected the Hunkpapa medicine man, but, as far as he was concerned, that was no reason to sit back and wait for the Long Knives to attack.

He pointed toward the encampment. "Many people could get hurt if Long Knives attack us here," he pointed out.

"There are many warriors here," Rain in the Face rebutted. "More than I have seen in one place in a long time. Scouts are three, four days out in every direction. Long Knives would have a hard time getting close without being seen."

Not wanting to push the issue, Little Big Man fell silent. He had considered leading a secret raid against one of the Long Knife outposts along the Shell River to prove his point. If he succeeded, the old men and Crazy Horse would listen to him—if he succeeded. It would be a risk, and he wondered how many warriors would follow him. A few, perhaps, but probably mostly young and inexperienced men eager to prove themselves and not enough experienced veterans. Nothing would be proved if all he managed to do was get a few boys killed.

He flipped the rein over his horse's head and mounted. "Perhaps you are right," he said. "But if we are to believe Sitting Bull's vision, Long Knives will be in our camp. That is the part of the message I do not like."

Little Big Man rode down the hill, angry and perplexed. He wanted to believe in the vision because he wanted a victory over the Long Knives. *If it does happen*, he wondered, *what would come after that?*

CHAPTER TWENTY-FIVE

The Absence of God

West of the Powder River, a thousand-man column arrived at the site where Fort Reno once stood. Scattered debris lay about, suggesting that it had been an active outpost at one time, but not even the wooden markers in the post cemetery were still standing.

A bearded man sat on his mule for several minutes before he dismounted to stretch his legs. Brigadier General George Crook knew that the Lakota and their Cheyenne and Arapaho allies had obliterated the post in the summer of 1868, not long after it and one of the other forts along the Bozeman Trail, Fort Phil Kearney, had been abandoned by the army. The Indians and the elements had done a thorough job. A sudden breeze flung dust pellets as if to remind him of this.

Taking off his narrow-brimmed hat, he wiped the sweat from his forehead and walked ahead slowly, looking west toward the Bighorn Mountains, trying to ignore the utter desolation all around him. It wasn't difficult to understand why the Indians had laid waste to the place, but he still resented them.

He pulled a watch from his shirt pocket and absently stroked his beard. "Lieutenant!" he called without looking up.

There was a quick shuffle of footsteps, and a slender young man appeared. "Sir?"

"Inform the troop commanders that we will bivouac here for one night. We will move out at dawn."

"Yes, sir. Will there be anything else?" The lieutenant glanced around nervously.

"No. Well, ah, would you see to it that my tent is pitched at once? And bring me my valise." He glanced at his watch again. "Officers Call in an hour."

He noticed the apprehension in the younger man's expression. "Nothing to worry about," he assured the man. "The Sioux are farther north. They will not bother us here."

The lieutenant nodded but did not appear convinced as he left to carry out his orders. As soon as he was gone, another man, one more self-assured, joined the general.

"You think the lieutenant never seen an Indian in the flesh," Sergeant Major MacAllister commented with a wry smile. His uniform tunic was unbuttoned because of the heat. "Maybe he got his fill with Colonel Reynolds up on the Powder." He watched the young officer for a few moments before he turned his weathered face back toward Crook.

"I think he did," the general replied. "That was not the way for an inexperienced officer to learn about fighting Indians."

"Been soldierin' for a lot of years, sir," the sergeant major said, already putting the lieutenant out of his mind. He waved an arm at the landscape. "Never have I laid eyes on hard country like this. I like it now no better than the last time we was here. Doesn't hold a candle to Virginny."

"My sentiments as well, Benjamin," Crook agreed. "Guess they pick old salts like you and me for postings in places like this because we've seen it all."

"If I was to decide the issue, General, I'd say let them Sioux have it."

"Couldn't agree more. But as you well know, there is more involved to this whole affair, and most of it, soldiers like us will never know. When the president and his generals, with more stars than I will ever have, say to round up the hostiles, that is exactly what we do."

The sergeant major chuckled, his raspy voice matching the dry breeze. "Beggin' your pardon, sir, but do they know what it takes, any of 'em? Guess they don't care that my old bones ache."

"No, Benjamin, they don't give a damn."

"Wal, half the blame is mine. It was me who decided soldierin' was what I wanted. I forget why, now." The sergeant major glanced around at the desolate landscape. "Times like this, I could kick myself," he said caustically.

"Aching bones and all, Benjamin, I'm glad you're along on this sortie."

"Thank you, General. In the end, I wouldn't trade it for anything. Maybe that's all us old soldiers can expect, sir, to look back at the trail we rode and wonder how we did it."

Crook nodded. "Careful, Benjamin, someone might mistake you for a wise man."

"No chance of that, General. Speakin' of hostiles, when will them friendlies be joinin' us?"

The general looked toward the mountains. "The Shoshone and the Crow? I expect any time. You might want to pass the word. We don't want the sentries getting nervous. Or the lieutenant to have apoplexy."

The heat of the early June day disappeared with the sun. A cool evening turned into a chilly night. Sentries on the second watch were forced to put on overcoats to stay warm. In spite of a bit of nervousness—most of the sentries were wondering how to tell a friendly Indian from a hostile one—the expected contingent of Shoshone and Crow scouts did not show. By nine o'clock the next morning, under a bright sun, the ponderous column was heading out once again, moving only as fast as its slowest wagon. The scrape of iron-rimmed wheels on the sandy ground and the clunk of wooden wagon boxes mixed with the jingle of metal bridle bits and the squeak of leather harnesses and saddles.

Second Lieutenant Edward Monseet Holliman rode next to the general near the front of the column. "Where were you ten years ago, Lieutenant?" asked the general.

The young officer found the sudden inquiry somewhat disconcerting, but he was also acutely aware that it had come from a general who outranked him by five grades. "Ah, sir, I was in my first year at the College of William and Mary."

"Oh? I was under the impression you graduated from the Point?"

"I did, sir. The appointment came through during my first year in college. I transferred."

"Ah, yes, of course." The general waved a hand at the dim trail they were following across the sandy landscape dotted with occasional clumps of sagebrush. "Ten years ago," he went on, "this was a well-traveled road."

"Yes, sir. Known as the Bozeman Trail?"

"Precisely. There were three outposts. We just left Fort Reno, or what is left of it. We will pass the site of Fort Phil Kearney, along Piney Creek. Nothing left of it either. Beautiful spot, however. Farther north was Fort C. F. Smith."

"I read something in a newspaper about 'Red Cloud's War.' It said he defeated the United States," the lieutenant recalled. "Was that true, sir?"

"Not in my opinion. That old rascal Red Cloud may think he won, and perhaps some people in the East think so also. But it was a tactical withdrawal on our part. Someone realized that a rail line could be laid in along the Yellowstone River, and that made the Bozeman Trail unnecessary, so the posts were abandoned."

"What about the Fetterman incident, sir?"

Crook glanced over his shoulder, making sure no one was within earshot. "Lieutenant, honest appraisal of an enemy's capabilities is a soldier's duty. Make no mistake, our weapons are superior and we are better organized. However, the Sioux are skilled fighters and they are better cavalry than we are. Their boys are placed on the back of a horse at the age of three or four. Although he gained experience in the war against the South, Fetterman knew nothing of the Sioux. He thought of them as inferior."

"But, sir, I thought he was hopelessly outnumbered."

"He was. What you must realize is that the Sioux understood that the best way to change the odds against an enemy with superior weapons is with superior numbers and the willingness to take losses."

Holliman glanced at the sawtooth ridges toward the west, their eastern slopes shadowy in spite of the morning sun. "I suspect, sir, they know this country as we never will."

"Astute observation, Lieutenant," Crook replied. "This is their home."

"Sir, I have always wanted to be a soldier, and I know a soldier must follow orders, but there are moments when I wonder why we are here."

The general glanced at the young lieutenant and immediately saw the confusion etched on his clean-shaven face. "Well," he replied after a moment, "a soldier does follow orders. Like you, Lieutenant, I have given thought to the task that lies before us. Like you, a part of me does wonder why. But then I remind myself, as I shall remind you now: civilization has always brought change, and at times we act for the later benefit of those who resist."

"Are you saying, sir, that the Sioux will benefit from what we are doing?"

"They can, if they so choose. Many of them have already made the sensible choice. Red Cloud and Spotted Tail and their subordinates have seen the writing on the wall. They have chosen to accept civilization. It is sad they cannot convince Sitting Bull and Crazy Horse to do the same. Therefore, it is up to us to compel them by force."

The lieutenant shook his head. "General, do you think we can?"

"There is no doubt in my mind that we will prevail, but they will bloody our noses. You can be sure of that."

Holliman nodded thoughtfully and said no more.

Crook knew that, in spite of his boyish appearance, the lieutenant was nearly twenty-seven and was reputed to have been one of the most scholarly graduates of West Point. His only experience in the field had been as part of Reynolds's unfortunate escapade against an Indian camp on the Powder River nearly two months earlier. After his troops had stormed the village, Reynolds had left dead soldiers, and one wounded, behind in the face of a Cheyenne and Sioux counterattack. Crook had been impressed with the young officer's comportment during Reynolds's court-martial hearings. Although Holliman testified to the facts as he knew them, he refused on several occasions to assess Reynolds's actions, stating that his own inexperience disqualified him from making tactical judgments. Because of that, Crook decided to assign him as his aide.

"As we speak," the general continued, "Major General Terry is on a westerly route from Fort Abraham Lincoln with nearly two thousand men. Colonel John Gibbon is proceeding east from Fort Ellis in Montana Territory with nearly five hundred under his command. Combined, we are a force of over three thousand, better armed and better supplied than the Sioux can ever hope to be. Furthermore, we do not have women and children to worry about. We have the advantage, Lieutenant, and we shall press it."

"Where are they, sir? The Sioux, I mean?"

"I suspect north of us, below the Yellowstone River and northwest of the Powder River. We have reason to believe Crazy Horse will not wander far from what he considers his home territory. Sitting Bull will be close by, if they have not joined forces already. We and Major General Terry and Colonel Gibbon will drive them before us. Then we will close the trap."

At midday, from their vantage point on the south ledge of a sandstone outcrop, Black Lance and Flood noticed the low cloud of pale brown dust at the edge of the foothills.

"Only hundreds of hooves could raise that kind of dust," Flood said.

"Hooves that are not moving very fast," observed Black Lance. "I have a bad feeling about this. I think we will see Long Knives before the afternoon is over."

A moment later, they spotted four riders, advance scouts far ahead of the dust. Through his field glasses, Black Lance noticed that two of them looked like Crow.

After the scouts passed west of their position, the front of the dark column finally came into view. Black Lance was right—they were Long Knives. Perhaps Sitting Bull's vision was on its way to coming true.

Black Lance glassed the open landscape northeast of the approaching column for any other outriders. With some irritation, he saw several riders some distance from the main body. "We should move our horses or one of those riders might find them," he said.

"I will move them farther east. That way, you can stay here and keep an eye on those Long Knives," Flood suggested.

Black Lance pointed to the outrider who was farthest from the column, though still some distance behind the scouts. "Go, before he gets closer."

Like water trickling down a rock, Flood worked his way down the low bluff and was out of sight. Through his field glasses, Black Lance could now see wagons. He guessed the Long Knives would stop soon and make camp, since it was already late in the afternoon. Their four scouts would certainly find the creek north of the sandstone bluffs. For a column with more animals than people, plentiful water was always a necessity for making camp.

With a growing sense of annoyance, Black Lance watched the plodding column getting closer and closer. It suddenly dawned on him that they were following the Powder River Road, the one the Long Knives called the Bozeman Trail. It had been years since a column of this size had used this trail. There was a reason those Long Knives were here, and it was not to protect gold seekers, as they had done years before, Black Lance guessed. From the looks of things, the Long Knives in this column were armed and equipped to do battle. He slid back until he was wedged in a deep fissure behind the lip of the ledge, just in case one of the outriders happened to look closely at the sandstone bluffs. Noting that the intruders were riding four abreast, Black Lance began counting.

Just as silently as he had climbed down from the ledge, Flood reappeared.

By then, the long line of mounted Long Knives and several wagons were passing the bluffs and the end of the column was in sight. Behind the wagons were some walking Long Knives, with a mounted rear guard behind them.

"That is a lot of Long Knives," Flood whispered.

Black Lance nodded as he scratched another line on the surface of the ledge in front of him. Each line represented a row of four, and there were already over a hundred lines scratched on the rock.

"How many?" Flood asked.

"Over four hundred so far. I think there are two times that many."

Flood let out a low whistle. "What are we going to do?"

"I think we should see where they camp for the night. I have a feeling they will stay on the Powder River Road. We need to get word to Crazy Horse. I will stay and keep an eye on these intruders."

Black Lance's hunch was right. The Long Knife column stopped at the creek north of the bluffs and turned itself into a wide, sprawling camp of square white tents on both sides of the fast-flowing stream.

The two Lakota scouts made their own cold camp to the northeast. Cloud and Yellow Wolf were probably close by, ready to relieve them. At the first hint of dawn, Flood was prepared to leave.

"When you see them," Black Lance said, "let them know that the Long Knives are following the Powder River Road."

"I will. Will you keep heading north?"

Black Lance nodded. "I will go as far as the plateau with the red streaks in the stone."

It didn't take long for Flood and his fast little bay gelding to fade into the hazy shadows of dawn. When he couldn't see them any longer, Black Lance grabbed his flat, braided buffalo-hair rope and expertly looped it around the gray mare, turning the braid into a neck and girth rope. From it, he hung his encased rifle and bullet bag, the water flask, his bow and quiver of arrows, and a badger-hide case. Across the mare's withers, he draped and tied the rolled-up elk hide. Next, he untied the horse's hobbles. Looking around to make sure that he had left no obvious sign of human presence, he mounted in one swift motion and rode off.

Holliman finished saddling his tall bay horse. From a trooper waiting nearby, he took the reins to Crook's favorite mule, also saddled and ready for the day. He led both animals up a slight incline to where the general was waiting.

The lieutenant had slept only fitfully through the night. At the first sign of daylight, having gone to bed dressed, he had arisen and changed his shirt, removing only his outer uniform tunic. The ankle-length nightshirt his mother had sent him he had left behind at Fort Fetterman, wrapped and hidden in a trunk. He felt that a long Quaker nightshirt did not fit in with the spartan existence of a frontier post. Besides, he didn't want to risk becoming the butt of jokes from other officers.

In the ice-cold waters of the creek, he washed and shaved his face, washed his feet, then slipped on a fresh pair of socks.

Monseet had been his mother's maiden name, and it was a custom in his father's family to bestow the eldest son with his mother's surname as his second name. He was the first in his father's family to serve in the army, having secretly asked his maternal grandfather, Major General Hiram Monseet, to petition on his behalf for the appointment to the United States Military Academy. Monseet had been only too happy to comply. Unfortunately, the letter of appointment had arrived at the Holliman residence and was opened by his father, Isadore Holliman. Consequently, young Edward had to endure an entire evening of his father's angry tirades. On advice from his mother, he had not uttered a word, to avoid further enraging the Quaker minister. Two days later, he turned nineteen and accepted the appointment.

Holliman glanced toward the mountain ridges gnawing at the sky. He did not wonder about the presence or absence of God in such desolate landscapes, but he did doubt the wisdom of anyone who thought white men belonged here in this country. In his opinion, it was a savage land meant for savage people.

Crook turned at his approach, an unlit pipe clenched in his teeth. "Good to see you up and about, Lieutenant. I trust you rested well."

"Yes, sir," Holliman lied.

"I wish I could say the same," the general admitted. "An uneasiness awoke with me."

"Uneasiness, sir?"

"I cannot fathom the reason for it, but it bothers me still. When the sergeant major arrives, I shall order him to extend our defensive perimeter. What is the date today, Lieutenant?"

"The twelfth, sir. June twelfth."

CHAPTER TWENTY-SIX

Night Riders

From the red rims of the high plateau, Black Lance watched three riders coming south, following a dry creek, working their way to the northern base of the plateau. He knew who they had to be, but he wanted to make certain. Pulling out his field glasses, he watched until the distant, dark figures of men and horses slowly took on color as they came closer and closer. Finally, Black Lance recognized the light bay horse belonging to Flood. The other two men were Cloud and Yellow Wolf.

By nightfall, Cloud, Black Lance, Flood, and Yellow Wolf were camped in a deep, grass-filled gully east of the foothills of the Shining Mountains. For most of the afternoon, until the Long Knife column encamped once again for the night, this time near Goose Creek, they had shadowed the slow-moving formation.

The pine-covered slopes and gullies in the area around Goose Creek were very familiar to the Lakota scouts. It was Lakota territory, after all, but more than that, Goose Creek was a special place. Ten years ago, it was in the cold waters of its upper reaches where the bodies of warriors killed in the Battle of the Hundred in the Hand had been washed. So the hundreds of Long Knives camped along its banks now were more than an intrusion; they were an insult.

They were far enough away from the column to have a small fire. The hot tea along with the friendly orange glow of the low flames was a comfort, especially in the chill of the evening.

"Little Feather told us that the Long Knives plan to round us all up like their cattle and take us to the agencies," Yellow Wolf told Black Lance and Flood.

Flood smiled. "They have to catch us first."

"How are your horses?" Cloud asked them.

"Good," Black Lance replied. "They have been resting. Do you want us to take word to Crazy Horse?"

"You must leave as soon as it gets light enough," Cloud replied. "Go to the west of the Wolf Mountains. From there, head straight north until you reach Ash Creek. Knowing our headman, he will want to do something about these visitors right away. My guess is they will stay on this trail. Crazy Horse might want to flank them from the east, and that would mean crossing over the Wolf Mountains. Be sure to mark the trail so that you will be prepared to lead them here, if that is what he decides to do."

Flood carefully added several small dry twigs to the fire and looked in the general direction of the Long Knife camp. "What about Sitting Bull's dream? Does it mean that we cannot stop these Long Knives before they get to our encampment?"

Cloud shook his head. "No. Things happen the way they are meant to happen, but that does not mean we do nothing about these intruders. With their wagons, they have to move slowly, so that means they are three to five days from Ash Creek, maybe more. I know Crazy Horse will want to stop them, and so will Sitting Bull. As warriors, that is our responsibility."

The three of them, all younger than Cloud, nodded, acquiescing to his experience and status as a proven warrior, and a Crazy Dog warrior at that. They all knew that he was more than capable of taking his place as a war leader alongside Gall, Black Moon, Good Road, and several others if he wanted to. In spite of his reluctance to assume leadership, he had the respect of many young warriors.

"As for Sitting Bull's vision," Cloud went on, "I have never questioned the power and wisdom of men like him, or High Eagle, or Crazy Horse's father, Worm. They know things and see things the rest of us cannot. So we must trust them and be ready for whatever we have to face."

Yellow Wolf suddenly stiffened and pointed to the horses, only a few paces away. All of them were peering north, their ears forward and nostrils flaring. In an instant, Black Lance extinguished the fire with handfuls of dirt, covering it thoroughly to dissipate the smell of the smoke as well. In the next few heartbeats, all four men were standing with the horses, straining to hear what was out there.

There was no moon yet. Except for the distant, faint chatter of coyotes, the night lay in utter silence. The darkness was pervasive, but not impenetrable. Shapes could be discerned in various shades of black.

All the horses were still intently gazing to the north, but whatever they were hearing or smelling was not yet detectable by the weaker senses of their human companions. So the warriors waited. Eventually, they heard the first soft scratches of horses walking on soft earth, with occasional *clop-clops* of unshod hooves stepping on stone.

The noises grew louder, indicating that the horses in the darkness were approaching the scouts' position. There had to be twenty or thirty, perhaps more. The steady pace clearly indicated that the horses were being ridden, not wandering in the darkness of their own accord.

Cloud drew his bow from its case, which was attached to his buckskin's neck rope, strung it, and draped the strap of the quiver full of arrows over his shoulder. The others followed his lead. If they had to defend themselves, an enemy would have difficulty discerning from which direction silent arrows were coming. The muzzle flash of a six-shooter or rifle would give away their position, but they could always resort to guns if necessary.

The noises were steady now and almost on top of them. They had chosen their camp because it was in a deep, narrow gully with a north wall of sandstone where a now dry but ancient creek had carved a bend. The wall was no higher than the withers of a horse.

Cloud whispered to the others, "Put your horse up against the bank and stand against him on this side."

After a few moments of quiet shuffling, everyone was in position, the horses standing nose to tail.

Now they could hear low, muffled voices intermittently and an occasional clink of metal, but they didn't hear the consistent rub of metal on metal that would indicate that the riders in the dark were Long Knives. Whoever the riders were, they were extremely cautious. In another moment, they began to pass on either side of the gully.

The riders on the north side of the dry creek wall would not have been able to see the hidden Lakota scouts, even in bright moonlight. It was those who were passing on the south side that Cloud was worried about. If any one of them stopped to look into the gully, it would be but a moment before he would discern four horses standing end to end. Luckily, no one stopped. But the flow of riders around the gully was like a slow, meandering stream, a maddeningly slow stream.

To a man, the Lakota scouts kept a steady, reassuring hand on the side of the neck of each horse. Years of patient training were paying off. Every one of the horses stood quietly, knowing that the steady pressure on the neck meant to stand quietly and motionless as long as the hand was there, whether it was during a driving rainstorm, a blizzard, under a blazing sun, or on a dark and moonless evening.

There was no way for Cloud or the others to know how many riders were passing in the dark. No one spoke or moved, and everyone kept a wary eye beyond the low bank to the south. They could see only shadows passing.

Finally, the last whispery scrapes of unshod hooves faded into the darkness, but still the scouts remained motionless, straining their ears for every sound they could catch. There could be stragglers.

After a long, long interval, Cloud whispered to Yellow Wolf, "Follow them on foot for a while. They have to be Crow heading for the Long Knife camp."

"They are Crow," whispered Black Lance. "I could smell the bear grease they use in their hair."

Yellow Wolf handed the rein of his horse to Cloud and blended silently into the darkness.

"If they are joining the Long Knives, that means they are looking for us. Our encampment, I mean," Flood whispered angrily.

"You are right," Cloud replied. "At dawn, you must head out. When you get home, find Crazy Horse immediately and tell him."

Just as the three men began to relax somewhat, from nearby came the bark of a coyote. A soft, inquisitive bark. Cloud was quick to respond with his own bark. Moments later, Yellow Wolf crawled down the embankment and rejoined them.

"They are headed for the Long Knife column," he reported. "No way to tell how many, though."

"Had to be fifty, at least," Cloud estimated. "Maybe more."

At dawn, the four scouts were moving. First, they followed the hoofprints of the riders that had passed the night before. They had come from the east, and without a doubt were Crow, hired to scout for the Long Knives. The riders had wisely stayed in a file in the dark, so it was difficult to estimate their numbers. But the impressions of sets of unshod hoofprints over others hinted that there were more than fifty.

"I think the Long Knives will stay on the gold trail because they know it," Cloud told Black Lance. "That means they could cross the headwaters of the Greasy Grass River. That is too close. They could turn and follow it downstream. The Crow scouts will think that we could be in the Greasy Grass valley and tell the Long Knives. They have to be stopped before that happens."

"Our horses are rested," Black Lance replied. "We should reach the encampment before sundown. We will pass the word to Crazy Horse."

As the sun rimmed the eastern horizon, Cloud and Yellow Wolf parted company from their fellow scouts and turned northwest. From the top of a low, grassy hill, they paused to look back toward the Long Knife camp.

Cloud cleared his throat after a moment of looking through his long glass. "The Crow are still in the gullies and breaks east of the Long Knives," he said to Yellow Wolf. In the circle of his glass, he could see the sprawling camp of white tents around Goose Creek. From among the gullies and hills to the east, he saw several thin lines of smoke rising from campfires. A cold feeling returned to the pit of his stomach. The Crow knew this country well—it had been theirs before the Lakota pushed them north.

Cloud glassed the landscape to the east and south. Nothing large was moving. Only hawks, eagles, and falcons prowled the skies. A silence lay over the land, as if it was waiting for something to happen. And something was going to happen; Cloud could sense it. What it was and where, he did not know, but something was in the wind.

At midmorning, Cloud and Yellow Wolf came to an area of low, broken hills with plenty of cover. They stopped inside a small grove of scrub pine below a small butte. Leaving the horses in the pine grove, they climbed the butte and picked a spot in a low thicket of sagebrush. From there they had an unobstructed view of the Powder River Road. As Cloud settled in, Yellow Wolf returned to the horses and took them to water in a small creek nearby.

At about the same time, Black Lance and Flood were following the lower fork of the Tongue to the point where it joined the north fork. The main stream was running full, so they backtracked and crossed the narrower forks. Although no less full, they were at least narrower and not as deep.

On the north side of the upper fork, they rested the horses briefly and then started walking, leading their mounts. All morning they had been alternating their gaits, mainly from a low lope to a trot. In between they would dismount and walk, as they were now, or run with the horses to lessen their load. Unceasingly, they stayed alert, keeping watch on the ridgelines all around, not forgetting their unexpected nighttime encounter with the Crow.

They were headed in a northwesterly direction for the southern end of the broken line of high ridges known as the Wolf Mountains, the divide between the Greasy Grass River and Rosebud Creek. Once there, they would turn north until they came to the lower fork of Ash Creek.

"What if Crazy Horse is not in camp?" wondered Flood.

"Then we get word to Gall," Black Lance replied. He pointed to a dip in the ridge ahead. "From there, we ride. How old is your horse?"

"Six," Flood said. "I raised him from a colt."

"Mine is eight. They are both in good condition, so I think we can push them a little harder. We have to reach home before the sun goes down."

Far to the south, Cloud tapped Yellow Wolf on the shoulder. The younger man had spread out his elk-hide robe beneath the sagebrush and was napping in the shade.

"Something is happening," Cloud told him. "The Long Knives have not moved all morning, and I think the Crow are finally joining them."

"Then they were waiting for the Crow," Yellow Wolf said, sitting up. "That means they had a plan to meet there."

"It might be good to have a closer look," Cloud suggested. "You can stay here with the horses. I will see how close I can get on foot."

Yellow Wolf squinted against the bright sun, his expression indicating some disagreement with the idea. But he knew there was no chance of dissuading Cloud from doing what he wanted. "Signal me with your glass when you return, so I will know that it is you."

Cloud pointed to a winding gully that followed the small creek below them. "I will follow that," he told Yellow Wolf, "and return the same way."

"Good. Be careful."

Checking to see that the loads in his six-shooter were still in place, Cloud tucked the gun into his belt and grabbed his encased, unstrung bow and quiver of arrows, leaving his rifle. After taking a short drink from his water flask, he tied it to his belt and picked his way down the back of the slope. In a moment, Yellow Wolf could see him trotting along the creek bed, and then he was out of sight.

Holliman watched the approaching Crow horsemen with more than a little apprehension. He turned aside to the sergeant major. "How many?"

"Over a hundred, I would say," the noncommissioned officer replied, noting the young officer's nervousness. "These people, the Crow, have been on our side for a long time," he added.

"How do you tell them apart from the Sioux?"

"Well, I'll tell you one thing, Lieutenant: do not ask them that. The Sioux and these here Crow are blood enemies, have been from before we came 'round. They hate each other."

Led by Crook's chief scout, the new arrivals rode toward the head of the column. "It strikes me, Sergeant Major," Holliman said, "that these people might have an ulterior motive for being on our side."

"Sir?"

"One of the vicissitudes of human nature."

"Beggin' pardon, sir. I got no notion of what you jus' said."

"Look at it this way," Holliman patiently replied. "It seems to me these people are using us to get at their ancient enemies. That being the case, we are a convenient tool, or a means to an end, more so than friends."

"That I can understand, sir, and I be agreein' with you on that score."

The lieutenant had to admit one thing. These brown-skinned men rode like they had been born on a horse. If their fighting abilities matched their horsemanship, they would be valuable allies. Secretly, however, he wondered how far their loyalty could be counted on.

Farther down the line, clusters of troops, along with civilian teamsters, watched the arriving Crow with no less apprehension than Holliman. To more than a few, all Indians were alike, and none of them were to be trusted.

"Best keep both eyes on all your possibles," growled one grizzled veteran.

"I thought they was here to help us," whined a young infantry soldier.

"Likely they help themselves to yer hair," snickered another standing beside him.

An unenthusiastic burst of laughter was short-lived. All eyes were on the parade of slender, lithe riders glancing neither right nor left and moving in total unison with their horses. There was no noise except for the soft plop of unshod hooves on the gravelly soil—no persistent jingle of metal bits or squeak of saddle leather. Most of the Crow warriors were dressed in tanned leggings and animal-hide shirts; some wore necklaces of large beads. A few wore a cloth shirt, and all had nearly waist-length black hair worn in two tight braids, many with a single eagle feather or a cluster of two or three hanging down from the back of the head. Rifles were carried across the withers of the horse, or hung in a hide case. Many of them also carried a single lance tipped with a long iron point or an encased bow and a quiver bristling with arrows hanging across their back. Nearly all of them carried a pistol tucked into a belt. All in all, it was a colorful display of military precision and neatness.

"That be more Indians in one bunch than I ever set eyes on," admitted one of the civilian teamsters, his hand seeking the reassuring feel of his rifle.

"They got no saddles," observed another soldier.

Up the line, Sergeant Major Benjamin MacAllister heard his name called out. He hurried to the general's tent.

"A nice, tight regimental formation, if you please, Sergeant Major. As fast as you can make it happen," Crook said, smiling, as he watched the Crow riders.

The sergeant major was never one to question an order, and certainly not one from the commanding general. In this instance, he clearly understood the general's intentions.

"Right away, sir!" MacAllister ran for his picketed horse and was soon loping through the encampment, looking for the company sergeants. "Regimental formation, on the double!" he called out. "Inform your troop commanders, now! General's orders!"

Word spread quickly, but the reaction did not match. The strident barks of company sergeants rang through the camp. Initially, a confused melee ensued, with men going in every direction; however, the relaxed atmosphere inevitably changed, and hundreds of soldiers sprang into action.

Cloud had finished covering himself with the branches he had cut from the sagebrush nearby when he heard and saw the sudden frenzy of activity in the Long Knife camp. He had crawled to well within arrow-shot of the camp and found a brush-covered knoll just high enough to allow him a wide view. The line of Crow riders had arrived, apparently stirring the Long Knives into sudden motion, as hundreds of blue-clad men were running in every direction. For a moment, Cloud thought the two groups would fight.

With a bemused smiled, he watched through his looking glass. The long line of Crow riders stopped and turned their horses left and waited. Mounted Long Knives finally began moving in organized lines. Those on foot formed in lines behind them.

Cloud heard the strident calls of Long Knife voices. He would have laughed at the entire incongruous scene unfolding in front of him except for the real fact that, no matter how they stumbled about, the several hundred Long Knives he was watching were a serious threat to the lives and well-being of his own kind. Finally, after the mounted Long Knives and those on foot formed into lines and sat stiffly on their horses, or stood, facing the Crow, the sudden activity settled.

His smile faded as he began to count the Crow riders, but he lost count at one hundred sixty. Because the Crow blocked some of his view, he had to stop counting Long Knives at just over seven hundred. He knew there were more, however, perhaps closer to one thousand.

Vivid images and sounds from past encounters with Long Knives pushed their way into his memory: the crack of gunfire, the rumble of charging horses, blasts of wagon guns, the concussions of explosions, the moans of wounded men, and the screams of dying horses. After a deep breath, he began to count again.

Through his glass, he saw Long Knives and Crow look suddenly toward the south, then he saw the reason why: there were more new arrivals. Another long line of dark-skinned riders was approaching. After a moment, he knew who they were: Shoshone, at least fifty or more.

The new arrivals filed in between the Crow and the Long Knives. As he neared the end of the line of Crow, the lead Shoshone rider spun his horse on a quarter turn to the left and stopped. Each rider behind him did the same, one after another, in a display of precision horsemanship. After the last rider turned his horse, the Shoshone ended up in front of the line of Crow riders facing the Long Knives.

Cloud ignored the ants crawling over his legs and paid no mind to the sand lizard that dashed between his elbows as he steadied the glass in his hands. Again, he started counting the enemy gathering on the plains between the two forks of Goose Creek. Letting out a slow breath, he hoped that Black Lance and Flood were pushing hard to take the news to Crazy Horse.

There was no doubt now: the Long Knives were hunting the Lakota. There was no other reason for the presence of the Crow and Shoshone warriors.

CHAPTER TWENTY-SEVEN

Strong Hearts

Black Lance glanced over his left shoulder at the bright sun hanging halfway between the middle of the sky and the western horizon. To the east were the undulating ridges of the Wolf Mountains. The encampment on Ash Creek was far over the northern horizon, but the horses were still strong.

He pointed to grassy knoll ahead. "We can walk from there and let them catch their wind, but we cannot stop to rest," he said to Flood. "We need to keep moving."

"Yes," Flood agreed. "And I think we should keep a straight line, as much as we can, toward home. I think the chances of encountering enemies are less now. We can avoid having to stay out of sight so much."

Black Lance nodded as they reached the knoll. They dismounted and began walking. Both horses were sweating but were not overly winded.

"Do you think these are the same Long Knives who attacked Two Moons and He Dog last winter?" Flood wondered.

"They have to be, since they are coming from the south, more than likely from the outpost farther up the Shell River from Fort Laramie."

"Have you ever seen that many of them at one time?"

"No, I never have."

"I keep thinking that every one of them has a rifle and plenty of bullets. If each of them has, say, twenty or thirty bullets..." Flood's voice trailed off.

"Long Knives always have more guns and bullets than we do," Black Lance quickly pointed out. "But, as my father told me, a gun and a bullet by itself is useless. It is up to the man who shoots the gun. He said there is more to being a warrior than holding a gun in your hand. You have to keep your head in a fight, overcome your own fears and doubts, and use the skills you were taught. A warrior with three bullets who kills three enemies because he stays calm and steady is more effective than one who has twenty bullets and hits nothing."

Flood walked in silence for several long moments. "I think my father said those same kinds of things," he finally said. "I can remember some of it; I was twelve when he was killed in the Battle of the Hundred in the Hand."

"I remember your father," Black Lance replied. "He always had a smile on his face."

"At times like this," Flood admitted, "I miss him most of all. He would be forty-four if he was still alive."

"He had time to teach you things," Black Lance reminded his friend, "the same kinds of things my father taught me. All we have to do is remember their teachings, and use them. We are the warriors now, and there is an enemy back there who must be defeated."

They walked in silence again, their moccasins softly scratching on the grass, glancing back frequently to make sure no one was following them and keeping wary eyes on the ridges around them. Behind them, the horses also stepped lightly on the soft earth.

Black Lance pointed ahead to the end of a long meadow. "We can ride again from there," he said. "And I think we should step up our pace."

At about the time Black Lance and Flood remounted and urged their horses into a lope, Cloud rejoined Yellow Wolf. "From here, they looked smaller than ants to me," the younger warrior complained, "but they seemed to be moving around."

"They were," Cloud affirmed. "I will never understand why Long Knives do the things they do. But I know Shoshone when I see them."

"Shoshone? With the Crow?"

"They arrived after the Crow finally showed up in the Long Knife camp. I tried to count them all. There are about a hundred and fifty Crow, maybe more, nearly a hundred Shoshone, and perhaps nine hundred Long Knives."

Yellow Wolf let out a low whistle. "What are we going to do?"

"Keep watching them. Whatever they do, wherever they go, we will be their shadows, and we wait for Crazy Horse."

Yellow Wolf glanced toward the Long Knife camp. "They are looking for us."

"They are, so we have to stop them in the next day or two."

"How many fighting men do we have? Does anyone know?"

Cloud smiled wryly as he handed his glass to Yellow Wolf. "Seven hundred, maybe."

Yellow Wolf stretched out the glass and pointed it toward the Long Knife camp. "Some men are always away hunting," he muttered.

"Yes, and there are maybe fifty scouts scattered in all directions. That means a few hundred are in camp. But the more important thing to me is when."

"When?"

"Yes. Say Black Lance and Flood get home after sundown and find Crazy Horse as soon as they do. Crazy Horse will gather all the men he can and head out at first light. That means he will reach here, or farther north, just before sundown tomorrow. At least I hope so."

The younger man was puzzled. "Why?"

"Because we need to attack these Long Knives and their Crow and Shoshone friends while they are still together in one group."

"But that way, they outnumber us for sure."

"I know three things about Long Knives," Cloud pointed out. "There are two kinds: those who walk and those who ride. The walking ones are slow; that is the second thing. The third thing is that those on horses cannot fight very well from the back of a horse."

"I thought you said 'when' was the important thing."

"It is. As one large column, they are slow and get in each other's way. The last thing I want to see is for them to split up into smaller and faster groups. So we need to attack them before they do that."

"Look!" Yellow Wolf pointed and then handed the glass back to Cloud. "The Long Knives are breaking camp!"

Black Lance looked down from a sandstone bluff in the direction of the sprawling encampment south of Ash Creek. Long shadows were stretching across the valley. Horses were grazing in the meadows below, with guards positioning themselves for the night. People were moving about among the lodges. It was the most peaceful scene he had ever seen, and it made him despise the Long Knives on Goose Creek. He reached down and stroked the powerful neck of his horse, whose ears pointed forward as he picked up the scent of other horses.

Flood pointed to the sun sitting on the western horizon. "By the time we get to the camp, it will be down," he said.

At the bottom of the slope, they met two young horse guards setting up their camp for the night beneath two bent and gnarled pine trees. The teenage boys stared at the trail-worn scouts and their horses stained with sweat.

"Do you know if our headman is in camp?" Black Lance asked them.

They both nodded. "I saw him in the afternoon," one of them said. "He was watering his horses in the creek."

Although they were anxious to deliver their news, they were not anxious to cause any panic. They rode toward the west end of the encampment, where the Oglala lodges were situated. A small crowd outside the Oglala headman's lodge was a sure sign he was home. Crazy Horse glanced up from his chair and spotted the scouts immediately.

They dismounted as the man stood and walked forward to meet them. "You look like you have had a hard journey," he said.

Black Lance rubbed his horse's neck. "Not as hard as they have," he replied. "My friend, we have news."

Crazy Horse looked at the two scouts and walked a few paces farther from the group of people sitting near the door of his lodge. Black Lance and Flood followed. "What is your news?" he asked.

"Long Knives," Black Lance said in a low voice. "Nearly a thousand of them, with Crow scouts. When we left this morning, they were still at Goose Creek."

"They came up from the south, following the Powder River Road," Flood added.

Crazy Horse stared at the ground for a moment. "You counted them?"

"As many times as we could to make sure," Black Lance assured him. "Cloud and Yellow Wolf are watching them now. Cloud is sure they are looking for us. He thinks it would be best to cross over the Wolf Mountains and come from the east."

"He is right," Crazy Horse agreed. He turned and caught the attention of a boy in the crowd at his door. "Go to the lodge of Sitting Bull," he said after the boy came to him. "Tell him I am asking the old men to gather, right away, as soon as they can get to the council lodge. Hurry, but do not run or speak to anyone else."

The boy, about twelve, nodded and hurried away.

The headman turned to the two scouts. "I am grateful for what you have done," he said. "Now you can rest."

"No," Black Lance protested. "No, we want to go back. We marked a trail."

Crazy Horse glanced around. "From Goose Creek, those Long Knives can reach the Greasy Grass valley in three days, maybe two. We cannot let them get that close. As Cloud said, it would be best to cross over the Wolf Mountains and come at them out of the morning sun."

"You mean leave tonight?" Flood asked.

Crazy Horse nodded, deep in thought. "Yes, as soon as we can. The days are long, so we have daylight left."

"We will be ready," Black Lance said. "We need to get supplies and fresh horses."

Black Shawl knew something was happening. She heard her husband tell the small crowd sitting outside that he had to meet with the old men in the council lodge. As he ducked through the doorway and stood, their eyes met.

"What is it?" she asked.

"I am going to talk to the old men," he said. "Long Knives are on Goose Creek, below the headwaters of the Tongue River. The scouts said there are nearly a thousand of them."

Black Shawl could feel a change in her husband's demeanor. Only a moment ago, he had been sitting with the people outside, listening politely. Now there was a coldness, and she could feel it filling the room. She knew, however, that it was not directed at her. The warrior inside him was emerging. "What will happen?" she asked.

"I will leave this evening with as many warriors as want to follow. Some…some food would be good. After I talk to the old men, I will catch my warhorse and come back for my weapons."

She crossed the room and put her hand in his. "I will have your things ready," she told him.

He reached up and touched the side of her face. "Maybe Grandmother Corn can stay with you." He lingered for a moment, looking around the lodge as if gathering his thoughts, and then ducked through the door.

The council lodge was nearly full when Crazy Horse arrived. Old faces glanced up politely and expectantly. At a nod from Sitting Bull, the war leader began to speak, not bothering to take a seat.

"Grandfathers," he began, after softly clearing his throat, "two of our scouts have brought news. There are Long Knives to the south along Goose Creek, perhaps as many as a thousand."

Murmurs coursed through the circle of old men. Polite expressions turned to concern and anger.

"We should not wait," Crazy Horse went on. "They must be stopped."

Old heads nodded in agreement, and more murmurs rumbled, like the beginning of a low growl.

"I would ask the camp criers to put out the call for warriors to prepare themselves. We must leave as soon as we are ready."

Sitting Bull rose and faced Crazy Horse. "It will be done," he said.

"Pray for us, Uncle," Crazy Horse asked.

"We will do that most of all," the medicine man promised.

With a soft swish of leather, the war leader ducked out through the door.

Sitting Bull glanced around at the circle of old men. "My friends," he said, "it is time for us to be strong."

True to his word, the Hunkpapa medicine man sent four old men with strong voices to announce Crazy Horse's call for warriors. Mounted and waving eagle-feather banners signifying their important status as heralds, the men started from the council lodge in four directions, turned with the sun, and rode through the sprawling village. "My friends and relatives," they called out, "it is time to be strong! We need our warriors to be strong! We need our warriors to stand between us and our enemies!"

Star Woman arrived just as Sweetwater Woman stepped out of her lodge. They listened to the crier coming nearer. "What is happening?" Sweetwater Woman asked her mother.

"Trouble, I think," Star Woman replied. "They are calling for warriors. Someone told me two scouts just returned and went to the lodge of Crazy Horse."

"Who?" Sweetwater Woman wanted to know.

"It was not my son-in-law," her mother said. "But the word is that Long Knives are coming."

"Long Knives are at Goose Creek!" the crier shouted. "We need our warriors! Long Knives are at Goose Creek!"

"Goose Creek," Star Woman repeated. "Good! They are not close."

Song arrived, nearly out of breath from running. "Mother, where is my father?"

Star Woman pulled her granddaughter close. "Seeing to his responsibility," she said in a reassuring tone.

"Where is Goose Creek?" the girl persisted.

"To the south," her mother replied. "Two days away."

"Is that where my father is?"

Sweetwater Woman knelt in front of her daughter and took her hand. "Yes, that is probably where he is. But do not worry. Your father knows how to take care of himself."

The girl nodded, though the shadow of concern did not fade completely from her usually bright eyes.

Earlier, as the sun had dipped closer to the western horizon, the village had begun to settle down. Women had been taking down meat racks and mothers were looking for their children. Men were leading buffalo runners and warhorses from the herd to picket them at their lodge doors. But as the criers rode through the village, a renewed energy flowed through the sprawling encampment, like a hawk that had found a current of rising air and stretched out her wings to ride it upward.

Now women set aside the fears that always nibbled at them when they knew their warriors were about to put themselves in harm's way. Many prayed silently even as they packed food in small rawhide cases and filled water flasks, tossing glances at their husbands and sons as they worked.

Men took stock of their weapons, gathered tools and equipment, and rigged neck and girth ropes on their horses. Young boys, not yet warriors, watched their fathers, uncles, and grandfathers prepare, holding onto a small hope that they would be asked to go along.

Little Bird finished tying his weapons onto a solid bay with black stockings while his oldest son, Ashes, held the rein to the gray warhorse. Two Horns stood with his mother, ready to hand a bag of food to his father.

"I am depending on the two of you," Little Bird said to his sons, "to look after your mother and your grandmother while I am gone. Keep your weapons close, and picket your horses at the lodge every night."

Although both boys were inwardly disappointed, they knew their father fully expected them to do as he asked. Their family's safety and well-being was their responsibility until he came home.

"We will," Ashes promised.

Stands on the Hill tapped her youngest son on the shoulder, and Two Horns took the hint to hand the bag of food to his father.

"Come back to us," she said to her husband.

Little Bird took the bag and stepped toward his wife, caressing her cheek. "I will," he said. "Until then, our sons will watch over you."

A stone's throw away, in the next row of lodges, Black Shawl waited. She had her husband's weapons hanging and leaning against the sturdy red-willow tripod to the right of the lodge door. Containers holding food and paint, a folded elk-hide robe, and his tools and equipment were piled near the weapons. His favorite horse, a yellow-and-white mare, waited patiently but seemed to sense the change of atmosphere in the village. Soon, Crazy Horse appeared, leading a sorrel warhorse.

There had been many partings such as this for them, but neither one felt any less anxiety each time it happened. Crazy Horse immediately set about loading and arranging his weapons and other gear on the mare and the sorrel. Everything except for a lance. Taking it, he impaled it point first into the ground near the tripod.

"Keep it there until I am home," he told her. "Until we all come home."

She nodded and waited for the next part of their ritual.

Unfolding the elk robe, he covered them both in the manner of a young man courting the object of his heart. "I hope I have been a good husband to you," he said gently.

"You have been the best of husbands," she assured him.

"Someday, we will go away together somewhere, to some secret place."

"I will hold you to that," she replied softly. "In the meantime, remember, it is better to lay a warrior naked in death than to be wrapped in finery with a heart of water inside."

"I will endeavor never to forget."

"Come home to me," she whispered.

"My footsteps will always turn toward you," he replied. "And my last thought will be of you."

In a moment, after a long embrace, he stepped away and folded the elk robe and tied it across the withers of the mare. Swinging up on the paint, he took the lead of the warhorse from his wife. With a wave and shy smile, he turned and rode away.

Somewhere nearby, an old woman began to sing a Strong Heart song, lifting her small but determined voice to the wind, encouraging all the fathers and sons and grandsons riding away to face the enemy.

Crazy Horse rode past the council lodge, through the opening between the rows of lodges, and turned his horses south. But instead of heading across the valley, he began to circle the village.

Kills Two, a very old man, watched him, and amid the unbearable desire to mount a horse and follow the war leader, he realized what was happening. He turned toward several mounted warriors nearby. "Follow him! Follow him!" he shouted to them. "He is doing an old, old thing. He is Gathering the Warriors. Follow him! He will circle the village four times!"

Small points of orange light in the valley below them were easier to see with each passing moment. Just now, the sun had slid behind the western horizon and shadows were deepening. The Long Knives were in a wide valley with clusters of trees and shrubs on either side of Rosebud Creek. The Rosebud was west of the Wolf Mountains and flowed into the Elk River far to the north. On the east side of the Wolf Mountains was the Greasy Grass River, into which Ash Creek flowed. Along its banks was the Lakota encampment.

"They moved a long way faster than I thought they could," observed Yellow Wolf.

"Because they left their wagons behind at Goose Creek, with some of the walking Long Knives. The others rode the mules that pulled the wagons," Cloud pointed out. "They left Long Knives behind to guard the wagons. When they need new supplies, probably food, some of these Long Knives will go back."

Yellow Wolf spat into the dirt. "That means they can move faster, and then they might do what you said—break up into smaller columns."

The two scouts were belly down on a high ridge overlooking the valley. Here, the stream bent straight north, for the most part. There was a wide bend, however, where the Long Knives and the Crow and Shoshone friends had made camp.

"They are a hard day's ride from Ash Creek," Cloud said.

"Do you think Black Lance and Flood have reached the village by now?" Yellow Wolf asked hopefully.

"Yes, they should have. Now it all depends on what Crazy Horse decides to do." Cloud pointed down into the valley. "I have a feeling they will move out at daylight. How do you feel about riding at night?"

"I can do it. What do you have in mind?"

"I will stay here and watch them. You should leave soon. When you get back to Ash Creek, tell them where the Long Knives have moved. Whatever this bunch does, I will stay ahead of them. Where they will go, exactly, is hard to know, except that it will be north. Tell Crazy Horse there is no time to lose. I will stay ahead of these Long Knives and watch out for our warriors."

Yellow Wolf looked behind them as the dusk deepened. "Do not show yourself. The Crow and the Shoshone will have scouts out."

"Do not worry about me," Cloud replied. "You have the more difficult task. Push hard. Take my horse and change off when yours gets tired."

"What? No! What if—"

"Take him! That way, I do not have to worry about finding a good hiding place for him."

Yellow Wolf reluctantly yielded to the older man's logic. "Do you need my bullets?"

Cloud shook his head. "No. I will watch them, not get into a fight with them. Now go!"

Yellow Wolf patted Cloud on the shoulder. "I will see you soon," he promised.

"I hope that will be tomorrow by noon," Cloud said.

CHAPTER TWENTY-EIGHT

The Middle of the Whirlwind

As the line of mounted warriors began the third circle around the sprawling village, Kills Two looked to his grandson. "How many?" he asked the boy.

"Four hundred," came the reply.

"It is good," said the old man. He leaned on his cane and watched, savoring the sight of the passing warriors. Nearly every old man, woman, and child in the camp was watching, it seemed, standing as Kills Two was, just inside or just beyond the outer row of lodges around the circle of the village.

Mounted warriors were still joining the procession, after gathering their weapons and standing quietly for a moment or two with their families.

Near the council lodge stood the lodge of the Kit Fox Warrior Society. Just outside its door, an old man stood waiting. In his hand was a red lance with eagle feathers tied along its entire length. The tapered black-stone head of the lance glistened, even in the dimming light. In a moment, a young warrior appeared, leading his horse, an older man with him as well.

"This is my son, Black Wolf," the older man said to the keeper of the eagle-feather banner.

The old man stepped forward. "In the old days," he said, "it was our way to keep this banner close to the war leader, so that all the warriors knew where he was during the fighting. Since our war leader is reviving the old custom of Gathering the Warriors, we want to revive our old custom as well. Therefore, I ask you to carry this for us. If you agree to do this, and there is fighting, you must remain at our war leader's side at all times, no matter what happens. Can you do that for us?"

Black Wolf, tall and with chiseled features, looked at his father, Tools. Turning to the keeper, he nodded. "Grandfather," he said, "I would be honored to do this."

The keeper was pleased. "The last man to carry this banner in the old way was your grandfather, when I was a young man. That is why we ask you."

"I will do the best I can," Black Wolf said.

"Good," the keeper said, smiling. "That is what your grandfather said."

Another old man stepped forward with the long tanned-hide case for the lance and a covering for the lance head. "You must keep it covered," he instructed as he put the lance in its case and the covering over the point. "When the fighting starts, take it out and hold it high."

"I will."

"It is time to go," Tools told his son.

After the young warrior swung effortlessly onto the back of his buckskin horse, the keeper handed him the encased feathered banner. "Catch up to Crazy Horse and tell him. He will understand," the keeper said.

With a final backward glance, Black Wolf rode forward to join the procession of warriors.

The line of men and horses stretched for nearly one-quarter of the circle of the village. From among the people watching, young women trilled and old men sang warrior songs while old women sang the Strong Heart songs. Somewhere, a drum pounded the rapid beats of a sneak-up dance.

Many of the passing warriors led a warhorse and rode another. A thin cloud of dust, stirred up by thousands of hooves, floated above the ground in the calm air of dusk. The bottom half of the procession was a blur of legs, while the upper half was a continuous flutter of feathers, worn in scalp locks or hanging from victory lances, and red, yellow, and blue streamers and long, thin strands of hair waving from the tops of war lances. Shields in painted cases were tied to the neck ropes of warhorses, and every manner of hand weapons could be seen: war clubs, some with stone heads or the sand-filled tips of buffalo horn, some carved from a single piece of hardwood with a wickedly sharp iron point embedded like the blade of an axe; all manner of rifles, old and new, some in elaborately decorated cases, some not; war bows, short and stout and backed with buffalo sinew; and quivers bristling with war arrows. The deadliest weapon of all, however, was in the mind and the heart of each warrior fully committed to whatever lay ahead—the will to fight and not back down from the enemy.

Black Wolf urged his sturdy buckskin into a lope as he drew closer to the front of the procession and saw Crazy Horse riding alone. Moving past other riders, he maneuvered until the war leader glanced over.

"Uncle," the young warrior called out, "the men of the Kit Fox Warrior Society sent me with this eagle-feather banner," he explained, holding up the encased lance. "They asked me to carry it and ride with you, the way it was done in the old days."

"That is good," Crazy Horse replied. "Old ways are what made us strong. I am honored you would do this."

It was the first time Black Wolf had ever been this close to the most revered fighting man among the Lakota. Many times, he had been within earshot, but never as close as this. From a distance, the man looked young, and the scar on his face was not very visible. But up close, the scar was easy to see, and so, too, were the worry lines around his eyes. But it was the look in those deep brown, almost black, eyes that made Black Wolf's stomach flutter. In them was an intensity, a fierceness, that he had never seen or felt from any other warrior.

Young Black Wolf cleared his throat, trying to relieve the sudden dryness. "No, Uncle," he managed to say, "it is I who am honored."

"Then we will do this together," Crazy Horse replied.

Three horse lengths behind, Two Moons, the Cheyenne war leader, rode alongside another venerable Cheyenne warrior, Bobtail Horse. Behind them was another war leader, Comes in Sight.

Two Moons leaned over toward his friend. "I have a feeling about this," he said. "There is a power here that I have never felt before, or at least not for many years."

Bobtail Horse nodded thoughtfully. "Yes," he agreed, "there is something here, and we must make the most of it. This cannot be the last time we will feel this kind of power."

As the procession of warriors approached the end of the fourth circle, Kills Two turned to his grandson. "How many?' he asked.

"Five hundred, I think," the boy replied.

"That is good. That is good," the old man rejoiced. "We are powerful again." With all his heart, the old man wished for the weakness in his thin body to be gone, if only for a few days.

"I know what you are thinking," a voice behind him said. Kills Two turned and saw an old Cheyenne named Shadow Wolf, once a fearsome Dog Soldier. "I would give anything to go with them." He paused and chuckled. "But I am a poor man, so I have nothing to trade."

"Yes," Kills Two replied, "it is the curse of old men to die in our sleep without taking several of our enemies with us."

"But we have taken a few in our day," Shadow Wolf reminded Kills Two. "So when our time comes, we can join our fathers and grandfathers on the other side and say, 'This is what I have done.' And then ask them to forgive us for dying in our sleep."

The two old warriors laughed together and watched the military might of the Lakota and Cheyenne nations flow past.

Black Shield and Grey Bull watched as well, with the same regret at not being part of it. But they, like Kills Two and Shadow Wolf, also understood that each time the younger warriors were away, the defense of the village was on the shoulders of those men past their prime. The responsibility of the warrior never ended.

"It is hard to know when the first Lakota war leader gathered the warriors in this manner," Black Shield said. "But I have heard it is taken from the whirlwind, because it gathers its power as it spins in a circle."

"And the middle of the whirlwind is the safest place to be," Grey Bull added. "That is why the warriors circle the camp."

Kills Two grabbed his grandson's arm. "Grandson, the warriors will leave when they ride past the opening. Come, let us get closer."

With an old warrior on either side, the boy worked his way carefully through the throng of people. "This is good," Kills Two said after they reached a point just outside the outer row of lodges on the east side.

People moved forward with them and formed their own long line, and waited for the warriors to pass by.

Crazy Horse completed the final circle and extended the line of men and horses south toward the low ridges in the distance and passed by the growing crowd pouring from the village. Honoring songs and trills and shouts filled the air as the departing warriors smiled and waved at friends and relatives.

High Eagle and Worm had been watching the spectacle from a ledge on the sandstone rims north of the village. As the procession of warriors stretched away, from the ledge it appeared to resemble a long lance. Worm bent to the small fire they had made and added a twist of sage and then assembled his pipe, fitting the stem into the bowl. As white smoked billowed, High Eagle smudged pinches of tobacco. The first he raised to the Sky, the second he touched to the Earth, the third he offered to the West, the fourth to the North, the fifth to the East, the sixth to the South, and the seventh and last he offered to the Great Spirit. Each pinch was placed in the bowl of the pipe, and with an ember from the fire, Worm lit the tobacco and began to pray.

The two medicine men planned to remain on the ledge through the night, praying for the warriors.

Cloud was within a short arrow-cast of the Long Knives on the north side of the creek. From there, he could hear voices. He covered himself with his robe and settled in for the night. He noticed that the Crow scouts were making their camp on the north end. The light was fading quickly, however. The shadowy shapes of men and horses gradually blended into the growing darkness until the only indicators of the scattered camps were yellow pinpoints of light from nearly a hundred fires.

He knew the Long Knives and their allies would move north, probably soon after sunrise. More than likely, they would cross the Rosebud before it bent to the northeast. Given how far they had managed to proceed downstream even after starting late in the day, he guessed they would not turn and cross the Wolf Mountains. Had that been their plan, Cloud was convinced they would have done so while still on the upper reaches of the Tongue River.

His plan for tomorrow was already worked out, and he went over it again. It was simple enough. Cloud was reasonably certain that Crazy Horse would take his suggestion to cross over to the east side of the Wolf Mountains. If Cloud stayed far enough ahead of the Long Knives, he would eventually meet Crazy Horse. Then he could guide them to the enemy. If, however, it was apparent that Crazy Horse had not crossed the mountains, Cloud had only one alternative—to start a grass fire. A grass fire would, he hoped, accomplish two things. First, it would probably confuse the Long Knives. Second, the smoke would serve as a marker for Crazy Horse—if he was close enough to see it. Whether he was close enough or not would depend on when he left the encampment on Ash Creek.

In the wide valley below, the campfires went out one by one. A wise thing overall, since the light from a single fire could be seen from great distances. Besides, the night air might turn cool, but fires were not necessary to keep warm. The Moon When Berries Are Good was nearly over, and the Moon When the Sun Stands in the Middle would soon begin, so the nights were warmer. Eventually, all the fires were gone and darkness hid the large camp. Cloud pulled the robe higher over his shoulders and decided to doze for a short while, praying that Crazy Horse and his warriors would move out at first light and travel as fast as they could.

Crazy Horse had sent word for Black Lance and Flood to join him. The first stars of the night were appearing as the group's pace settled into a fast walk. Wolf Eyes, a battle-hardened veteran known for his ability to find his way anywhere, anytime, and in any weather, had taken the lead. Living up to his name, he picked a way over the rough and broken ground.

Black Lance and Flood caught up to Crazy Horse and Black Wolf. "On your way back, did you cross over the divide?" Crazy Horse asked in a low voice.

"No," Black Lance replied. "We turned west and then north from the Tongue and came up along the western slopes."

"I know of a way through the ridges," Flood said. "It is not a hard climb, but it is rough ground. Not far from here."

Crazy Horse thought for a moment. "I think we should cross there, then strike east, away from the deeper gullies. Once on the other side, we can move faster. Perhaps you can tell Wolf Eyes, and the two of you can lead us through that pass."

A lone rider came down from a hill and joined the shadowy procession, matching the pace but staying just off the right flank. Slowly, almost imperceptibly, the horse and rider increased their pace and moved gradually closer to the front.

Word was passed back again, this time alerting everyone that they would turn east and cross over the Wolf Mountains off to their left. "Follow the riders in front of you, and be prepared to dismount and walk" were the instructions.

With Wolf Eyes and Flood leading the way, the procession turned easily toward the east. Their eyes had grown accustomed to the darkness, and the forms of men on horses were not difficult to discern. In any case, riders trusted their mounts, knowing a horse's night vision was much sharper than any man's. After a long and gradual climb with only an occasional switchback, they gained the crest of the ridge. From there, they began to descend.

With coyotes barking all around them, horses and men kept moving. Now and then came a low, muffled cough or the soft snort of a horse. Otherwise, the crunch of hooves on rocks and loose dirt was the predominant noise.

Above them, the tail of the Great Bear in the night sky had turned on its nightly swing around the North Star. The night was passing, oblivious to the comings and goings of the beings who walked the Earth.

The lone rider had blended into the procession, hiding in the anonymity accorded by the night and the silence.

All of the Lakota bands were represented, though most of the riders were Oglala and Sicangu, with a smattering of Nakota and Dakota. There were over one hundred Northern Cheyenne.

Every man rode alone with his thoughts. Most of them were not new to the prospect of combat, but even the most experienced and battle-hardened men wondered if they would see the sunset of the day yet to dawn. They were riding to face an enemy who, by all reports, outnumbered them.

Crazy Horse caught up with Wolf Eyes and Flood after they had reached the end of the gradual downslope. There, they turned south. "I think we will stop soon to rest the horses," he told them, "as soon as everyone reaches the bottom of the slope."

He moved toward Wolf Eyes. "Darkness is good cover, but it can hide trouble. Still, we have to move as fast as we can without injuring any horses. After we rest, we need to increase our pace, so I must depend on you to find the easiest and safest path."

"Then we should turn east," Wolf Eyes replied, "away from the deep gullies coming off these ridges, then turn south. I will do my best."

There was no way to know when the last man had reached the bottom of the slope, so Crazy Horse could only guess. Word went back quickly through the line, and the procession came to a quick halt.

Dismounting, Crazy Horse handed the reins of his horses to young Black Wolf. "I will return," he said.

Up and down the line, men dismounted and walked a few steps to stretch their legs or flexed their shoulders to loosen stiff muscles. Many of them offered water to their horses, pouring it from their water skins into their hands or scooping out a bowl in the ground and lining it with an oiled elk or deer bladder made just for that purpose and then pouring water into it.

Even in the dark, Crazy Horse was a recognizable figure as he walked among the warriors and horses. He spoke in a low voice. "It is good you are here with us," he said. "We will rest the horses a few times before we get to Goose Creek. Is there anything you need?"

"To be remembered well by my children," came the low, earnest reply.

"That you will," Crazy Horse said. "That you will."

A few men approached, offering water. "How many Long Knives are on Goose Creek?" one wanted to know.

"Perhaps a thousand, and they have Crow with them," he told them, and took a drink.

"I once thought the Crow were honorable enemies," said another man. "Maybe they no longer want to be human beings."

"How many and who they are, or what they are, does not matter," Crazy Horse said, handing back the water flask. "It is more than a matter of defeating them. We must get rid of them."

"Then we will start with those on Goose Creek," said the man with the water flask.

Something woke him, a shout or the clink of a metal bit. Instantly alert, he listened. There were noises, voices, and the squeak of leather, consistent enough to indicate that something was happening—the Long Knives were moving around. Cloud rolled onto his side for a moment to see where the Great Bear was in the night sky. According to its position, dawn was not coming anytime soon. The noises persisted, and he decided to move closer.

Sitting up, he worked quietly. He tucked his six-shooter into his belt next to the knife in its sheath, both at the small of his back. That way he could crawl and his weapons would be out of the way but easy to grab.

Getting down on his stomach, he reached forward to brush aside grass and twigs, hoping he wouldn't grab a sleeping rattlesnake. Clearing the area ahead of him as he went, he crawled slowly and silently until he could plainly hear voices and people moving around. He could not understand the words, but the tone was easy to discern. Someone, more than one someone, was speaking commands. He could only assume the Long Knives were moving out.

He moved forward again, trying to pick out shapes and movement in the dark. Cloth scraped against sagebrush just ahead of him; someone was approaching. Not four paces in front of him, someone relieved himself; Cloud plainly heard the soft thud of water hitting the ground. In a moment, the man finished and returned to the camp.

There was only one thing to do. Cloud had to shadow the Long Knives, move with them until dawn. Crawling back to his hiding place, he rolled up his robe and slung the encased rifle over his shoulder.

A tall man with broad shoulders and powerful arms carefully ducked through the doorway of the council lodge and looked quizzically at the man sitting next to the fire pit. A soft glow from the coals filled the room.

"Is it true?" Gall asked as he took a seat. "When I got home from hunting, one of my wives told me."

"Yes," Sitting Bull replied, looking up. "They left at dusk."

"Where are the Long Knives?"

"Goose Creek, the scouts said. A thousand of them."

"Then I will leave right away. There have to be a few men who want to go. I saw Hawk Eagle on his way home."

"Wait until daylight," the medicine man advised. "That way, you can find their trail. You will not see it in the dark."

"Yes, you are right."

"We can send the crier around at dawn and gather as many as we can. I will go with you."

Gall settled back against the willow chair, obviously agitated. "How many men rode out with Crazy Horse?"

"Five hundred, I think, perhaps a little more."

"That means they will be outnumbered. We have to leave at first light."

Wolf Eyes smelled the water as the first faint hint of light began to define the eastern horizon. He knew it had to be a creek, though it was probably a small one from a spring that seeped out of the Wolf Mountains. But water was water, and he knew the horses were thirsty.

"Creek ahead," he said over his shoulder. "We should stop here and cool the horses down before they drink."

As word was passed back, the procession slowed and then came to a halt. Men dismounted and walked about to loosen stiff joints, glad for the light in the east.

A small, slender figure slowly led a horse along the line of men and horses, casting inquisitive glances. Near the front, the figure stopped, staring at one man in particular for a moment, and then wove through the maze of four-legged and two-legged bodies.

Comes in Sight, one of the Cheyenne war leaders, felt the tug on his sleeve and immediately recognized the person standing there. "What are you doing here?" he asked in a surprised whisper.

"I needed to come," Buffalo Calf Road replied.

"You needed to come? Did you tell Mother? Does your husband know?"

In the growing light, Comes in Sight could see the amused expressions on the faces of the other Cheyenne warriors standing nearby. His younger sister stood defiantly, her chin thrust out against his impatience.

"My husband went hunting yesterday," she said, her tone defiant as well. "I will not go back."

He sighed. "Did you at least bring a gun this time?"

She smiled, her teeth flashing in the dim light. "Yes, Father loaned me his, and fourteen bullets."

"Stay close to me," he said, trying to sound as though he was still angry.

"I will. That is why I came, to keep watch over you," she retorted impishly.

"You could have gotten lost in the dark," he said, trying to recover some semblance of control.

"No. I was waiting in the trees on the ridge south of the village. When you came by, I rode down. Nobody noticed me, especially after it became dark."

Comes in Sight shook his head in exasperation and looked at his sister's horse, a dark bay with speed to burn. "At least you brought the right horse. They told us a creek is up ahead. Watch him. You know he likes to bloat himself with water."

The valley of the Rosebud was still in dark shadows, though Cloud could see grass and rocks outlined on the ridges around him. Dawn was sliding over the eastern horizon, so he decided to move farther away from the slow-moving Long Knife column. He did not want to take the chance of one of the Crow or Shoshone scouts spotting him.

He was just about to break into a run when he heard strident shouts from the column. Ducking down behind a clump of soap weed, he strained his eyes and ears. Even in the dim light, he could see that the Long Knives were stopping.

CHAPTER TWENTY-NINE

The Long Ride

Through the night, Yellow Wolf had been guiding by the North Star. He was east of the Wolf Mountains, and at first had angled away from the rough terrain of its slopes and then back north. But the horses had not been able to safely maintain anything more than a fast walk. At a trot, they were snorting nervously at every shrub or sudden drop-off, and once, both shied from a prairie hen they had disturbed. Fortunately, he had hung onto the rein as he fell, and except for a sore left shoulder, he was none the worse for wear. At a walk, the horses were not as nervous.

He saw stars reflected on the surface of a narrow creek and stopped to water the horses and refill his water bag. As he was about to remount, his gelding swung his head around to look west into the darkness, ears turned forward. Cloud's horse did the same. Standing between them, Yellow Wolf stroked their noses to keep them quiet. Neither of them exhibited signs of fear, thus a bear or a mountain lion could be ruled out, but they were very curious. That left anything from deer, elk, and antelope to other horses. If other horses were nearby, it would mean people were nearby as well, since there were no wild herds around. Unless possibly it was a loose horse.

Yellow Wolf strained to hear but detected no sounds, yet the horses were still peering intently into the dark. Something or someone was there.

Two men waited at the southern edge of the village, watching the last of the night's stars in the western quarter of the sky. Gall and Rain in the Face each held the reins to a warhorse, their packs and weapons tied on for travel. A teenage boy stood with Gall. Hawk Eagle arrived, leading a second horse.

In the dim light of dawn, people were already moving around inside the sprawling village, and a few dogs barked here and there. By the time the sun rose, new horse guards would be relieving those who had stayed with the herds through the night, and the village would be awake and starting the new day.

Sitting Bull, limping slightly, joined the small group. The old hip wound from his younger days as a warrior bothered him most when the weather was cold or when the morning air was cool. Both Gall and Rain in the Face noticed the encased rifle tied onto the medicine man's horse. It was unusual these days to see him equipped and ready for battle.

"There are more coming," he said to Gall. "Hard to say how many of us there will be, but I think we should not wait too long."

Gall agreed, patting the shoulders of the boy with him. "My nephew will wait here after we have gone. If anyone else comes, he will point them in the right direction."

They did not have to wait long, however. The group rapidly grew to a little more than forty men, armed and equipped for whatever lay ahead.

"It is time to go," Gall announced, then waited for Sitting Bull to mount before he jumped on his horse.

In the next instant, everyone was mounted. Gall moved to the center of the group. "The last we heard, the Long Knives were camped at Goose Creek," he told them. "But I think they will be moving north. Our intent is to catch up to Crazy Horse. We will pick up his trail and move fast. Follow me!"

The big Hunkpapa war leader nodded to the medicine man and both turned their horses and immediately led out at a low lope. Close on their heels were swift, shadowy forms of men on horses.

On a narrow sandstone ledge on the rims to the north, Worm added small pieces of wood to the dim embers still glowing inside the ring of stones. "Gall is leaving," he commented, indicating the dark shapes moving away south of the village.

The two medicine men had spent the night next to their fire on the ledge, meditating and praying. High Eagle stretched his legs and arms and leaned back against his willow chair. Sitting Bull had been with them for part of the night, before he left to prepare for travel.

"There will be a fight," High Eagle said, "but it will not be the fight he saw in his vision."

"That worries me," Worm replied. "I think there will be more than one fight. We should be watchful while most of the fighting men are gone."

The pinpoints of light in the valley of the Rosebud faded as the daylight increased. Through his looking glass, Cloud could see thin columns of smoke, which meant that the Long Knives were still encamped. He sat up and stretched his arms, then quickly checked his weapons. His water skin was over half full, though water was not a problem—Rosebud Creek was nearby. From a bag, he took a handful of pounded, dried meat and ate. Finishing the small meal, he shook the dirt out of both moccasins and slipped them back on, tying them tight since he expected to do more than a little running. Standing, he arranged his unstrung bow and quiver of arrows across his back and tied them securely.

As the light improved, he took out his glass again and made a quick but thorough visual reconnaissance of the Long Knife positions along the creek. He could see dark shapes of men moving around and horses standing quietly on picket lines. He waited as the light improved and looked again. Still, he saw no signs of the Long Knives organizing themselves into lines as they always did when preparing to move out. Putting away his glass, he began working his way down the slope.

At the bottom, he headed east toward the creek, deciding to fill his water flask while he could, but just as importantly, he decided to stay on the floodplain west of the stream. There were fewer hills and rises he had to climb.

At the wide creek, he filled his flask and took a drink, then splashed water over his face. He felt good, strong, and confident in his abilities. Turning from the bank, he walked at a fast pace for a while before he broke into a trot, holding the encased rifle in his right hand.

Although it looked less broken from a distance, the creek bottom was not totally flat and even ground. Consequently, it was next to impossible to set a consistent pace, so the best he could do was to keep moving at a trot and extend his stride where the terrain allowed. He glanced constantly to the right and left at the skylines, and, as much as he could without losing his footing or breaking his stride, over his shoulders behind him.

At the age of thirty-seven, he didn't have the endurance he had had as a teenager or in his early twenties, but he had always been a good runner and was known for his stamina rather than speed. Today, he would need whatever endurance he could muster.

By the time the first bright rays of the rising sun shot across the sky, he estimated that he had trotted well over a thousand paces. His breath was coming faster. Not wanting to wear himself out, because he had no way of knowing how far he had to run, he slowed to a fast walk to let himself recover.

Walking backward for several paces, he checked his back trail, especially the ridge he had just left. He expected Crow or Shoshone scouts to ride out in advance of the column. Reaching the lip of a low, grassy plateau, he walked across it and started to jog again when he reached the end. Ahead, he picked out a low ridge that gradually angled down to the creek bottom, and he decided not to stop until he reached it.

By the time the last of the horses reached the creek, the water was muddy from the thousands of hooves that had walked across it. The last group of warriors took their mounts upstream to drink from water that was still clear, then led them into a broad meadow to catch up to the rest of the column. As the growing light defined the landscape and chased away shadows, all the warriors were mounted. Energized by the brief rest and refreshed by cool water, nearly seven hundred horses went from a fast walk into a high lope. A soft rumble rolled across the ground.

A shout went up, and several of the warriors pointed to the east. The shadowy outline of a rider leading a second horse stood out plainly against the growing light. Rifles were pointed, and six-shooters were yanked out of belts.

The rider lifted a hand, and a shout came thinly across the distance. "I am Yellow Wolf!"

Crazy Horse broke from the column and rode out to meet the approaching scout. "Where are you coming from?" he asked.

"I left from north of Goose Creek. Cloud sent me because the Long Knives broke camp. They are probably moving farther north."

"Cloud is still there?"

"He was going to stay ahead of them."

By now, the procession had stopped and several men approached: Good Weasel, Black Moon, and He Dog, as well as Two Moons and Bobtail Horse of the Cheyenne.

"He thought you would not leave until this morning," Yellow Wolf continued.

"We left at dusk," Crazy Horse told him. "What is Cloud planning to do?"

"As I said, stay ahead of the Long Knives and look for you."

Crazy Horse looked around at the brightening landscape. "We are west of Rosebud Creek," he decided. He looked at the war leaders gathered around. "I think we should send scouts east. If they see Long Knives, or a trail of any kind, they can send a messenger back to us. Meanwhile, we can keep going south and look for Cloud."

The men nodded in agreement.

Four scouts were selected and moved out at a lope, riding more confidently in the growing daylight. The main body continued south.

At the end of a long meadow, Cloud once again slowed to a walk. When he reached a slight depression choked with sagebrush and grass, he stopped to rest and turned to study the southern horizon through his glass. By now, he expected the first Crow or Shoshone scouts to be out ahead of the column. He put away his glass and wiped the sweat off his forehead with the back of his hand. Then he felt it through the soles of his moccasins—the barest of tremors.

He immediately looked south, thinking the Long Knives were on the move, but he realized there were too many intervening ridges and hills. Kneeling down, he laid an ear to the ground. Someone or something was moving, and it had to be very heavy or very many. It wasn't buffalo. That was the only thing he knew for sure.

For several more moments, he kept his ear to the ground and the light rumble did not diminish. Cloud looked around. There was no cover, not enough for an adequate defense, in any case. His next best alternative was to find a place to hide, a place where he could disappear completely.

Staying down behind some sagebrush, he could feel the tremor through his feet growing stronger. Whatever, or whoever, it was, it was getting closer. He took his time and glassed the southern horizon but saw nothing. Turning slowly, he checked the skyline all around. When he swung the glass around to the north, he saw a thin, dark, uneven line appear just over a ridge. A line that had motion.

Deducing, or at least hoping, that the Long Knives could not have circled around him that fast, he allowed himself to consider that they might be Lakota and Cheyenne warriors. It was probably too late to find good cover, and he could not hope to outrun whoever was approaching, because the tremors he felt through his moccasins meant that horses were approaching.

Pushing his way in between two thick stalks of sagebrush, the best cover he had, he steadied his glass and looked. Framed in the circle were the dark outlines of men on horses, but they were still too far away for him to know who they were. There was nothing to do but wait. In the meantime, he pulled his rifle out of its case and loaded it.

The sun was over the horizon now, and in the bright light he saw the approaching riders topping the ridge and moving down a slight incline. It was a long, wide line of men and horses.

Patiently, he watched the front of the column until he recognized the yellow-and-white paint belonging to Crazy Horse. No one but Crazy Horse ever rode that mare.

Cloud went weak with relief. He had not expected to see anyone until past midday at the earliest, if at all. Wiping the surface of his looking glass clean, he sat up and angled it toward the sun and then aimed it at the approaching column.

Yellow Wolf pointed at the flashes of light. "Cloud!" he shouted.

Cloud was glad to see Yellow Wolf leading his horse, but he was even happier to see the sheer number of fighting men. They slowed and gathered around him in a wide front.

"My friend," Crazy Horse called out, "if you are looking for Long Knives, there are none in the direction we came."

"I believe you," Cloud replied, "but I know where there are a few who seem to have lost their way."

Good-natured laughter rolled through the rows of warriors who had heard the banter between the two men.

"Where are these lost souls?" Crazy Horse asked as Yellow Wolf led Cloud's horse to him.

Cloud turned and pointed to the southwest, to the peak of the high hill where he had spent the night. "Over that hill to the south, on both sides of the Rosebud. They started out before dawn and stopped there."

"How many?" Two Moons asked, moving up beside Crazy Horse.

"Almost a thousand, I think. Over a hundred Crow, and maybe sixty or seventy Shoshone."

Crazy Horse turned to the young Black Wolf, who was waiting not far away. "My friend," he said, motioning to him, "unfurl that banner. It is time."

Black Wolf complied. Removing the lance case and the covering for the point, he lifted the banner high above his head. The line of eagle feathers twirled and fluttered in the soft breeze. At the signal, all the war leaders gathered around Crazy Horse.

"We'll split into two columns," Crazy Horse said. "My friend Cloud will lead one and I the other. I will go around to the west of that hill to the south, and he will go around to the east. I will attack first," he said to Cloud. "As soon as I do, you attack. That way, we will force them to split, and then we keep them that way."

Crazy Horse looked around at the circle of determined faces. "Take the time to pass the word. We will allow for our warriors to prepare themselves, and then I will ride forward. Look for this banner," he said, pointing toward young Black Wolf. "That will be the signal to move out."

The war leaders hurried back to the waiting warriors, and the call to battle flowed through the line of anxious men like a rushing spring flood.

Cloud pulled Crazy Horse aside. "My friend, send a man ahead of us up to the top of that hill," he suggested, pointing south. "From there, the Long Knife camp is easy to see. He can stay there until they move, then flash a signal to us with a looking glass."

Comes in Sight found his sister standing next to her horse. He wanted to send her home. "I know you would follow if I left you behind," he said. "So if you care how our mother and father feel, stay next to me. If you do not, I will tie your hands and legs and leave you hidden in some gully until it is all over."

Buffalo Calf Road nodded. The look on her brother's face left no room for defiance or stupidity. "I will go where you go," she promised.

"Good." His tone softened. "Load your rifle, and tie your bullet bag in front of your left hip. That way, you can grab the bullets faster."

Little Big Man was ready for battle. Although the morning air was still cool, he had removed his shirt, as many warriors did, disregarding a slight and short-lived discomfort in favor of freer movement. Two six-shooters were tucked into the soft leather sash tied around his waist. A second belt he wore over one shoulder, this one with double slits to hold the thirty-two bullets he had for his breech-loading rifle. With a discerning eye, he inspected his horse as well as the girth and neck rope. Two small bags, one containing his shirt, were tied to the rope, and tucked beneath the rope was his long-handled stone-head war club. Hanging by a loop over his right wrist was a riding crop. With rifle in hand, he led his horse slowly through the maze of men and horses until he found Crazy Horse.

"We have never faced this many enemies at one time," he commented offhandedly.

"True," Crazy Horse agreed. The left side of his face was painted with a yellow lightning mark. Like Little Big Man, he was shirtless, and blue hailstones were painted across the top of his chest. A round red stone hung from his left ear. To the back of his head he had tied four tail feathers from a red-tailed hawk, all pointing down in attack position. All the symbols worn or painted were elements from his dream.

"But we are many as well," Crazy Horse pointed out. "And our speed and movements will make the Long Knives think there are more of us. Besides, they are not true horse warriors. We are, so we will be the victors this day."

Cloud led his horse through groups of men preparing for battle. Some were tightening their horses' neck ropes or counting bullets. Many were painting their faces and bodies. Still others were taking a quiet moment to pray. Young horse holders, brought along to watch over the riding horses, were gathering them on connected leads after the warriors had transferred equipment and weapons to their warhorses.

Cloud found Little Bird, Yellow Wolf, and Goings together, as they always were during moments such as this.

"It is good you will lead us," Little Bird said.

"Then you should point me in the right direction," Cloud replied, grinning.

Goings nodded toward Yellow Wolf. "He told us about the Crow and the Shoshone with the Long Knives. If there are that many, they are not only scouting. They have thrown in with the Long Knives because they cannot wipe us out on their own."

"That means the Long Knives have supplied them with guns and bullets," Little Bird added. "So there are over a thousand guns waiting for us over that ridge."

Cloud nodded slowly. "It seems all of our enemies are uniting against us. Think about this: if it were only us, the Crazy Horse people, against that many, we would be hard put. But because Sitting Bull brought us together, there are more of us to fight them." He pointed back over his shoulder toward the ridge to the south. "It seems likely that the Long Knives and their friends have not moved, because they were preparing cooking fires. And they are scattered on either side of the stream. That is good, because Long Knives organize themselves before they do anything. When we come from two directions, it will be too much for them. We will defeat them."

Gall led the group of warriors over the divide, following the trail of hoofprints. At the bottom of the slope, the trail widened and he once again increased the pace to a low lope.

Wolf Eyes climbed to the crest of the hill and looked south. The floodplain was not hard to discern as it curved to the southwest. Below him, he caught glimpses of a narrow little creek that probably flowed into the Rosebud, and beyond the creek were dark spots. He took out his glass, and through it the spots turned into men and horses. As an experienced scout, he had long ago learned to look for the subtleties, the small signs that were always hidden in the broader view. But it was as Cloud had described. Small groups of Long Knives were scattered on either side, and he could see saddled horses. Long Knives were standing or sitting, many without rifles in their hands.

Nothing indicated that they were preparing to move. On the north end, a small knot of Crow scouts stood together, their horses picketed nearby. Just west of them, other groups that Wolf Eyes guessed were Shoshone were congregated among the sandbar willows. Glancing back down the steep slope to make sure his horse was still tied to a sagebrush, he settled in to wait. Once the Long Knives started moving, and there was no doubt they would eventually, he would flash a signal to Crazy Horse and Cloud.

In order to prevent a telltale dust cloud, the warrior columns moved out at a slow, deliberate walk, like two wolves relentlessly stalking prey. Anxiety rode with them like an unwelcome companion, always there when battle was nigh. But overshadowing the anxiety, at least for a few moments, were thoughts and images of family, of wives, children, mothers and fathers, and grandfathers and grandmothers. More than a few of the Lakota and Cheyenne warriors remembered a father, brother, uncle, grandfather, or friend who had died in battle.

For Crazy Horse, it was Little Hawk, always carefree and smiling, and recklessly brave. Then Hump, not only a stalwart warrior, but a beloved friend. And also Lone Bear, who had died in his arms.

Cloud could feel the presence of his father and grandfather, both Crazy Dog warriors, and, of course, Rabbit. Those thoughts and feelings mingled with the images of Sweetwater Woman and Song. Reluctantly, he let them go to focus on the task at hand.

He felt the power behind him. It was more than an awareness that over two hundred fighting men were following him. It was their determination, their willingness to face an enemy who had more men and guns. Glancing left, he saw Crazy Horse at the head of the column heading in a southwesterly direction. Both columns kept to the low, wide gullies and openings that permitted easy passage and hid them from any scouts who would be watching.

Wolf Eyes saw movement from several of the Crow or Shoshone scouts probing the brushy draws and gullies north of Rosebud Creek. Along the stream, however, the main body of the Long Knife column was still at rest. West of his position, Wolf Eyes saw Crazy Horse's warriors move beyond his hill, following a winding gully. To the east, Cloud and his warriors were about to move beyond him as well. If he used the looking glass, there would be a chance the enemy scouts would see it, since he would be flashing it in a southerly direction.

Bounding down the steep slope as fast as the terrain allowed, Wolf Eyes reached his horse and mounted and threw caution to the wind as he galloped over the broken ground to catch up to Crazy Horse.

A whistle alerted Crazy Horse as Black Wolf pointed to the rider approaching at a gallop. Wolf Eyes and his winded horse caught up.

"The Crow and Shoshone are moving toward you!" he reported.

"The Long Knives?" Crazy Horse asked.

"Still along the creek."

Crazy Horse contemplated for a moment and turned his horse around, then motioned for Good Weasel and Black Moon. "Take your men and spread out through these gullies," he told them when they rode up. "Watch for Crow and Shoshone. The Long Knives might be on the move."

A line of twenty to thirty warriors followed each of the two war leaders as they dropped down into the gullies and pushed slowly toward the south. Waiting only a few moments longer, Crazy Horse signaled an advance.

Staying in between the low rises and hills, the Lakota and Cheyenne warriors moved forward, rifles ready, eyes sweeping the skyline for the enemy. A short distance behind Black Wolf and Crazy Horse, a warrior grunted in surprise at the same instant a gunshot popped from the south. The warrior's mount jumped sideways as a bullet grazed the man's left hip, then sliced its way through the horse's rump. Other shots followed.

The front ranks of the advancing warriors fanned out, looking for the shooters. Behind a rise, a dark form scurried through the brush. A Lakota shouted and fired.

Cloud and his men heard the distant, thin cracks of gunfire. He quickly signaled for a halt and motioned for Yellow Wolf to look from the rise in front of them. The warrior dismounted and scrambled to the top of the rise and quickly pointed to the southeast.

Cloud spun his horse and went back down the line of anxious, wide-eyed men. "We wait! We wait!" he called out. "When Crazy Horse is fully engaged, then we attack! Hold yourselves back, there are plenty of Long Knives to fight in that valley. Think of the helpless ones! They are why we are here!"

From over the intervening ridges, the gunfire was sporadic at first, and then came faster. Cloud held up his arm, holding his men back, his stomach fluttering with each shot he heard.

CHAPTER THIRTY

The Screams of Horses

Grey Bull sipped his morning tea and looked at the brightening sky. A sudden breeze tossed about grass and other small debris and fluttered the long streamers hanging from the tops of lodge poles. The old warrior sat in front of his willow chair, just outside the door of his lodge. His wife, Red Leaf, was seated next to the fire, preparing a bundle of food for the two medicine men. He watched the debris fly about. Something was happening, somewhere, and he couldn't help but glance toward the southern horizon, in the direction the warriors had gone last evening, and then the additional men at dawn.

He was about to stand when a woman appeared, a look of concern on her pale face. "Uncle, Aunt," Sweetwater Woman said in greeting.

"Good to see you," Red Leaf replied cordially. "Have you eaten?"

"Niece," Grey Bull said, "you are up early this morning." He pointed to the robe next to the small fire. "Sit down, sit down."

"Yes," Sweetwater Woman replied politely, "I have eaten." She took a seat on the robe, folding her legs to the side in the proper manner of a married woman.

"Then have some tea," the old woman said, pouring from the pot and handing a cup to Sweetwater Woman.

"Thank you," Sweetwater Woman said.

Sensing some worry on the part of the younger woman, Grey Bull waited only a moment longer. "What brings you to our fire this morning?" he asked gently.

Sweetwater Woman stared into her cup. "My husband has been gone for five days, and I know we will not see him today. I was wondering if you had any thoughts about the news that came back last evening."

"You know us old people," Grey Bull teased, trying to put her at ease. "We are either thinking about something or sleeping."

Sweetwater Woman smiled, and the tension on her face faded a little.

"I have been thinking about that news," he told her. "For one thing, it is like your husband to send someone else back while he stays and keeps his eyes on our enemies."

"What do you think will happen?"

"Our men will fight the Long Knives. I am sure of it. They are too close, and we are all angry about what has been happening. Most of our people have given in to life at the agencies, and the buffalo are gone. Those are reasons enough."

Sweetwater Woman glanced at a boy leading horses toward the edge of the village. "I am afraid," she admitted hesitantly, "as other women are. We are afraid to lose our husbands, the fathers of our children."

"Ah, yes," Grey Bull replied gently. "In a strange way, it is easier for a man to die fighting our enemies. Then his purpose is fulfilled, his work is done. But those he leaves behind have to pay the price." He paused for a moment, recalling the grief of many generations. He then took a deep breath and looked at Sweetwater Woman again. "But I have always had a feeling about my nephew, your husband. I am sure he will live to be an old man."

Sweetwater Woman nodded. "Thank you, Uncle," she said. From her belt she untied a small bag and laid it on the ground by the fire. "Peppermint," she told Red Leaf and Grey Bull. "My daughter and I picked it yesterday by the water."

Worm and High Eagle watched the man picking his way slowly up the slope to the sandstone ledge. He was carrying a bundle and carefully balancing a pot to keep the liquid contents from spilling out.

Grey Bull reached a narrow ledge below them and handed up the articles. "Some elk meat my wife roasted," he said, "and tea. She wondered if you thought to bring anything to eat or drink."

He climbed the ledge after High Eagle took the meat and pot, slightly winded at the effort. "I know you probably circled the camp and came from the north, just so you would not have to climb this slope," he teased, pointing back at the way he had come.

"Better to travel a long, slow road than a short, slippery slope," Worm teased back.

Grey Bull chuckled as he made himself comfortable.

High Eagle pointed to the encased rifle as Grey Bull slipped the strap over his head and laid the weapon down. "What is that for?"

"To remind me that I was once young and strong," Grey Bull retorted as he caught his breath.

High Eagle and Worm chuckled sympathetically. In his prime, Grey Bull had been a tough and competent warrior, and could still be a skillful tactician if called upon. He said often that at the age of sixty, he still had one good fight left in him. Both of the old men knew that their friend had passed the word among the old warriors still in camp that weapons should be kept close at hand. Grey Bull was simply taking his own advice.

High Eagle opened the bundle and handed a piece of roasted elk to Worm.

"Tell your wife we are grateful," Worm said, taking a bite.

Grey Bull waited while the medicine men finished eating. From the sandstone rim, the sprawling village looked normal enough. Horses were grazing peacefully in the meadows to the south and southeast. Although the day was still new, people were already moving around, going about their tasks. Streamers on the lodge poles were still fluttering, whipped about by an occasional gust. Visually, there was no way to perceive that nearly six hundred men were absent. Six hundred men out of five thousand or more people was like a tree losing a few of its many branches, but the emptiness and uneasiness in the hearts of those who waited could not be so easily measured.

"There is no doubt that our fighting men will find the Long Knives," High Eagle said, interrupting Grey Bull's thoughts. "The one thing I am not certain of is how many of our men will fall. That is always the worry."

"Guns and bullets can be found, or traded for, or taken from the enemy, and they can be replaced," Worm pointed out. "A warrior is not so easy to replace. There are many boys here," he went on, gesturing at the village. "Although they are eager, they do not have the experience, and will not for several more years."

"We can be successful at driving out the white people and their Long Knives," Grey Bull added. "But I am worried that it will happen at a high cost. A thousand Long Knives at Goose Creek will not be easy to defeat. How many more thousands of them will we have to fight? We may win in the end, but we may also lose those strong men who should father the next generations."

"Then there have to be other ways to fight them," Worm suggested.

"That must be a thought for us to talk about," Grey Bull agreed. "We must do what they have done to us. They killed our buffalo, the one thing we depend on most. Likewise, we must take from them what they need most, what they depend on most, especially those things they need and depend on to wage war against us."

High Eagle nodded thoughtfully. "These are thoughts that need to be spoken to the gathering of the old leaders," he advised. "What you have said is the plain truth, much the same as the nose on the front of a face. It is so plain to see that many cannot."

"We must find ways to fight the whites that do not put our warriors in harm's way each time," Grey Bull concluded.

"As I fear they are at this moment," Worm said quietly.

Cloud was mildly surprised as he watched a group of dismounted Long Knives, about two hundred paces away, advancing on foot toward the attacking Lakota and Cheyenne. He sent Yellow Wolf with at least twenty men to a low ridge to the left, with instructions to pick their targets carefully and make every shot count.

Meanwhile, he and thirty or forty warriors positioned themselves behind cover and waited for Yellow Wolf to open fire. Peering between rocks and sagebrush, they waited. Yellow Wolf and his men were at least a hundred paces off the soldiers' right flank. Cloud saw eruptions on the ground among the Long Knives, even as they turned toward the boom of gunfire. Rising, Cloud aimed and fired and heard the blasts of gunfire on either side of him.

Most of the Long Knives ducked down behind rocks or brush. Others returned fire toward Yellow Wolf's position. Firing from the north, from Cloud's warriors, made them turn back. But even as the Long Knives on foot retreated on the run, Cloud could see mounted Long Knives far to the south forming for a charge.

Crazy Horse and his warriors had immediately and swiftly beaten back the scouts who had opened fire on them. The Crow and Shoshone had put up a stiff resistance but had fallen back, badly outnumbered, toward the main body of Long Knives. Behind them, many of the Long Knives had managed to take positions on hills and ridges on either side of the stream.

A fierce exchange of gunfire occurred as Good Weasel and Little Big Man led a charge at a defended hill from the east after crossing the creek. The Long Knives stayed on the hill, perhaps because many of their horses had scattered in the confusion. Several of the Lakota chased the runaway mounts, making sure the Long Knives could not recover them. After that, they joined the other warriors as they withdrew to regroup.

Crazy Horse watched the initial stages of the battle, realizing that their attack had caught the Long Knives scattered in several groups. It would be to their advantage to keep them from regrouping. Ducking behind a rise, he motioned for a young warrior, named Yellow Earrings, who had paused to reload his six-shooter.

"Find all the war leaders," he instructed, speaking calmly in spite of the continuous gunfire from the south. "Tell them we cannot allow the Long Knives to regroup. We have to keep them separated. Our warriors must keep moving. Let the Long Knives attack and wear out their horses and use up their bullets, then turn back on them. Do you understand?"

The wide-eyed young man nodded.

"Go. Find them all and tell them."

Crazy Horse watched the young messenger for a moment, then dismounted and tossed the rein of his horse to Black Wolf, waiting nearby. "Stay here in this gully," he said, and climbed the rise with his field glasses to take another look.

North of the stream, several lines of mounted Long Knives were moving north, forming a charge, though many of their horses seemed reluctant to stretch out into a gallop. He watched a moment longer, then jumped back down into the gully and remounted. He pointed south and shouted to the warriors all around him, "They are charging! Let us see how far they can go! Follow me!"

Crazy Horse led them north at a high lope, following the low gullies and washes but occasionally going over a rise to reveal themselves to the oncoming Long Knives, who were still far behind but firing as they came.

The Lakota and several Cheyenne with them reached the crest of a long, low ridge and strung themselves out, many in the rear of the line firing toward the Long Knives. When the blue-coated enemy reached the base of the ridge, Crazy Horse started north along the ridge and then led his men down the side, their horses raising dust into the morning air as they practically slid down the slope. When they reached an old stream bed, they turned north again and headed for the base of the sharp hill that both Cloud and Wolf Eyes had used to scout.

Reaching the hill, Crazy Horse halted and picked several of the younger men to hold horses while the others climbed the hill and dug in to fire at the Long Knives, who were slow to keep up. "Hit their horses," he called out. "Hit their horses!"

Sniping from the elevated positions on the hill, the Lakota and Cheyenne killed or wounded several of the Long Knife horses, causing considerable confusion and forcing a brief retreat. The Long Knives eventually gained the top of the long ridge and halted there, as if uncertain. In a while, they were joined by another group.

Crazy Horse looked through his field glasses, then handed them to Good Road. "It looks as though they are catching their breath," he said. Then he noticed a gash in the warrior's left side. "My friend, you have been shot, I think."

Good Road looked through the lenses. "It is not as bad as it looks," he said. "The wound, I mean. Only a scratch. You are right, they have stopped. What should we do?"

"Rest," Crazy Horse replied. "Rest while we can, and reload and see if anyone might be hurt."

After Cloud and Yellow Wolf had stopped the dismounted Long Knives, Cloud regrouped his men and circled around to the west, charging the Long Knives still hiding among the sandbar willows. Initially, they scattered picket lines of mules and many of the workers who traveled with the Long Knives, then engaged the Long Knives when a large group of them counterattacked. Cloud gathered his men and charged again, a broad front of warriors firing as they galloped at the line of mounted Long Knives, forcing them to drop back, unable to maintain their lines. Those in the center stopped first and then wheeled about, followed by both ends of the line. But as those Long Knives fell back, another group crossed the creek and charged.

Cloud and his men exchanged fire with the new chargers and turned northeast, staying ahead of the pursuit. Although these Long Knives kept coming, their pursuit slowed considerably over the rough, uneven ground. Cloud, Yellow Wolf, Goings, Little Bird, Taken Alive, and ten other men spread out in a long skirmish line and fired steadily. Long Knife horses balked; two or three went down, taking their riders with them. Cloud saw one Long Knife flip backward off his horse as if struck by a giant hand.

Throughout the open, broad valley of the Rosebud, there was hardly a place where something wasn't moving in one direction or another, be it Long Knives on foot or mounted, loose horses, or mounted warriors. Gunshots cracked and boomed in every space of time. The heavier blasts were rifles, and the high-pitched cracks were six-shooters.

Crazy Horse and his men had vacated the high hill and probed south, eventually charging the Long Knives who had occupied the ridge southeast of the hill. They stopped a large bunch of Long Knives, forcing them back up the ridge. Groups of warriors broke off, charging or engaging scattered bunches of Long Knives. Crazy Horse dismounted and crawled to the top of a rise to have a quick look around. The tactical situation was as he had hoped. Long Knives were scattered about, fighting in separate groups. All the Lakota and Cheyenne had to do was maintain the pressure and keep the separate enemy groups apart. At this point, he realized, the numerical superiority of the Long Knives was not giving them any sort of distinct advantage. At best, it was saving them from being overwhelmed.

He noticed a line of Long Knives west of his position, moving northwesterly along a narrow creek. Strung out as they were, they were ripe for attack. Crazy Horse scrambled down the rise and remounted, calling out and pointing to the enemy. "There! Follow me!"

With the standard bearer, Black Wolf, at his side, the Lakota war leader took the lead, galloping his horse but allowing him to weave and dance his way past boulders and sagebrush. Behind him came seventy or eighty men, fanning out to form firing lanes as they drew closer to the enemy. Crazy Horse lifted his rifle and fired, and in the next instant, gunfire blasted behind him, adding to the staccato of booming and cracking throughout the wide valley.

To the south, a line of Cheyenne warriors splashed across the creek and raced toward a knot of Long Knives crouching in a stand of willows, scattering them and forcing them to move to thicker cover, firing erratically as they ran. Bobtail Horse and Comes in Sight took their men past the willows and up a low hill and then behind it. There they stopped to give their winded horses a brief rest. Many of the warriors took the opportunity to quickly count their ammunition and reload. However, they all kept an eye out for any counterattacks or sudden movements by the enemy.

Earlier, they had turned back on a large group of Long Knives pursuing them, fully intending and expecting to engage them in close, mounted combat. The Long Knives, however, opted to turn and find cover and dismounted behind scattered boulders. Bobtail Horse led his men past them, engaging in a fierce exchange of gunfire, and then crossed the creek.

Bobtail Horse watched the Long Knives still firing from among the boulders, some two hundred paces to the northeast. Those who scattered into the willows were off to the west at about the same distance. He tapped Comes in Sight on the arm. "I will see to those over there," he said, pointing toward the boulders. "You can do something about those in the willows."

Comes in Sight nodded. "When our horses have caught their wind, we will go," he replied, glancing over at his sister to see that she was unharmed.

The sun was high now, well past the quarter point in the sky, the point halfway from sunrise to noon. For the Lakota and Cheyenne warriors, time seemed to pass quickly, interspersed with moments when things seemed to happen in slow motion.

Goings realized he was falling but didn't know why until he felt the searing pain in his left side. He managed to grab a handful of mane with his left hand to stop his fall while reaching out with his right to brace himself for the collision with the ground, all the while fighting to take a breath. Something had taken the air out of his lungs. An arm suddenly reached out and hooked him under his right armpit and stopped his forward momentum. He saw another arm grab the horse's rein. Someone shouted, but Goings could not make out the words.

"Hang on!" Little Bird shouted, trying to slide Goings back onto the loping horse and slowing the horse down at the same time. Pushing his horse up against the other, he managed to keep Goings from falling.

Riding to the right and a little behind his friend, Little Bird had heard the bullet hit and saw a spurt of blood and tissue from Goings's lower left abdomen. Vaguely aware of the gunfire all around, Little Bird managed to slide his rifle beneath his horse's neck rope and somehow pulled both horses to a stop. Dismounting, he reached up and let the inert form of his wounded friend drape itself over his left shoulder. Then, grabbing the reins to both horses, he led them down into a wash among some brush and shrubs. Picking a bare spot, Little Bird lowered his friend to the ground, disregarding the blood that had wiped off on his own shoulder.

In an instant, he tied the reins to a bush and bent down to look at the wound. The bullet had entered just above the hip bone in the back and came out the front, closer to the left side. The hole in the front was big enough to put two fingers in and was bleeding profusely.

Goings tried to sit up, pain evident in his eyes.

"No," Little Bird warned, gently pushing him down. "Stay down. Stay still. You are hurt and bleeding."

Goings's right hand instinctively reached toward the wound.

"No," Little Bird said again. "Put your hand down. I will wash the wound."

Less than three paces away, both horses kept watch toward the sounds of gunfire.

"I hurt," Goings muttered, somewhat confused.

"I know. Stay still, stay still."

Goings lay back, his shoulders tense and his lower jaw trembling.

"Good, good," Little Bird said. "I will pour water on it to clean it out, then I will cover it—somehow."

To the south, Comes in Sight watched Bobtail Horse heading for the Long Knives in the boulders. Turning, he looked to see that his men were loaded and ready. Then he had a thought. He rode to the middle of the line of thirty or so men and waved an arm at the warriors to his right, including his sister.

"I will charge with this group," he said, indicating the men on his left. He looked at Stands in Timber and Fire Crow, with the other group. "When we are down there and have their attention, then the rest of you attack," he instructed.

Heads nodded in understanding, some turning north, where a distant burst of sudden firing could be heard.

Comes in Sight wheeled his horse and urged it into a high lope around the hill, fourteen warriors hard on his heels. They broke from around the hill like an arrow flying off the bow and thundered toward the willows south of the creek, quickly closing in on the enemy. They fanned out and opened fire. For a brief moment, there was no return fire from the Long Knives, but then it came. Surprisingly, there was fire from the other side of the creek as well, from a small group hidden in the brushy creek bed. Suddenly, Comes in Sight and his warriors were caught in a cross fire. With a scream, the war leader's horse pitched forward and rolled, sending its rider sliding across the rock-strewn ground. The other warriors charged past him.

Stands in Timber and the others had ridden to the top of the low hill and saw their leader go down. Buffalo Calf Road gasped in disbelief, then watched her brother roll and lay motionless. She cried out when he turned over, gained his feet while holding his arm, and scrambled for the thin cover of a clump of willows.

Before anyone else could react, she kicked her horse and was down off the hill, galloping across the open ground toward the willows. Long Knife guns boomed from the willows and from the brush across the creek, some of the fire directed at the rider racing across the open.

"Brother!" she yelled at the top of her lungs, her voice drowned out by the guns. "Brother!"

From between the willows, Comes in Sight saw his horse struggling to rise and fall back down on one side, his legs twitching. A hot anger in his chest overwhelmed the pain in his right shoulder, though he was aware that he couldn't lift his arm. Suddenly, he realized he didn't have his rifle. Behind him, the rocky soil erupted as bullets tore into the top layer of dirt. Then he heard a thin shout through the din of gunfire, or whatever was roaring in his ears. In the next instant, he saw a horse and its small rider in a flat-out gallop heading directly for him.

In one of those incongruous moments in the midst of combat, although she knew the distance she had to cover was about a hundred long paces, she didn't seem to be getting closer. Buffalo Calf Road instinctively leaned low over the withers of her horse, her fingers curled around the neck rope and mane with a death grip, and the rifle in her right hand. She shouted at the horse and kicked him mercilessly to coax more speed. Strangely, she could not hear herself shout, or any other noise for that matter.

But close the distance she did. A few paces from the willows, she leaned back and yanked on the rein, and the horse squatted in a sliding stop, spewing rocks and dirt. She saw her brother looking up in total disbelief.

"Get on!" she screamed. "Get on!"

At first, he seemed to be moving in slow motion. In the next instant, however, he managed to jump up behind her, his left arm wrapping around her waist. She felt his weight pulling on her, and heard him grunt with the exertion, and her ears seemed to suddenly open. Gunshots boomed all around them, something buzzed by her head once and then again. She kicked the horse and felt his powerful lunges as he hit full stride in only a few jumps, in spite of his double load.

They reached the low hill and went around it and slid to a stop. Stands in Timber and some of the men were cheering; others were firing on the Long Knives from the crest of the hill. Several men quickly helped both of them down from the winded horse.

Buffalo Calf Road leaned and put her face against the horse's neck. "Thank you," she told him. "Thank you, my friend."

She felt a hand on her arm and turned to face her brother. His shoulder was obviously dislocated. He stood with his right arm draped over his left wrist, his mouth set against the pain. She noticed the scratches on his face and upper torso.

"Sister," he said softly, his lower lip trembling. His left hand reached up and wiped away the tear sliding down her cheek.

"You would have done the same for me," she told him after taking a deep breath. "Yesterday, someone, something, whispered in my ear. It told me to follow you, to go with you wherever you went. Now I know why."

Comes in Sight nodded, tears welling up in his eyes.

Black Moon found Crazy Horse watching from a rise as the fighting continued all around. "They are still scattered," he said to the war leader. "They are on that ridge to the north and are staying on the high ground near the creek. Some of them keep trying to charge us and then turn around."

Crazy Horse pulled down his field glasses. "Yes," he said, "and we must keep them scattered, make them run around like confused rabbits and use up their bullets."

"Cousin," Black Moon said, "we have many wounded."

"I know," Crazy Horse replied. "They must be taken from the field." Then he pointed to a line of Long Knives far north of the creek, strung out in single file and appearing as though they might be withdrawing. "There," he said. "We have to split them, cut them off so they cannot rejoin the others!"

In the next instant, with Black Wolf and Black Moon behind him, as well as nearly thirty warriors, Crazy Horse headed for the column of Long Knives.

Little Bird finished tying the ends of the cord he had wrapped around Goings's waist to hold the strip of torn shirt over the wound. He was relieved to see that the makeshift bandage had slowed the bleeding.

Goings had recovered his senses, his jaw set against the pain. "Thank you," he said through clenched teeth.

"You have to stay still and calm. When the bleeding stops, we will move away to the north and find a place to hide until this is over."

"No," Goings protested, "our friends need our help. I can hear the guns. Those stupid Long Knives do not know when they are defeated."

Little Bird glanced up at the horses, both still looking intently toward the sound of gunfire, and shook his head. "No," he said to his friend. "For now, we are out of the fighting. I have to move you, after a while, when the bleeding stops. If you start riding and get back in the fighting, you will bleed to death."

Although Goings did not reply, Little Bird saw the gleam of defiance in his friend's eyes.

"Think of your family," he said.

Goings nodded, his jaw still set against the pain.

In the distance, the sound of gunfire did not cease, and now and then came shouts of men. But the worst were the screams of horses in pain.

CHAPTER THIRTY-ONE

The Broken and Uneven Ground

Two Bulls, one of the four scouts Crazy Horse had sent east, lay belly down between a clump of grass and a small boulder and watched the line of riders going south. He knew who it was. The big man in the lead was Gall, the Hunkpapa war leader, and he was in a hurry. Since Two Bulls had first spotted them, the riders had kept their horses in a steady lope.

He hurried down the slope to the other three scouts waiting in the gully. "Forty men," he told them, pointing a thumb toward the west. "Gall is leading them. I think we should join them, since they are going toward Goose Creek and we have not seen any Long Knives."

Hawk Eagle saw the four riders as soon as they topped the rise and knew immediately that they were Lakota.

Gall signaled a halt as the riders arrived. "Where are you coming from?" he asked immediately.

"We were east of the stream," Two Bulls explained. "Crazy Horse wanted to make sure the Long Knives would not go that way. We saw nothing." He suddenly realized that the man next to Gall was none other than Sitting Bull. "Good to see you, Uncle," he added.

The medicine man smiled and nodded, but said nothing.

Gall pulled out his field glasses and looked to the south, focusing on the summit of a sharp hill. "I think I see a little dust," he said. "Something is moving down there." He glanced up at the sun and then at Sitting Bull. "It is just past the middle of the day. If that dust is nothing, we go on, and I think we can reach Goose Creek by the middle of the afternoon."

Eight teenage boys encircled the herd of horses left behind by the warriors, nervously riding guard. Now and then, they could hear pops of gunfire thinned by the distance. Badger suddenly whistled to the others and pointed north. The line of riders was already within six-shooter range. Badger was surprised and irritated that he had not heard them coming, but the men at the head of the group raised their hands high in greeting.

"Gall!" Swimmer, one of the other boys, called out. "It is Gall!"

The approaching riders slowed to a trot, and the Hunkpapa war leader stopped in front of Swimmer. "Where is your father, and the others?" he asked.

Swimmer pointed south.

"How long?" Gall went on.

"After sunrise," Badger replied.

Sitting Bull moved past Gall and looked thoughtfully at Badger. "Tell us, Grandson. What is happening?"

Badger glanced toward Swimmer and took a moment to think. "Cloud met us here. After that, they prepared themselves and rode for that hill over there," he said, pointing to the sharp hill to the south. "Crazy Horse took one group east of it, and Cloud took another group to the west."

"Has anyone come back?" Gall asked.

Badger and Swimmer shook their heads. "No one. Sometimes we can hear guns, I think."

Gall held up a hand for silence, and everyone listened. Soon enough, faint cracks of gunfire could be heard. He looked at Sitting Bull, who nodded and dismounted.

Gall rode up the line of warriors. "I think there is something happening beyond that hill," he told them. "Prepare yourselves. We will take only our warhorses from here."

As the Crazy Horse warriors had done before, Gall's men prepared themselves, checking their weapons and their warhorses. Most of them took the time to paint their faces and chests and pause for a moment of prayer.

Sitting Bull walked among them. "It is time to think of the helpless ones," he reminded everyone. "Your families expect you to be strong and brave, but not reckless. They want you to go home to them. And remember, fighting Long Knives is not for glory or honor. We must destroy them."

More horses were added to the waiting herd as Gall and his men loped toward the sharp hill.

Little Bird returned from his brief scout. "There is a deeper gully just north of here, and a hill behind it," he told Goings. "Good place to hide. When you are ready, we can go. I think we should walk and stay to the gullies and low areas."

Goings nodded, his face still pinched with pain. "I am ready," he said. "Help me up."

After a few steps, Goings settled into a slow, comfortable pace, using his rifle as a cane while Little Bird led the horses. The firing to the south had not dissipated, though now there were more frequent intervals without gunfire, and fewer sustained volleys. What it meant, Little Bird wasn't certain. Perhaps the fighting was changing from the initial frenzy of charges and counterattacks. It was probable that the Lakota and Cheyenne were saving ammunition. In between the gunfire was the thud and scramble of hooves and yelling voices.

Little Bird tied the horses to a sturdy sagebrush stalk, then helped Goings recline against the sharp slope of the gully. He built a makeshift shade over the wounded man by piling brush over the tops of sagebrush. The sun was high, leaning over into the afternoon half of the sky, and it was hot. Finishing the sunshade, he checked the wrap over Goings's wound. In spite of the movement, it did not seem to be bleeding heavily. But Little Bird could tell the pain was nearly unbearable. Suddenly, he remembered the red-willow medicine in his bullet bag. Reaching in, he probed among the bullets. It was there, in a small bag. Pulling it out, he showed it to Goings and poured the pieces of dried bark into his palm. "Suck on this," he said. "It might help with the pain."

Of course, Goings knew what it was, and he put the dried bark in his mouth. His saliva would soak the bark, and the juices would help alleviate the pain. He nodded his thanks.

Little Bird crawled to the top of the hill, careful to stay low among the brush and sage. He wanted to take a look at what was happening.

Cloud, Taken Alive, Yellow Wolf, and several other men were spread out, crouching behind and along the lip of a ravine. Farther down, in a deeper part, two men were guarding the horses, letting them rest.

Cloud trained his glass on the higher ridge to the west, where many Long Knives had gathered and taken cover. Occasionally, some of them would snipe at someone. All around, the firing had noticeably lessened, and shouts and running hoofbeats came thinly. The battle had settled down into isolated pockets of fighting. The initial surge of adrenaline that had driven them hard and sometimes recklessly had now thinned somewhat, and warriors were now thinking and acting deliberately, carefully considering each move and shot.

Suddenly, firing from the Long Knives on the ridge increased and return gunfire could be heard. Cloud turned his glass to the north and saw a line of warriors riding south at a gallop, ducking and dodging through the gullies and drawing fire from the ridge. He kept his glass trained on the warriors, wondering who had been able to circle to the north. After several moments, he saw the broad-shouldered man in the lead. It was Gall, with reinforcements. He obviously had started south from Ash Creek sometime after they had.

"Gall!" he said to the others. "It is Gall!"

As the new arrivals came closer, firing up at the ridge as they rode, Cloud continued to watch, and noticed the man behind Gall—Sitting Bull. He was riding and shooting like the warrior of his youth. At the sight of the old warrior putting action behind his words, Cloud felt a surge of energy coursing through him, even as a lump came into his throat.

Little Bird saw the line of warriors below the ridge and heard the gunfire. At that distance, they were nothing more than dark forms against the landscape. "It looks like someone is going after the Long Knives on the ridge to the west," he called down to Goings.

As the charging warriors drew close to his position, Cloud pulled out his looking glass and signaled. Taking the right fork of a dry watercourse, Gall and his warriors pulled to a dust-raising halt in the ravine, their eyes wide with energy and excitement.

"What is happening?" Gall called out.

Cloud ducked below the lip and climbed down the incline. "We have been fighting since this morning," he told the fresh and eager line of warriors.

"I think Crazy Horse is across the creek, and so are the Cheyenne. The Long Knives are scattered in several groups, mostly near the creek. That bunch on the ridge is the largest group."

"Have we lost many men?" Sitting Bull asked cautiously.

"We have wounded," Cloud replied somberly. "Hard to tell how many, but many, I think. I know of only two men who have been killed."

As Cloud talked with Gall and Sitting Bull, Taken Alive knelt down next to Yellow Wolf. "I have not seen Goings and Little Bird for a while," he said. "Do you know where they are?"

Yellow Wolf shook his head. "I have not seen them since we came this way," he said. "They were behind us, I think."

Taken Alive looked worried. "I think I will go back and look for them," he said in a low voice. "Something might have happened."

Yellow Wolf nodded. "Want me to go with you?"

"No, stay with Cloud. I think he plans to keep watch on things on the ridge. I will be back, whether I find them or not."

Little Bird kept a close eye on the man leading a horse who appeared now and then in the gullies and in the dry washes. He seemed to be tracking something. The man's outline did not have the distinctive upswept hair-style of the Crow, and his movements were familiar. In a while, he appeared in the gully where they had stopped to treat Goings's wound. At a distance of something less than a hundred paces, Little Bird recognized Taken Alive and whistled sharply, using the call of the quail three times in a row.

Taken Alive immediately looked to the north, in the direction from which he thought the whistles came. Three calls of the quail, meaning someone was wounded or injured.. Throwing caution aside, he mounted and urged his horse into a lope and followed the gullies.

"Here!" Little Bird called out.

"What is it?" Goings wanted to know, reaching for his rifle.

"It is Taken Alive. He is coming," Little Bird told him.

Crazy Horse and his nearly one hundred warriors had been harassing a column of Long Knives who, for some reason, were moving northeast along Rosebud Creek. One Lakota mounted charge had been met with fierce resistance and quickly bogged down until Crazy Horse regrouped and led another charge that forced the Long Knives to dismount and fight from behind whatever cover they could find. Gunfire filled the air for several long moments.

As the charge turned left and away from the creek, Black Wolf whipped his horse to keep up with Crazy Horse, who emptied his six-shooter, sending Long Knives scattering out of the clumps of sandbar willow, even as his sorrel warhorse was at a full gallop. The standard bearer fired his own six-shooter and felt a sting just below his ribs on the right side. Disregarding it, he followed the war leader as the line of warriors made a wide circle and regrouped.

Gall suddenly pointed south toward the creek at several lines of Long Knives riding hard toward them. Where they had come from was anybody's guess. Gall smiled in eager anticipation.

"I think we will let them chase us for a while," Cloud suggested, "let them wear their horses out. Then we will turn back on them."

"Good!" shouted Gall. "Let them come!"

Cloud's men remounted and joined Gall and his newly arrived warriors, who were eager to tangle with the Long Knives. Eighty or so warriors, Sitting Bull among them, strung themselves out to the north, apparently in full flight, like the prairie hen dragging an injured wing and drawing the coyote away.

Taken Alive watched the warriors in the distance galloping north, bobbing along through the gullies. Behind them came the Long Knives, their bigger horses not as nimble as the smaller and more sure-footed Lakota mounts.

"That is Cloud and Gall," said Taken Alive, pointing.

Against the haze of the ridge to the west, they could see muzzle flashes as the Long Knives in the front of the column fired at the Lakota.

As they neared the sharp hill, the Lakota split into two groups, one suddenly veering east and the other west, and both quickly angled back toward the Long Knives, attacking both flanks and catching them in a deadly cross fire. The Long Knives returned fire, but the fast-moving warriors proved to be elusive targets. As the Lakota warriors bore down on them, the enemy column turned and followed a narrow stream that emptied into Rosebud Creek.

Meanwhile, a small column of Long Knives came down off the ridge and charged toward the pointed hill.

Taken Alive trained his field glasses on the hill, surprised that more than a few warriors seemed to be on its summit and on the steep slopes. How and when they had gotten there, he didn't know, but they were outnumbered by the advancing column. As the Long Knives got close to the base of the hill, the warriors left the hill and disappeared from view.

As Taken Alive and Little Bird continued to observe, another column of Long Knives came off the ridge and joined the other that had turned back, south from the hill. The now larger column moved toward Rosebud Creek. From out of the earth itself, it seemed, mounted warriors suddenly appeared, and once again gunfire filled the air and every heart beat in time.

The two warriors watching sensed they were witnessing the heaviest fighting of the day. The Long Knives were dogged and, for reasons unknown, apparently trying to hook up with those along the creek. Lines of walking Long Knives also got into the fray, and the broken and uneven ground north of the creek became a frenzy of motion and noise.

Crazy Horse and Good Road led a contingent of warriors at the left flank of the Long Knives. There, groups of Crow and Shoshone saved their allies from complete collapse as they put themselves in between them and the charging Lakota and Cheyenne.

Horses collided, and for the first time this day, ancient enemies came face-to-face, and the presence of the confused Long Knives was temporarily unimportant. War clubs were swung and six-shooters were fired at point-blank range. Dust rose from hundreds of horses until Long Knives could not discern which of the brown-skinned and -braided fighters were enemies or friends.

Crazy Horse was in his element. With his long-handled buffalo-horn-tipped war club in hand, he threw himself into the fray. In the space of moments, as his horse spun and dodged, his weapon crunched into an arm, expertly parried a blow, and punctured an enemy's lung. In the next instant, he landed a blow into the spine of a Shoshone, stunning the man and rendering his arms useless. All the while, young Black Wolf stayed near him, using the feather banner to parry and thrust, ignoring the pain in his side.

Gall and Cloud threw themselves into the fight, galloping into the confused array of whirling men and horses, grunting and yelling as they and their warriors waded in.

Taken Alive and Little Bird came off the hill. "We have to go," Taken Alive explained to Goings, putting his rifle close to his side in case he needed it. "Something is happening over there. We have to help." Little Bird grabbed his horse's rein.

Goings smiled weakly and nodded. "I will be here," he said. "Take care of yourselves."

In the next moment, they were mounted and gone.

"Grandfather," Goings prayed, "watch over my friends. Keep them safe."

Buffalo Calf Road waited on a rise south of Rosebud Creek with her brother and watched the fighting. Comes in Sight's dislocated arm had been pulled back into place, but he was still unable to grasp with his hand. He could still ride and fight with one hand, if need be, but with one arm he would be at a disadvantage. Furthermore, if he went, he knew his sister would come along. Besides, he didn't want to diminish or insult her act of bravery by putting himself, or her, in harm's way again.

"Brother," she said, "what has happened here this day?"

Comes in Sight thought for a moment. "We have met this enemy," he replied. "I think whites and Long Knives have to learn that we will stand and fight. I think we are showing them today. To defeat an enemy, it is necessary to defeat him in his mind, so that his will is weakened."

She stared across the creek as a thin cloud of dust arose, raised by the hooves of hundreds of horses. "I do not think this is over yet," she whispered.

The crack of gunfire indicated there was still a hard fight, perhaps several. Goings crawled carefully up the incline and reached the top. The pain in his side had subsided to a persistent, hot throbbing, and he kept a careful eye on the wrap. It didn't feel like the wound was bleeding as he settled himself carefully to have a look over the hill. Behind the pain, he was thoroughly exhausted. He wanted to sleep. The nightlong ride followed by a day of battle did not seem real. Images tried to push their way into his awareness, past the pain and utter fatigue—flashes of men and horses falling, Long Knives fumbling to reload rifles, a black-tailed deer bounding away from the noise and chaos, the long, dark shadows of early morning.

The gunfire was subsiding, however. From his vantage point, it seemed that the Long Knives had crossed to the south side of the Rosebud, but there was no way to know for sure. He could see groups of warriors breaking off and moving west and north. In a while, he saw three of them coming in his direction. Other warriors probed the draws and gullies behind them, looking for the dead and wounded.

From the creek and the open valley came sporadic gunfire, and a column of Long Knives was still moving south. But Goings had a feeling that the battle was over.

Goings was immensely relieved to see his friends Little Bird, Yellow Wolf, and Taken Alive. It was easy to see that the battle had taken a toll on them. Not only did they look exhausted, there was already a haunted look in their eyes.

"It is good to see you," he said as they arrived.

"I think it is over," Taken Alive said.

Nearly thirty warriors proceeded north in the washes and gullies east of the ridge where some of the Long Knives were still situated, heading toward the waiting horse herd to help the horse holders drive it north. The main body of Lakota and Cheyenne warriors moved rapidly toward a narrow canyon that guarded both sides of Rosebud Creek. An advance group had been sent ahead to take up positions on the slopes and ridges of the canyon and wait to ambush.

Like Goings and everyone else, Cloud was exhausted. His arms and legs felt heavy as he and several Lakota Crazy Dog and Cheyenne Dog Soldier warriors rode in a long line as the rear guard. Behind them, at the edge of six-shooter range, followed a column of Long Knives.

As most of the main body of warriors entered the canyon, the Crazy Dogs and Dog Soldiers dropped back a little, close enough to see which of the scouts at the front of the column were Shoshone and which were Crow. Suddenly, it seemed, the Long Knife column had stopped.

Cloud looked through his glass. A small group of scouts and Long Knives were gathered together, and the column behind them was halted. He could see several of the scouts pointing north, toward the canyon.

"My friends," he called out, "they have stopped."

"They are afraid of the canyon," one of the Dog Soldiers replied. "They know we will wait for them there."

The warriors waited, sitting quietly, introspectively, on their horses, somewhat oblivious to the hot sun. Each of them was assailed by the images and noises of combat that played over and over in their minds. They stared at the distant, dark column without really seeing it.

In a while, after the shadows below shrubs and rocks grew a little longer, the Long Knives were moving. The front of the column turned south, away from the canyon and the waiting Crazy Dog and Dog Soldier warriors. Like a ponderous, dark snake, it doubled back on itself, causing a thin dust cloud to rise as it moved away.

CHAPTER THIRTY-TWO

There Has Been Death

Sweetwater Woman saw the war lance impaled in the ground near the lodge of Black Shawl and Crazy Horse. Nearby, under the frame covered with willow branches, Black Shawl sat with a small, squarish stone in her hand, pounding dried elk hamstring into sinew atop a larger, flat base stone. The long, thin cord, as wide as a child's little finger, turned white and fibrous as she pounded it. When she finished, she would then separate the fibers into very thin strips to use as thread.

"Sister," Sweetwater Woman said in greeting, "I have brought a little dried meat for you and your husband." She placed a canvas bag next to Black Shawl.

"You are kind," Black Shawl said, smiling.

"It is elk."

Black Shawl pointed to a spot on the buffalo robe. "Sit," she invited. "Thank you. Elk stew is my husband's favorite."

Sweetwater Woman sat down on the robe. The meat containers in the lodge of Black Shawl and Crazy Horse were almost always empty—not because he was not a good provider, but because they gave things away to other people who had little or nothing.

Black Shawl set aside her task, glad to have her own visitor. When her husband was home, there seemed to be an endless procession of people who came to see him.

Black Shawl was thin and had been for several years now, since her bout with the coughing sickness, which had also taken her daughter. Sweetwater Woman was concerned when she noticed that Black Shawl's cheeks looked especially hollow. These days, she seemed to look tired as well.

"I wanted to thank you for staying with me when my daughter was stolen," Sweetwater Woman said, "but it seems I did not have the chance until now." Truthfully, she had not wanted to broach the sensitive topic of lost children, for fear of reminding Black Shawl of her own loss.

"How is your daughter?" Black Shawl asked.

"She is well."

"There was nothing my husband and I could do to save our daughter," Black Shawl went on. "That illness was beyond his power, beyond anyone's power. That is why he was so driven to help you and your husband. He could make a difference there."

"And he did. All the men did."

A moment passed. A sudden playful whirlwind danced between the lodges and was gone.

Black Shawl smiled. "Speaking of men," she said, "I hope they return soon, and safely."

"Waiting is hard to do," Sweetwater Woman admitted. "It is so different from anything else—the more I sew, the better I become, but the more I wait, the more I hate it."

"Waiting is our battlefield," Black Shawl pointed out. "We may not face death or injury, but sometimes other things can be wounded. We rejoice when we see them return alive, but there is always the prospect that one day…one day, they will not."

They heard soft footfalls, and a figure came around the lodge. It was Stands on the Hill, wife of Little Bird, carrying a small kettle in her hand.

"Cousin," she said to Black Shawl, "I made more soup than my sons wanted to eat. I hope you can help make sure it does not go to waste."

"Thank you," Black Shawl said, taking the kettle. "Join us, we are just talking."

Stands on the Hill, who had large brown eyes and a ready smile, took a seat next to Sweetwater Woman. "Ashes and Two Horns went to the creek," she said. "They are restless."

"I think we all are," Black Shawl said. "The last time so many of our men went off together to fight was ten years ago, when they surrounded the Long Knives near Prairie Dog Creek."

"Yes," Stands on the Hill recalled. "The Battle of the Hundred in the Hand. That was the coldest winter I can remember."

"This bunch of Long Knives is near there, according to what the scouts said yesterday," Black Shawl said.

"Yesterday…," Sweetwater Woman mused softly. "It seems longer than that since they left. I wonder where they are now."

"Probably at Goose Creek," Stands on the Hill guessed.

An anxious silence descended for a few moments. If the warriors were at Goose Creek, where the Long Knives had been seen, that meant there was probably fighting, likely at this very moment, or else there certainly would be before this day was done.

Black Shawl pointed north. "My father-in-law and High Eagle have been up there praying since last evening. I think they have not slept, at least not for very long."

"I did not sleep well," Stands on the Hill admitted. "I kept seeing the warriors circle the village, and hearing the old women sing the Strong Heart songs. There was a feeling of strength from seeing so many warriors. The scouts said there are a thousand Long Knives."

Black Shawl reached into a case nearby and took out a short braid of sweetgrass, handed it to Sweetwater Woman, and pointed to the gray ashes in the fire pit under the shade. "There are still coals from this morning," she told her.

Sweetwater Woman took a stick and stirred the dimly glowing coals, dislodging the ash. From a nearby pile, she took a handful of twigs and dropped them onto the coals and leaned over, blowing until the twigs caught and erupted into low flames. When the small fire burned steadily, she held the end of the braid of sweetgrass in the flames until it glowed. Withdrawing it, she waved it gently, causing a thin plume of smoke to rise.

Smudging with sweetgrass was an appeal for the good spirits to come, to gather and hear the prayers—spoken and unspoken.

"Watch over them," Sweetwater Woman whispered. "Keep them safe."

The three women watched the thin wisps of smoke rising into the air between the lodge poles.

"My friend," High Eagle said to Worm, "something has happened. I feel something stirring."

Worm nodded in agreement, staring south toward the hazy, bluish outline of the Shining Mountains.

High Eagle's shoulders sagged, his eyes shut tightly as he looked inward, trying to see something, to visualize whatever it was he was feeling. After a deep sigh, he said, "My friend, I am afraid there has been death."

While the rest of the rear guard warriors waited behind a rise to the northeast, Cloud, Wolf Eyes, and Tall Bull, a Cheyenne, squatted behind the crest of a hill. The three scouts had followed the Long Knife column but were mindful to stay beyond rifle range. Like wolves watching a wounded deer, they stared intently at the small dark figures to the southwest.

The Long Knives had fallen back to the sparse meadows on either side of Rosebud Creek, where they had stopped sometime after dawn to build fires and eat. Much had happened since then.

"I think they are gathering dead and wounded," Tall Bull surmised. "But from this distance, they are nothing but black specks."

"I am confused as to why they made camp farther south last evening," Cloud mused, "but for some reason, they broke camp in the middle of the night, came here, and stopped."

Wolf Eyes shaded his eyes with both hands as he studied the movements in the distance. "It looks like they are rounding up loose horses too," he said. He pointed. "And those six specks there, I would guess they are watching in this direction with their far-seeing glasses."

"Good!" Tall Bull exclaimed. "That means they are afraid of us. The question is, what will they do now?"

"I think they will make camp there for the night," Cloud said, looking up to see that the sun was well past the middle of the afternoon sky. "Whatever they do, we will keep an eye on them."

"Do you suppose they will follow us north?" Tall Bull wondered.

"They might," Cloud replied. "They were hunting us, and now they know we are somewhere in the area."

"I wonder," Tall Bull said, "if they think they won today."

"Who understands how they think?" Cloud replied and shrugged. "Let them think they won. They would only be lying to themselves. The fact is, they had more guns and bullets, but they could not defeat us. If that does not make them stop and think, they are foolish, and the only thing the foolish can rely on is luck. Luck is a good thing, but it is never dependable."

Each of them suddenly, instinctively, reached for a weapon, startled by the thin pops of hoofbeats behind them. Cloud immediately raised a hand, reassuring his companions that the approaching rider was not an enemy.

Yellow Wolf dismounted, and Cloud noticed that even the stalwart young warrior walked with a slow shuffle, reflecting a bone-deep weariness they all felt.

"Crazy Horse is leaving forty men in the canyon, just in case the Long Knives follow," he told them. "Drag poles are being prepared to haul the wounded and those who were killed. When everything is ready, they will move out."

He looked directly at Cloud. "Goings was wounded, but he is insisting on riding home. His wound is not bleeding now. He is being a little stubborn about riding. Little Bird thought maybe you could talk to him."

Cloud nodded. "I will. How many…how many were killed?"

"Ten or twelve, I think. Someone said there are over eighty wounded. Some of them probably will not make it home."

Cloud accompanied Yellow Wolf back to a meadow west of the creek and the deep canyon. Although there were hundreds of horses and men, activity was minimal and quiet. Worn-out horses stood quietly with their heads down, and exhausted men moved about slowly. Many were at work constructing drag frames. The wounded were being treated and helped. Sitting Bull and a helper were sitting and praying near three hide-covered bodies.

The mood was one of relief more so than elation. In the minds of most of the warriors, they had won the day, but it had worn them down physically and emotionally. Many sat or reclined, simply resting and trying to ignore the lingering sights and sounds of battle. Conversation was at a minimum. Eyes stared ahead to some distant point, searching for peace and solace, not seeing the rock or the bush they seemed to be looking at.

Goings sat against a rock beneath a makeshift shade of elk hide and bare branches. Nearby, Little Bird was helping Taken Alive coax a fire to life to make tea.

Goings looked up sheepishly as Cloud cleared away a space in the grass and sat. "My father said life and death are sometimes both a matter of being in a certain spot at a certain moment," he said, grimacing a little. "Now I understand what he meant."

"My father said getting shot would hurt," Cloud said, half smiling.

"I can understand that too," Goings replied.

"And home is a long way," Cloud said, glancing at the binding around his cousin's waist.

"Little Bird got some tobacco somewhere and made a poultice," Goings explained. "It stopped the bleeding."

"Good," Cloud replied. "And if you stay off your horse, it will stay that way."

Goings glanced at Yellow Wolf and Little Bird. "I knew they would say something to you," he complained.

"Look at it this way, Cousin," Cloud warned, smiling, "if you insist on riding, there are three of us. We can tie your hands and feet and then tie you down to the drag poles."

Goings sighed. "Hard to say which is worse," he groused, "getting shot or being cared for by the bunch of you."

Cloud chuckled and heard soft footfalls behind him. Crazy Horse squatted on one knee beside him, gazing intently at Goings. "My friend," he said, "how are you?"

"Good," Goings replied. "I am good. My wound is nothing compared to some others I have seen. And I am sure that if those who were killed could speak, they would rather be alive and in pain."

"You are probably right," Crazy Horse agreed. He paused for a moment to look around. "When everyone is prepared, we will move out," he said to Cloud. "I wonder if you can stay behind with the scouts. We need to know what the Long Knives do as soon as they do it."

"I was planning on it," Cloud assured him.

"I think we hurt them," Crazy Horse said. "At least we made them use up their bullets. They will take time to regroup, and then they will probably head north. If they do, we will turn back. We will travel slowly to rest the horses and to take care of the wounded. Forty men will stay in the canyon, but if the Long Knives move north, do not engage them the way we did today. Harass them, run off their horses, snipe at them from long distances, but do not engage them. And send a messenger as soon as anything happens."

Cloud nodded. "I will."

After Crazy Horse left, Cloud looked toward Taken Alive. "I wonder if you could take word to my wife. Tell her I am staying behind. Let her know that I am not hurt."

Taken Alive nodded. "How many bullets do you have left?"

Cloud touched the bullet bag hanging near his left hip. "Plenty for my six-shooter," he said, feeling the one hanging near his right hip. "A few for my rifle."

Taken Alive handed him four large bullets for his rifle, as did Goings and Little Bird. Yellow Wolf grinned. "I am going to keep my bullets, because I am staying with you," he said.

Under the hot late-afternoon sun, the lines of warriors started home. Cloud and Yellow Wolf watched for a little while before they turned south to join the scouts who were keeping an eye on the Long Knives.

To keep the wounded men as comfortable as possible, the column of warriors started out at a slow pace. A few of the less seriously wounded rode, but most were carried on drag frames behind horses. With Little Big Man at his side, Crazy Horse rode some distance behind the column, occasionally glancing back over his shoulder.

"Do you expect the Long Knives to come after us?" Little Big Man asked.

"Any enemy can surprise you," Crazy Horse replied. "They might not send a large force, but they might decide to send a smaller and faster column at our left flank, from the west."

"Maybe we should turn back on them instead," Little Big Man suggested.

"They would be expecting that," Crazy Horse pointed out. "And our men are worn out. We will turn and fight if it is necessary. But I think it is wiser to go home and prepare to defend the village. By sundown, if the Long Knives do not follow, we will stop to rest."

As the sun began to set, Crazy Horse called a halt near a narrow, fast-flowing creek and posted sentries. He sent messengers to tell the exhausted warriors that they would start again sometime in the night. Then he found Lone Hill and pulled him aside.

"I know you are as tired as the rest of us," he said. "I want you to water your horse and get some sleep, and then leave early. Take a message to my father, as well as to High Eagle, Black Shield, and the old men. Tell them about the battle, about the wounded…and about our dead. Their families need to be told."

The young warrior nodded. "I can leave now," he offered.

"No, get some rest first, and let your horse rest."

A shout came from the south. "The horse herd! They are bringing the horses!"

The horse guards and the warriors helping them arrived amid all the rumbling.

Lone Hill turned to Crazy Horse. "My other horse has more endurance," he said. "I will catch him."

Nearby, Walking Eagle leaned over a young man lying on a drag pole frame. "Little brother," he said hopefully, "can you hear me?"

Yellow Earrings stared upward. Walking Eagle put his hand on his brother's chest; it was no longer moving. Walking Eagle covered his face with his hands, his broad shoulders shaking as he sobbed quietly. Then, reaching over, he gently closed his brother's eyes and prayed he would find the right words to say to their mother and father.

A few fires were lit as, here and there, men took the opportunity to brew tea and eat before they slept. Crazy Horse found Sitting Bull tending to the more seriously wounded men, and Gall was not far away. The three of them gathered around a fire when Sitting Bull was finished.

"I am afraid we will lose a few more before we reach home," Sitting Bull told them.

Crazy Horse nodded grimly.

"Uncle," Gall said to Sitting Bull, "what happened today is not what you saw in your vision, is it?"

The Hunkpapa medicine man slowly shook his head. "No, it is not. That is yet to come…"

At dusk, the Long Knives faded from sight, blending into the shadows. Even with his looking glass, Cloud could not see them.

"Do you think they will follow Crazy Horse?" Yellow Wolf asked.

Cloud shook his head. "Not in the dark, but in the morning, maybe. I think they will see to their wounded first. So we will take turns on watch. Two of us at a time will stay awake while the others sleep. In the morning, I want us all to be rested so that one of us can catch up to Crazy Horse, if it is necessary."

Not long after sunrise, the Long Knives began moving upstream, back toward the Shining Mountains to the west. However Cloud was not convinced that retreat was their real intent. He sent Yellow Wolf to alert the warriors in the canyon.

Then he turned to Wolf Eyes and Tall Bull. "Flank them to their right," he told Wolf Eyes. "I want to be sure they do not turn. And you," he said to Tall Bull, "flank them to their left. If they turn, I want to know."

"What if they keep going?" Wolf Eyes asked.

"We will follow them as far as they go."

At Goose Creek, the site of their previous camp, the Long Knives stopped.

At about the same time the Long Knives started west, Crazy Horse and his warriors arrived home. Lone Hill had already delivered his message, and word had swept through the village faster than a wind-driven fire. Many of the women and children were waiting at the edge of the village, anxiously watching the mass of returning warriors for signs of their loved ones.

Lone Hill had also told the story of Buffalo Calf Road, the young Cheyenne woman who rescued her brother. Many were already calling the fight along Rosebud Creek the Battle Where the Woman Saved Her Brother.

Crazy Horse couldn't bear the looks of anxiety and dread on the faces of the wives and mothers. Three of the wounded had died during the night, and he was not looking forward to what lay ahead of him—visiting the families of the dead warriors. At least thirteen families would have a hole in their lives.

Taken Alive waved at his wife, then broke from the line and took her up in a long embrace.

Nearby, he saw Sweetwater Woman and worked his way through the crowd toward her. "Your husband is well," he said quickly. "He was not hurt. He stayed back with the scouts."

Sweetwater Woman closed her eyes in relief and nodded, biting her lip to hold back the lump in her throat. "Thank you," she whispered, and turned away.

For two days, Cloud and his scouts stayed hidden and watched the Long Knives carefully. They almost couldn't believe that their enemies showed no apparent inclination to go anywhere, except for a few hunters who had been sent into the mountains.

At dawn on the third day, Cloud sent two of the younger scouts back with word for Crazy Horse, and he called the remaining warriors together. "I think they might be waiting here for something. Perhaps wagons with more supplies, or more Long Knives," he told them. "So I want ten men to go south for two days, following the Powder River Road, to see if anyone is coming north. Wait for two or three days. If there is no one, then come back. In the meantime, the rest of us will be here, making life uncomfortable for the Long Knives as long as they are around."

Just after sundown, White Wing found Crazy Horse in the council lodge.

"Uncle," White Wing said, "Cloud sent us back to tell you that the Long Knives went back to Goose Creek and stopped there. Cloud and the others will make sure they do not come north."

"Good," said Crazy Horse, looking around at the circle of old men. "That is good to hear, but I think we should move the village."

Sitting Bull, Black Shield, and Grey Bull nodded in agreement.

"Yes," Black Shield said. "We have already scouted the site near the Greasy Grass River. When the families of the dead have had time to bury them, we should move."

CHAPTER THIRTY-THREE

The Foolish

Sergeant Major MacAllister waited patiently just outside the general's tent. A subdued atmosphere lay over the camp, which was situated on both sides of cold Goose Creek. Sentries were posted all around the perimeter, but the Sioux and Cheyenne, who had more than adequately demonstrated their tenacity, were out there watching, so the sergeant major did not feel assured that the camp was safe. He glanced at his watch, noted the time, and looked across the camp. He heard the general's pen scratching across the pages of his journal. The sergeant major knew Crook was writing his battle report.

"We beat those Indians and drove them away," the general had commented last evening. Perhaps he would state that in so many words in his report, but MacAllister did not share his sentiment. Nor were there such feelings among the men, as far as he could tell.

Almost exactly thirteen years ago, MacAllister had been a corporal of artillery at Gettysburg. His battery had been in support of the Union army's Iron Brigade under the command of Major General John Fulton Reynolds. Seminary Ridge was the place, one of the spots where thousands of men in blue fought thousands of men in gray. He could still feel the tins of canister shot he shoved down the barrel of his cannon time after time, and he could still hear the ear-concussing *whump* as the gunpowder was ignited. But it had done little to stop the Confederates' advance, it seemed. First the men of the Iron Brigade had pushed them back, then the Confederate soldiers had pushed back and the cannons had to be moved. But there had been definable lines—the enemy advanced and retreated and you could see where they were. Fighting the Sioux and the Cheyenne was nothing like that. They were like bugs on the water, and by all that was holy, they could ride and fight from the backs of their small mounts. They were true horse warriors.

Not once did the sergeant major feel that Crook or any of his company commanders were in control of the situation. It was all a reactionary fight on their part. There was no choice. It was hard to see, but there couldn't have been more than a few hundred Indians, though it seemed like there were more because they were scattered all over the place. If the scouts hadn't convinced the general to countermand his own orders to follow the hostiles, Colonel Anson Mills and his force would have been cut to pieces in that narrow canyon. No, not by any means did they defeat the Indians. If anything, it was the other way around.

A small, wiry man, the surgeon's orderly, approached and stopped. "Sergeant Major," he said, "Lieutenant Holliman is awake."

"See to the lieutenant," the general called out, "and let me know."

"Yes, sir!" MacAllister replied.

A man was bent over the lieutenant's cot as MacAllister ducked into one of the infirmary tents a minute later. "Opiates," the doctor explained to the young officer, "for the pain."

His hand trembling, Holliman reached for the cup and drank the liquid, then carefully laid back against the rolled-up blanket behind his head. A flicker of recognition flashed through his pain-glazed eyes as he saw MacAllister.

"Edward," the sergeant major said gently, "glad to see you back among us." The lieutenant had been unconscious for several hours, likely as a result of the loss of blood from his lower-leg wound.

"Sergeant Major," the young officer replied hoarsely, "they tell me I have a broken leg." He pointed at his right shin and ankle elevated on folded blankets and bound by a wooden splint on both sides. Blood soaked through the bandages.

"That is the case," affirmed the sergeant major. "A big round hit you in the leg."

The surgeon stood for a moment, carefully observing the wounded man, and then pointed to a low stool. "Have a seat, Sergeant Major."

"Thank you, sir."

MacAllister waited until the surgeon left the tent. "No use asking how you feel," he said. "Might be a while before you can stand on that leg."

"Never knew anything could hurt this bad," rasped the young man. "The doctor told me I would probably have a limp."

"One of the dangers in our chosen line of work, Edward," MacAllister said, smiling. "That and low pay and bad dreams, among other things."

"I see you are full of joy and good news, as usual," Holliman teased. "Glad to be alive to hear it."

MacAllister chuckled.

"They whipped our behinds, Benjamin."

The sergeant major glanced cautiously around to make certain no one was within earshot before he leaned over to reply in a near whisper, "I think you are right, lad. Our losses were not as bad as they could be. Yet here we are, curled up like a dog that got kicked across the room."

"Colonel Reynolds underestimated them as well, back in January, up there on the Powder," Holliman pointed out. "He didn't think they could or would counterattack. We outnumbered them, but they outfought us."

"Aye, that was the case yesterday," MacAllister admitted. "Not that it is the opinion common among the higher-ups. The general thinks we beat 'em and sent 'em packin'."

The lieutenant shook his head. "I do not concur, but I am not writing the report." He held himself rigid against a sudden bolt of pain, then slowly relaxed. "What is the plan now? Are we to regroup and go north to rendezvous with the other columns in the field?"

MacAllister shook his head. "No word of that sort. I know for certain the general is not wantin' to move wounded men, nor does he want to leave you behind."

"I am grateful for that sense of humanity, though it may not be sound tactical thinking. One more thing—were our dead really buried back there along the Rosebud?"

The sergeant major nodded somberly. "They were. Their graves were dug in the dark, and any sign of 'em was wiped clean, so the hostiles don't find them and dig 'em up."

Holliman sadly shook his head. "Hell of a legacy—an unmarked grave far from home."

"Maybe, maybe," the sergeant major allowed. "On t'other hand, they might be the lucky ones. They got no more troubles."

They both looked toward the door at the sound of a mounted troop hurrying by, saddle leather squeaking and metal bits jingling. Returning his attention to MacAllister, the lieutenant asked, "What is our situation now?"

"We got ourselves a tight perimeter. The sentries were doubled last night, with orders to shoot at anything that moved."

The lieutenant sighed deeply. "That doesn't seem like the action of a victorious force."

For some strange reason, Holliman was bothered by the fact that he was not dressed. He recalled, more or less, that the legs of his uniform pants had been cut off, but he could not remember when his shoes, what was left of his pants, or his shirt and wool tunic had been removed. The right leg of his wool underwear had been cut off as well. All in all, he was not properly attired to receive guests. *But where did that thought come from? And why was it important?* he wondered.

The pain. It had to be the pain.

Unable to sleep because of the throbbing pain, Holliman listened to the sounds outside his tent. Horses were snorting and stomping and whinnying. Men were talking, coughing, walking by. Beyond them, in the hills and trees, he could see coyotes in his mind's eye. Their thin, almost tinny voices annoyed him. But they were not as annoying as the creak from the wooden frame of his cot each time he moved.

It was dark now. From a nearby tent, he heard the low moan of a man in pain, reminding him there were other wounded in the tents next to his. Suddenly, he heard running feet and shouts, and strident, panicked voices.

"Fire!"

Holliman smelled the smoke.

Shots boomed from what sounded like the northwest corner of the camp. Holliman looked toward the door of his tent; it was tied shut. Someone, an officer with a familiar voice, barked orders. The pounding of running feet increased, and more shots cracked and boomed.

The doorway of the tent was ripped open, and two men ducked in. "We've got to move you, Lieutenant!" one of them yelled.

A jolt of pain coursed through his leg as Holliman was unceremoniously lifted, cot and all, and hauled out into the cold evening air. Panic reigned outside. Men scurried, and rifles boomed. Holliman saw a glow to the northwest as he bounced along. He was deposited none too gently near other wounded. One of them was pointing toward the fire.

"Injuns! They's tryin' to burn us out!"

There was no way to fight the flames, which were crackling and rolling toward the camp. Officers and noncommissioned officers were organizing men to do the only thing they could—move away from the brush.

Consequently, tents, wagons, and other gear and equipment were being pulled, pushed, dragged, and carried toward the creek.

"The horses! The horses!"

The warning was too late. Holliman knew the horses and mules were being chased off into the brush. Men rushed forward, but they were unable to prevent the loss.

Dense white smoke billowed and filled the air as the fires continued to burn. Nothing could be done but to let them burn themselves out. The glow exposed much of the camp in an eerie orange light.

"We're sitting ducks!" one of the wounded men yelled.

Holliman shivered in the chilly night air and pulled the thin blanket over his chest and shoulders and wondered where his weapons were. He intended to tell the surgeon he wanted his revolver and plenty of ammunition.

As the flames burned down, the pain in his leg throbbed. The surgeon and his orderlies were walking among the wounded, checking bandages and providing more blankets.

Out of the corner of his eye, Holliman saw a figure arrive and pull the surgeon aside. "What do you need for these men, Doctor?" the man asked. It was Crook.

"Shelter," the doctor told him. "They need to be warm and comfortable."

"Very well. I will see to it that a detail is organized to put up tents around them, with a stove in each tent."

The general stepped carefully among the cots, which were scattered somewhat haphazardly. "Men," he said, "that was a raid to take some of our horses. They did, but it was that and nothing more. I apologize for the discomfort."

"That was a bit of excitement, sir," Holliman said, trying to minimize the situation.

"That it was. We will endeavor to see that it does not happen again. How is the leg?"

"I am certain it will heal, sir."

"Good. Good. Well, rest easy, son." The general, obviously distracted by the noise and activity happening all around, reached down and patted Holliman's shoulder and walked away.

How many people actually slept the rest of the night, Holliman couldn't guess. The best he could do was doze fitfully, bothered by the surrounding activity and by the pain. Sometime during the night, an uneasy silence settled in around him, but his pain persisted. He and another wounded man were placed practically side by side, and a tent was put up around them.

Through bleary eyes, he saw daylight growing ever so slowly, and then the noises started again. When the first rays of sunlight cast shadows across the camp, the tired-looking surgeon entered. The man next to the lieutenant, who had a shoulder wound, had finally fallen asleep. For several minutes, the surgeon carefully looked at Holliman's leg from several different angles.

"How is it, sir?" the lieutenant asked.

"We will need to wash it thoroughly," the doctor replied, still looking closely at the wound site. "Water is boiling. When it is ready, the orderly will remove the bandages and wash your leg. It will be somewhat uncomfortable, I warn you. But it is necessary."

Holliman sighed deeply. "Yes, sir. I understand. A cup of tea would be good, if it is not too much trouble."

The surgeon finally made eye contact and smiled. "We are working on that as well. Should be here shortly."

A hundred miles to the north, sunrise revealed the valley of the Yellowstone River and the encampment near the mouth of Rosebud Creek. The sprawling camps were already astir as a lone horseman waving a white flag approached the southern edges. After a brief exchange with a sentry, he was allowed to pass.

The Crow scout trotted through the rows of tents until he spied the one he was looking for near the south bank of the Yellowstone—the one marked by the guidon that identified the commanding officer.

Dismounting, he held out a leather pouch to one of the sentries guarding the tent. "To Gen'ral Terree," he said in an accent almost hard to understand.

Minutes later, after reading the dispatch from the pouch, Alfred Terry emerged and turned to one of the sentries. "Find my aide," he said cryptically.

An hour later, Terry sat under a canvas shade with several officers, including Colonel John Gibbon, Major James Brisbin, and Colonel George Custer.

"Major Reno will arrive before the day is out," the general announced.

"However, he has apparently decided to circumvent my orders. Instead of coming back down the Tongue, he has crossed over it and is at this moment coming down the Rosebud. If his reconnaissance reveals what I have suspected all along, we will press on with my plan to catch the Indians between the Bighorn River and Rosebud Creek."

"And hope that he has not alarmed every Indian in the region by going too far west," Custer observed.

"George," the dour Gibbon drawled, "they know we are in the area. My scouts have seen their scouts watching us, farther up along the Yellowstone."

Terry stepped in. "Armstrong," he said, addressing Custer, "I quite agree. They may very well know we are here, but they have no notion of our strength."

Custer shrugged. "Perhaps."

Later, Custer stood by as a weary Major Reno reported to Terry.

"Because we saw no sign of Sioux nywhere, not the slightest, I decided to cross the Tongue," Reno explained. "We did find a trail that the scouts thought was made by a large group. They were convinced that whoever made it was heading beyond the Tongue. If they were Sioux, that trail seems to suggest they are out of the area."

Custer could not contain himself. "Since you had already disobeyed your orders by that point, why didn't you follow the trail?" he snapped.

Terry, a patient man, intervened. "Armstrong, one trail does not indicate that all of the Sioux and their allies have left the area. I am still convinced that they are somewhere between the Rosebud and the Bighorn. I will send Gibbon's column to the mouth of the Bighorn today, as the first movement in the plan. Tomorrow, I will send you and the Seventh. I will give you your specific orders tonight."

The outline of the steam-powered stern-wheeler seemed out of place, moored by long lines tied to the closest trees. It didn't fit with the slopes and rolling hills on either side of the Yellowstone River. Loaded with supplies, the *Far West* had somehow made the two-hundred-mile journey upstream from Fort Abraham Lincoln, first on the Missouri and then up the Yellowstone to the mouth of Rosebud Creek.

Terry never understood how such boats could navigate the smaller, shallower rivers. A proud captain had once told him that the flat-bottomed boats could float in the tears of a weeping woman. But the strong current of the Yellowstone River was something more than that. He could feel a slight shudder now and then and a protesting squeak from the mooring lines as he sat in the *Far West*'s stateroom. It was far from stately, however, with stark wooden chairs and old wooden tables scarred by cigar burns.

Along the opposite shore, he could see occasional flashes of fireflies in the fading twilight. The three officers with him took no notice of anything outside the room and the issue at hand. Gibbon was pacing, and Brisbin, seated next to Custer at the table, seemed uncomfortable. Terry waited while the lamps were lit.

"Come to the table, John," he remarked casually, then waited while Gibbon took a seat. Terry looked directly at Custer. "I want you, and the Seventh, to go up the Rosebud to its headwaters and then swing west toward the Bighorn. Once there, turn north. Gibbon and his regiment will go south up the Bighorn. Between you, you will most certainly catch the hostiles. They must fight or surrender."

"What of General Crook, sir?" Brisbin asked.

"I know no more than you, Major," Terry replied. "I am sure he is following his orders, just as we are."

CHAPTER THIRTY-FOUR

Dreams

Cloud was puzzled. For four days now, the Long Knives had stayed on Goose Creek. He had expected them to be moving by now, but the scouts he had sent south had returned, reporting no sign of travel along the Powder River Road. During daylight, every other possible route leading to Goose Creek from any direction was being closely watched. No other whites had been seen.

Assuming that the Long Knives were regrouping and preparing to move north against the Lakota and Cheyenne, Cloud decided to harass them at every opportunity to keep them off balance.

Tall Bull and several of the Cheyenne Dog Soldiers followed three hunters working for the Long Knives. Along the upper reaches of Goose Creek, far up in the thick pine forest of the foothills, they drove off the hunters' horses and wounded one of the men with an arrow. To the surprise of Tall Bull and his companions, the other two hunters carried their wounded man back to the camp.

Late in the afternoon, White Wing arrived with eight men and a message for Cloud. Crazy Horse wanted news and Cloud's assessment of the situation. Before leaving, Cloud encouraged Wolf Eyes and the men staying behind not to let the Long Knives rest.

Yellow Wolf, Tall Bull, and several others accompanied Cloud north. At twilight, they crossed the Tongue and made camp. Just before sundown on the next day, they were home.

Cloud turned his horse loose in the herd and walked toward the southwest part of the village. It was a good feeling to see familiar lodges and know that he was back home, at least for a while. His footsteps quickened as he caught sight of his own lodge.

Song was playing in front of the lodge with her collection of bone horses and glanced up as the long shadow crossed over the ground. With a squeal, she was on her feet and jumped into her father's arms. "Father!"

He held her tightly, amazed at the strength in her arms as she squeezed his neck. "It is good to see you," he breathed into her neck. She nodded and did not let go. In a moment, he lowered her to the ground.

"How are you?" he asked, stroking her braids and touching her smiling face.

"Good! Are you hungry?"

Sweetwater Woman looked out the door and a hand went to her mouth as she emerged. "I thought I heard voices," she said.

Stepping toward her, Cloud embraced his wife, holding her for many long moments, silently reveling in the fresh scent of her hair and the feel of her body against his. He had been gone for so long.

"Nine days," Sweetwater Woman said, as if reading his mind. "We have not seen you for nine days."

"Too long, too long," he replied, finally letting go.

"It is good to have you home," she told him. "Crazy Horse stopped by two days ago and told us he was sending for you, so we have been preparing food."

"We have a new colt too," Song announced. "She came three days ago."

"Then we had better get acquainted with her," he replied.

"Me and Grandpa did already. We can go see her after we eat."

The fatigue in his body and the shadows in his spirit faded as he allowed himself to be led into the lodge. As far as he was concerned, the touch of a woman, young or old, was the best medicine for the troubled soul of a warrior.

Earlier in the afternoon, he and the other men had stopped to bathe in a small, busy little stream that flowed into Ash Creek. It was a small ritual the warriors tried to observe as much as possible, if circumstances allowed. The ceremony was to cleanse more than the body. Washing off the dirt and grime also symbolically washed off the difficult and even ugly things they had seen and done. After the bath, they smudged with sage. In spite of being anxious to get home, they finished the trip at a leisurely pace.

"Everyone is still talking about the Battle Where the Woman Saved Her Brother," Sweetwater Woman said as she handed him a slice of roasted elk skewered on a willow rod. "Was it as difficult as some are saying it was?"

He stared at the black hair of the buffalo robe on the floor before he answered. "It was a long fight," he told her, "the longest I have ever been in. I hardly slept the night before."

"And where are the Long Knives now?"

Cloud glanced at Song, who was rearranging her bone horses on the robe next to her father. "Goose Creek," he said.

"Will they stay there?"

"I think so. There is something strange about them. They are not going anywhere." He cut off a piece of meat and ate, chewing slowly. "How is my cousin?"

Sweetwater Woman poured tea and handed him the cup. "Frustrated," she replied. "Like you were ten years ago when you were wounded. He has to move slowly."

"Moving slowly is better than not moving at all," he said.

Cloud was physically tired. She could tell by his hand gestures, by the way his shoulders slumped. But she was more worried about the distant stare in his eyes, as if he were seeing something that was not part of the moment or the setting, but something that was part of him somewhere.

A soft scratch at the door caught their attention.

"Come in," she said cautiously, on the verge of irritation.

A young face looked in and glanced immediately toward Cloud. Sweetwater Woman recognized the young man but could not recall his name.

"Uncle," he said respectfully, "the old men and the war leaders will get together in the morning. Sitting Bull asks that you be there as well."

"Yes, I will be there."

Sweetwater Woman awoke in the middle of the night to see Cloud sitting up, staring ahead. She whispered softly so as not to alarm him, "Are you well?"

"Yes," he said quietly. "I think I was too comfortable."

"There is tea left in the kettle."

"No."

She sat up and moved closer, laying her head on his shoulder. "I want to know something," she said.

"What?"

"Sitting Bull's vision. Did it happen?"

He shook his head. "I do not think so."

Cloud was up at first light and walked toward one of the horse herds, curious about the grass. The herds were farther from the village; much of the grass had been grazed down. On the way back, he happened to notice the young man Little Feather, or Bug, sitting forlornly in front of his dome shelter. Not many of the single men living on the edges of the village were awake at this time.

"How are things with you?" Cloud asked, stopping.

Little Feather seemed surprised that Cloud was speaking to him. "Ah, I...good," he said. "Except for the mosquitoes."

"One of the bad things about summer," Cloud observed. He pointed to the rifle lying in the opening. "I see you got your rifle back."

"Yes, Uncle Grey Bull gave it back to me. Bullets too."

"Good. Good."

"But that was after all of you left for Rosebud Creek. I...I wanted to go."

Cloud nodded. He thought of Sweetwater Woman's question during the night. "Keep it close," he said. "The Long Knives are sneaky."

Little Feather watched the warrior walking away. There was something about the man that gave him a cold feeling in his stomach. Little Feather knew Cloud was downright dangerous, even without a rifle in his hands. After a moment, he glanced down at his rifle.

Cloud walked slowly along the curve of the outer row of lodges. Sweetwater Woman had told him last night that more people continued to arrive every day since he had left to scout to the south. He noticed there were more temporary shelters at the edges of the village. Although it was early, many people were awake and going about their tasks. Already there were groups of old men sitting together. Over it all, there still hung a sense of power Cloud had never felt before.

Twenty men or more were already in the council lodge, including Gall, Black Moon, Good Road, Good Weasel, Bull Bear, and Two Moons of the Cheyenne, among others. Red Butte of the Dakota and other old leaders sat with Sitting Bull on the north side of the room. With them were High Eagle and Worm. The talk as Cloud walked in and took a seat was about moving the village.

"Those who are grieving," Sitting Bull said, referring to the families of the warriors killed at the Rosebud, or those who had died of wounds later, "have had four days since they received the news. So I think it is time to move. The grass in the valley of the Greasy Grass is very good. We can send the camp criers out before the sun is high. By sundown, the village can be in place. My friends and I," he said, pointing to the two other medicine men, "have decided that the cottonwood grove west of the river is the place."

Heads nodded in agreement.

"Good," Sitting Bull said. "Now, what about the Long Knives to the south?" he asked.

Crazy Horse leaned forward. "Uncle, before we talk about that, some of the scouts who have been up near the Elk River think they have seen Long Knives up there."

"What did they see?" Sitting Bull wanted to know.

Good Road cleared his throat. "White men not dressed as Long Knives, two or three. Our scouts watched them until dark, and they seemed to be scouting out a trail north of the river, going east. That was three days ago."

Sitting Bull turned a questioning glance toward Crazy Horse and Gall.

"We will keep our scouts in that area," Crazy Horse said.

"If there are Long Knives to the north," Gall said, "I think it is a smaller column. The column we defeated at Rosebud was over a thousand. We cannot forget about them."

Heads turned toward Cloud, who took a deep breath. "Two days ago, they were still at Goose Creek. Two of our men went south but saw no other whites or Long Knives. I think they are waiting for other Long Knives to join them. About forty of our men are down there. We will hear if they move in any direction."

"My friend," Red Butte said, leaning forward and glancing toward Sitting Bull for a moment. The Dakota headman was the only one in the lodge who wore a cloth shirt and wool trousers, but his moccasins were made of elk hide and his long, thin braids were wrapped in otter fur. "Something has been on my mind since we received word of our victory several days ago. What you saw in your vision, I think, did not happen there. What do you think? What can you tell us?"

The sudden, deep silence indicated that Red Butte had spoken what was on all their minds.

The Hunkpapa medicine man sat thoughtfully for a moment before he looked up and glanced over the circle of faces. "As a man with a family, I do not want the Long Knives to attack. As a medicine man, with a gift that I did not ask for, the gift that helped me to see something I did not like, I have to say that what I saw has not yet come to pass. We must be ready at all times."

Gall made eye contact with Crazy Horse, who nodded slowly.

Word had been circulating for days that a move to the Greasy Grass valley would happen, so the women had been preparing, packing, and tying bundles to be loaded onto drag poles. Not long after the camp criers rode through the village announcing the move, the first lodge covers were pulled off and folded. The village came alive with an almost festive air. Movement was in the blood of the Lakota and Cheyenne; therefore, moving the village even a short distance was reason for excitement. Shouts of children filled the air, and women laughed as they worked.

Cloud and Song went to the herd and brought back their drag horses, four big geldings with quiet, patient dispositions, along with the horses they would ride and those that Star Woman and Bearface needed as well.

The horse herds began moving first. As the horse guards and young men began driving them west, most people paused to watch them go. They moved in a stream of colors over the land. The flow of manes and tails and the drumming of hooves stirred the soul, reminding everyone that their spirits were bonded to these relatives that carried them and shared their journey through life. Here and there, a warrior lifted a war cry and women trilled to acknowledge and celebrate the very image of freedom and strength. The Lakota were the Buffalo Nation, but they were also the people of the horse.

The landscape was now covered with thousands of people and nearly two thousand horses pulling drag poles. Singing a Moving the Camp song, High Eagle led the way, with Worm and Sitting Bull beside him. Behind them were several very old men. One of them, Elk of the Four Winds, carried the glowing embers from the council lodge in a turtle shell. At the new encampment, he would start a fire with them. This was an old custom symbolizing that the strength and spirit of the people would never die, no matter where they pitched their lodges. When the flames of the new fire burned strong along the Greasy Grass, they would ask for blessings on the new site.

Cloud decided not to join the procession of warriors riding guard on either side of the long column. He rode with Sweetwater Woman and Song instead.

"Where are we going?" Song asked, squinting in the bright sun.

"To the valley where Ash Creek empties into the Greasy Grass River," he told her.

"Is it a good place?"

"There is plenty of grass, and our lodges will be close to the river, in the shade of very large cottonwood trees. It has always been one of my favorite places."

"Are there good places to play?"

"Many," he replied, smiling. For the first time in days, he felt good.

South of Ash Creek, the column found a crossing upstream from where the creek flowed into the Greasy Grass River. The spring snowmelt from the mountains made the stream deeper than usual, but a few young men had already found a fairly shallow crossing and piled stones on each bank to mark it. The playful atmosphere did not subside. At the riverbank, many women and girls removed their moccasins and leggings and held their dresses up to their knees as they waded across or helped balance loads on the drag frames being pulled by the current.

Turning right beyond the west bank of the river, the horses and men, women, and children on horseback and on foot moved across a broad green floodplain. Breezes whispered through the tall grass and shook the leaves of the giant cottonwoods west of the river, giving them a soft, beckoning voice.

As the last of the column gained the west bank, Worm and High Eagle led the front of it into the wide grove of tall trees. West of the grove, thousands of horses were already grazing, their heads down in the thick grass and their tails flicking at bothersome flies. The lush bottomland along the river seemed like a different world compared to the uneven prairies and sparse grass along Ash Creek. Here, there was a sense of peacefulness that the previous village site did not have.

Two men sat on the sandstone bluffs north of the now empty village site. Only a lone burial lodge and the poles of the Sun Dance arbor were signs that people had lived here for a month. The last of the departing line of humanity had long since disappeared over the rise. The men's horses grazed below them on a slope.

Stands in Timber looked over at Crazy Horse. "I have never seen so many people in one place," he observed. "More have come in the past ten days, many of them young men."

"Yes, and there are more horses than people," Crazy Horse replied. "I think they will graze the Greasy Grass valley down in less than a month." The shrill of a hawk in the high, cloudless sky drew his gaze upward. Shading his eyes, he found the form soaring effortlessly, riding the breezes on outstretched wings.

"I had a dream," Stands in Timber said. "I was driving a wagon pulled by horses, the way white men do. There were women and children with me in the wagon. That bothers me. I have never been in a wagon."

"That is the funny thing about dreams," Crazy Horse replied. "They come when you least expect and do not when you seek them. And they bring messages you do not want."

"I cannot see the time when I would ever ride in a wagon," Stands in Timber said. "Why it comes in a dream, I do not know."

"I can tell you this: the reason or the answer will come in time. It will come to pass. That is the terrible thing about dreams."

Stands in Timber nodded silently. "Driving a white man's wagon is not a bad thing, as it stands. What the dream means is what I am afraid of."

"I, too, have been having a dream recently," Crazy Horse admitted, "about a snake."

"A snake?"

"Yes. Like your wagon, the snake in my dream has a meaning, and I think it is a warning about enemies," Crazy Horse speculated.

"You mean like the Long Knives or the Crow? Those kinds of enemies?"

Crazy Horse shook his head thoughtfully. "No, other kinds. The kind that hide behind smiling faces. The kind that hold their true feelings back."

"You have those kinds of enemies," Stands in Timber said angrily.

"The good thing is, most of them are at the agencies near Robinson, not here. What was your dream?"

"A snake follows me in the grass, and then in the air. When I turn, it flees. But it comes back again."

"In the air?" Stands in Timber asked. "A snake that can fly. Perhaps it means that your enemies will do something unexpected."

Crazy Horse looked back and stood. "I think I will draw it, my dream, on this rock." He pointed at the low sandstone wall behind them. Choosing a bare spot the size of a man's chest, he traced over it with his finger, then pulled out his knife. With the tip, he began to scratch at the surface of the soft stone.

The young Cheyenne watched as his friend concentrated on his task. First, the outline of a horse appeared on the rock face, seeming to move to the left. Stepping back for a moment, Crazy Horse then scratched out the outline of a long snake, behind and slightly above the horse, bent forward at the middle, with a well-defined head and eyes. He then added stripes across the middle of its body.

Stands in Timber did not tell his friend that a shiver went up his back as he gazed at the sketch.

"I hope that the spirits look at this and know that I bear no ill will toward anyone except the whites," Crazy Horse declared.

The young Cheyenne stepped forward. "In that drawing," he said, pointing, "that snake will never catch that horse."

Crazy Horse put away his knife and pulled out a sprig of sage from the pouch hanging from his belt and laid it gently on the narrow ledge. "My friend," he said quietly, "it is time to go."

They crossed over the north fork of the creek and put their horses into a lope. By the time they reached the bluffs north of the confluence, it was the middle of the afternoon. All along the crests of the hills to the north, warriors—mounted, sitting in the grass, or standing next to their horses—were looking intently into the trees below them and across the river. Through the trees, many of the hundreds of lodges that had already been erected could be seen. On the other side of the cottonwood trees, horses—thousands of horses—dotted the flat land.

Turning north, Crazy Horse and Stands in Timber rode the crests until they were even with what they thought was the middle of the new encampment. A man standing by himself on a gentle slope, holding the long rein to the horse behind him, caught their eye. It was Gall.

The Hunkpapa war leader nodded as they arrived. He seemed glad for the company, and pointed toward the village. "I never get tired of watching how quickly the women can put up the lodges," he said.

Crazy Horse grinned. "As long as we stay out of their way," he said.

Because of the trees, the village could not be arranged in one large circle, as it had been along Ash Creek. Instead, the medicine men had let each group pick out their own sites and form smaller circles.

"Your people are on the northern end, past the Medicine Tail crossing," Gall said to Stands in Timber. He turned to Crazy Horse. "South of them are your people, and then the Sicangu, along with the Oohenunpa. Below them, the Ihanktunwan and the Isanti. Next, the Sihasapa, then the Mniconju and Itazipacola. My people, the Hunkpapa, are at the end, as we always are. In that open area between the Sicangu and the Sihasapa, close to the river, the council lodge and the warrior society lodges will be put up."

"That is a long village," Stands in Timber pointed out. "Someone should walk from one end to the other to see how many paces that would be."

"I would guess at least four thousand," Gall ventured. "It would take a very good horse to gallop that far before it had to reach for its second wind."

"Look!" Stands in Timber called out. He pointed at the giant cottonwoods as the breezes suddenly grew stronger, loosening the tiny white puffs of silvery cotton that carried the seeds. Before long, the air was filled with them, looking like a sudden snow squall.

"Life goes on," Gall said loudly. "Life goes on."

CHAPTER THIRTY-FIVE

Worms in the Grass

Leading their horses, two men moved tentatively up an uneven slope. In the dark, the ridge ahead of them appeared as an ominous black shadow.

"Higgins," one of them whispered, "stop! I thought I heard somethin'."

"What?" Higgins replied cautiously.

"A voice, I think," Blake said, lowering his whisper even further.

Higgins was immediately worried. "Could be Indians."

"No. I think it be that feller that do na' speak English so good."

"How can you tell? There be more than one—that cannot speak English, I mean," Higgins pointed out.

"The man has a whiny voice, like a woman," Blake asserted.

"Then where he be?"

"Ahead of us, down below," Higgins replied.

The two privates stopped and listened intently. A faint clink reached their straining ears.

"There!" Blake whispered again. "That got to be them!"

"That was no voice," Higgins cautioned.

The column had been awakened after dark, after scouts had reported seeing an Indian trail that led into the valley of the Bighorn River. Custer ordered Officers Call and divulged his plan to follow the trail. Maintaining direction proved to be difficult, however, during the moonless night. Several soldiers dozed in the saddle and lost their way.

"Shh!" warned Higgins. "It still might be Indians."

"Why? You think they can see in the dark?"

"Sure they can. That's why they don't use lamps and lanterns."

"Yeah? How do you know?" Blake was skeptical, but still worried.

"The barkeep, back at Watts Landin' in Bismarck. He tol' me."

"How he know about Indians? He never been west of the river," Blake reasoned.

"They is Indians east of the river," Higgins pointed out.

"Those kind don't scare me. The ones out here, they scare me," Blake admitted.

The slight clink was heard again. It seemed to be coming from somewhere below the ridge.

"There!" Blake whispered fiercely.

"A tin cup," Higgins was certain. "Sounds like a tin cup."

Clink.

"Yeah, that be it," Blake decided happily.

One of their horses neighed softly, affirming his assumption. The two lost privates carefully descended the incline and rejoined the column. "Troop G!" Higgins whispered. "We is from Troop G!"

"Behind us," came a low voice with authority. "This is E! Get yourselves lost?"

"Yes, sir," Higgins replied meekly.

"Damn lucky you found us," said the voice. "If Indians was to get you…wal, fall in. Find your troop. We're beddin' down for the night."

"Tha's good," Blake replied. "I could use the sleep."

It was well after midnight when the column finally halted. Amid the sighs of relief were low grumbles of complaint—it was about time. Most of the soldiers took a moment to loosen saddle girths and to hook horses together, four in a picket line. Then, after a quick swallow of water from a canteen, each soldier found the closest likely spot on the ground to sleep. The need to sleep and rest trumped the prospect of insects and snakes as boots scraped and cleared away rocks. Even a rocky slope was a welcome bed—for everyone, that is, except Lieutenant Varnum, four Crow scouts, guide Charley Reynolds, and the half-breed scout Mitch Bouyer. By dawn, they were several miles ahead of the column.

As first light turned shadows into recognizable shapes, the Crow picketed their horses in a pine grove on the eastern slope of the highest point south of Ash Creek. White Man Runs Him led the file of silent men up the slope. Halfway up, Varnum paused to remove his spurs, then hurried to catch up to the other men.

In the cool air on the summit, the officer and the scouts sat and waited for sunrise. North of them was the valley of Ash Creek. To the northwest, behind the shadowy intervening ridges, was the valley of the Little Bighorn, familiar ground to the Crow. It had been their land before the Sioux had pushed north and forced them beyond the Yellowstone River.

Varnum pulled his field glasses out of their case and slowly panned the landscape. "Where the hell are they?" he muttered to himself.

Two of the Crow who knew a smattering of English glanced at one another and grinned; they understood the tone of frustration. One of them chuckled.

The lieutenant looked over at them and saw one of them make a sign as if cutting his own throat—the sign other tribes used for the Sioux.

"Sioux there," the man said, pointing to the south. "There and there," he went on, pointing north and then west.

Varnum ignored the teasing. He liked the Crow, respected them for their skill and knowledge, but he had no inclination to be drawn into a personal conversation. The line had to be drawn somewhere. They worked for him, after all. "Then find them," he admonished.

The grin faded from the scout's face, and he turned to White Man Runs Him, lapsing into his own language. "This man will not be happy to see them face-to-face," he said.

White Man Runs Him nodded knowingly. "I would be happy not to see them at all," he replied.

He glanced at the fourth scout, who sat quietly listening to the conversation. He was a young man who had not been anxious to wear the blue coat the soldiers had given him. On the side of his face was a wide scar that ran from the corner of his eye to the corner of his mouth. "What do you think?" White Man Runs Him asked. "Where are the Lakota?"

Broken Hand looked toward the west, toward the distant, hazy landscape slowly being revealed in the growing light of dawn. "The soldier glass sees far. Look there," he said, pointing toward the valley of the Little Bighorn.

The older scout, hard-bitten and cynical at times, stared briefly at the younger man. "And what if they are there?"

"Then this will be a day we will not forget."

White Man Runs Him suddenly felt a cold shiver run down his spine. Broken Hand was right—the Lakota were not to be taken lightly. They chose when and where to fight, and they knew how to fight. Like the Crow, they were true horse warriors. Long Knives were not.

Somewhere above the ridges, the shrill cry of a hawk already on the hunt broke into his thoughts. It sounded like a war cry.

The scout pulled his field glasses from their case and looked west. Many times in his life, he had been awake before dawn and watched the daylight reveal the land, but today, for some reason, he was almost afraid to see what the light might show. Tentatively, he lifted the field glasses to his eyes.

Morning shadows were long, stretching east to west, and the contrasts were extreme. Sunlight on open areas was bright, and low spots were hidden in blue-black obscurity. The valley of Ash Creek was easy to discern, a dark, swerving east-west line. It led west to more dark and uneven north-south lines that White Man Runs Him knew were the hills, ridges, and trees next to the Little Bighorn River. The tops of the hills and ridges were slowly becoming visible.

Boot heels and soles grated on the gravelly soil as Varnum and Reynolds moved up the crest. White Man Runs Him liked Varnum because he treated him and the other scouts like men, but he did not trust Reynolds—or the half-breed Bouyer, because he was part Sioux. That man was always watching everyone out of the corner of his eye.

"What do you see?" Varnum asked.

"No Sioux," White Man Runs Him replied.

"Do you think they are out there?"

The Crow nodded in affirmation.

"Close? Are they close?"

White Man Runs Him had a feeling. "Close," he said.

"Will we see them today?" the lieutenant persisted.

The scout nodded slowly.

Varnum glanced sideways at Reynolds and Bouyer. "Yeah, I think you may be right."

Broken Hand moved up beside White Man Runs Him and motioned to use the field glasses. The other two scouts, Curly and Left Hand, waited nearby, sitting on their haunches. After riding for nearly three days, both white men and the half-breed looked as tired and saddle worn as they all felt.

Broken Hand was certain the Lakota were close. They had to be. The soldiers might have missed the signs, but he had seen plenty of indications: tracks of elk and deer they had come across were old, as were the few bear droppings he had seen. This told him, and the other Crow, that people were in the area, and had been for quite some time. It was very likely that it was a large group, with hunters who went out every day, far and wide. In the interest of survival, the deer, elk, and bears moved away, beyond their usual trails and grazing areas.

He pointed the field glasses west, toward the hills and flatlands growing lighter by the minute. Some of the dark areas were now turning green. He moved swiftly over the circle of land inside the field glasses, wondering if birds had the same view. Then, just beyond a line of trees, he saw something in a wide meadow that was not grass—there were faint splashes of color, barely visible even with the powerful lenses.

For a long moment, he kept the field glasses steady and studied the thin, faint smears on the land. At this distance, movement was difficult to perceive unless it was a large herd of antelope or buffalo—or a long column of people. The smears weren't moving, but there was something there.

The thought flashed in his mind quite suddenly, unexpectedly, like a distant bolt of lightning: horses!

It had to be. Broken Hand lowered the field glasses and looked over his shoulder to the east. In a moment, he saw thin columns of smoke several miles away, coming from the cooking fires the soldiers had started. There was no smoke to the west, perhaps because the Little Bighorn Valley was too far away to see well.

White Man Runs Him turned and saw the smoke as well. Anger clouded his dark face. He motioned to Varnum. "Sioux will see that," he said.

Varnum swore under his breath. "Damn fools!" he spat. "Might as well wave flags from the hilltops."

Broken Hand lifted the field glasses again and found the meadow in the distance. The faint smears were still there. He didn't expect otherwise. Now he was certain. Turning, he touched White Man Runs Him lightly on the elbow. "Look west," he told him in a low voice. "There are hills on the other side of the line of trees. Something is there, between the hills and the trees."

The older scout took up the field glasses. He looked for nearly a minute, and then cast a narrow-eyed glance at Broken Hand. "Horses," he whispered.

Broken Hand nodded slowly.

White Man Runs Him thought for a moment, and then stood to approach the chief of scouts. "Varnum," he said, "we see something."

The other scouts sensed something immediately and looked questioningly at Broken Hand. White Man Runs Him pointed west. "Trees," he told Varnum. "Past trees."

Seeing the sudden alertness in the scouts, Reynolds and Bouyer moved in closer. Varnum raised his field glasses and looked hard. "What did you see?" he asked.

"Horses," White Man Runs Him replied.

"No," the officer said. "I see nothing."

After another minute, he turned and passed the field glasses to Reynolds. The guide moved to the edge of the crest and stood next to the Crow scout. "Where?" he said.

"Little Bighorn Valley," White Man Runs Him said, pointing. "Hills back, trees front. Between is something."

Reynolds adjusted the field glasses. "Lieutenant," he said, after a moment, "something is there."

"What? What do you see?"

"Like the man said," Reynolds replied, "horses."

"How many? Where?" Varnum asked skeptically.

"On the other side of the line of trees. I expect them trees is along the Little Bighorn," Reynolds said. "Hard to say how many."

Meanwhile, White Man Runs Him handed his field glasses to Left Hand. After a long moment, the young scout nodded. "Worms in the grass," he said in Crow to the other scouts.

"What did he say?" Varnum asked.

White Man Runs Him translated. "Worms in grass."

Bouyer took a look and agreed, nodding silently.

Varnum grabbed the field glasses again and tried to see what everyone else apparently could. "Damn!" he exclaimed, after another fruitless effort. "I see nothing!"

"They are there," Reynolds assured him. "Trust me."

Varnum looked at White Man Runs Him. "Horses mean a village. Many horses mean a large village."

The scout nodded patiently.

"You are certain? There are horses there?"

White Man Runs Him looked toward the other scouts. They all nodded. "Many horses," he told Varnum.

"Very well," the man said, reaching into the pouch hanging from his belt. Taking out a short pencil and a small notebook, he knelt on one knee and carefully wrote a message. Finished, he ripped out the page and held it toward Curly. "Tell him to take this to Long Hair," he said to White Man Runs Him. "To Long Hair, and no one else."

White Man Runs Him pointed to the folded paper in Varnum's hand and translated.

Taking the paper, Curly, the youngest of the scouts, barely twenty and very slender, trotted down the slope to his horse. In a moment, hoofbeats drummed the ground as he loped away.

Atop the butte, Varnum was still trying to find the worms in the grass.

A pair of cold, blue eyes read Varnum's message a second time and then glanced to the man waiting at his side. "Lieutenant," Custer ordered, "Varnum and his scouts may have found something. We move out now. Pass the word."

"Right away, sir." Lieutenant W. W. Cooke spun on his heel and was gone.

Custer turned and found Bloody Knife sitting a few yards away, sipping on coffee and eating some concoction of dried meat and berries. He motioned for the Arikara scout to follow him and walked up a slight incline, out of earshot of the nearest soldiers. "Varnum's Crows saw horses in the Little Bighorn Valley," he told him.

The scout arched his eyebrows, but said nothing.

"Could they be right?"

Bloody Knife nodded. "Good place for Sioux to go," he said. "Good grass, good hunting. Sioux put village there…before."

"Yes, of course. We will move out and find Varnum."

The respite had been an all-too-brief four hours. More than a few soldiers grumbled as the column began moving, slowly stretching itself out.

Close to the head of the column, but not too close to Custer, Benteen put his horse into a trot and caught up to Reno. "What have you heard, Marcus?" he asked.

"Lieutenant Varnum may have found something. I have heard nothing more."

"That would explain this," Benteen said, gesturing at the column. "First he was excited about the trail yesterday—or was it the day before? Then he did not feel inclined to scout it as General Terry ordered. If this proves to be real, I suspect we shall be chasing Indians before the day is done."

"Then I say, let us finish this and go home to our station," Reno said drily. "Let our illustrious general have his glory, so long as we live to tell about it."

Benteen chuckled humorlessly. "I fear that it will not be that easy." He turned aside to rejoin his troop, leaving Reno to wonder at the remark.

The column moved slowly, owing mostly to the rough and uneven terrain, but also because its commander was reluctant to raise a dust cloud. After several miles, growing impatient, Custer ordered yet another halt.

Custer turned toward Bloody Knife and Curly. "I want to go ahead and see for myself what Varnum is talking about."

The Arikara scout nodded.

"I want the two of you to take me there." He turned to Cooke, behind him. "Dismount the column and stay in this ravine. Post sentries and wait for me."

At a gallop, Bloody Knife, Curly, and Custer departed.

Broken Hand heard the approaching horses. Before a minute passed, three men climbed the slope and gained the crest. Varnum saluted his commander and waited.

"Where are the horses, Lieutenant?" Custer wanted to know.

"According to my scouts, in the valley of the Little Bighorn, sir. I have not been able to see anything." He handed Custer the field glasses. "There is a broad tree line," the lieutenant went on, "and a plain beyond that. That much I have seen."

A long minute passed. Custer's posture indicated that he did not see the horses the scouts said were there. He passed the field glasses to Bloody Knife and turned to White Man Runs Him, who was standing quietly to one side. "There are horses?" he asked the leader of the Crow contingent.

White Man Runs Him nodded patiently. "Many horses," he said resolutely. "Many horses, many Sioux warriors."

Custer turned to Bloody Knife. "What do you see?" he asked.

"Something," the Arikara replied. "Horses, maybe. Something in the grass."

"General," Reynolds ventured, stepping up, "we seen them," he said, pointing to Bouyer. "We did. Somethin' is there."

The colonel took the field glasses again, squared his shoulders, and took another long look. "Nothing. I cannot see anything to suggest the presence of the Sioux." He gave the field glasses back to Varnum. "Nonetheless, I shall move the column forward. Rest your men before you go on. Get word to me immediately if you see anything more definitive."

"Yes, sir," Varnum replied.

Custer and Bloody Knife departed from the hill. White Man Runs Him watched them go. He did not like Bloody Knife, or trust him. Like Bouyer, he was part Sioux. Anyone who turned against his own kind could not be trusted. Besides, the man was always close to Long Hair. White Man Runs Him had heard that he was Long Hair's favorite. Why Long Hair and the soldiers did not use only Crow scouts was a mystery.

Custer and Bloody Knife returned to find a group of men huddled around a sergeant, among them his brother, Captain Tom Custer, with Lieutenant Cooke and Captain Thomas Weir, along with several troop commanders, including Reno and Benteen.

"Sir," Tom said, "this sergeant rode back to recover a pack that fell off a mule during the night. He found the pack, and Indians going through it."

Custer's gaze zeroed in on the sergeant. "Indians? Are you certain?"

"Yes, sir. Three of 'em," the sergeant replied nervously. "They rode off when they saw me."

"Sir, what did you see up ahead?" Cooke asked Custer.

"Nothing. Varnum's scouts insisted they saw horses in the valley of the Little Bighorn. I saw nothing to indicate a village. But given what the sergeant is reporting, they have to be close." He glared at the sergeant, as if the Indians were his fault. "Where there is one Indian, there are more. We have lost the element of surprise!"

Custer turned to Cooke. "Prepare a message for Varnum, Lieutenant. Tell him we have been spotted, and I want him to find that village! Tell him we are moving out immediately and will attack when we find it."

Then he stepped toward Bloody Knife. "Send a man with that message now."

He turned to the circle of officers. "Get this regiment moving!"

Reno stepped up. "General, I think it would be wise to wait for Colonel Gibbon."

"You do, do you? Do you know where the colonel is, Major?"

"Not exactly, no."

"I thought not," Custer snapped condescendingly. "The situation is, if we do not find the Indians and engage them, they will escape, they will scatter."

Benteen stepped forward and stood next to Reno. "Sir, I agree with Major Reno."

"Captain, your opinion does not surprise me. In spite of it, we have a duty, and we are capable of carrying it out. Of course, if either one of you have no stomach for it, you can be relieved of duty."

Startled, Reno took a step back. "No, sir," he said.

Benteen glared back at Custer for a moment before he turned his gaze aside.

"Very well," Custer said, softening his tone somewhat. "Then I would appreciate your cooperation."

As Reno and Benteen turned away to join their troops, Tom and Weir waited for the colonel to join them. Tom watched until Benteen and Reno were out of earshot. "Sir," he said in a low voice, "those two may have a point."

Custer nodded. "Perhaps," he allowed. "But it has been our experience that Indians have run anytime they are confronted by a large force. You know that. If they know we are here, they will scatter." He paused and stepped next to his mount as it was being saddled. He had ridden bareback to the crow's nest and back. From a saddlebag he took out a blue uniform shirt.

"Furthermore," he went on, as he pulled off the striped shirt he had on, "I am confident in our ability to find and engage them."

The two captains nodded and waited for the colonel to finish dressing. After Custer donned the blue shirt, he tied a red scarf around his neck. Running his hands through his hair, he put on his wide-brimmed hat.

"We will move out, gentlemen," he continued, smiling confidently. "We will bring the Indians to bear, and we will win the day. Mark my words."

CHAPTER THIRTY-SIX

A Thin Veil of Dust

Black Shield stood outside his lodge as dawn chased away the dark hues of night. A soft morning breeze caressed the leaves of the giant cottonwoods that stood all around. He offered tobacco to the Sky, the Earth, the Four Directions, and then to the Great Spirit. Finishing his prayer, he began his morning stretching ritual, starting with his legs. Like the great mountain lion, he stretched his legs behind him, one at a time. Then he bent over slowly, working his back muscles. Upright again, he twisted deliberately from side to side. After that, he rotated his head, loosening the neck muscles. He finished with his arms, reaching for unseen points until his muscles began to protest, and then he rotated them slowly.

Black Shield had performed his stretching ritual nearly every morning for the past twenty years, beginning in the days when he was no longer an active warrior. Although he was one of a few men his age who could still swing up on a horse, he was finding it more difficult as the years went by. But he was not yet ready to use a mounting step, a simple, short, hardwood stilt.

Most elderly people had some kind of morning ritual, whether to stretch or meditate or pray. Black Shield meditated as he stretched. This morning, he was contemplating the future. He didn't like what he had been hearing since the battle along the Rosebud, eight days ago. Many of those who had broken away from the Spotted Tail or Red Cloud agencies were talking of going back, worried that the Long Knives would exact retribution. Sitting Bull had invited the old men leaders to a meeting today around noon. Black Shield knew the Hunkpapa medicine man was worried that many wanted to leave and the only way to prevent them from doing so was to talk them out of it.

Black Shield turned at the slight rustling noise and saw his wife setting up his willow chair to the right of the doorway, next to the willow tripod. He retrieved his pipe bag from the tripod and took a seat. It was on his mind to have a smoke. More than once a good smoke had relaxed his mind and enabled him to think. And there was much to think about.

All around, the village was awakening. Black Shield heard the sound of hand axes cutting firewood and smelled smoke from cooking fires already started. The early part of morning was one of the most peaceful periods of the day, before the busyness took over. He leaned back and opened the pipe bag. Later, he intended to have a talk with Grey Bull.

Farther south, Sitting Bull emerged from a lodge, pipe bag in hand and a rolled-up bundle under his arm. Through most of the night he had been treating a very ill elderly woman. Before that, he had crossed the river and climbed to the top of a ridge to spend the evening praying. So he was emotionally and physically exhausted. The old woman was sleeping now, and he wanted to go home and have a good, strong cup of coffee to revive him. There was much to do today.

As he passed between lodges, two teenage boys were about to cross his path but paused when they recognized him. "It is good to see you, Grandfather," one of them said shyly.

"You are awake early," the medicine man replied.

"We were watching the horses last night," the older of the two said. "We are going home to sleep."

"Yes, yes. I remember those days, watching horses, listening to nighthawks, and chasing away mosquitoes."

The boys smiled. "Our mother is Stands on the Hill, our father is Little Bird," the older one told him.

"Yes," Sitting Bull replied, "I know them. Tell me your names."

"I am Ashes," the older boy said. "This is my brother, Two Horns."

"It is good to know you, Grandsons. Now, you need sleep. I need coffee." Sitting Bull looked around at the brightening sky. "It will be hot today, I think. Or maybe it is something else I feel in my bones."

For a moment, the boys stood and watched the Hunkpapa medicine man trudging away, limping slightly.

As soon as dawn came and the land grew bright, the night guards around the herd were relieved; fewer guards were needed during the day. Already they were letting the herd spread out across the lush river bottom, though they would keep watchful eyes to the west and north.

In the northern half of the village, a lodge stood beneath an especially tall cottonwood tree. Because of the camp's location in the long and wide cottonwood grove, many lodges were pitched next to trees to take advantage of the shade they provided. This morning, a young man lay beneath his elk robe and looked up through the smoke hole and saw leaves wavering in the breeze. His father was already outside; Black Wolf heard him blowing on the kindling to start the cooking fire. Near the door, his mother was gathering food containers to take outside.

"Are you awake?" she asked.

"I am," he replied. "I thought I would take a walk and see to our horses."

A worried frown creased her forehead. "Your side was still bleeding a little yesterday," she reminded him.

Black Wolf smiled. "But not too much, and it was because I rode."

"Have something to eat first," she asserted. "Rest and good food will help you heal faster."

He had been wounded at the Battle Where the Woman Saved Her Brother. A bullet had torn through his side, and the pain was bothersome on the ride home. It was likely the loss of blood that had caused him to faint and fall from his horse, much to his embarrassment. But Crazy Horse had been quick to help him. As a matter of fact, he had stopped by last evening.

As smoothly as he could manage, in spite of the dull ache, Black Wolf sat up, mainly to indicate to his mother that he was well.

"I will make some tea and cook soup," she said, ducking out through the door.

After a moment, he arose slowly and followed her.

As he went out into the cool dawn air, his eyes were immediately drawn to the willow tripod to the right of the door. His weapons had already been placed there; his mother had done that. For some reason, his gaze moved over the breech-loading rifle in its case and the unstrung bow in its case, but what caught and held his attention was the quiver bristling with war arrows.

In the Hunkpapa camp to the south, a woman hung a kettle filled with water from the iron tripod standing over the fire. She turned in time to see Sitting Bull, with a bundle under one arm, enter his lodge. She saw him leave the evening before around dusk; her husband, Gall, had told her the medicine man was going across the river to pray.

High ridges on the east side of the river cast long shadows and hid the large encampment. From atop those ridges, the lodges were easily seen, but from the floor of the floodplain, only a few were visible, the rest hidden by the cottonwood trees and thickets.

Lazy breezes wandered through, and more and more people began to emerge and move about. Near the council lodge, the remains of a large fire were still smoldering. One of the warrior societies had put on a victory celebration, and the dancing had gone on most of the night.

Cloud had been invited and had attended, but he did not stay long. He wanted to work with a yearling colt that was showing promise as a runner. From the silence in the lodge, except for Song's even breathing, he knew Sweetwater Woman was already outside. Someone was chopping wood.

When he stepped outside, he smelled the coffee first, and then the meat roasting over the flames. It had been a while since they had had coffee.

"Sit," Sweetwater Woman told him. "My mother traded for coffee and gave us some."

He could see bits of the pulverized black seeds on her pounding stone, where she had ground them down. It was a bitter brew, a favorite among the people, but hard to obtain. After the water in the blackened pot had boiled, she had simply added the black powder.

"I saw your cousin walking around by himself yesterday," she mentioned as she finished cutting strips of fresh elk meat, "after we moved. It is good to see that his wound is healing."

Cloud smiled as he took a seat. "My sister-in-law is probably the happiest about that," he said. "I think he is making her crazy."

"Yes," she replied, concentrating on her task. "It is not easy to keep a home in order when a man is underfoot."

"Even a wounded man?"

Sweetwater Woman looked up for a moment, her eyes twinkling over a smile. "Especially a wounded man. They can be more needful than a small child, and sometimes behave like one."

Cloud chuckled softly. "He who protects the home gets restless when he is there too long."

"It is one of the strange things in life," Sweetwater Woman said.

A dove suddenly cooed somewhere in the branches above them. For a moment, its soft, mournful call silenced every other sound. Sweetwater Woman paused and glanced toward her husband. "For some reason," she said gently, "that makes me feel sad."

Something in her tone seemed like a warning. Cloud glanced to the side at the willow tripod, where his weapons were already hanging. Overhead, the dove cooed again. Its voice was not loud, but somehow it evoked a sense of deep melancholy, something akin to grief.

After a moment, Cloud shook his head and looked toward his wife. "It is their purpose to remind us there is sadness in the world," he said. "Perhaps it is nothing more than that."

Sweetwater Woman was motionless, staring into the flames of the cooking fire. "Perhaps," she allowed. "But right now, it annoys me."

Soft gurgles from the blackened pot interrupted the moment, and both of them looked at the coffee boiling over, out of the spout. Sweetwater Woman quickly grabbed a piece of hide, folded it over the handle, and removed the pot.

"My mother wants to move her lodge," she commented as she tried to move her thoughts to the day ahead. "I think she put it over an old creek bed, and there is a hole in the floor. I will help her."

"Good," Cloud replied, and watched as she poured coffee into a metal cup. He waited to hear the dove again, but it was silent. "I want to work with that yearling colt, the buckskin. He is fast, but he also has a quiet way about him. He might be a good horse for Song."

Sweetwater Woman nodded and sent a quick glance up into the tree branches.

Rising above the ridges across the river, the sun illuminated the cottonwood groves and thickets along the Greasy Grass in less than a heartbeat. The encampment of a thousand lodges or more instantly felt the warmth of its life-giving rays. Throughout the village's length and breadth, elderly men and women lifted their gray heads and turned deeply seamed faces to the east to pay homage to the light, acknowledging that another day had been added to their lives.

Low shelters stood among the shrubs and thickets near the river's edge where it meandered east of the encampment. Here, men, mostly young and unattached but some older and without their families, made their camps. Most of the shelters were simple triangular or dome frames covered with blankets or robes to keep the occupants dry if there was rain, and to act as enough of a windbreak to take the bite out of a chilly breeze. At one such shelter directly east of the Sicangu camp, two young men were already sitting at their fire.

Horn Tail was in the last phase of making arrows, attaching iron points to eight willow shafts onto which he had already tied and glued feathers. His cousin Bear counted again the number of round lead balls he had for his old muzzle-loading rifle. They had arrived the day before, following the wide trail from the site on Ash Creek. It had taken them twenty days to get that far, traveling from the White Earth River valley west of the Great Muddy River on the northern fringes of Sicangu Lakota territory. Their families and a few others had chosen to take their chances and live apart from the agencies.

The two young men, not yet twenty, had been impatient to join the gathering since the winter, when they had first learned of Sitting Bull's message. But because of their meager circumstances, there were no horses to spare. A month ago, Horn Tail's father had found two wagon horses wandering along a creek and decided to give his son and nephew his only riding horse, a slow but steady gelding. Over the journey, they alternated using it as a packhorse and riding horse.

Their weaponry had consisted of Horn Tail's two bows and nearly forty arrows and Bear's old muzzleloader and twelve balls. Along the way, Horn Tail had cut enough willow stalks to make twenty more shafts. Yet, they were less concerned about being poorly armed and more concerned about missing the excitement. At the victory celebration last night, they both listened to story after story about the Battle Where the Woman Saved Her Brother.

"How long do you think we should stay?" Bear asked, already acquiescing to the end of their adventure.

"We need to hunt," Horn Tail replied, "to make enough meat to last through the winter. Our fathers want us to hunt with the bow."

"Yes, I know," Bear replied. "A bow is quieter and we can make as many arrows as we need, but shot and powder are hard to get."

"We have to hunt along the Great Muddy this fall," Horn Tail said. "The big gullies and breaks there have more deer and elk. I have heard that the people have been here for over a month, but no one is certain how much longer they will stay."

Bear sighed as he moved a small kettle over the flames. "I wish we could have been here several days ago," he said.

Horn Tail looked up from wrapping sinew around the tip of the shaft, binding it to the point. "We are here now," he stated patiently. "We have missed the battle, but we can learn what the old men are thinking, what they want our people to do. That is what our fathers wanted to know."

"Do you think your father will join Sitting Bull and Crazy Horse?"

"It is what he said, and what your father said too. They both think we will be stronger if we stay together. They hate the agencies, but they also know it is a risk to live the way we do, always on the lookout for whites and Long Knives. If they knew the people would band together, they would join."

Bear looked at his cousin. "Yes, I think you are right…" He watched Horn Tail's skillful fingers. "Why are you so good at making bows and arrows?" he asked.

Horn Tail shrugged. "My grandfather taught me."

"If you could make guns, that would be better."

Far to the east, in the bottom of a deep gully, several men stood quietly with their horses, their weapons drawn and ready, listening for the sound of galloping horses.

"I saw only one rider," Bear Robe whispered. "I found some things—a bag and a container made of wood with hard bread in it. The rider was a Long Knife. I left because it was hard to know if there were others behind him."

"What about tracks?" someone asked.

"Horses, with iron on their feet, the way whites do," Bear Robe replied, "going east."

"Crazy Horse needs to know," Two Bulls, a tall, gangly young man said.

"I will go," Bear Robe volunteered.

"Go north and cross Ash Creek and then circle to the east," Two Bulls advised. "If these are Long Knives, they will stay in the low areas, out of sight."

At a nod from Two Bulls, a lithe teenager climbed to the lip of the gully and slipped in between two boulders and scrutinized the wider gully that stretched east and west. "Nothing," he whispered fiercely. "I see nothing. No riders."

"Good," Two Bulls said. He turned to Bear Robe. "Stay in the low areas until you are north of Ash Creek. We will wait and then follow the tracks you saw and see who or what made them."

At midmorning, Rain in the Face finished his walk around the Hunkpapa village circle. A brisk walk helped to loosen the stiffness in his leg, a consequence of an old wound that bothered him more and more these days. The long ride to Rosebud Creek and back, not to mention the fighting, had aggravated the injury. He was glad for the warm days of summer; they helped his stiff hip and knee joints. Already it was evident the day would be hot, and he would not complain.

A few girls and young women who were gathering twigs and firewood in the brush smiled and waved as he passed. Their long braids glistened as sunlight struck them.

The Hunkpapa warrior glimpsed the high ridges just east of the river between the trees as he stopped south of his own lodge. A ride across the river and up to the ridges would be in order, he thought. But first he wanted to talk with Gall.

On the opposite end of the encampment, north of the Cheyenne lodges, several women were walking leisurely, chatting as they went.

"I heard a branch crack in the night," Good Plume said. "A big branch just above the lodge. I saw it this morning. If it falls…anyway, I will move today."

Good Plume was a widow, as were her three companions, Little Creek, White Crane, and High Voice. They had been friends for many years, drawn even closer now by their common status. Good Plume had lost her husband at the Battle of the Hundred in the Hand. High Voice's husband had been killed by Crow horse raiders when he pursued them alone. White Crane's husband had gone hunting west of the Shining Mountains and never returned. For years now, they had pitched their lodges next to one another and helped each other with raising children and other responsibilities that had grown heavier because of their losses. Where Good Plume went, the others followed, and so they would move their lodges, too.

"Then we should move your lodge first," White Crane decided.

Good Plume pointed northwest of the Cheyenne lodges to an area between two thickets. "That looks like a good place," she said.

They stood for a moment, planning. Good Plume noticed that High Voice had been unusually quiet. "Sister," she said, "is there something on your mind?"

High Voice nodded. "What do you think will happen after this summer?" she wondered.

"Hard to say," Good Plume replied. "Why do you ask?"

"My cousin came from the agency," High Voice said, "but she and her husband plan on going back. She thinks…she thinks I should go with them."

The other three women exchanged surprised, troubled glances.

"Why would you do that?" Little Creek asked timidly.

"It would be easier on the children, my cousin said. At the agency, we would be safer—safer from Long Knives attacking us, the way they do out here," High Voice said.

"But our men stopped the Long Knives who tried to attack us," Good Plume protested.

"Yes, this time. But what about the next time? What if they send more Long Knives than we have men? What then?" High Voice demanded, an edge of distress in her usually soft voice. "None of us have husbands to protect us and our children, and I do not think I could stand it if one of my children was killed."

Good Plume reached out and took her distraught friend's hand. "My husband died to keep his family free, away from the clutches of the whites," she said. "Every night I go to bed with a memory, but for me it cannot be any other way because here I am free to do what is best for my children."

"Sister, you cannot leave us," Little Creek pleaded. "We have taken care of one another, and we always will, no matter what happens."

High Voice looked around at the circle of worried faces. "Yes. Yes, you are right," she admitted.

White Crane smiled and pointed toward the horse herd, almost numberless, grazing the plush bottomland. "Look. Look at them. That is how strong we are. Who will dare to give us trouble here?"

North of Ash Creek, past the point where the middle fork joined the north fork, Two Bulls and his companions saw the smoke from the area near where the encampment had stood only three days before. Someone had started a fire, and they suspected it had something to do with the thin dust cloud hanging over the middle fork. Loping their horses up a gully, they topped the narrow opening onto the valley and saw a lone rider on a horse on an opposite hill. Below him was a column of Long Knives.

"Get back over the hill," Two Bulls said. "If they follow us, we will lead them away. If they do not, we need to see where they are going."

They turned, and Two Bulls led them along the slope, heading northwest in full view of the column on the other side of the valley. But no one was chasing them. They finally crossed over a ridge and down onto the north slope. Two Bulls signaled a halt.

"No one is following," someone said.

"Then we stay here and watch them," Two Bulls decided. "Bear Robe should be getting close to the encampment, if he is not there already."

Circling back and remaining behind intervening ridges, the warriors gained a brushy ridge and stopped. Climbing to the crest, they saw the column in the distance, continuing west along the creek.

Beneath the shade of the cottonwoods, as they finished staking a fresh elk-hide, hair down, to the ground, Black Shawl and Looks Back Woman heard the soft footfalls of a man and a horse. Sunbeams were streaming nearly straight down through the tree branches; it was the middle of the day. Crazy Horse returned to the lodge leading one of his favorite horses, a fast sorrel gelding. Black Shawl knew what her husband was planning.

"I think she will like that horse," she told him.

Looks Back Woman looked at her, puzzled.

"My husband is giving that horse to the Cheyenne woman Buffalo Calf Road," Black Shawl explained.

The older woman nodded.

"And this," Crazy Horse said, pulling a large eagle feather out of a painted case hanging from the willow tripod. "I will not be gone long," he added, then left.

"He always says that," Black Shawl said, smiling patiently as she watched her husband leading the horse away. "I probably will not see him until sundown."

Looks Back Woman stood. "I will go get water from the river so we can soak the hide before we rub in the brains," she said. "Wait, and rest until I get back."

At the river, Looks Back Woman met Sweetwater Woman and Song, who were busy filling three water bladders. A man on horseback passed behind them, leading a packhorse laden with his belongings. Bird stopped at the bank and dismounted to water his horses.

A young man sitting somewhat disconsolately at his brush shelter looked up from his fire and recognized the man with the horses as one of those who had recently come from the Spotted Tail agency, then stared at the loaded packhorse. "Are you leaving?" Little Feather asked.

Bird nodded. He was a widower with no children, and he had grown to like the easy life at the agency.

"I hope they do not punish you for leaving," Little Feather cautioned.

Bird shrugged as he watched his horses drink. He had never liked this young man, the one everyone called Bug. He was a lackey for the one called White Hat Clark. What he was doing here was a mystery to him.

"I do not think so. They will punish those who stay away," he retorted.

"I am staying," Little Feather replied haughtily. "I like it here."

Bird chuckled under his breath, but said no more. Mounting his bay riding horse, he grabbed the lead rope to the packhorse and began crossing the river.

Little Feather watched the man pick a way across the strong current.

Behind his brush shelter, the village was busy with all the things of living. Horses were led to water between the lodges, passing those already picketed next to lodge doors. Bands of children roved; young boys dashed about like flocks of birds. Women were busy with the endless chores of seeing to their families. All in all, there was constant motion beneath the whispering leaves of the cottonwood trees, standing guard with their thick branches spread protectively, like the wings of the mystic thunderbird.

From the front of the council lodge, High Eagle and Worm watched the man crossing the river as well. They knew that some people were planning on leaving. "I think that is not the last of it," High Eagle said, pointing toward the rider leading a packhorse across the water.

Worm nodded. "I think you are right."

Many hills to the east, a young man knelt on one knee and gazed at the swelling of his horse's front left ankle. A dirt ledge had crumbled beneath them on a downhill slope, and they had tumbled. Bear Robe dusted himself off. He reached over and retrieved his rifle from the grass, checked himself over, and adjusted his belt and clothing. He sighed dejectedly and looked around.

He had a long way to go, and his horse was hurt. In an instant, he decided what to do. Removing the neck rope and the long rein, he coiled them and draped them over his shoulder.

With an experienced eye, he watched for signs of other injuries as he pushed the gray sideways. The ankle seemed to be the only one, but the gelding favored it noticeably. Bear Robe knew he was lucky he had not suffered any injury himself.

"I have to leave you here, but I will come back for you," he said. "You can eat all you want. There is water nearby; I know you will find it."

Bear Robe turned away reluctantly, looking back. The gray watched him, its ears perked forward, apparently puzzled by the turn of events.

At the bottom of the slope, Bear Robe got his bearings, picked out a butte in the distant greening landscape, and broke into an easy trot. He knew the rifle would get heavy after a while.

Bird climbed the ridge at an angle to avoid having to go straight up the slopes, some of which were steep. He was in no particular hurry. The weather was good, and once over the ridges, the horses would settle into a fast walk.

At the top, he paused to look back over his shoulder. He had never seen an encampment with so many people, or one as long. Countless circles of lodge poles poked up through the openings in the tall trees, reminding him of the antlers of a herd of elk he had seen once near the Shell River. For a moment, he wondered if he was doing the right thing by going back to the agency.

There was nothing keeping him here, he decided. He had no one. He clucked to the bay he rode and tugged on the lead rope of the packhorse. In a way, he was looking forward to the long journey.

Bird didn't immediately see the dust cloud to the south. It was barely noticeable, a low, thin veil hanging over a dark line of trees. But after a moment, he realized that a dust cloud might mean something. He reined his horses to a halt.

It was a ways off, but Bird could tell that whatever was making the dust was at the junction where Ash Creek flowed into the Greasy Grass River. And the dust was moving. In near disbelief, he saw a long line of dark figures, people on horses, crossing the river. The front of the line gained the west bank of the Greasy Grass and turned north.

Long Knives!

Momentarily stunned, Bird watched the line stretch out as more men continued crossing. Shaking his head, he jerked the rein of his horse and turned him, kicking him savagely. The bay broke into a lope, but the packhorse was reluctant, and Bird realized he had to leave it behind, so he let go of the lead rope.

At a gallop, he retraced the trail down the slope that he had ridden up leisurely, sliding to a stop on a bank high above the water. From there, he could still see the Long Knives in the distance on the green floodplain.

He was across from the southern end of the village. Throwing caution aside, he forced the bay down the bank and hit the water with a splash, sending white spray in all directions. With powerful lunges, the horse surged across the current and scrambled up the bank.

"Long Knives!" Bird yelled. "Long Knives are coming from the south!"

CHAPTER THIRTY-SEVEN

Death in the Wind

A narrow ditch, filled with backwater from the Greasy Grass River, undulated through the brush far southwest of the Hunkpapa camp circle. Much like a lake, its water didn't flow. Along its grassy banks grew peppermint, a favorite for tea. Several women and girls were picking leaves from the low-growing plant with the pleasant, refreshing aroma, laughing and conversing as they moved about in the bright noonday sun. From their location, they could neither hear nor see the frantic rider as he careened down the slope east of the river. In fact, the thickets of chokecherry and buffalo berry shrubs around them obscured the floodplain to the south and prevented them from seeing the narrow column of riders charging across the open ground toward the encampment.

One of the women glanced up in surprise, startled by the sound of an angry hornet buzzing by her ear. She was worried they might stumble onto a nest in the brush. Another one buzzed by, and as she paused to look for a nest, something popped behind her and the woman only a few paces away gasped sharply. Then one of the girls nearby cried out.

Red Quill turned and saw a woman on the ground, and another bending over her with her face contorted with shock and disbelief. Several girls and young women dropped their bags and willow baskets and ran toward the woman lying in the grass. It was then that Red Quill heard faint cracks. For a moment, the sounds and the shocking scene in front of her had no connection. But in the next instant, she knew what the faint cracks were—gunfire!

Horrified, Red Quill looked south between the thickets and saw the bobbing line of riders and an occasional flash followed by the sound of gunfire.

"Run!" she shouted. "Run back to the village! Run! Run!"

Another woman cried out, then stumbled and fell to the grass. A girl turned to help her and suddenly flew backward as if bowled over by a horse. Red Quill threw herself to the ground next to the girl. There was blood oozing out of the hole in her dress between her breasts, and her dark eyes stared vacantly at the sky.

Immobilized by fear and indecision, Red Quill couldn't take her eyes off the dead face. The only thing she knew for certain was that Long Knives were charging the village.

Just outside the first group of lodges, two young men, Stabs and Yellow Eyes, were braiding twists of buffalo hair into a long rope. First they heard the screams and shouts of women, and then they saw several running in panic toward the lodges.

"Someone is shooting at us!" shouted one woman as she dashed by.

"Long Knives!" said another.

Then came the sound of distant cracks of gunfire. The young men dropped the rope and stared at each other.

"Get your weapons!" shouted Stabs as he bolted toward his lodge. "Long Knives!" he shouted as he ran. "Long Knives! From the south!"

Yellow Eyes was hard on his heels and turned toward his own lodge. Behind them and beyond the thickets, the cracks of gunfire were steady, one after another. Overhead, bullets slammed into branches and tore through leaves.

Bug was bent over his small fire pit, blowing at the kindling, coaxing his fire to life, when he heard the shouts from the south end of the village. He sat up, thinking a horse was running loose or that boys were starting a mock battle. The shouts were faint, but persistent. After a moment, he stood to get a good look and thought he saw people running between lodges and through the thickets and trees.

Stabs saw his mother standing in front of the lodge, puzzled by the noise and trying to see what the excitement was about. He stopped at the willow tripod and grabbed his rifle and bag of bullets and turned to his mother. "Long Knives!" he said, panting from the hard sprint.

Her hands flew to her mouth and she looked around.

"Find father!" he said, tying the bullet bag to his belt. "Find father and go north!" He stepped over and embraced her, taking a moment to caress her gray head.

"Find a place to hide, Mother."

Letting go, he turned and ran a few steps and stopped to look back.

She was staring after him. Waving, he turned and sprinted toward the sounds of gunfire, which were growing louder.

Instinct kicked in for every man, woman, and child in the Hunkpapa camp who heard the commotion. Mothers and grandmothers looked for their children and grandchildren, calling out to them as all protective mothers do when danger is approaching. Children waited for their mothers and grandmothers to find them, or ran for home. Men, young and old, went for their weapons. The younger men ran, as Stabs did, toward the gunfire or for their horses; the older men gathered their families to them, grimly determined, knowing they were the last line of defense for the women and the very young and very old.

Being attacked by enemies was nothing new in Lakota life. They had enemies all around them, and many people in the encampment had experienced the confusion and melee of attacks in the past. As the alarm spread north, slowly at first, the instinct to survive would flow with it. After the initial panic and uncertainty, a grim sense of calm would take hold in every man and woman. Anything less was not the way to survive.

Stabs and Yellow Eyes were at the front of the first wave of warriors, most on foot, who were responding to the attackers. The intensity and confusion of the moment, not to mention the constant movements of the defenders, made it difficult to determine their numbers. Out of the corner of his eye, Stabs thought he saw two blue-coated riders race through the thickets toward the village, but they had disappeared from his view by the time he turned to get a better look.

Stabs ducked behind a shrub to take a good look at the enemy. Because the gunfire had steadily grown louder, he assumed the Long Knives were charging toward the village. He was relieved to see them in a long line stretching east to west, with the east end near the river. Horses were being led to the rear in bunches; a single man was leading each bunch of several horses. The Long Knives on the line were mostly kneeling or lying prone and firing at will.

He estimated the distance to the line of Long Knives at about a hundred long paces. From the edge of the last line of lodges, they had run at least that far, so the Long Knives had stopped far short of the village.

On either side of his and Yellow Eyes's position, more and more warriors were arriving. Several were mounted, and most of them dashed into the open and charged the Long Knives, drawing their fire and getting off a few shots. Stabs and Yellow Eyes and the other warriors on foot took careful aim and fired. Neither side was doing much damage to the other, however.

By now, bundles in hand, women and children from the Hunkpapa camp were fleeing northwest, most of them passing west of the Isanti and Mniconju lodges and reaching the edge of the horse herd.

Last Horse, an old Sihasapa warrior, was on his way back from the river after watering his horse when he saw two very strange-looking men riding toward him. One was bearded, and both were sitting off balance and wide-eyed. They were Long Knives, bearing down on him at a gallop.

The old warrior had two choices: stay where he was and be trampled, or run. Knowing there was virtually no time to get out of the way, he did the only thing that came to mind—he jumped up and down and yelled at the Long Knife horses.

"Hah! Hah!" Last Horse shouted at the top of his lungs and waved his arms. One of the horses stopped suddenly, spilling its rider. The other veered left toward the river, its rider hanging off to one side.

His shouts had drawn the attention of the people running past. Like a family of foxes after one mouse, everyone pounced, reacting out of confusion and anger. Last Horse saw a woman grab her skinning knife from its sheath hanging at the small of her back. At the same time, a man yelled and thrust a deadly war lance downward. The blue-coated Long Knife threw up his arms and cried out, and his shout of fear turned into a weak gurgle. Then he was silent and still.

In a moment, Last Horse realized what was happening—the village was under attack! He yanked at his horse's lead rope and ran home to his lodge in the Sihasapa camp and found his wife. "Long Knives are attacking!" he told her.

She was standing in front of the lodge, watching people run. Women and children were going north, warriors were going south. Dogs were barking, and horses that were picketed at the lodges were nervous.

"We need to leave now!"

"Where will we go?" she asked calmly, ignoring the increasing noise. "Perhaps it is better if we stay. We have faced everything together, and if our lives are meant to end here, then let us stare death in the face together."

Last Horse looked at his wife's lightly seamed face. She had always been steady, never one to give in to the stress of any difficulty, even when death was in the wind. "We can do that," he said gently.

Noticing a young man running by, an old rifle in hand, he turned and reached out to him. "Grandson, take this horse! The Long Knives are attacking from the south. Before you join the fight, go to the next camp and warn them. Tell someone to take the warning to the other camps."

The young man, Red Bow, took the lead rope and swung onto the horse. "Thank you, Grandfather! I will warn them!"

Last Horse hurried to grab his rifle and pointed to the two willow chairs in front of the door. "We will sit," he said. "If trouble comes, we will face it, side by side."

Red Bow rode Last Horse's bay mare toward the Sihasapa, Mniconju, and Itazipacola camps. His warning was simple, but it struck fear and motivated everyone to take immediate action: "Long Knives! Long Knives are coming from the south!"

North and adjacent to the Sihasapa camp stood the warrior society lodges. In the middle of them was the large council lodge. Sitting Bull and several older men and warrior society leaders were inside making small talk.

Outside, a woman finished rolling up the bottom of the covering to allow air to flow through. It was already hot. The woman poked her head in the east-facing door. "Uncle," she said to Sitting Bull, her eyes wide, "people are running. Someone is shouting that Long Knives are coming!" Then she was gone.

In the silence of the ensuing moment, faint shouts were heard. The men exchanged glances and stood, exiting one by one. Outside, the sounds persisted, shouts of warning and women calling for their children. In between the lodges and trees to the west, women and children could be glimpsed heading north.

Good Weasel turned to Sitting Bull. "Uncle, I think this is your vision coming true!"

"Go," Sitting Bull responded calmly. "Go, see to your families, and get the warriors together."

Little Feather had a feeling. A sudden sense of calm washed over him. He had been listening to the shouts and cries coming from the south end of the village. He had been watching women and children fleeing north and men running and riding south toward the faint pops of gunfire. Kneeling in the opening to his shelter, he grabbed the small bag decorated with quills, pulled out the bullets, and counted them—eleven. Putting them back, he took hold of the breech-loading rifle, stood, and trotted toward the sound of the guns. For the first time in years, he knew he was doing something right. For the first time ever, he felt like he belonged.

Riding the bay mare loaned to him by the old man, Red Bow continued north after swinging through the Isanti and Sihasapa camps. Skirting west of the warrior society lodges, he loped toward the Ihanktuwan and Sicangu lodges.

"Long Knives!" he shouted. "Prepare yourselves! Long Knives are attacking from the south!"

Reaction was instantaneous. Men went for their weapons and their horses. Women looked around for their children and called out if they were not near. But Red Bow was already continuing toward the Sicangu and Oglala lodges, and beyond them to the Cheyenne.

Black Wolf stood with one armed draped across the withers of a mare, watching Cloud lifting the feet of a yearling colt one at a time. Behind Cloud, Goings was leaning on a lance that he was using as a cane. The colt tolerated the handling patiently and seemed to be enjoying all the human attention. Black Wolf was about to say as much when he noticed a sudden movement out of the corner of his eye. Horses nearby turned to look, and some moved away from a sudden intrusion. Women and children, some carrying bundles, were running toward the herd.

"My friends," Black Wolf said, "something is happening."

Goings and Cloud looked toward Black Wolf and they, too, saw the women and children approaching in a hurry.

"What is happening?" Cloud called out. "Where are you going?"

"Long Knives!" a woman said, with two small children at her heels. "They have attacked!"

"Where?" shouted Cloud.

"South!" came the reply. "At the Hunkpapa lodges!"

More and more women and children and elderly poured out of the thickets at the edge of the tall cottonwood groves.

Cloud quickly released the colt. "Come, my friends! We must see about this!"

A long arrow-cast to the north, west of the Cheyenne lodges, a boy ran to a group of men standing with four horses. "Long Knives!" he announced excitedly. "A man said that Long Knives are attacking from the south."

Gall looked at the boy. He knew in his gut that what he heard was true. Swinging up onto his black gelding, he turned to three Cheyenne who were watching him. "Get your weapons and your horses!" he told them. With that, he spun his horse and put it into a gallop.

East of the Cheyenne lodges near the river, Red Bow burst through a thicket and immediately recognized Crazy Horse and the Cheyenne woman who had saved her brother, and there were two other men he did not know.

"Long Knives! They have attacked at the south end!" he shouted.

Crazy Horse approached. "Give me a ride to my lodge," he said. "I came without my horse."

Red Bow reached out his hand and helped the war leader swing up behind him. After a short gallop, they arrived at the Oglala camp.

"Thank you, my friend," Crazy Horse said, sliding off. Quickly, he ran toward his wife, who was standing at the front of their lodge holding the rein to a bay horse. He grabbed his rifle and bag of bullets from the willow tripod.

"I have heard," Black Shawl said quietly.

"I will get your horse. You must go with the other women and children."

"No! No, I will wait here. The wife of the greatest Lakota warrior will not run."

He grabbed her gently by the shoulders and looked into her eyes. "My other rifle is hanging inside. Load it," he told her. "Keep it at hand."

Crazy Horse pulled his wife close and held her for a moment. "The only way we can be defeated is when the hearts of our women are on the ground," he said. "That is not this day."

Letting go, he mounted the bay and rode away and caught up to Red Bow. Together, they stayed to the west of the encampment, maintaining a slow lope in order to guide their mounts through the groups of women and children fleeing to the northwest.

Along the river east of the Sicangu camp, Bear turned to Horn Tail. "The gunfire is not letting up," he said.

"We should go see what is happening," Horn Tail said, reaching to the back of their shelter for his bow and quiver of arrows.

"We have only one horse," Bear pointed out.

"Then we ride double."

As Horn Tail and Bear headed south along the river, Gall jumped off his horse and pushed his way into his lodge. He had expected his wives and children to be waiting inside, since he hadn't seen them anywhere else.

Stepping back out, he ran over to an old woman sitting in the shade of a nearby lodge. "Grandmother," he said, looking about, "why are you still here?"

Rounds whined overhead, tearing through the trees, and the gunfire from the south was now a steady exchange.

The old woman shook her snow white head. Her face was deeply lined. "Oh, Grandson, my legs are not strong. I would only slow everyone down."

Gall pointed to a large cottonwood tree not far away. "Then let me take you over there," he suggested. "At least you can sit behind it, where bullets cannot hit you."

"That would be good," she said weakly. "I may not be able to run, but that does not mean I am ready to leave this world."

"Have you seen my family?" he asked.

She nodded. "Before the guns started, I saw your wives going toward that creek with their baskets."

Scooping her up gently, he carried her toward the tree. She was thin and not heavy at all. Putting her down carefully, he trotted toward the backwater creek. In the distance, he saw a line of Long Knives out in the open between the thickets. Mounted warriors were riding back and forth while others on foot were firing at the enemy.

Gall circled several thickets quickly, thinking that his family was likely among the first groups to flee north. He was about to turn away when he saw a spot of color in a stand of tall grass closer to the creek. Something caught in his throat, and his heart began to beat heavily. As he stepped closer, he saw a swatch of blue calico—one of his daughters wore a calico dress. After another step, he collapsed to his knees. It was his daughter, her arm stretched out, her hand reaching toward another body in the grass.

Horn Tail, Bear, Red Bow, and Crazy Horse reached the first line of defenders at the same time. Crazy Horse saw flashes and immediately noticed part of the line of Long Knives, with the rest of his view blocked by trees. In another instant, he heard the booming of rifle fire and instinctively took cover behind a tree. The firing from the Long Knives was consistent. From the Lakota defenders, it was sporadic, and louder.

He noticed Good Weasel and Black Moon not far away in the middle of the thicket and rode over to them. "What is the situation?" he asked as the firing continued.

Good Weasel pointed south. "They have formed a line," he said. "One of our young men told me they were charging and then stopped."

"How many?"

Good Weasel shook his head. "Hard to tell. Some of them are holding horses. There could be some from the Rosebud fight because they have Crow with them."

"Does that matter?" Crazy Horse asked. "Long Knives are Long Knives, and we must defend our people. Many of them are running to the north already."

He moved around, trying to get a glimpse of the western end of the enemy line, and finally urged his horse through the thickets. Good Weasel and Black Moon were close behind him. They dismounted and remained in the thickets, and they were surprised to see that the line of attackers stretched far to the west. At that end were the Crow scouts.

"If we scatter the Crows," Crazy Horse said, "it will weaken the line. We can try a mounted attack."

"I think we have fifty or sixty mounted men," Black Moon said.

"That will have to do," Crazy Horse decided. "The other men can keep firing. We can take our mounted warriors behind the cover of the trees and charge the west end of the line. Gather the men."

Returning to a relatively protected area behind the firing lines, Crazy Horse was surprised to see Sitting Bull alongside Cloud.

"They have stopped," Sitting Bull said, "but is that all of them?"

"As far as I know," Crazy Horse replied, and told him the plan.

Cloud was the first to notice the man who rode up and joined them. His shirt was hanging in tatters, obviously sliced with a knife, and there was blood on his arms. In his right hand was an iron hatchet, his only weapon.

"I heard," Gall said in a hollow voice, his eyes haunted and distant. "I will lead it. Whoever wants to follow me can." Without another word, he urged his horse forward. As he went, he pulled off his tattered shirt and tossed it aside.

Sitting Bull watched the broad, muscular back of the departing warrior. "He has a story to tell," he said gravely. "I hope we will hear it one day." He glanced at Crazy Horse and lifted a hand, then turned to ride back toward the village, leaving the fighting to the younger men.

"Something bad has happened," Crazy Horse said. "Right now, he is about to charge the Long Knives alone." He turned to Cloud. "We must gather all the mounted warriors and follow him."

In an instant, both men led their horses toward the lines of warriors hidden in the shrubs, behind trees, or using the slightest mound of earth as cover.

"We will charge on horseback!" Crazy Horse shouted. "Keep shooting! Keep the Long Knives down if you can!"

Meanwhile, Cloud was galloping toward the mounted warriors, his six-shooter in hand. "We are charging!" he yelled. "We are charging!"

As warriors spun to look at him, bullets tore the air above their heads.

"There!" Cloud pointed to the lone figure of Gall galloping into the open and toward the far end of the enemy skirmish line. He kicked his horse into a gallop, and as he looked right and then left, he saw that more warriors were turning to follow. To his far right, Crazy Horse already had his horse flying low through the tall grass of the floodplain.

Far ahead of all of them, Gall was nearly upon the Crow scouts, riding headlong into the teeth of their gunfire.

CHAPTER THIRTY-EIGHT

The Death Lodge

Like a hawk focused on a hapless rabbit, Gall steered his black gelding toward the middle of the group of Crow scouts, staying low over the horse's neck and drumming both heels against the animal's sides. His right arm hung loosely, somewhat relaxed, gripping the handle of the hatchet. His left hand held the braided rein and a clump of mane.

Pinpoints of light flashed in his eyesight—muzzle blasts from rifles aimed directly at him. Low, angry hums buzzed past his head—*zoom, zoom*—near misses. As he raced closer and closer to the enemy, the blasts grew louder.

Boom! Boom! Boom! A few lighter cracks were pistols shots. Gall felt his horse's hooves thudding on the ground.

Nothing deterred him; nothing would deter him. The image of the bodies of his wives and daughter would not go away—bullet holes in them, their blood seeping into the green grass, their blood even now drying on his arms. He might die today, sometime in the next few moments, but first someone would pay for the gaping hole in his heart.

Judging that his horse would put him on top of his quarry in the next three to four strides, Gall extended his right arm back in preparation for a blow. The figures in front of him were somewhat of a blur as they scrambled, dove, or sprinted to get out of his way. Picking out a scout wearing a tanned shirt and running away, he swung his hatchet.

Gall felt a jolt in his right shoulder and heard a grunt of pain and surprise, but he did not see the man tumble to the ground. Veering his horse to the right, he intended to make a wide turn and charge again. Reaching a low clump of snake berry bushes, he allowed the horse to slow down of its own accord. He saw the swatch of bright red on the blade of his hatchet and wondered why the scouts or Long Knives were not shooting at him. Then, as he finished the turn, he saw why.

The west end of the enemy skirmish line was scattered. Scouts and Long Knives were running in several directions to avoid the onslaught that came behind Gall—mounted warriors swinging war clubs and firing six-shooters at point-blank range, their horses trampling a few unlucky scouts.

Many of the scouts remounted and raced east. Some of the Long Knives were trying to remount, or trying to catch their horses.

Crazy Horse had been right—the instant the Long Knives saw their scouts scatter, they were not far behind. Cloud burst through the line, trying to count his shots while staying focused on the moment. Swinging left, he realized that none of the scouts or Long Knives on the west end of the line who were still standing were facing them. They were retreating, running away, some mounted and others on foot. Taking advantage of the lull, he slowed his horse while glancing at the cylinder of his six-shooter to see the number of live rounds—he had two left. Feeling along his belt, he reassured himself that he had two spare cylinders. On his left, a rider caught up to him.

"Crow and Arikara, I think," Black Moon said, pointing at the departing scouts.

"I noticed," Cloud replied. "This is a different bunch of Long Knives."

Another rider appeared. Crazy Horse was checking his ammunition as well. "We need to keep after them," he said.

Some of the Lakota chargers had already turned and were whipping their horses after the fleeing enemy. A broad-shouldered rider with braids flying behind him flashed past them on a black horse. It was Gall.

"We need to follow him," Crazy Horse said, and put his horse into a lope. Cloud and Black Moon did the same.

The east end of the enemy line was near a group of low-growing oak trees and thickets of chokecherry. Horn Tail was belly down in tall grass, crouching behind a low thicket. He had been helping Bear pick out targets because the enemy was far beyond effective bow range. As his cousin took time to reload, Horn Tail kept his eyes on the Long Knives. "Something is happening," he said, craning his neck above the grass.

"Be careful," Bear cautioned as he rammed the ball down the barrel.

"They are not firing this way," Horn Tail told him.

"What does that mean?"

Horn Tail lifted himself higher above the grass and looked west. He had a notion that the mounted charge might have disorganized the Long Knives, and he was right. The enemy skirmish line was in disarray. Riderless horses were running east toward the river. Behind them came several mounted Long Knives.

"I think they are running," Horn Tail said.

They heard running footsteps swish through the grass, and then Little Feather ducked down beside them. "See that?" he asked. "What should we do?"

Horn Tail looked back toward the trees where they had tied their horse. He was gone. He had probably broken or slipped out of his halter, frightened by the gunfire. He was not a trained warhorse.

More and more warriors were arriving from the camps, most of them mounted and heading directly toward the enemy.

"Look!" shouted Little Feather, pointing.

To the south, the Long Knives were in full flight, some turning back to fire at their pursuers.

Shouts arose along the line of the warriors on foot and they rose out of the tall grass to join the pursuit.

Little Feather jumped to his feet. "Come on!" he shouted and started running.

Horn Tail took a moment to string his bow and hang the quiver of arrows in place. "Come on!" he urged Bear. "We will not miss out this time!"

Rising, their first steps were hesitant, but they were soon running through the tall grass.

To the north, Goings looked at his two daughters and his son, all of them young. They were afraid and trying not to show it. He grabbed his older wife, Gathers Medicine, by her shoulders. Behind her stood Walks in the Night, his young Cheyenne wife. She was trembling; she had a morbid fear of Long Knives ever since she had witnessed unspeakable things at Sand Creek. Most of the movement around them now was coming from men heading south toward the distant gunfire.

"I will send someone to find you when it is over," he told them. "There are hills to the northwest. Find a gully covered with brush and thickets and hide there."

"You are not coming with us?" Gathers Medicine worried.

"I will stay here. I cannot ride, and I would slow you down walking."

"You will stay? You will not join the fighting?"

"I cannot. It would be stupid for me to try."

"Maybe I should stay with you," she protested. "Walks in the Night can take the children—"

"No," he said firmly. "We agreed. It does not sound like the gunfire is getting any closer. Still, I would feel better if you would do as we agreed."

After a deep sigh, Gathers Medicine nodded reluctantly. "Yes. Yes, we will go."

"Good." Goings helped his wives mount their horse, and then his children theirs. "Do what your mothers say," he told them. "They will keep you safe."

Goings watched them all ride away but lost sight of them as they moved beyond the horse herds. He returned to the lodge, its doors tied shut, and it seemed more than physically empty. Grabbing his rifle, he took a seat. With every fiber of his being, he wanted to join the fighting, but he knew he would be slowed by his wound. With a disappointed sigh, he loaded his rifle. Suddenly, it seemed, he noticed the sounds of men shouting and running and he heard the thud of hoofbeats on the grass.

Several lodges away, Black Wolf's mother handed her son's weapons up to him after he mounted his horse. His father, Tools, was holding the horse's halter, and his grandmother was standing nearby. His mother, usually placid, was on the verge of weeping.

"Mother," the young man said, looking at the women's worried faces, "I am well enough to fight. I will do that, and I will come home."

"We will wait here," his grandmother replied softly, her gray-streaked hair framing her narrow face. "Your father will protect us."

She was more than seventy, Black Wolf knew, but he always marveled that she did not look that old. Her eyes were still bright and vibrant.

His father stepped forward, a six-shooter tucked into his belt, a muzzle-loading rifle in his hand, and a bow and quiver of arrows hanging across his back, the very image of a tough, competent fighting man. "As your grandmother said, we will be here." While he was still a very young warrior, a Shoshoni bullet had shattered his knee. Now it would barely bend, making walking awkward and mounting a horse a chore. "We know you will do your best," he said.

Black Wolf looked back and waved once as he rode away. Then he loped his horse toward the sounds of gunfire. He veered to the right of an old woman hurrying toward the river.

As he passed, he heard her call out, "Granddaughter!" looking among the brush as she went. "Granddaughter, come out!" Then she saw a slight movement in a thick stand of reeds closer to the river's edge and saw a tiny form rise to look. "There you are!" the old woman said, immensely relieved.

"Grandmother!" the girl shouted and ran into the old woman's waiting arms. "I was afraid!"

"Yes, but I think we are safe now," Yellow Leggings said, brushing the leaves and mud from the girl's tanned deer-hide dress.

"Who was shooting?" the girl asked.

"Enemies, Long Knives," the old woman replied disdainfully. "But our warriors are there now, your father among them. Come, we will go home and wait for him."

Hand in hand, the old woman and her five-year-old granddaughter walked toward the village, mindful of the riders hurrying south to join the fighting.

Black Wolf kept close to the Greasy Grass and rode past the edge of the Hunkpapa lodges, past the mouth of the backwater creek, and onto a scene of chaos. Most of the firing at this point was coming from the pursuers. As far as he could tell, the only bodies lying in the grass along the path of the enemy retreat were clad in blue. Black Wolf knew that in another instant, the fighting would take place at close range.

The young warrior paused to tie his encased rifle, stock upward, snugly to the horse's neck rope, where he could pull it out quickly and easily. After feeling to make sure the war club was tucked in just behind his right hip, he yanked the six-shooter from his belt and dug his heels into the horse's sides. He ignored the dull ache and discomfort from his wound as he leaned forward and urged his horse to charge.

Little Feather, Horn Tail, and Bear were also in the same general area and pursuing the fleeing Long Knives.

Like a covey of scattered quail, the Long Knives were desperately trying to outrun their pursuers. Somehow, most of them managed to make it to the dubious safety of the trees near a bend in the river. The cover enabled them to regroup, so the mounted warriors veered to the north and south of the grove, forcing the Long Knives to fire.

South of the council lodge and east of the Itazipacola camp, Black Shield and Grey Bull paused inside a thicket as Grey Bull looked south through his glass. "I can hear the shooting," he said, "but there are too many thickets and trees in the way to see anything."

"Crazy Horse and Cloud told me that at the Rosebud the Long Knives had several different groups, large groups, scattered all over the valley," Black Shield recalled. "I wonder how many Long Knives are in this group, and I wonder if they are the only bunch."

"That is something to keep in mind," Grey Bull agreed. "Uncle, we need to get closer."

They moved farther south and turned right at a bend in the river and followed it until it veered briefly to the southeast. Finding a thicket of tall chokecherry trees, they paused as Grey Bull looked through his glass again.

"I think they have the Long Knives trapped inside some trees," he reported to Black Shield. "Some of our men are on foot. Those on horseback seem to be charging at the trees."

Meanwhile, Black Shield kept on eye on the high ridges to the east across the river. High ground was always an advantage, if for nothing else than as a place to observe. He wondered if someone should cross the river to see if there were other Long Knives around. "Nephew," he said, "perhaps you should take a look at the hills above the river."

Grey Bull quickly took the older man's suggestion and turned his glass. He knew there were slopes behind the ridges that descended to the east as well as deep gullies that could hide hundreds of enemies or more. Black Shield had enough reason to be concerned.

He slowly panned the glass from north to south and then back again, holding it as steadily as he could. On the third sweep back to the south, dark forms appeared. Grey Bull paused, his shoulders and arms rigid. He took a deep breath and held it.

The forms were men. He could see their shoulders, and an occasional horse's head and neck. On the heads of the men seemed to be Long Knife–style hats. He exhaled. "Uncle," he said evenly, "you are right! There are Long Knives on the hills above the river!"

"Ha! I was afraid of that. We have to let Crazy Horse know!"

"I can do that," Grey Bull replied. "The people in the camps should be warned too."

"I will do that," Black Shield said. "We must go now!"

Grey Bull watched a moment longer, until the dark forms on the ridge disappeared behind it, then he put his glass away. "Take care of yourself, Uncle."

"You, as well," the older man replied.

As the two men parted company, Sitting Bull emerged from his lodge with his shield and a rifle in hand. In front of him waited nearly twenty mounted warriors. The medicine man handed the shield and the rifle up to one of his adopted sons and swept his gaze around the semicircle of men. "Have courage!" he said to them. "Remember the helpless ones!"

At a signal, the warriors turned their horses and departed at a gallop, the thundering of hooves rumbling for a few moments.

Sitting Bull watched them go, then noticed an old woman sitting behind a tree and walked over to her. "Grandmother," he said, kneeling in front of her, "you are still here. I thought you would have left with your family."

The old woman smiled, the corners of her eyes crinkling. "No, Grandson," she said, "I am too slow. I told them I would be safe here."

"What can I do for you?"

"I was just thinking of going back to my lodge," she said.

"I will help you. Our men have stopped the Long Knives."

He stood and helped the old woman to her feet. She stood a moment to steady herself, then looked toward the lodge of Gall. "Grandson," she said softly, "something terrible has happened. I saw something that makes my heart sad."

Sitting Bull looked in the direction of her gaze. "What? What happened?"

"I saw my grandson, the tall warrior, carry several people into his lodge. Women, I think. My eyes are not very clear anymore. Then he came out with his shirt cut into shreds, like a man in mourning."

A cold feeling settled in Sitting Bull's stomach. "Come," he said, "I will take you to your lodge, then I will see."

Several moments later, with the cold feeling still there, Sitting Bull went to the lodge of Gall and his family and immediately saw the brush piled in front of the door—a sign that no one was home, or that the family did not want to be disturbed. Ignoring protocol, he bent over and slowly pushed aside the door covering and put his head and shoulders inside. "Haun!" he exclaimed softly.

Near the fire pit lay three bodies, all of them covered with robes. Although their eyes were closed, he recognized them. He had seen them only this morning. Now they were so still, and the medicine man knew they were not sleeping the sleep of this world. Death was in the room; he knew the feeling all too well.

Now he knew the reason for Gall's deeply haunted, almost shocked expression earlier—his wives and one of his children were dead. Exactly how they might have died was not important, except that Sitting Bull guessed it was from Long Knife bullets. It had to be. He pulled back out of the lodge, put the covering in place, and stood, not fully believing what he had just seen.

"My friend, you look like you have seen a ghost," came a deep voice.

Sitting Bull turned and saw the horse and rider and looked up at Black Shield. "I have," he said softly. "My nephew's wives and one of his children have been killed."

Black Shield knew the truth when he heard it, and the look on the medicine man's face was proof enough of the awful reality of which he spoke. There was nothing he could say.

In a moment, Sitting Bull shook his head slightly and looked up at Black Shield again. "How goes it?" he asked, pointing south.

"It appears that the Long Knives have been chased into some trees along the river," Black Shield replied. "But Grey Bull saw others on the ridges above the river. We need to be ready because they might come down the hills and cross the river. Grey Bull went to find Crazy Horse and tell him."

A look of worry crossed the medicine man's face. "Yes, that could happen," he agreed. "I will find some boys, anyone, to spread the word to the people still here."

"I will go north and warn everyone there as well," Black Shield said. Then he had a thought. "If the Long Knives do not come down the hills, they might cross at the dry creek, Medicine Tail. Their scouts would know that crossing."

"Yes, that is true," Sitting Bull affirmed. "That crossing should be watched."

"I will see to it," Black Shield said.

After he was gone, Sitting Bull stood for another moment, staring at the door of the death lodge, for that's what it was. Most of Gall's family was dead. Along with the pity and the grief that arose in him came anger, anger directed at a despicable enemy. Not even the certain knowledge that his vision would come to pass and the Long Knives would be defeated could assuage his grief or cool his anger.

As Black Shield headed north, pausing to warn anyone he found, Grey Bull worked his way south, trying to pick out any of the war leaders. But there was too much movement. It was easy to see that all the fighting was in one area, a grove of trees near the river.

Somehow, Little Feather, Horn Tail, and Bear stayed together. They and other warriors crossed the river and moved up to a protective bank. From there, they had a good view of the Long Knives and their horses in the grove. A lot of gunfire came from the grove, directed mostly at warriors in the open areas to the west and south.

"That is less than a hundred paces, I think," Horn Tail said to Bear and Little Feather. "Too far for my bow, but not for your rifles."

Little Feather nodded nervously. Bear yanked out clumps of grass from the edge of the bank to give himself a clear shooting shelf. "Do the same," he said. "Rest your rifle on the bank. You can aim better that way."

As Little Feather pulled grass, an older warrior crawled to them. "Do not bunch up so close to each other," he advised. "Spread out. That way, a close miss will not hit anyone else." After delivering that bit of chilling advice, the warrior left.

Little Feather stared after him for a moment before he moved farther down the bank. "Have you ever been in a battle?" he asked Bear and Horn Tail.

"No," Horn Tail replied. "This is the first time for both of us. What about you?"

"Me too," he said. Pulling open the breech, he reached into his bullet bag for a shell but dropped it into the sand. Retrieving it, he carefully brushed off the sand and slid it into the chamber. "If nothing else, I know how to fire this rifle."

After clearing an area to rest the stock of his rifle, he hunched down and aimed toward the trees, then realized he had to pick out one target. For the first time in his life, Little Feather pointed a weapon at something other than a deer or an elk. He lined up the sights on the dark outline of a Long Knife and took a deep breath.

CHAPTER THIRTY-NINE

The Desperate Trail

Strangely, Little Feather did not hear the thunderous crack of his rifle, but he did feel it slam into his shoulder. Whether it had been a hit or a miss, he did not know. Although he could not define it in so many words, he felt changed by the simple act of firing at the enemy. He was not brash enough to think that he had suddenly become a warrior, a full-fledged fighting man, but he had become a defender of the people. Ducking below the edge of the bank, he opened the breech, took out the empty round, and slid in another.

Boom!

He jumped at the sudden blast. Nearby, Bear had fired his old muzzle-loader. Blue smoke still hung in the air. Farther down the bank, other warriors opened fire at the Long Knives in the grove.

B-boom-boom-boom!

A voice came from somewhere down the line. "Get down! The Long Knives will return fire! Keep your heads down!"

In the next instant, rounds tore the air above their heads or ploughed into the soil in front of the bank, followed by muzzle blasts from within the trees.

Horn Tail and Bear stared at one another. Their complaints about missing out on the Battle Where the Woman Saved Her Brother seemed so foolish now.

Looking for Crazy Horse or Gall, Grey Bull loped his horse in a south-westerly direction, away from the trees where all of the Lakota firing was directed. Strangely, he was drawn to the sounds of gunfire and the life-and-death struggle ensuing on the floodplain. But even as he wished for the strength of his youth, he was subdued by the sight of some Lakota and a few Cheyenne warriors helping wounded men.

Because of the constantly moving mounted warriors, he couldn't immediately see either of the war leaders. He guessed that Gall was riding his favorite black gelding. He saw several black horses, but none of them was carrying a big man. Grey Bull reined his horse to a stop in the meadow where the Long Knives had their skirmish line. He could see blue-clad bodies in the grass where they had fallen, forming a haphazard line leading to the river. The man closest to him had been stripped of his rifle, six-shooter, and bullet belt. A particularly sharp exchange of firing pulled his attention to the east. Grey Bull knew he had to get closer if he wanted to get a glimpse of Crazy Horse or Gall.

Northwest of the village and southeast of the Greasy Grass River confluence with the Bighorn River, a hunter was heading home, leading a packhorse carrying a gutted elk. The air was hot, though an occasional breeze brought momentary relief. Nuances of weather never bothered Taken Alive. It was part of life.

He had left the village well before dawn, riding out quietly past the horse herd and the guards. Someone had told him that the black-tailed deer along the Bighorn were fat, and his wife's meat containers were nearly empty. Incredibly, he had all but stumbled onto the cow elk grazing along the river bottom soon after he had hidden his horses.

At a narrow creek, Taken Alive stopped to let the horses drink. Strangely, he thought he heard a man's fingers tapping on a dry log. Tilting his head, he listened, but all he could hear was the breeze whispering through the grass and the horses sipping water. Ever watchful, the warrior scrutinized the surrounding prairie. Nothing was out in the open; on a hot day, animals stayed in the shade.

The tapping came again. Taken Alive sat motionless. This time, the noise persisted longer, and then it was gone. Something in the distance was making the noise. At first he thought a woodpecker, but it was not a uniform tapping; rather, it was like several woodpeckers tapping at once, and not in unison.

Taken Alive clucked to his horses and pulled them away from the water. If he put them in a low lope, he would be home shortly.

As Black Shield rode north, more and more men were moving past him, heading toward the southern end of the camp, drawn toward the gunfire.

But, surprisingly, many women and children and old men and boys were still in camp. He motioned to an old warrior sitting next to a lodge with a rifle at his knee and stopped. "My friend," he called out, "we think there may be Long Knives on the other side of the river, behind those hills."

"I have thought about that," the old warrior returned.

"They might come down the slope," said Black Shield.

"They might," the old man agreed. "But that would expose them too much. I think they will look for a crossing," He pointed north. "The one up there."

"I think you are right, so we must watch that crossing."

The old warrior smiled. "My legs are not as fast as they once were, but my eyes still see well enough," he said. "Well enough to aim this rifle."

"Good! We need as many men as we can find to help keep watch." Black Shield turned his horse north. "I will meet you at the crossing, and anyone else you can bring."

As Black Shield continued north, stopping to talk to any old man who had a weapon and could help watch the Medicine Tail crossing, he didn't see the faces of the two riders who flashed past him, or realize that one of them was a woman. Buffalo Calf Road, armed with two six-shooters, rode with her husband, Black Coyote.

To the south, along the riverbank north of the grove of trees where the Long Knives had found cover, a warrior crawled along the line of men scattered behind the bank. "Take careful aim," Blunt Arrow advised. "Do not hurry your shot."

Little Feather noted the look of experience and air of competence about the man. "Shoot, get down, reload, and wait for them to return fire," the man went on. "Then fire again. Do not show any more than your head and shoulders over this ledge. Many of our men are in the open on the other side, with no cover. Make the Long Knives shoot at us and use up their bullets."

As Blunt Arrow went past, Little Feather glanced at Bear and Horn Tail, then cautiously raised himself up above the edge of the bank. Sliding his rifle forward, he took careful aim. In his side vision, he saw Bear doing the same, and other men as well farther down the line. Then the rifles blasted. Little Feather heard screams from inside the grove, screams of men and horses. He ducked down again quickly.

Grey Bull recognized the man galloping toward him. Yellow Wolf slid his horse to a stop. "Do you know where Crazy Horse is?" he asked the younger man immediately.

Yellow Wolf shook his head. "I just got here," he said. "He is probably over there, where all the shooting is."

"I need to find him. We saw Long Knives on the hills across the river," Grey Bull explained. "We need to tell him and Gall. If all of our fighters are here, there will be no one to defend the east side of the village. But Black Shield thinks the Long Knives will go to the Medicine Tail crossing, the dry creek. He is gathering men to wait there, just in case."

Yellow Wolf pulled out his six-shooter to check that it was loaded, and then his rifle. "I will find one of them, Uncle," he assured the older man, "and tell them. Where will you be?"

"I have a feeling Worm and High Eagle and the other medicine men will need help treating our wounded," Grey Bull replied.

"Watch yourself, Uncle," the younger man said, and rode toward the fighting.

Cloud joined Crazy Horse and several other warriors south of a low rise that was slightly more than a hundred paces from the trees. It did not provide complete cover, but it was enough to prevent the Long Knives from seeing them.

"Our men are firing from the north side of the trees," Crazy Horse said. "We need to get word to them to increase their firing and keep it up. It would give us a chance to move in close from the west and south."

"I will find a messenger," Black Moon offered.

"Good. As soon as we hear sustained firing, we will charge," Crazy Horse said.

Grey Bull reached the end of the Hunkpapa circle. Along the way, he passed men helping wounded comrades back to the village. He stopped at Sitting Bull's lodge and noticed that a few boys were digging a large fire pit and others were bringing stones from the river. Still others were gathering piles of dry firewood. Nearby, Sitting Bull, with two women helping, was already leaning over a wounded man.

"Uncle," Grey Bull called out, "do you need my help?"

After a moment, the medicine man looked up. "Perhaps. Later, when the enemy is driven away, I will have a cleansing ceremony, so I will need to build a sweat lodge."

Grey Bull dismounted. "I can help with that," he said.

The medicine man pointed toward a pile of freshly cut red-willow saplings, which would be the frame of the dome-shaped structure.

After retracing the route he had taken early that morning, Taken Alive gained the top of a hill northwest of the sprawling village. With the mid-afternoon angle of the sun, he had a clear view of the village site. Although he could not see the lodges in detail, he was able to pick out the nearly numberless dark specks that indicated the horse herd, which was scattered farther about than it had been this morning. His eyes roved south, beyond the large groves of cottonwood trees, where some kind of movement was noticeable. As he was about to ride down the hill, a slight movement inside some shrubs to his left caught his attention.

As his hand grabbed the handle of his six-shooter, he saw it again—a horse flicking its tail. Peering into the trees, he saw the outlines of people.

A slender young warrior galloped his horse into a thicket at a bend in the river. After dismounting smoothly, he fashioned a bridle from the rein and tied the lead to a branch in practically the same motion. Long black braids bouncing, he dashed toward the warriors positioned along the riverbank, keeping low. Little Feather watched him come, envious of the slender but muscular frame and the young man's fluid, catlike movements. He stopped next to Blunt Arrow, his face intense but his manner calm.

"Black Moon and Crazy Horse sent me. I am Red Horse," he said, hardly panting. "They want you to increase your firing and keep the Long Knives engaged with you. Keep their attention. When you do, Crazy Horse and the men on horseback will charge them from the other side."

Blunt Arrow nodded. "I am Blunt Arrow. As soon as I inform every one of these men, we will do it."

Taken Alive looked at the ten or twelve faces all around him, mostly children and four young women. He didn't know any of the women. They told him they had been hiding after they had fled from the village. "So they attacked on the south end?" he asked.

"Yes," one of the women replied. "They told us to take the children and run in case the Long Knives broke through."

"A wise thing," he told her. "But from what I could see, something is happening at the south end. I do not think they broke through." He paused, mentally planning even as he talked. "I see you have food and water. I have a large flask that I will leave with you, and I will leave the packhorse and elk here. Do not worry, we will drive them away, if they have not done so already." He stood to leave, looking for a last time at the small faces, uncertainty and apprehension reflected in their dark, innocent eyes. "It will be all right," he promised. "It will be all right."

Red Horse found Black Moon and Crazy Horse. "A man named Blunt Arrow is there," he reported. "He will make it happen."

"Good," said Crazy Horse. "Now we must gather our men and prepare to charge."

Grey Bull worked quickly to bend the red willow saplings and tie them together. Most of the frame was already completed, bound together with thin strings of green bark. After Sitting Bull had blessed the site and the wood, Grey Bull had started his task, trying to concentrate. But it was difficult not to think of the battle raging near the Hunkpapa camp. As he bent down to grab another long sapling, the few quick, sporadic shots he had been hearing evolved into a continuous barrage.

Blunt Arrow had devised an effective plan, knowing that the forty or so men along the bank were using a variety of weapons. One other man had a repeating rifle, while everyone else had a single shot. However, the breechloaders could be reloaded much faster than the muzzleloaders. Every other man in line would fire simultaneously, and the other men would fire together while the first group was reloading. Consequently, the first few volleys became unrelenting fire poured into the grove of trees, effectively providing no chance for the Long Knives to return fire. Bullets tore through the leaves and shrubbery, most of them striking flesh or tree trunks. Men cried out in surprise and pain, and horses screamed as well.

Crazy Horse launched his charge from the southwest, knowing that Blunt Arrow's men were firing from the north. The thunder from the hooves of nearly a hundred horses could not be heard, as they were masked by the continuous gunfire. As a wide front, the charge advanced swiftly. Crazy Horse held his fire until he could plainly see the dark outlines of the enemy inside the sheltering trees. Then he opened fire. At that signal, nearly a hundred muzzle blasts rent the air, propelling death.

Before the chargers reached the grove, Long Knives burst out of it, heading in a southeasterly direction. Crazy Horse and his men veered right in pursuit.

At a flat-out gallop, Cloud slid his rifle into its elk-hide case and drew the six-shooter from his belt. Closing in on the fleeing enemy, he saw several of the scouts. He despised them, though he understood why the Crow and Arikara would work for the Long Knives. As a nation by themselves, they could not defeat the Lakota and Cheyenne alliance, and thereby hoped that the Long Knives could do it for them. But he had heard that a few Lakota were scouting for the enemy as well. That he could not understand at all.

He took aim at a Long Knife mercilessly gouging his spurs into his horse's already bloody sides and fired. The man jerked from the impact of the bullet and flopped from the saddle. Like wolves after a herd of hapless deer, the warriors swept in among the Long Knives. Slightly ahead of him, Cloud saw a warrior swing a horn-tipped club and knock a man off his horse. He had the sensation of being part of a surging flood sweeping away everything in its path.

A lone warrior swept in from the west and joined the charge. Taken Alive had stripped off his shirt and was leaning over as his horse flew across the open floodplain. Like Cloud, he quickly put away his rifle and drew the six-shooter, knowing that close combat was imminent. He had seen the Long Knives streaming out of the trees like a flock of sparrows trying to elude an attacking hawk.

Blunt Arrow was the first to jump up over the bank, realizing that the Long Knives were fleeing, though all the men along the bank followed in an instant. Little Feather reached into his bullet bag as he ran—he had two bullets left. Horn Tail had always been a good runner and soon outdistanced most of the others, his bow ready.

Shoulder to shoulder with Blunt Arrow, Bear entered the grove and saw the bodies of men and horses scattered in the grass and shrubs. "Look out!" Blunt Arrow warned.

A body was moving and a shot blasted from behind Bear, startling him. The body jerked. As he stepped forward, Bear saw that it was a black-skinned man. The dying man reached up a hand and spoke in Lakota, "Help me! Do not kill me!"

Another shot boomed, and the man jerked once again. This time his dark eyes turned blank. "I know him," Blunt Arrow hissed. "He should have known better than to throw in with the Long Knives!"

Warriors quickly stripped rifles and pistols from dead Long Knives and unbuckled the black belts to which bullet cases were attached. Bear grabbed one of the square cases and took out the bullets. Horn Tail took a rifle and a bullet case and knelt to load it. Little Feather was momentarily immobilized, staring at the dead bodies.

"Come on!" Blunt Arrow shouted and pointed southeast. "The battle is going that way!" Without waiting, he ran out of the grove, other warriors close behind.

Horn Tail grabbed Little Feather and then saw what the young man was staring at. It was a dead scout. Most of his head was gone, likely splattered by a bullet. Blood was splashed over the grass, as if poured from a bucket. "Come on," Horn Tail said gently. "I guess we will see more of that sort of thing."

Emerging from the grove, the three young men saw that the fleeing Long Knives and the relentless pursuers were moving away swiftly. Several horses with saddles and without riders were caught in the flow, and Long Knife bodies already dotted the plain.

Gunshots reverberated along the river. Cloud veered left to get out of the way of a knot of warriors. Angling for a clear shot, he fired and quickly picked another target. He heard a hollow thud and felt his horse begin to stumble badly. Instinctively, he clinched with his legs and grabbed a handful of mane. In the next instant, he knew he was going down.

Cloud rolled free of the horse, but he felt the hard jolt forcing the air from his lungs. He gathered his knees beneath him, still bent over, with his forehead in the grass. He was trying to catch his breath. The horse was dead, he knew. Somewhere in the back of his slightly dizzy mind was a thought to grab his rifle from the neck rope of the dead animal. Moaning in pain, he saw the cylinder from his pistol lying in the grass next to his knee. As he reached for it, noise and motion suddenly crashed into his awareness. Something was moving on his left. Something was bearing down on him.

Finally drawing a breath, he rolled over. As his vision cleared, he saw the outline of a man with the hairstyle of a Crow.

Cloud rolled left over his shoulder and reached out toward the horse and his rifle, but it was beyond his reach. Pieces of grass and clods of dirt rained on him as a horse slid to a stop. Remembering the knife at his belt, he reached around for it. Still shaken by the hard, jarring fall, he was able only to rise to his knees, and he saw the black muzzle of a rifle less than a hand's width from his face. His instinct was to grab the rifle and pull it aside, until he heard a voice.

"Friend," the voice said in Lakota.

Cloud looked up and saw a scar on the Crow's face that ran from his right ear down to the corner of his mouth. There was recognition in the intense, dark eyes.

"Friend," Broken Hand repeated.

The muzzle of the rifle lifted. For an instant, Cloud locked eyes with the man. Images of snow and a young man leading a horse with buffalo meat loaded on drag poles rushed in. And then he was gone. He watched him go. Broken Hand did not look back as he galloped away.

Drawing deep breaths to gather himself, Cloud crawled toward the dead horse to retrieve his rifle. Every part of his body ached. Loose horses were running about nervously here and there. He would need to catch one, somehow.

Taken Alive watched warriors ahead of him ride in among the Long Knives and fire at close range. Some of the Long Knives fired back, but ineffectively. Inexorably, the enemy was being pushed toward the river.

Beyond the northern end of the large encampment, Little Bird and his family walked leisurely along the river. They had been picking peppermint and trying their hand at fishing with a trap. When they came to the clearing at the northern edge of the Cheyenne camp, he immediately noticed some activity. Cheyenne warriors were mounting their horses, weapons in hand.

Little Bird hurried forward. "What is happening?" he asked a young man near a lodge.

The young man seemed surprised at the question. "Long Knives," he replied. "They attacked the Hunkpapa camp."

Little Bird turned to Stands on the Hill and his two sons. "Come," he said, "we have to get back to our lodge!"

The young Cheyenne warrior mounted his horse and loped past them as they ran.

To the south, Yellow Wolf rode into a thicket above the river to see a man he recognized standing beside a horse. "Uncle," he called out, "I was sent to find you."

Gall looked up, forearms leaning across the withers of his horse, watching the Long Knives crossing the river. His only weapon was the small iron hatchet in his hand, and he was shirtless, sweat dotting his face. The gunfire was steady, mostly coming from the warriors in pursuit.

Yellow Wolf could immediately sense the man's deep anger. "Grey Bull saw Long Knives across the river, up on the hilltops," he told him. "He is afraid they might cross the river and attack the camps."

"Then we must do something," Gall replied, but it sounded more like a growl. "I will take a few men and have a look."

With that laconic reply, he mounted his black gelding and turned northwest, oblivious to the gunfire. Something about the big man's demeanor sent a shiver up Yellow Wolf's back.

In the next instant, Gall was out of sight and Yellow Wolf turned his attention to the raging fight on both sides of the river.

Long Knives had crossed and were climbing a steep slope on the other side. Exposed on the slope, they were easy targets. The gunfire did not let up, and Long Knives cried out and fell. The east bank of the river was bare, with very little cover, and low thickets grew on the west side. On both sides, there were dead Long Knife horses. Wounded horses stood motionless, some with their heads down and quivering, immobilized by shock and pain, or by a badly shattered leg. Many were bleeding profusely.

And everywhere there were warriors pursuing relentlessly, mercilessly killing the enemy.

Little Bird finished tying his encased rifle to the neck rope of his horse and turned to face his anxious family. He pointed to the six-shooters he had given to each of his sons. "You know how to use those," he said. "Take care of your mother."

They nodded silently, their eyes wide.

Even as far north as the Oglala camp, the gunfire from the south could be heard, though faintly.

He stepped in front of Stands on the Hill. "I heard that many women and children fled northwest. Perhaps you should as well," he suggested.

She shook her head. "We will wait for you here. Take care of yourself."

Bear and Little Feather moved out of the grove as Horn Tail stopped to take a last look at the dead Long Knives. He knew his friends were in the trees somewhere ahead of him, but he couldn't see them, so he trotted through an opening to his left and emerged in a small clearing just north of where the Long Knives were fleeing across the river. As he started to quicken his steps, he almost stumbled over a very young warrior curled in the grass who was holding his arms across his abdomen, his breathing labored as blood oozed out of him. "They shot me," he moaned. "I am shot."

Horn Tail looked around and saw a loose horse, a Long Knife horse with a wound of its own, but it was moving. He walked over slowly and grabbed its reins. It walked with a slight limp, but it moved well enough. Horn Tail led it to the boy. "My friend," he said, bending down, "I want to put you on this horse, and you can go back to the village."

The boy looked up, his eyes clouded with pain. He was too far gone.

"I will put you on the horse and take you back," Horn Tail said, leaning down to speak directly into the boy's ear.

Laying aside his newly acquired rifle, Horn Tail slid his forearms under the wounded warrior's legs and back and lifted. It was an effort to lift him up to the saddle of the tall horse, but with a mighty grunt, he did it. All the while, the boy kept his arms across his bloody abdomen. Horn Tail took a brief moment to slip the boy's feet into the stirrups to help him balance. Taking up his rifle, he led the horse away, hoping the boy would not fall.

He turned and glanced briefly over his shoulder. Long Knives were still scrambling up the steep, broken slopes on the other side, the desperate trail marked with their dead. Mounted warriors splashed across the river after their stumbling and falling enemy. Punctuating it all was the gunfire.

Far downriver and up another steep slope, ten riders urged their tired horses up the incline. Gall led the way. Their horses winded, they reached the crest of a ridge and went down the east slope. Breezes whipped around them, bending the tall grass to and fro. As the slope leveled into a narrow plateau, Gall stopped and pointed.

In front of them was a trail of matted grass, and from the direction the flattened grass was facing, it looked like many horses had gone north. Grey Bull *had* seen something.

Gall said as much, but the horses and their riders who had made the trail were nowhere in sight.

"Shall we follow that trail, Uncle?" asked a young Hunkpapa warrior.

"No," Gall replied. "Our ammunition is low. There are only a few of us, and we do not want to give the Long Knives the advantage. No. We will cross back down to the village, gather more men and ammunition, and then head for the Medicine Tail crossing. That is where these Long Knives are going. It is an easy crossing, and it would put them in the middle of the village. We cannot let them do that."

South of them, guns were still firing.

CHAPTER FORTY

The Long Knives Are Crying

Black Shield could see the open coulee on the opposite side of the river. South of the crossing, the ridges ended with a cut bank that angled steeply down to the floor of the coulee. There were no trees and no place for Long Knives to hide, unless they came in on foot and stayed down in the gullies and the old watercourse. But somehow, he doubted they would do that. They would be in a hurry to kill the Lakota and Cheyenne, as had those who had been to the south, so they would be on horseback.

On this side, just east of the council and warrior society lodges, there were stands of sandbar willow, very good cover. "Prepare your weapons and find a place to hide," he said to the several older men and boys with him. "Get behind something," he instructed the boys. "The Long Knives will come from the east. When they do, I will shoot first. Pick a target; do not shoot just to be shooting. Aim at their chests."

Most of the group was made up of boys, aged perhaps thirteen or fourteen, including Little Bird's sons, Ashes and Two Horns. They all nodded, their eyes wide in anticipation, mixed with more than a little fear of the unknown.

Near his lodge in the Oglala camp, High Eagle saw the young man leading a Long Knife horse with a figure slumped over in the saddle. As they came closer, High Eagle saw that it was a boy who was bleeding heavily from his abdomen. He quickly helped take down the injured boy.

"There, put him there," he indicated, pointing to a bed of cottonwood and willow leaves he had already prepared.

"I found him near the water, Grandfather," Horn Tail explained. "I do not know his name."

"I will see what I can do," High Eagle said. "Are you hurt?"

"No. I must get back. The Long Knives are fleeing up a hill. We have driven them away."

"That is good to know. I will tell everyone," High Eagle replied. "Take care of yourself."

As the medicine man bent to the wounded boy, Horn Tail wiped the blood from the saddle with a handful of dry grass, and then mounted. Now he had his own horse.

Like Horn Tail, Cloud was riding a Long Knife horse. The saddle felt awkward and the stirrups were too short. He looked at the scattered bodies of men and horses on the slope across the river. As he crossed and urged his horse up the bank, he looked down at a man facedown in the grass. Because of the long, dark braids and the white-man clothing, Cloud assumed it was one of the enemy scouts. The weapon in the grass near the body was a Long Knife weapon, but the moccasins on the man's feet were Lakota.

Cloud dismounted and turned the body over. The exit wound near his shoulder blade was large, and blood stained his shirt. Cloud's heart fell. He knew the man—it was Little Feather, the one called Bug who had come from the agency and who had spied for White Hat Clark. But here was no spy. Here was a man who had given his life facing a Lakota enemy.

Cloud closed the man's eyes. He would come back later and take him to the village. This man would have a warrior's burial.

He was about to mount when he saw a Lakota warrior galloping toward him from the north. It was a Hunkpapa whom he recognized, but he could not remember his name.

"My friend!" the man called out, sliding his horse to a stop. "Gall sent me. We saw a trail behind those hills above the river. There are more Long Knives there, heading north!"

"Are you certain?"

"Yes. The tracks are of horses with iron on their hooves."

"I see. We need to find Crazy Horse and spread the word. The east side of the village must be protected! I will find him."

"Gall is going back into the village for more men, and then he is going to the crossing, where the dry creek goes down to the river."

"Good! Good!" Cloud yanked out his glass, surprised that it was still intact in spite of the fall he had taken, and pointed it up the slope. He was convinced Crazy Horse was up there, near the fighting. The Hunkpapa whirled his horse around and galloped away.

On the west bank of the river just north of Cloud, a man crawled out of the water, his legs trembling and his chest heaving. He lay in the grass for a moment, panting, and then sat up on his knees. Bear glanced toward the water, where he saw the body of the Long Knife floating away, and looked at the war club in his hand.

He had never touched a white person, much less fought one hand-to-hand. The man was no fighter, but he was strong. A wicked blow to the side of his head with the stone-headed club had finally stopped him. Bear could still feel the skull caving in where he had hit him.

He had lost his old muzzleloader, but nearby was the Long Knife's rifle. He wondered where Horn Tail had gone. Behind him and to the south, the battle seemed to be going up the hill.

Taken Alive jumped off his horse to take aim. Even as the rifle boomed and slammed against his shoulder, he saw the Long Knife in his sights flail his arms and fall back down the slope. As the warrior shifted to his right and opened the breech of his rifle, he suddenly felt himself falling. He felt the grass on his bare back and saw the blue sky above. There were a few clouds.

"Come with me," a voice said. Strangely, it was a woman's voice.

Taken Alive sat up. His weapons were gone, and so, too, was his horse. He felt a warm, gentle breeze on his face. In front of a light, perhaps the rising sun, he saw the outline of a woman.

"Where are we going?" he said. He felt something below his feet, but it was not firm like the earth.

"To the other side, Grandson," the woman said.

He shaded his eyes from the light and saw her face. It was his grandmother, smiling patiently. "What are you doing here?" he asked, confused.

"They sent me for you," she replied.

"Who? What do you mean?"

"All of your relatives. You are coming with us."

"Where are we going? I have to…," he paused, suddenly not able to remember where he had come from.

"To the other side," she replied patiently.

Suddenly he realized he must follow her, so he did. He was walking, putting one foot in front of the other, but he felt like he was floating. Taken Alive looked around and saw forms all around him. In a strange way, he felt their presence more than he could see them. Ahead, he saw his grandmother walking slowly toward the light. He followed her, anxious to reach the light.

The horse lowered his head and sniffed at the feet of the body in the grass, at the body of Taken Alive. His eyes stared up toward the blue sky, and the breeze tugged at the blades of grass around his face. There was a hole in his chest, just above the breastbone. There was blood, but the hole was no longer bleeding.

Gall took the rifle and the belt of bullets that Rain in the Face had picked up off the battlefield before joining the group of warriors. After a quick glance around, he estimated that there were sixty or more men with him, mostly Hunkpapa and a few Isanti Dakota as well. If they were not enough to stop Long Knives from crossing at Medicine Tail, they would at least slow them down.

"Come on," he said, turning his horse north, "we have to hurry!"

From the east side of the Hunkpapa camp, they thundered north, following the river.

Several moments after they were gone, three warriors galloped by—Crazy Horse, Cloud, and Yellow Wolf. They stopped at the lodge of Sitting Bull.

"Uncle," Crazy Horse said, "did Gall come by here?"

"Yes. He took men toward the dry creek ford," the medicine man replied. Several helpers were treating nearly twenty wounded men under his direction. "He thinks the Long Knives will try to cross there."

"He is right," Crazy Horse replied. "It is an easy crossing."

"What happened to the south?" Sitting Bull asked.

"We chased them across the river. They have retreated to the top of a ridge. They are in a bad way, I think. I left men to keep them there," Crazy Horse said.

In the next instant, he and the others were gone, heading north.

High Eagle and Worm were working together, with the help of several women, to tend to the wounded men who were beginning to pour in. Sitting Bull had sent many to them, and in their treatment area, under a couple of makeshift shades, there were more than twenty men. All of them lay quietly; no one was crying out in pain. Those who could were sitting up, comforting their fellow warriors. Horn Tail was there again, with more wounded men.

High Eagle looked at him. "How many have you brought?"

"Two here. Six to Sitting Bull," the young man replied. He looked worn, his arms and clothing spotted with dried blood. "I have not done much fighting," he admitted.

"There are many ways to face death and to fight for life," High Eagle said, offering the man a dipper of fresh water.

Black Shield touched the boy's shoulder. "What is that?" he said, pointing to the gully on the other side of the Greasy Grass.

The boy gasped involuntarily. "Long Knives!" he whispered loudly.

"How many?"

"Four, maybe five," the boy replied. "At the water's edge. I…I think there is another one up on that hill."

"Yes, I see them. Get ready!" he called to the old men and boys hidden in the willows. "They are at the river's edge!"

Black Shield wiped his old eyes and lined up his sights on the Long Knife in the lead, perhaps less than a hundred paces away. The man was wearing a light-colored shirt and a big hat.

Boom!

The rifle bucked against his shoulder as the man in the light shirt toppled sideways.

B-b-boom!

Other shooters in the willows opened fired. The boy next to Black Shield stood up. "Look! They are taking that first man back across!"

Black Shield pulled him down behind the willows. "Get down!" he warned, expecting return fire. But nothing came.

Gall glanced sideways at Rain in the Face. Gunshots!

"Prepare yourselves!" he shouted. "They are at the crossing! Come on!"

Without slowing down, the black gelding plunged into the water. An instant behind him, hundreds of other hooves hit the water and then churned it as they raced across to the other bank.

Ahead of them, they saw a few Long Knives galloping away. To their left, a line of mounted warriors swept in from the north. Where they had come from, Gall did not know, but he was relieved.

They raced up out of the dry watercourse and saw the thin column of Long Knives east of them, just now turning north and riding toward a long upward slope. There was open area to the east, and no hills. Gall wondered why the Long Knives were heading for the slope, and then he saw—another line of warriors, though far back, was sweeping in from the southeast. There were hardly more than twenty, but they were firing furiously.

Two Bulls and his scouts had been following the Long Knife column. It had split while still along Ash Creek. Part of it went to the southeast and two columns continued east along the creek. Pack mules brought up the rear. The Lakota had stayed in the hills until the column north of the creek turned north. Staying behind the low hills to the east, they had shadowed that column until it had descended into a broad gully, a gully that narrowed toward a crossing.

Two Bulls knew that the column was planning to cross the river at the Medicine Tail Coulee. He was not about to let them do that. Staying back and hidden in the low hills to the east, he waited until the column was strung out. Surprisingly, it had stopped. Two Bulls knew they were badly outnumbered, but it was his intention to attack and divert the Long Knives' attention, knowing that someone from the village would hear. He launched his charge, surprised and relieved when he saw other warriors charging down a northern slope toward the Long Knives.

Now the Long Knives were heading up a long slope, pursued by mounted warriors.

Several hills farther to the east, a young warrior sat beside a soap weed, hands shading his face as he watched the moving black figures in the distance. There were many figures slowly moving up a slope. Bear Robe knew he was watching men and horses. He was on foot, and it would be a long run to get there. His shoulders slumped and he hung his head. Whatever was going on, it would probably be over before he got there.

A shout erupted from the old men and boys in the willows as they stood from their hiding places. They watched the group of warriors crossing the stream and could hear the horses splashing. They could also hear the gunfire cracking from across the river.

In the Oglala camp, an old woman heard the guns firing. Yellow Leggings looked toward her young granddaughter. "Do you hear that?" she asked.

The little girl nodded. "Grandmother, where is my father?" she asked in a small voice, her eyes round, desperately wanting reassurance.

In the Cheyenne camp, a man looked south toward the river and turned to another next to him. "Guns!" said Bobtail Horse. "It has to be at the crossing, or near it. Come on!"

Rifle in hand, he swung up on his horse, followed by the other man, Fire Crow. They rode south along the river toward the crossing. "Come on!" Bobtail Horse shouted to every warrior they passed. "Something is happening!"

Before they reached the crossing, they saw the lines of mounted men crossing the water, and across on the open meadow, there were more. The gunfire was coming from across the river.

Crazy Horse took the reins of a second warhorse from his wife. After a brief embrace, he mounted and raced toward the crossing. Gall had been right—the crossing was an obvious place for an attack on the village.

Other warriors followed him. By the time they came to the sandbar willows, the firing was moving away. A man waved, and Crazy Horse saw Black Shield standing with a group of men.

"They came and we stopped them!" he said, pointing to the group of old men and boys. "After that, our men crossed in pursuit. See? They are going after them, up that long hill!"

Crazy Horse slid out his field glasses and looked across. Black Shield was right—the Long Knives were heading north. Why, he didn't know. But no matter; he had an idea.

He turned and saw the warriors gathered in the trees. He guessed there were close to a hundred, Cloud and Yellow Wolf among them.

"North," he said. "We will go north on this side of the river, and then cross ahead of those Long Knives and double back to the southeast."

Black Shield watched the warriors striking east of the Cheyenne lodges. He almost felt sorry for the Long Knives.

Yellow Leggings watched the warriors. They were moving north now, and in a hurry. She looked down at her granddaughter. They were a small family. Strange illnesses had taken a toll on them. Now they were only three: her granddaughter, herself, and her son. "Grandmother," came the small, scared voice, "where is my father?"

Yellow Leggings reached to wipe away a tear sliding down the tiny face. "I think he is over there, across the river, with all the other warriors." A thought entered her mind. "Go and get my cane, and that bag of dried meat, and a water skin."

"Why?" the girl asked.

"Because you and me will go find your father."

The girl smiled.

As it turned out, Two Bulls and his men found themselves far behind the warriors chasing the Long Knife column. Warriors were to the right and left of the Long Knives, though still behind them.

This second group of Long Knives was no longer a threat, if they ever had been. They were in full flight, no longer in control of their own situation, trying to reach the high ground.

Gall felt no sense of urgency, however. He noticed that the Long Knife mounts seemed to be straining, some stumbling up the long slope. Crazy Horse was right—Long Knives were not true horse warriors. Some of them were barely staying in the saddle. Their shooting from the back of a galloping horse was ineffective. Furthermore, there was no cover to fight from once they reached the top of the slope. With the Lakota steadily gaining on them, the Long Knives would not have the advantage of high ground.

Somehow, the Long Knives did manage to gain the top of the hill before the first one was shot off his horse. He was at the rear. Two Bulls saw him fall and bounce.

Gall turned his head and shouted, "Shoot ahead, not across! Our men are on the other side! And spread out!"

The warriors spread out into a long file to avoid accidentally hitting one of their own as they fired. Now the firing was constant, and the Long Knives were beginning to fall. Horses were being hit as well. One seemed to curl its legs up and crash to the ground, sending its rider sliding across the uneven ground. The man was pounded to pulp under the hooves of the horses coming behind.

A dust cloud began to rise as the pursuit and running battle continued.

His horse was tiring; Gall could feel him straining. He was not surprised. They had galloped up and down several ridges and slopes since the first attack. He raised his rifle and snapped off a shot, grunting in satisfaction as a Long Knife tumbled down.

The warriors on fresher horses were leaving everyone behind. Those on the right side of the Long Knives were consistently hitting their targets. On a horse, it was more natural for a right-handed man to aim across toward the left. Warriors riding on the left side of the column had to twist slightly to aim, which was awkward.

A thought suddenly struck Gall. He waved his arm in a circle as he slowed to a stop and allowed his horse to rest.

Warriors drew up around him. "The Long Knives will stay on that ridge," he said, pointing. "It is the only high ground. Some of you should shadow them on the left; get ahead of them if you can. Then dismount and take good aim from the ground. Hit their horses, knock them down, and then the men."

"What about from the other side?" asked a young warrior.

"No," Gall replied quickly. "We do not want to hit each other in a cross fire. Besides, on this side we are between them and the village, if they decide to turn. We defeated the first attackers. We will defeat these as well."

From behind a clump of soap weeds along a ridge, Stabs and Yellow Eyes watched the activity south of them. They were surprised that the Long Knives could put up what was obviously a defensive barricade after they had been chased across the river and up the ridge. They could see hats and the tops of heads moving around.

"What is that?" Yellow Eyes wondered.

"Something for them to hide behind," Stabs assumed. "Pieces of wood, saddles, and dead horses. They are digging in behind that."

A shot popped from a hill north of them. They saw the ground erupt behind the barricade. All the heads behind the barricade ducked down.

"Those Long Knives are not going anywhere," Yellow Eyes observed. "Whoever is shooting is very good. Anyone who peeks up will be dead."

Yellow Leggings sat down on a grassy bank on the east side of the river just below a low hill and put her moccasins back on. "You too," she said to the girl. "Put your moccasins back on, and we will go see what is around this hill. I know your father is over there somewhere."

They had found a crossing near the north end of the Cheyenne camp and slowly walked across. The old woman was careful not to lose her footing on the uneven bottom.

Yellow Leggings held her granddaughter's hand firmly as they skirted the low hill and climbed an incline. They stopped on a small, grassy mound. The angle of the afternoon sun shone brightly on the west-facing slope in front of her. On the long ridge of the slope, there were men on horses moving north. In a moment, she realized what she was seeing: the men and horses on the ridge were Long Knives. Those on the slopes below them were Lakota and Cheyenne warriors. Her heart pounded. "Stand behind me," she said to her granddaughter. "Stand behind me."

Unlike the old woman and her granddaughter, Crazy Horse and his warriors had slashed across the water. Nearly a hundred strong, they were galloping across a wide bench, heading for the ridges and hills to the east.

Gall's plan was working with deadly effect. On the slope below the fleeing Long Knives were at least twenty warriors, dismounted and firing from sitting or kneeling positions. When the Long Knives passed out of the effective field of fire, Gall jumped on his horse and moved ahead. On the ridge, Long Knives were falling like dry leaves in a rainstorm. Other warriors were shooting from the east side of the ridge.

Another group of warriors swooped in from the south, unaware that some of Gall's warriors were sniping at long range. On fresher horses, it seemed they flew across the slopes and slashed into the Long Knife column, decimating it further. In the process, they scattered a dismounted skirmish line that was hastily trying to form. The warriors went over the ridge and circled back around to the south.

Farther south, Two Bulls saw another group of Long Knives dismount and form a line to face his oncoming warriors. "Spread out!" he shouted. "Spread out!" Steadying himself over the withers of his galloping horse, he raised his rifle and fired. To his right and left, warriors' rifles boomed.

The Long Knives in the skirmish line returned fire. Two Bulls saw the muzzle flashes but didn't slow his horse.

Like the shadow of a cloud moving swiftly across the land, the warriors bore down on the dismounted Long Knives. After another volley, they broke and ran for their horses. A horse or two got away from the holders, and some of the Long Knives ran after them. In the next few moments, they fell.

Across the ridgetop, the firing did not cease.

Crazy Horse and his warriors gained the top of a hill and saw several Long Knives loping north toward them. In an instant, however, the group of four or five turned and galloped away. "We'll follow them," Crazy Horse shouted. "They will lead us to the others."

They heard the firing before they saw the first large group of Long Knives about to reach the end of a long ridge. Crazy Horse noticed a group of Long Knives in tight formation behind the front of the column, obviously holding their own. There was no way to know how many men were in the column, but he could see loose horses and many dead, or at least wounded and immobilized, on the slopes.

He turned to face the men behind him as they pushed in close to hear him. "We need to scatter that group," he said, pointing over his shoulder. "And then we'll finish off anyone else. Gall is pushing them from the south. We'll crush them in the middle."

Spinning his horse, a muscular buckskin, Crazy Horse put him into a flying gallop. In a few heartbeats, he was far out ahead, alone.

"Come on!" Cloud yelled. Thunder from hundreds of hooves began slowly and built to a rumble as Lakota and Cheyenne warriors swept south. Crazy Horse reached the end of the long ridge and passed the first small scattered groups of Long Knives at the head of the column. Cloud and the others were not far behind as Crazy Horse opened fire. He emptied his rifle and pulled out his six-shooter.

Their attention diverted and focused on the lone warrior, the Long Knives in the group somehow failed to see Cloud and the other warriors coming behind. Stretching out in a long line and swerving left, the warriors poured forth a devastating round of fire.

Warrior bullets slammed into the flesh of horses and men. Some impacted with a hollow pop, others with a sharp thud. Long Knives and horses fell. Crazy Horse's objective was achieved—the last group of Long Knives fighting in any organized manner was scattered.

Yellow Leggings sang at the top of her lungs. Strong Heart songs rose and fell as the battle raged before her, moving north. Her little granddaughter clung to her skirts, seeing but not comprehending the images before her.

To her left, the old woman noticed a group of Long Knives break from the main body and head west down the slope. Men fell from their horses, and horses fell with their riders still on them. A few Long Knives were running. A trail of dark bodies, both horses and men, was left behind. In a moment, those Long Knives who had made it to the bottom of the slope passed behind an intervening hill.

Yellow Leggings kept singing.

Warriors were moving north along the east bank of the river below where the old woman stood with her granddaughter. Others were crossing in front of her, sweeping north along the slopes toward the end of the ridge.

Yellow Leggings paused to take a breath. She heard two blasts of gunfire, which seemed to come from nearby. Then she noticed that the gunfire was diminishing, becoming sporadic.

Crazy Horse veered left and circled back. As he approached the ridge from the east, he saw dead Long Knives all along the back of it, as far as he could see. Cloud caught up to him. Gunfire had fallen off, except for a few muffled blasts here and there. Killing shots, fired downward, finishing off wounded Long Knives.

Yellow Wolf arrived, rifle in hand, looking around in disbelief. "I think…I think they are all dead," he said, incredulous. "All of them. Their horses too."

Gall sat on his horse and patted the gelding's strong neck. The animal had stamina. The warrior looked around. Only Lakota or Cheyenne warriors were moving around. He closed his eyes tight, but the images came. He couldn't stop them. The faces he loved, the blood on their dresses. They had seemed so small, so fragile, when he had carried them home. His broad shoulders slumped and shook. He covered his face and wept.

A man approached Yellow Leggings, a Cheyenne Dog Soldier. "Grandmother," he said gently, "I heard you singing and praying." He dismounted and unwrapped the long red sash from around his waist. "I want you to have this," he said, draping it around her neck. "You did a brave thing. As brave as anything I saw today."

The old woman wiped away the tear from the corner of her eye. "Thank you," she said, touching the sash, then looked down at her granddaughter. "We came looking for her father, my son. Do you know him? His name is Red Lodge. He is Oglala."

"No, I do not," the Dog Soldier said. "Can I help you back to the village?"

"In a while, perhaps. I think we will wait here and see if anyone knows of my son."

From around a hill, a rider appeared, loping his horse toward the old woman and the girl. Stopping near them, he jumped down. "Mother! What are you doing here? They told me you were standing here!"

From behind her grandmother, a small form dashed out and threw her arms around the young man's legs. Red Lodge looked down. His expression softened. "What are you doing here?"

"Looking for you," the girl replied shyly.

The Dog Soldier stepped forward. "I heard your mother singing a Strong Heart song. You know as well as I do that when our women are strong, we cannot be defeated."

Red Lodge glanced at the sash hanging around his mother's shoulders. "Thank you," he said to the Cheyenne. "Thank you."

Stepping forward, he embraced his mother, caressing her graying head. "I think we should go home," he said.

Horn Tail added wood to the fire and looked across it. Bear sat looking into the flames. The sun had gone down behind the mountains far to the west.

"Are you hungry?" Horn Tail asked.

Bear shook his head.

"Me neither."

"What shall we do?" Bear said suddenly.

"I do not know. I am very tired."

"No, I mean shall we go home, or shall we stay here?"

Horn Tail looked off toward the sounds in the village. Someone was crying. "There are Long Knives on the hill. I think tomorrow something will be done about them. After that, we can decide."

"That sounds…it sounds good," Bear agreed.

Several large fires burned, all to heat stones for the sweat lodge ceremonies that would be conducted throughout the night by Sitting Bull, High Eagle, Worm, and the other medicine men. There were many wounded to be treated, over a hundred, someone had said. And forty dead. Many families were already in mourning, and other families were praying that their son, their father, their uncle, their brother, their grandfather would recover from his wounds.

Not until Cloud had recovered the body of Little Feather did he hear about Taken Alive. Sweetwater Woman, Gathers Medicine, and Stands on the Hill were with his wife, who had fainted when she was told.

The victory they had won this day was a hollow one for Cloud, as well as for Goings and Little Bird. The price had been too high. They would sit through the night with their friend's body. High Eagle had already prepared it for burial. In the next few days, they would take him to the Shining Mountains, where he loved to hunt.

On the hill across the river to the south, the Long Knives had dug in and were surrounded. In the council lodge, the old men were talking even now, deciding if those Long Knives would live or die. Among the war leaders in the lodge, Crazy Horse listened. Little Big Man was haranguing the old men, trying to convince them that all of the Long Knives should die.

Gall was not in the council lodge. He was sitting in front of his lodge, staring into the night.

A man stepped out of the darkness and approached the fire in front of Horn Tail and Bear. It was Yellow Eyes.

"I recognize you two," he said. "I saw you in the fighting, in the first fight. They are calling it the Valley Fight."

"Sit," Horn Tail invited. "I am afraid we have no food to offer you. Not even tea."

Yellow Eyes waved a hand as he sat on the grass. "No, I am not hungry. I was just walking around and I saw your fire."

"What is happening in the village?" Bear asked.

Yellow Eyes shrugged. "The medicine men are busy. Some boys were dancing, but an old man scolded them. When I was walking by, I heard an old man singing very softly. He was sitting in front of his lodge."

"Singing?" Horn Tail asked.

"Yes, a victory song. I liked it and asked him to teach it to me. Would you like to hear it?"

Horn Tail and Bear glanced at one another and nodded.

Yellow Eyes cleared his throat softly and began patting his leg, as if hitting a drum, then began to sing softly:

The Long Knives are crying. The Long Knives are crying.
We went on a charge. We went on a charge.
We went on a charge. We went on a charge.
We went on a charge. We went on a charge.
The Long Knives are crying. The Long Knives are crying.

CHAPTER FORTY-ONE

The Moon of Hard Times

Cloud looked up at the steep, narrow trail and wondered how Crazy Horse's mare had climbed it. To the west, beyond the broad, snow-covered valley, stood the dark and hazy Shining Mountains. Their jagged outline cut across the deep blue hue of deepening dusk.

He pulled the buffalo robe higher until his ears were covered against the pushy breeze that was making the air feel uncomfortably cold. For a moment, he debated whether to dismount and walk, but he decided to ride.

Cloud was familiar with this ridge and this particular trail. Farther up, it turned sharply left at a narrow ledge that became a small plateau with a grove of stunted pine trees. In the summer, there was grass around the trees. Behind the trees was a cave that opened to the north, overlooking the valley. But there were ghosts here as well. He could feel them. They were going up the trail with him. The buckskin knew they were there; its ears perked up as it glanced to the side of the trail.

Eight hard months had passed since the Greasy Grass Fight. Most of the people who had broken away from the agencies to join Sitting Bull and Crazy Horse had returned to Fort Robinson, afraid that the Indian Bureau would punish them if they did not. For some of them, joining the summer encampments had been nothing more than a brief taste of freedom, something to break up the monotony of agency life. Those people had never really intended to stay on the northern prairies. To them, the victories at Rosebud and the Greasy Grass were a reason for fear, not pride. But most disheartening of all, Sitting Bull and his Hunkpapa people were in Canada, having crossed the Medicine Line hoping to find peace and plenty, and to be free of the Long Knives once and for all. No one had heard about them for months. No one knew if they were living in peace or had plenty to eat.

Cloud gained the ledge and dismounted. From inside the narrow grove, a yellow-and-white mare looked their way. Cloud tied his buckskin next to the mare and unfastened the bag of food from his bundle. The fire's glow inside the cave promised warmth.

As the sun set, they finished their meal of elk and turnip soup, and Crazy Horse prepared his short-stemmed pipe for a leisurely smoke. "I know the old men probably sent you," he said. "They do not like it when I go away to think. Perhaps I should not do that so much."

"No," Cloud replied. "I just wanted to see my friend. My wife and yours gave me food to bring." He had not seen Crazy Horse looking so haggard and worn, and he knew it was the burden of worry, of trying to see the future. Now that Sitting Bull had gone north, Crazy Horse's small band of nearly a thousand—with only one hundred twenty-eight warriors—were the only Lakota not on an agency. Cloud had immediately noticed that his friend's hair was loose, unbraided, as if he were in mourning.

"How is it down there?" Crazy Horse asked.

"Another message came from White Hat Clark. Another promise about our own agency up here, in the Powder River country. The people are losing hope, I think."

"We are defeated when the hearts of our women lay on the ground," Crazy Horse said quietly.

"My friend, it is getting close to that."

"I know. And the buffalo are gone and the next generation of Lakota warriors are on the agencies eating longhorn cattle and wearing white-man shoes. I do not think I could ever wear white-man shoes."

Cloud added wood to the fire and leaned back against the wall of the cave. "I have never seen the old ones so mystified by anything," he admitted. "Many of them say they can see no future ahead of us."

"That is why the people are losing hope," Crazy Horse replied, "because the old ones, the wise ones whom we have always depended on, have no answers."

"Speaking of answers, I have been meaning to ask you something," Cloud remembered. "Sitting Bull's vision from the Sun Dance. I heard—we all did—the warning that came with the vision: 'Do not take what belongs to them.' I think that means the Long Knives."

"Yes," Crazy Horse recalled, "that is what he told us. Why do you ask?"

"At the Greasy Grass, during the battle and after, men took rifles, six-shooters, and bullets. I took a horse. I have been wondering if because we took those things, we are somehow being punished for it. Our victories were reasons to remain united, to stay together. Yet now we are scattered. We are certainly not united—"

"I do not know," Crazy Horse interrupted. "I asked my father, but he said nothing. He did not have an answer." He paused for a moment and lit his pipe with an ember on the end of a twig.

"The second day," Crazy Horse went on, "we let them live, the Long Knives on the hill. We had to because of the others coming down from the north. But when we struck our camps and left, I never felt so powerful. I watched our people and our horses fill that valley as we rode away. And we rode away as victors, as a strong people. I thought it would be enough to keep the people together, to teach them that strength comes from unity." He paused again and took a deep breath. "But I was wrong. So that leads to the answer I do not like to think about.

"The messengers who have come to us from Robinson, they think they have the answers for us," he finally said. "Think of it. Sword, and then even Spotted Tail and Red Cloud have told us that life is good on the agencies. When men like that say those things, it is hard to ignore it.

"And our people look around and see empty meat containers and thin, ragged blankets," Crazy Horse added. "Then they hear that Sitting Bull has taken his people to Grandmother's Land. I walk through the village and I see the looks on their faces—part prayer and part blame."

"There is something I have come to understand, I think," Cloud said. "We have defeated those people, the whites and their Long Knives, just about every time we have met them in battle. When Bear Coat Miles attacked us a month ago, we outfought him even though he had more men and wagon guns. My father said that if you defeat a man's spirit, a people's spirit, you own him. I have decided that white men have no spirit, no soul where they can feel the important things in life."

Crazy Horse nodded slowly. "You are right, my friend. That is why it means nothing for them to be defeated. Less than a year ago, on the Rosebud, and then on the Greasy Grass, we outfought them, we killed many of them. We can kill all their Long Knives, but they will send more—until they kill all of us. They cannot stand the fact that some of us want to live as free people. They do not know, or care, that our spirits will wither if we cannot live free. They want to herd us and control us, like so many cattle."

Crazy Horse paused and ran his hands over his face. "The trouble is, many of our relatives and friends are on the agencies. That makes it very difficult. The whites send Spotted Tail up here spouting good words, and he brings blankets and food and tells us his people want for nothing. That is why those few families sneaked away. I took their horses, I killed their horses, but they still went. Sometimes hopelessness can be just as powerful as hope, perhaps even more."

The fire crackled inside the little cave. Cloud leaned forward toward the fire to catch some of its heat and looked up at his friend. "What are we to do?"

"Keep our feet on the Red Road," Crazy Horse replied softly. "The Long Knives could never defeat us in a fair fight. We cannot let them defeat us now, even though it is not a fair fight." He waved toward the opening of the cave. "This land has bred us to be strong. Now I am afraid that strength will be tested." He took a deep breath. Lack of sleep had left dark circles under his eyes.

"You and me and all our warriors can fight and die," he continued. "But if that happens, who will protect our women and children? They will suffer in the end, as they are suffering now.

"My father taught me that the Red Road is narrow and very, very difficult. I have tried to follow it all my life. That is what is ahead for us. We will be tested like never before, even more so than we have already been tested by the bullets and arrows of our enemies. We must put our feet on this new Red Road. It is the only way to make certain there will be Lakota in this world. We must endure, because we can. We are stronger than anything the whites can do or say to us. I am afraid, however, that this will go on for several generations."

Cloud stared into the fire and suddenly noticed the charred bits of sage and sweetgrass on a flat stone next to it. Clearly, Crazy Horse had spent his time alone thinking and praying. "Why do you suppose, after Greasy Grass, that even Sitting Bull could not keep the people together? Why did most of them hurry back to the agencies? Are they afraid of this new road?"

"No, it is not so much that they are afraid of it, but that they do not understand it," Crazy Horse replied. "It is easy, too easy, to put on the white man's clothes. After that comes the white man's ways. Clothes and kettles and iron knives are things. We can wear them and use them and still feel and think like Lakota. But if we follow his ways, then we are walking the Black Road, we are taking the easy way. Those people who left surrendered to the lure of new things and the easy way. So they mimic the whites, and even stop speaking their own language, thinking it will be easier for them. It will not be, and they will end up losing who and what they are."

"So, my friend," Cloud said gently, "are you saying that the Red Road begins at the agency, under the thumbs of the whites? Why do we not go to Grandmother's Land, like Sitting Bull?"

Crazy Horse nodded slowly, somberly. "It is the reality that faces us. Grandmother's Land is not known to us. How is the hunting up there? I do not think the whites up there can be trusted any more than those down here. Besides, this is our land, here, and perhaps the whites would keep their promise and give us an agency here in Powder River country, but somehow I do not think it will turn out that way. I know this for certain: if…if we do not go down to the agency, the Long Knives will hunt us down. To save our women and children, we must go down to the agency."

"When?"

"In the spring, after the weather is good, we will start for Robinson," Crazy Horse replied, his voice tinged with sadness. "The next messenger who comes can take that word back to White Hat."

Cloud sighed deeply. "My friend," he said, his voice strangely hoarse, "I cannot go with you."

Crazy Horse looked up, the low wavering flames casting light and shadow over his face. He didn't seem surprised. "I think I understand," he replied.

"Yes," Cloud said. "My wife and I have talked about this many times. She is afraid they would take her away."

"They would. They would never understand that she is a Lakota woman on the inside, where it counts. Where will you go?"

"To my father's country, near the Great Muddy River, south of the White Earth River."

Crazy Horse smiled. "Ah, yes, that is good country. My other mothers came from there. There are many good places to hide, and plenty of deer, I hear."

"We have to wait until the spring. She is due to give birth next month."

Crazy Horse smiled again, his eyes twinkling. "That is good. One more Lakota in the world is a good thing."

The light inside the shallow cave took on a yellowish orange hue as the darkness of a moonless night settled across the land outside. In the valleys below them, coyotes barked, and somewhere a wolf howled.

"It is good to know that some things will not change," Crazy Horse observed. "I cannot imagine a world where the coyotes do not laugh and the wolves do not sing." He paused. "But then, who could have imagined that the buffalo would be gone in our lifetime?"

They listened to the coyotes for several moments. "My friend," Cloud said, "I felt the presence of other beings when I started up this trail."

"Yes," Crazy Horse replied, "they have been visiting me day and night. First it was my friend, he who taught me the path of the warrior. Then it was my younger brother, and then my best friend, who was killed at the Hundred in the Hand. They come often."

"Did you see them?"

"Yes, as clearly as I see you."

"Do they speak to you?"

"No. They just come and sit at my fire, as if they are waiting. I wonder if they are waiting for me."

CHAPTER FORTY-TWO

The Hunter in the Sky

Cloud stayed close to the river because the trees provided cover and it was the best place to hunt, although the cover was not as good now because the leaves were falling. After nearly an entire day in a blind, he had been able to ambush a white-tailed deer. Now the doe was tied across the back of a tall sorrel horse. Cloud picked his way through the fallen leaves in the cottonwood and oak groves near the river, trying not to make too much noise. Noise was a giveaway, so he had hunted with his bow, as all the men did. Rifles, it was decided, were for defense only.

No whites or Long Knives had been seen since they had arrived in the valley of the Smoking Earth River five months ago. They were a day's travel west of the Great Muddy River and thirty days east of the Shining Mountains. There were no mountains in this country, only rolling hills. But Yellow Wolf had found the tracks of shod hooves, likely a small Long Knife column.

Cloud wasn't certain what would happen if they did encounter whites. Knowing whites, there would be a confrontation, possibly even a fight. Because of that probability, they had taken pains to hide their little village the best they could. They had decided to build dome shelters, which blended into the surroundings easier than the tall lodges. And, although four of the dome dwellings were taller than a man and nearly as wide as a buffalo-hide lodge, they were located and arranged in such a manner that they were not easily seen, even from a few paces away. They had been placed in a wide gully among tall buffalo berry thickets.

It seemed somehow sadly appropriate that they had cut up their lodge poles for firewood and used the buffalo-hide lodge covering on their new type of dwelling. Since the buffalo were gone, Cloud reasoned, perhaps there should be no more tall lodges.

In addition to white people, food was also a concern. Being constantly alert and watching the skyline was the price of the life they had chosen. They knew it would be that way. All the men—Cloud, Yellow Wolf, Goings, and Fast Horse—had decided they would always have a plan in case something did happen, and they would fight, if necessary, to protect their families. Part of the plan was for everyone to wear white-man clothes in case someone saw them from a distance.

As far as food, they were relieved to find white-tailed deer in abundance. There were catfish in the river and sage hens all around on the flatlands, and they had been able to pick and dry turnips and a variety of berries. But they had yet to face winter here, and things could change next year. They were willing to face whatever lay ahead, yet each and every day they wondered and talked about how it was with their friends and relatives at the Spotted Tail and Red Cloud agencies. They hungered for news.

Cloud thought of these things as he headed home. The Smoking Earth River and White Earth River area was home, at least the home of his father, who was Sicangu. Their little village was south of where the Smoking Earth flowed into the White Earth. His father had told him that in the old days, before the first Long Knives had come up the big river in a big wooden boat with white wings, bands of Sicangu would camp in this area to trade furs to whites who had come up the Great Muddy. From the mouth of the White Earth River, those traders had pushed their canoes up the chalky river. Perhaps because of all of that, there were ghosts here; he could feel them.

Shaking these thoughts from his head, he looked down at the slaughtered deer. He would share the fresh meat with everyone. That was the way, without it being spoken. Crossing the river carefully, he wove his way through chokecherry thickets losing their leaves and saw the horse pen in a small grove of oak. Eleven horses looked his way, not overly alarmed. Behind and to the right of the pens was the first dome lodge. In front of it, a gray dog watched him and the horse intently but did not bark. There were four dogs in all.

Cloud suddenly noticed a different horse in the pen, a small buckskin. Still eyeing the horse, he hung the carcass from the sturdy branch of a short oak tree near the pen. Two of the dogs watched his progress with curious, hungry gazes.

Goings stepped out of his dwelling and approached slowly, a somber expression on his face.

"What is it?" Cloud asked.

Goings drew a long breath and exhaled. "We have a visitor," he said.

"A visitor? How did anyone find us here?"

Goings shrugged. "We have a visitor," he repeated. "He is waiting in my lodge, with news."

It was Ashes, the oldest son of Little Bird and Stands on the Hill, dressed in white-man clothes. He looked weary, but there was something else etched on his boyish face.

"It is good to see you, Nephew. You had a long journey," Cloud said. "I hope you did not have difficulty."

"No," the boy said. "My father drew out the route for me. "

Cloud pointed to the empty metal plate in front of the boy. "I am glad to see you were fed." For some reason, he didn't want to ask any more questions, but he knew it was expected. "Ah, Nephew, what brings you here?"

Ashes stared at the glowing coals in the fire pit. His lips grew thin, his jaw set tight. "Uncle," he said, "I have bad news."

Cloud glanced at Goings, who had obviously already heard the news. "What is it?"

The boy's lower lip quivered, and he took a deep breath. "They…they have killed him," he said, as if afraid to hear his own words.

Goings put his face in his hands.

"Who?" Cloud asked. "Who killed who?"

"The Long Knives, the whites," Ashes replied, trying desperately to keep his composure.

In the back of the lodge, Goings's Cheyenne wife was quietly weeping, her head on the shoulder of Gathers Medicine.

"They killed our headman, your friend, over a month ago. My father sent me to find you, to give you the news." Ashes stifled a sob.

Cloud sat back against the side of the dome lodge. He could feel the grass already stuffed between the dew cloth and the outer lining. When he lifted his eyes to look at Goings, his cousin was quietly weeping, tears sliding down his weathered face.

Crazy Horse was dead? Cloud felt sick to his stomach. He shook his head. It was the truth, an awful truth. This boy would not have been sent on a dangerous, nearly monthlong journey if it were not true. He could feel the tears building up in his own eyes, but he did nothing to stop them. He could not.

"You are brave, Nephew," he said hoarsely, "to make such a journey."

The boy nodded and wiped away a tear.

"Can you tell us how it happened? Do you know?"

Ashes nodded. "Yes, I do. My father told me what to say." He drew another deep breath and exhaled. "There was bad trouble. Many of our people were jealous of him. The Long Knives and the other whites were afraid of him. They tried to put him away in the house of iron doors. He fought. Little Big Man held his arms—"

"Little Big Man?" Cloud interrupted. "Held his arms?"

"Yes, from behind. He was working for the whites. I saw him in one of their blue coats. He held his arms after they came out of the house with iron doors. A Long Knife came and…and stabbed our headman with the knife on the end of his rifle." The boy paused to wipe away another tear. "They took him to the white medicine man's house. The knife went through his kidneys. He was singing, or trying to, my father said. Later, they let his father, Worm, sit with him, and Touch the Clouds. They were with him when…when he died."

Cloud glanced at Ashes. "What about Black Shawl? What happened to her?"

"He took her to his mother and father's lodge, over in one of the Sicangu villages to the east," the boy replied. "That was the day before. Touch the Cloud's people took her in for a time, after…after…" Ashes paused to sigh. "To keep her safe. My father said she has been sick."

"At least my friend did not die alone," Cloud said in a near whisper. It was all he could think of to say. There was nothing more that could be said.

Fast Horse and his wife, Walks Alone, took in the young traveler. They had no children and plenty of room. The next night, the four men conducted a sweat ceremony to pray. Not wanting to build one large fire that could be seen from a distance, they heated stones in their fire pits all day, then carried them to the sweat lodge. Goings, as the oldest man and a Sun Dancer, poured the water.

They took Ashes in with them as they sang and prayed to honor their beloved leader, to help send him on his next journey. There would never be another like him, they all agreed. And they all wept, some with tears quietly streaming down their faces, others shaking with sobs of grief.

Before the sun came up the next morning, the men were at the corral as Fast Horse was preparing to walk up to the sentinel post atop the ridge above them.

"I still cannot believe it," Goings commented. "I did not sleep all night."

They all shook their heads in affirmation.

"What will happen now?" Fast Horse wondered.

"The Long Knives must feel powerful now," Cloud said. "Sitting Bull is in Grandmother's Land, and Spotted Tail and Red Cloud will do what they are told."

"What will we do?" Yellow Wolf asked.

"We made a choice," Cloud reminded them. "We made a choice to stay free, away from the agencies. If Long Knives or other whites come and give us trouble, I am prepared to take my family to Grandmother's Land."

"My wife and I will go with you," Yellow Wolf vowed.

At midmorning, Cloud slipped away from the camp, telling only Sweetwater Woman that he was taking a walk into the hills east of the river. He wanted to be alone, to face and think about the gut-wrenching news brought by Ashes.

Out of habit, he took his bow and arrows and a six-shooter and felt adequately armed against anything, or anyone. But he was also armed with anger, a deep, seething anger that was trying to work its way past the grief. Part of him was looking for a fight, some kind of confrontation, and wishing that a white man would appear on the horizon. Yet deep down he knew that taking revenge against one or all the whites he could find would never replace his friend.

On a long, gradual slope he sat down in the middle of a low, leafless sumac thicket. There he had a view of the valley and the confluence of the Smoking Earth and White Earth rivers. A cool freshness was in the air. Ordinarily, he would revel in it. Today, it annoyed him.

Like Goings, he had not slept during the night. Instead, he had lain staring up at the smoke hole in the ceiling of the dome shelter as images flowed through his mind. A sad and dreadful thought threaded the images together—the dream Crazy Horse had had as a young teenager. Crazy Horse had never told him the dream, but Cloud had heard of it from High Eagle.

In the dream, a young Lakota warrior rode his horse on the surface of a lake as enemies fired arrows and bullets at him. He was unharmed until he reached the shore and brown-skinned people rose from the ground and pulled the warrior down from his horse.

Several medicine men agreed on the interpretation of Crazy Horse's dream. To them, it meant he would die young and his death would be caused by his own kind. As far as Cloud was concerned, the dream had come true. He knew that as soon as Ashes had mentioned that Little Big Man had grabbed Crazy Horse from behind. Little Big Man had always wanted to be important and have power, so it was not completely surprising that he had gone to work for the Long Knives. Whatever his reasons, they had put him in the wrong place at the wrong time.

Perhaps Crazy Horse had been expecting something to happen in the way that it did. It was a terrible foretelling to have to live with. An unimaginable burden to bear. Crazy Horse was right, in a way, when he said the ghosts of his friends and his brother were waiting for him.

Cloud looked across the valley at the rolling hills turning yellow and brown. This was a different world. There were no buffalo, and there was no Crazy Horse. At this thought, he put his face in his hands and wept.

That afternoon, with a wooden bucket in each hand, Cloud walked with Ashes and Song to the river, which was not unlike the Greasy Grass River, though a little narrower. Sweetwater Woman and the other women were near the lodges, hard at work cutting and drying the deer meat Cloud had brought home. They Are Afraid of Her, now nearly eight months old, was propped next to her mother in a cradleboard. Cloud had wanted to name her after Crazy Horse and Black Shawl's only daughter. Now it seemed even more appropriate that they had done so.

Fast Horse was in the hidden pit atop a ridge to the west, in a spot that looked like nothing more than a clump of soap weed. It was the highest point; from there, a man with a glass could see anyone and anything coming. Yellow Wolf had spotted Ashes from there.

"My father said to ask if I could stay the winter," the boy said.

"Yes, you should. In the spring, one of us will go back with you," Cloud promised.

"There are other things about what happened that my father told me to tell all of you," Ashes revealed timidly.

"Yes, there is much we want to know, but there is time. Winter nights are long. There is time."

The land felt different somehow, and there was a heaviness in the air. It was the same earth, the same trees, grasses, and river. Cloud knew that everything was the same as it had been yesterday, but it felt different, and he was sad. Perhaps the land was sad as well. Or perhaps everything felt different because of the memory of a conversation had between friends in that cave above the Tongue River. Or perhaps it was because of the constant flow of images of a Lakota warrior flying across the prairies on his yellow-and-white horse.

They filled the buckets and started back as mostly bright yellow leaves from the tall cottonwoods fell from the top branches. Song looked up and watched, her eyes sparkling as the leaves spiraled slowly to the earth. Her sharp young eyes spotted a bright red leaf that seemed to ride the breeze better than the others. It glided down in smaller and smaller circles until she caught it in her hand.

Screee! Screee!

A red-tailed hawk shrilled its hunting cry in the cold autumn sky above them. Cloud looked up and saw its dark outline circling. Unlike the leaf, the hunter in the sky was going higher and higher.

They watched it until it was gone from sight.

EPILOGUE

When Old Men Outlive Their Time

A lone hawk rode a high wind beneath the cloudless blue sky. Somewhere, a meadowlark sang a soft song that rose and fell with the wandering breezes. The old man caressed the tall stalks of grass at his knees as he looked across the broad floodplain west of the river below them. He could still see the seemingly endless line of people walking or on horses, the drag frames piled high with packs or elderly passengers, and the lines of mounted warriors riding guard on either side of the long column. He had never felt so powerful as a Lakota as he had that evening, not because they had defeated an enemy, but because of the sense of belonging.

The breezes sighed through the grasses like soft, ghostly whispers from the past as the images faded from his mind, but not from his memory. Everything that had ever happened in his life, whether he could remember it or not, had brought him to this moment in his eighty-second year. Everything had made him who he was today.

Great Spirit, Grandfather, he said in his mind, *I am grateful to be Lakota.*

For a moment, he listened to the whispering breezes, then turned to his daughters and grandson. "I am happy you brought me here," he said to them. "I am grateful. I could not have made this journey alone."

"Oh, Dad, we are grateful too," Katherine replied immediately. "I will never forget hearing your stories here, at this place. I can almost see Mom and Anne down there, hauling water from the river."

"Yes," Anne agreed, "I, too, remember it all. I remember my moccasins getting stuck in the mud. I remember that the river was deep, and that all the cottonwood seeds were floating in the air and all over the ground. It almost looked like snow. And the horses—there were so many horses! But I remember the laughter too. People were always laughing. It was a good time."

A moment passed. Below them and across the river, hundreds of lodges seemed to materialize, with people of all sizes around them. Then the hazy image receded back to where it had come from. Katherine looked at her sister, a puzzled question in her eyes. Anne nodded silently; she had seen it as well.

Justin, deep in thought, had been staring at the shadowy, jagged outlines of the Bighorn Mountains to the south. "Grandpa, what would have happened if you had attacked the forts like Crazy Horse wanted to do?" he asked finally.

Cloud glanced at his grandson and nodded thoughtfully. He had asked himself that same question many times since that summer. "If we had had enough guns and ammunition, we could have beaten the soldiers," he asserted. "We were better fighters. But Crazy Horse had other plans, too. He wanted to send us out in groups of fifty to hit the soldiers at night, wherever they were. He was sure that if we kept them confused and afraid all the time, eventually we would have worn them down."

"Do you think that was really possible, Grandpa?"

Cloud reached down for a handful of soil and let it slide from his palm. "Perhaps for a while," he said. "But they would have sent more soldiers and more cannons until they killed us all. Spotted Tail was trying to tell us that—that there had to be another way to win, one without guns or bullets."

"How do you win without fighting?"

"He meant by hanging on to our ways, our language. But that has to be a war fought by each generation. They will not stop taking our lands or our ways. Last summer, the police surprised Louie LaFromboise at his camp when he was doing a healing ceremony. They took his pipe and all his things, and they warned him that if he did not stop doing Lakota medicine, they would put him in jail. But the other bad part, to me, is that the policemen were Lakota. The Black Robes from St. Ignatius Mission complained to the agent at the agency, so the agent gave orders to the policemen, who talked to their friends and relatives and found out where LaFromboise had his sweat lodge."

Justin shook his head in dismay. "What about LaFromboise? What did he do?"

"He is following in his grandfather High Eagle's footsteps," Cloud replied. "He found another place to build a sweat lodge. Maybe they will find that, too, but Louie is not afraid to go to jail. No one will scare him out of being Lakota."

"What can I do, Grandpa?"

"Remember," came the ready reply. "Remember what I told you about this place, and about the Hundred in the Hand. Remember all the stories you heard from different people. Those stories are how our people, our

Lakota nation, will keep going. We cannot fight with guns anymore, but we can still be a strong people if we remember our stories. That is how we remember where we came from, and that is how we know who we are."

Justin looked out across the land and listened to the wind whispering in the grasses. Although the land looked empty, it was not. Spirits lingered here, and his grandfather had reached back across the years to touch them, to revive them. He had recalled how he felt in the midst of battle in France. In the middle of unfettered violence, mayhem, and death, he had never felt so alive. It was a strange feeling, one that did not seem to belong, and now he felt it again. He felt his Lakota blood rising to the top and overwhelming every other part of him. Perhaps it was only momentary, but he liked it.

Justin felt the old man's hand on his shoulder. "There is something else I want you to do, Grandson," he said, a twinkle in his eye.

"Anything, Grandpa. Just tell me."

"Find a good woman and make many children and teach them how to be Lakota."

The young man smiled, a slight blush coloring his face. "I will try, Grandpa."

Anne and Katherine stood and brushed the grass and dirt from their clothes. Anne lifted the glass jar, still half full of water. "Dad," she said, "what do you want to do? We can find a place for the night and come back tomorrow."

Cloud shook his head. "No," he sighed. "I am done with this place. Time to go home."

At the bottom of the hill, near the highway, stood the small building they had passed when they first arrived. It was a general mercantile with a lone gas pump off its front porch. Because they had stayed on the battlefield for most of the afternoon, Anne worried about starting the long trek home without provisions. Although there were still several hours of daylight left, she wanted to find a hotel or camping accommodations.

Justin pulled in next to the gas pump and stepped out of the car. Images still swirled in his mind, and gunshots still echoed somewhere. He paused to look back toward the battlefield. Now he understood why the old man had insisted on coming to this place. This place and that long-ago battle were the turning points in his life. For Justin, it was a place called Arneau Plain, acres and acres of mud and trenches and shattered bodies. If it weren't for his own experience, he could not have understood his grandfather. But it was even more than that: this place was the turning point for an entire nation, for all of the Lakota people.

The young man pulled himself back to the present moment as he approached the mercantile. He was almost on the wooden porch when he noticed the man sitting on the bench beneath the window.

He was an Indian, wearing a threadbare coat in spite of the lingering heat. A gray hat was pulled low over his forehead, and he was sitting with his head down, his face obscured. But it was his hands that Justin noticed most. They were brown hands, weathered and worn from hard work, like his grandfather's hands, and they were curled over the head of a cane. Perhaps it was the hands that made Justin pause, or maybe it was his grandfather stepping down from the passenger side of the car.

At the same moment that Cloud stepped onto the wooden porch, the old man on the bench lifted his head. Justin saw a wide scar that ran from the corner of his right eye down to the right side of his mouth.

The two old men gazed at one another before the man on the bench pulled himself to his feet and took a step forward and removed his hat. Two thin gray braids hung down to the lapels of his coat, and his eyes were tired. It was easy to see he had lived a long life.

Cloud removed his own hat and stepped forward with his hand outstretched. "I am John Richard Cloud," he introduced himself, "from Smoky River."

A smile bent the other man's mouth, showing gaps where teeth were missing, and his eyes brightened. "I am Gabriel Broken Hand, from Lodge Grass," he said in a low, raspy voice.

They grasped hands, and the two seemed to blend, making it hard to discern which fingers belonged to which old man.

"The last time I saw you was in the trees by the river," Cloud recalled, nodding his head toward the Greasy Grass River. "You rode with the Long Knives, and you let me live."

"You gave me meat the winter before that," replied Broken Hand without hesitating. "Meat for my wife and son and mother. We ate good that time, for a while."

"How is it with you now, my friend?" Cloud asked.

Broken Hand smiled. "For some reason, I am still alive," he said. "My wife finished her journey fifteen years ago, and my daughter as well. My son has a family, and they have a room for me. And I have a horse. I think he is my only friend, but he is old, too." He let go of Cloud's hand and pointed at the bench. "Come, let us sit and talk."

Cloud motioned for Justin, who stepped up onto the wooden porch. "This is my grandson," he told Broken Hand as they sat. "He fought with the Long Knives in France."

Justin stepped forward to shake hands with the old Crow warrior. "Yes, a few of our young men were there," he said.

Katherine and Anne stepped out of the car, and Justin looked over and said, "Mom, remember the buffalo hunt that Grandpa told us about the winter before the battle? Well, that is the man who came to trade for meat. The Crow."

Katherine couldn't believe it. "No! After all these years?"

"It is, Mom. Look at the scar on his face."

Anne and Katherine stared at the man sitting with their father as Cloud looked up and saw them. He motioned for them to approach and introduced them to his old acquaintance.

Broken Hand nodded shyly. "You are all a long way from home," he said.

"Yes," Anne said. "We came with our father. He wanted to see this place."

Broken Hand nodded again. "I see it all the time," he told them. "And each time, I remember what happened here. It is good to see your father. It reminds me of the days when we human beings were strong."

After he paid for the gas, Justin returned to the car and parked it on the side of the building, then joined his mother and aunt as they stood listening to the two old warriors. He leaned close to his mother. "They have groceries, and a restaurant too. The man inside says there is a hotel in a town called Hardin, fifteen miles north."

Katherine nodded. "I will buy some supplies here, and if your Grandpa is tired and wants to stay the night, we can go to the hotel," she said.

After reminiscing with the other old man for almost an hour, Cloud stood up from the bench. "My friend," he said to Broken Hand, "it is good to see you. I have thought of you now and then, when I wish for a good cut of buffalo meat."

Broken Hand stood and reached into his coat pocket and pulled out a buffalo tooth. "I have carried this for over forty years. I never knew why, but now I do. This is yours. I took it from the carcass you gave me. Now I give it back to you to remember me by."

Cloud took the tooth. "I have never forgotten. Thank you. Can we give you a ride somewhere?"

Broken Hand shook his head. "No, my son will be along. Take care of yourself, and have a good journey home."

Broken Hand stood on the porch of the mercantile and watched the car carrying his Lakota friend drive away. Cloud put his head out the open window to look back and wave to the lone figure growing smaller each second.

"It is a hard thing when old men outlive their time," he said to no one in particular.

In the backseat, Katherine and Anne glanced apprehensively at one another.

"What do you mean, Dad?" Anne asked cautiously.

"It means that I am tired," he said. "But I was thinking. When we get close to home, I want to stop at Wounded Knee. I have not been there since I went looking for Little Bird and his family after…after all those people were killed."

"We can stop there, Grandpa," Justin assured him. "You have not talked about that time very much. But I think I understand why."

Cloud stared out at the passing landscape for nearly a minute before he replied. "The Ghost Dance years," he said softly. "If you want to listen, I will tell you."

Justin looked back at his mother and aunt. They nodded. "Yes, Grandpa, we want to hear about the Ghost Dance."

Cloud lifted his gaze to the far horizon. "Lots of songs were made and sung that time. They were songs of hope that turned out to be sad songs for the Buffalo Nation."

ACKNOWLEDGMENTS

Writing this book has once again put me in touch with countless stories from my childhood on the Rosebud Sioux Indian Reservation. My grandparents and their generation are always waiting in my memory, always ready to put me in touch with their memories. I shall always be grateful for that connection.

I am grateful to the readers who took the time to send notes and offer comments about *Hundred in the Hand*. It is reassuring to know that there is an audience that is sincerely interested in all sides of the stories that make up our collective past.

Once again, thank you to Fulcrum's publisher, Sam Scinta, for making the second installment in this series possible. Thanks also to Katie Wensuc and Haley Berry, my editors, who helped me enormously, and to everyone else at Fulcrum, including Michelle Baldwin, Erin Palmiter, and Shannon Hassan. I look forward to working with all of you on the next installment.

Finally, but most of all, a special thanks to my agent and chief motivator—and most important of all—my wife, Connie.

Donald F. Montileaux

"Long Knives." Prismacolor pencil and India ink on antique ledger paper dated April 3, 1936.

Donald F. Montileaux (Oglala Lakota) is a master ledger artist. Following in the footsteps of his forefathers, he has rekindled ledger art with his collection of striking images that capture the unique Lakota way of life.

Montileaux interned under noted artist Oscar Howe at the University of South Dakota at Vermillion in 1964 and 1965. He also credits his personal friend and mentor, the late Herman Red Elk, as his primary artistic muse. With work spanning the globe and numerous awards and commissions to date, Montileaux's art is represented in many private and public collections. He has illustrated covers for ten books and has been the featured artist in galleries in New Mexico, Minnesota, Arizona, Colorado, Montana, Illinois, and South Dakota.

Today, Montileaux dedicates himself to further exploring his gift and to introducing ledger art to new generations.